BEARINGS AND DISTANCES

Glenn Arbery

Wiseblood Books

Wiseblood Books
www.wisebloodbooks.com

Printed in the United States of America
Set in Georgia Typesetting

ISBN-13: 978-0692468203

ISBN-10: 069246820X

Fiction / Literary

Acknowledgments

Gratitude in the case of a novel like *Bearings and Distances* is complicated, because in many ways it is the inadequate return on a gift too substantial to repay. I am most grateful for the suggestions of those who read versions of this work, especially Bill Berry, David Spence, Robert and Melody Palmer, four of my eight children (Joan, Lucia, Therese, and Will) and one son-in-law, Matt Skidd, all of whom read the first draft; Teleia Tollison, who read the second draft (twice); Jeremy Holmes, who read the novel more or less as it now exists; and of course my closest reader, my wife Ginny, who has generously reread it at every stage. It has been a pleasure, too, in the last revisions, to work with Louis Maltese at Wiseblood Books. The suggestions (and occasional outraged objections) of these readers have contributed mightily to the final shape of the book. I also owe more than I can readily say to the generosity of my stepbrother, Hugh W. Mercer Jr., who introduced me decades ago, not only to the world of surveying that provides the book with its central metaphor, but also—through his example—to what it might mean to be a good man.

On the other hand, these fine people can in no way be held responsible for the many remaining flaws, both of the book itself and of its author. Those are all my own.

O God of our flesh, return us to Your wrath,
Let us be evil could we enter in
Your grace, and falter on the stony path!

—Allen Tate

Where were you when I laid the earth's foundation?
Tell me, if you understand.
Who marked off its dimensions? Surely you know!
Who stretched a measuring line across it?

—Job 38:4-5

BOOK I
The Undertaker's Daughter

PROLOGUE

November 5, 1976

The other children in first grade said she got her white hue and church-pew stillness from staying in a house of dead people. Nobody ever came to find out, but they were right, it was a hush-your-mouth place. Daddy could hush anybody. When her mama went out on her errands after supper, he would sit beside her while she made her ABCs on the tablet paper. The solid lines showed how tall a letter could grow and the dotted ones were for round parts. Did she know that in the Bible, Jesus himself was the alphabet? She shook her head. *Oh, yes,* Daddy said. He showed her the Alpha like an A and the Omega like a horseshoe. *The beginning and the end.* Daddy was a whispery man, so she whispered too, but this time she forgot. *What happened to Z?* she asked out loud; frowning, he put his finger to his lips and told her that if she talked too loud, the dead people might wake up. So she whispered, *What happened to Z, Daddy?*

Baby, Omega was the end of the alphabet back in the old days. If time was the alphabet, then Jesus was there at the beginning, that's the Alpha, and he'll be there at the end, and that's the Omega.

But time is numbers in a circle, Daddy. My teacher showed us.

They did things different back then.

So Omega was a Z?

Yes, honey, like Z, except it was Omega.

Is Z the end of the world?

Well, heh heh, I suppose so, sugar, but Jesus didn't say he was the A and the Z.

So that old alphabet was better for Jesus.

That's right.

But people go Z-Z-Z in the funny papers when they're asleep. Maybe that's why they changed it, so people would wake up after the end of the world.

Heh heh.

It was no wonder she liked school better. You could talk out loud in school. Not that she did. She loved sitting still at her desk in Mrs. Ziegler's classroom—a Z lady!—and forming the curves and lines of letters with the restless boys around her, grinning and squirming. Later, when she was older, she was going to learn cursive, and all the letters would hold hands like in Red Rover or Crack-the-Whip. She had seen older girls make a word without lifting the pencil from the page except to dot an *i* or cross a *t*.

It was Friday night, so she didn't have to do letters. Her mother was out on an errand, and she was at the kitchen table drawing the Queen of Sheba from the Bible when the telephone rang. Daddy grunted and got up from his chair in the living room and answered it. He had to talk out

1

loud on the phone and he didn't like it. After he listened he said, *Yes, sir.* That meant it was either a man older than he was (and she didn't know many), or it was somebody white. *Yes, sir, I'll help, of course. Yes, sir, I'll be right here.* He stood there quiet for a long time after he put down the phone. *Daddy,* she said, and he looked up at her as though he'd forgotten she was in the world. He told her that something terrible had happened. *Dead people are coming?* He nodded and squeezed his temples and then wiped his eyes. *Old dead people?* He shook his head and did not look at her eyes. He said, *No, baby, it's not old people,* and told her he had to leave her by herself. Would she be alright until her mama got home?

But he didn't wait for an answer. He went through the secret door she could never open, and she sat at the table in the kitchen, afraid to move. She meant to draw a golden crown for the Queen of Sheba, but she was so scared, she just held her crayon in the air. On the wall over the table was their picture of Jesus kneeling down and praying. His hands were in front of him on a rock and his face was lifted up, sad-looking, and light was shining down on his halo. Her friend Debra said it was supposed to warm her heart when she looked at it, but it didn't. That was because something was the matter with her. She heard a woman at church say so the time her mama took her. *Huh, something bound to be the matter with that child.*

On the other wall was Jimmy Carter, the brand-new president. He was from Georgia, and he had signed the picture himself. Daddy was so proud of it he stood and looked at it every night. But she liked the picture on the refrigerator best. Marilyn Monroe had on the reddest lipstick in the whole world. Her head was thrown back and her mouth was open laughing. Her white teeth gleamed, and the shiny black strap of her dress came over her pretty shoulder like good news at last, Mama said.

After a while, she heard the new dead people coming in. Marilyn Monroe was dead, too, Mama said. But not in the picture. Right now Marilyn was having too much fun to notice a scared little girl. Marilyn was so pretty and happy it always made her feel better just looking at her. But not this time. Now there was moaning and calling, and some of it sounded like Daddy. And what if it was dead people who didn't want to be dead? She sat there a long time, staring at the secret door.

Then it started to open. The back of her neck prickled with terror. All the air went out of the room, and when the crayon broke in her hand, she closed her eyes and screamed. There was a long hush. She could hear something near her breathing.

"Aw baby. Not again."

Mama. She had on one of her tightest, whitest errand dresses and her dark red lipstick and gold earrings, just like the Queen of Sheba, and she had that smell she said was what errands smelled like. *Mama!* she sobbed. She wanted to jump up and run to her but she was ashamed of the puddle she had made. Her mama held up her finger to her lips and went over and got a roll of paper towels and gave it to her.

"A terrible thing happened," her mama whispered. "The bus ran off the road on the way to the football game and five of the boys...." She fell silent. After a moment, she reached out her hand. "Now don't you be upset. There's not a thing we can do about it. Tonight Daddy's too busy to worry about what we're doing."

Then her mama talked out loud, so loud it startled her "We can watch anything we want to on TV" she said. She went into the den and brought back the *TV Guide* and flipped through it until she found the right page. Her mouth opened, a perfect O of pleasure. She tilted her head, teasing her. "Guess what's on tonight?"

But she felt small and confused and couldn't guess, and she was ashamed. She was trying to be happy, but she couldn't help thinking about what would make Daddy moan and cry. "*It's How to Marry a Millionaire!* It's Marilyn!"

July 15, 2009

Marisa talked the waiter into giving them the last outdoor table. She was sitting with her back to the street, and the sidewalk traffic of Rome broke steadily around her onto the strip of open pavement beyond the awning. Forrest caught fragments of dialogue from the passersby, some of it in English: *I told him I didn't want to shoot her but he said...*

Shoot her?

He leaned forward distractedly to hear what Marisa was saying, and just then a large, bald man in khaki shorts and a white knit shirt backed softly into her, whirling suddenly around as though she had tried to trip him. When he saw what he had done, he begged her pardon and held the back of her chair with his left hand as he faced away from her and pointed to the street with his cane. T-I-M was printed vertically down an old yellow strip of laminated poster board he had taped to it.

Forrest saw a group of tourists—large, round-faced, docile people—come up *en masse* behind Marisa. Tim released her chair and slipped into the street ahead of them. The group surged after him out onto the cobblestones like sheep. A boy on a moped went weaving carefully through the horde, revving his engine as they winced back from him, and just as he got to the edge of the group, he hooked the purse from a lady's shoulder and accelerated away amid the sudden outcry.

Forrest, enjoying the drama of it, turned back to Marisa just as a stocky African in a dashiki and khaki shorts materialized beside the table. The man gave a curt upward nod and gestured toward the goods he held above their pasta. "Eshu-Elegba," he said. He lifted the figure of a seated man with a disproportionately large head and held it about six inches from Forrest's nose. His fork still hovering in midair—he was hungry—Forrest stared at the man, momentarily panicked. Was this some relative of Natalia's?

"Eshu-Elegba," the man said again, this time with an accusing, aggrieved tone, as though Forrest had insulted his little idol. He was just trying to sell something. He bumped Forrest's shoulder with the tray and wagged Eshu-Elegba too close in front of his face. Forrest swatted the little idol aside with the back of his hand. The African's lip lifted and he thrust the tray at Marisa, insolently sweeping his hand above the small figures as if to demonstrate that the least thing there was worth any amount of American money.

"No," Forrest said. "Understand? *Capisce?*"

Unperturbed, the vendor held up a figure with a scimitar in one hand and an ax in the other. "Ògún," he announced. Now people at the other tables were turning to look at him. He felt himself reddening. People were bumping into each other on the sidewalk to try to keep from

5

jarring the African. Out on the street, a wispily bearded man in his twenties stopped and aimed his camera at Forrest and Marisa. *Shoot her.*

"Braxton," Marisa said. "Don't."

"These Africans think we're fair game," he said loudly. "We ought to re-colonize their black asses."

"Please don't do this."

"This your honey?" the man asked in his deep voice, cutting his eyes toward Forrest with a hateful half-smile. "Mmm, buy your pretty woman little Oshun." He had a peculiarly lilting British accent. He leaned close to Forrest and opened his eyes wide, waggling a female figure whose great breasts burst from the wood. "She be the honey tree."

Forrest stood up, looming over the man, and his chair tipped over backwards with a sharp clap. The African made a flipping gesture of contempt and quickly melted into the street. The restaurant owner, small and mournful-looking, was hurrying out, shouting after the vendor in rapid Italian.

"*Scusa, signore,*" he said to Forrest, spreading his hands and shrugging. He set the chair upright, beckoned a waiter, and pointed to the empty carafe of wine beside the bread basket. "*Gratuito,*" he said. "On da house."

"*Grazie,*" Marisa said and gave him the first smile Forrest had seen on her face all week, but as he sat back down, it faded and she stared across the table, the skin around her eyes already tightening with criticism. And that unbearable mouth.

"Imperialist complacency." A woman's voice, British. Forrest turned toward it, angry again. Sixtyish and stout, she raised a palm and smiled at him ruefully from the next table. "He comes in my bookshop," she said, in a voice clipped and ironic. "Particularly bitter about Americans. 'Imperialist complacency'"—she imitated his African accent. "You're so wealthy, you see, and here he is struggling to pay his rent by commodifying his culture, and you won't even deign to buy anything. Of course, he knows you won't before he tries, and he resents it, and that's why he's so rude that you would never even consider buying something, which just proves his point."

Marisa's mouth softened at this speech.

"He's trying to sell you his Yoruba gods, you know," the British woman said, lifting her glass to them. "They might feel a bit offended at your lack of interest."

"Yoruba?" asked Marisa.

"A Nigerian tribe," said Forrest, wanting to impress this British lady. "Wole Soyinka, Chinua Achebe. Ben Okri."

"Am I supposed to know that?" Marisa asked.

"Come on, I've taught Soyinka. You must have seen the books around the house."

"Well, I don't teach it. You teach it."

"Achebe is Ibo, actually," said the British woman mildly. "This gentleman you just encountered is a playwright, quite an intelligent man. He can't seem to sell his real work lately. The postcolonial day itself seems to be *post-*, too bad for him. Even the guilty interest in Islam is fading. Obama changes things. Here lately, though," she said, "I've had a run on Mahfouz."

"*Palace Walk*! Last week when we first got here," Forrest said. "You run the little bookstore in Trastevere."

"Yes, you remember my cat. And you said your daughters were in— Alabama, was it? Wasn't one of them named Dolores? With Charlotte Haze?" She sipped her tea with a wry smile.

"Cate and Bernadette. Cousin Emily Barron Hayes," said Forrest. "And they're in Georgia. How is that cat?"

"Speaking of imperialist complacency?" she said.

Just then, the waiter brought a fresh carafe of red wine and set it down, blocking their view of her, and asked with a look and a gesture of his open palm whether they needed more bread. "Sì, *grazie*," said Marisa and adjusted her napkin. When he left, she stared across the table at Forrest, rudely making no effort to resume the conversation with the British lady. Her eyes had no mercy.

Ever since Viterbo last week. Whole days of ice and accusation. Suddenly, the British woman stood beside the table, and Marisa started.

"Sorry," the woman said.

"I thought it was one of those gods," Marisa said, almost smiling again.

"No, all too mortal." She held out a card. "Please drop by and tell me how your girls are faring. Is it Forster?"

"Forrest. Braxton and Marisa Forrest." Forrest stood to take her card.

"Marisa Forrest. Lovely name. Oh!" she said. "I just made the connection. *Braxton Forrest*—I've seen your book. May I have the card back for a moment? Let me put my number on it." Marisa handed it to her, and she dug in her purse for a pen, found one, and leaned on the table to write her number on the back.

Forrest stood until she left, then sat back down, glancing down at the card.

"Elizabeth Spence," he said. "*Last relic of the British Empire.*"

"You seemed chummy enough."

"No, that's what it says. Last relic of the British Empire." He held it toward her.

Marisa shook her head and said nothing. She gazed down the street past him. Her face had lost the sharp, almost predatory clarity of line it had when he fell in love with her. Her hands lay in her lap; her pasta cooled untouched. She murmured something, still not looking at him, and he leaned closer.

"What did you say?"

She turned back and her eyes burned at him, her mouth bruised with disdain.

"You don't even—" She broke off and picked up her fork, twisted the spaghetti savagely, put it down. More boys on mopeds sped loudly past. A chorus of honking started up at some obstruction in the next intersection.

"Don't even what? Care? I do care," he said too loudly.

"*Care*," she said sarcastically. "That's not what I was going to say. You don't even let me finish my own sentences."

"What do you want, Marisa?"

"What do I want? Good God, Braxton. What do I want?"

"Okay, have at it. It's been—what?" He glanced at his watch. "Five hours and twenty minutes. I'm getting complacent. Imperialist and complacent."

"You don't *understand*. That's what I was going to say. What it's been like for me."

"I'm sorry. I've said I was sorry. I've said it over and over."

"You're sorry."

"Jesus, give it up, Marisa!"

"I'm standing there on the terrace with my aunt, and she's showing me the street, and there you are down on the corner with a sack of provolone in one hand watching that woman walk past. And of course you had to stop her and speak to her, you had to touch her arm, you had to look at her like, I don't know, and get your hand on her waist while you pulled her aside, even though you don't know Italian. Do you understand how humiliating it was? My aunt's hand was up beside her ear, doing that shaking thing old Italian women do. And this afternoon I remembered that email to Roger Carboys I read by accident. About the new 'succulents' on campus? At first I thought, *That's strange. They've planted cactus in New Hampshire*? But then I realized, *No, this is Braxton Forrest*. He means the coeds. Braxton among the succulents. The *succulents*, my god! A man with two daughters of his own."

Day after day—what did she want? Confession simply exacerbated her rage. His words had no effect, especially his attempts at honesty. He pictured some wild, flailing homunculus being pulled out of him with forceps, all blood and gristle. Then she would stab it through the heart with her fork.

"I like that noun. Succulents. Maybe you ought to think about what it means," Forrest said. "A thorny plant that grows in a very dry place."

"I know what a succulent is. I just said."

"As a metaphor. Some smart shy thorny one I don't even notice at first who raises her hand. Do you know how rare intelligence is?"

"Intelligence. Oh my God. Just shut up."

Forrest pushed his food away in disgust. She got up and made her way down the sidewalk and into the restaurant toward the restroom. Some gesture, maybe the way she dodged a table, made him remember seeing her from behind when she was twenty-two and painting the hallway of his office building at Georgia, part of a student crew. With her hair in a ponytail, she was reaching up as far as she could to make a big W with a roller and fill it in, her T-shirt lifting to show a crescent of tanned waist and the dimples of her lower back above the round bottom that shook with a little meringue of sweetness when she reached for the high part of the wall.

The light naiad carriage of her body had entranced him. He had wanted to beget on her. That was his exact feeling, an intense and unprecedented need to *beget*, not simply to bed her. He had foreseen a shining son out of her lovely body. Now he'd see her sometimes, her slightly thickening hips, and think that in fifteen or twenty years, Marisa would be like her Italian mother, but without the florid, exaggerated gestures, the conspicuous hospitality. A few years after that, she would shuffle through the kitchen hunched over like one of her peasant forebears, all warts and limp and varicose veins and evil eye.

Five or six years after they'd married, around the time of the third miscarriage, Marisa had gone pious. She was obsessed with saints who had suffered grotesque attempted rapes or mutilations or wasting diseases and had received some vision in return. She felt at home in the Catholicism of daily Masses, scapulars and miraculous medals, novenas and adorations and posters of twelve-week-old babies in the womb. Her candor with his colleagues embarrassed him. The fact that she refused to dye the grey from her hair embarrassed him. *You don't dye yours.* At least she wasn't a puritan. With everyone else but Forrest, she had a fine judgment, fair and wise, and often he'd actually wanted to talk to her about the college girls he sometimes slept with. Sometimes he'd caught himself about to bring one up. Natalia, the *raison d'etre* of this anniversary trip, wasn't one he'd care to discuss, not yet. What would Marisa have to say about the way she—

"This whole time," she said from above him. She sat down. Her eyes were red. She clasped her hands and loosened them and put them in her lap and stared at him, red-eyed, false-seeming, self-consciously dramatic.

"What?"

"Our whole marriage. Our whole so-called marriage. Have you ever loved me? You're just—my God, don't you even remember what I *gave up* for you? For your girls."

Gave up for him?

"Fifteen years I'll never get back, never." A hunted desperation crossed her face. "So much put aside, so much wasted. Friends who don't have half my talent, but they've had gallery openings in Manhattan. And for what? For you and your girls. We have nothing in common. Nothing."

"What are you talking about? *My* girls?"

She picked up her wine glass, drained it, and set it down.

9

"I want a divorce," she said in a strained voice.

"You don't believe in divorce."

"I'll get the marriage annulled. It will be easy. You're not Catholic. You never meant to be faithful."

"What about the girls?"

"Your girls, you mean? They don't even like me. My faith embarrasses them. I embarrass you. You take them."

"You're drunk, Marisa."

"Put your head down," she said.

"What?"

"Put your head down!" she hissed, ducking to one side to dig at something in her purse. "My cousin Mario is standing right there!"

Forrest examined his cooling fettuccini.

"What's he doing here?" he said to his plate.

Marisa grabbed a menu from a startled waiter. "He has pictures. He's—it's that bookstore lady! Oh my God, she's pointing at us. Something's happened! Oh my God!"

She pushed back her chair, half-rising to meet Elizabeth Spence as she approached the table. Forrest turned and saw Mario, an earnest young man who always wore white oxford shirts and black trousers, touch his forehead with his fingers and glance upward in relief.

"What's happened?" Marisa demanded.

"There was a phone call," Spence said tensely. "Your daughters have been calling urgently. Your relatives did not understand the message." She squeezed her hands together.

"Oh my God!" Marisa cried.

Forrest looked at Mario.

Mario said tentatively, "*La cugina vecchia*?"

"The old cousin?" Spence asked. "Your relatives didn't know what the girls meant."

"Cousin Emily Barron Hayes," Forrest said.

"*Sì, sì!*" said Mario.

"Cousin Emily Barron Hayes," repeated Forrest. "Something's wrong?"

Beneath his ribs, doubt spilled like burning oil.

"They haven't been able to get in touch with us!" cried Marisa. "We have to call right now! Right now!" She looked around wildly. The other patrons stared at them, and the owner approached again, mournful and anxious. Spence spoke to him in rapid Italian and mimed writing. He nodded and waved off the waiter approaching with the bread and the check.

"Let's go to my place. It's just across the river and you can make the call from there. It's five hours earlier here, I believe."

"Six," said Forrest. "So it's—?" He glanced at his watch. "It's almost seven here, so it will be one in the afternoon there. How long ago was the first call?" he asked Mario, glancing at Spence.

10

Spence repeated the question to Mario, who thought for a moment and said, "*Lunedi scorso.*" They moved out onto the sidewalk and into the flow of the crowd toward the piazza just beyond them.

"Last Monday," Spence said ruefully. "And I think he means Monday of last week."

"Last week!" cried Marisa, stopping. "That's the day we left Viterbo! Oh my God, that's over a week ago! Braxton, we talked to Cate and Bernadette that day, remember? We were out on that terrace, before Zia Maria sent you down to the store. That afternoon, that day you..."

Her face accused him. Mario spoke again, reproachfully, and Spence translated. "He says they've been calling everywhere they could think of."

For the past week, they had been touring through Tuscany, staying in convents and monasteries, visiting churches and museums. Assisi, Siena, Florence. Marisa burst into tears. Passersby swung wide around the little group.

"I told them we'd call, but we never did. We never did!" She struck him on the shoulder and sobbed openly. Spence tried to embrace her but Marisa broke free and cried, "You have to go home!"

"What do you mean, I have to? What about you?"

"Sending them there was your idea. They're your girls!" cried Marisa.

"What are you talking about?" said Forrest, shaken by her fury.

"It's your fault. You take care of it. I'm not going back." She turned and ran clumsily back in the direction of the restaurant, stumbling and falling with a cry, her handbag spilling a dozen gift rosaries in little plastic boxes on the cobblestones. Already she was scrambling up and limping on, leaving them there. Forrest stood paralyzed. After a moment, Mario glanced at him reproachfully and ran after her, scooping up a few of the little boxes on his way. Still Forrest did not move. Spence stirred anxiously beside him.

"It's not far to my flat, just over the Ponte Sisto," she said. "But how will she find you?"

Stupidly, he stared in the direction Marisa had fled. "I don't know," he said, but then came to himself and shook his head. "I'll catch up with her at the hotel," he said.

When they came out onto the main street beside the Tiber, the traffic was a constant surge of cars and motorbikes. By now, he had worked himself into a fury. The bitch, the righteous bitch. Finally, the traffic light changed, and they crossed the street onto the bridge, mercifully closed to cars, where several vendors had their wares spread out. Another African selling carved masks, a skinny man with knives who looked Eastern European. The dome of St. Peter's loomed in the distance. People glanced at Forrest towering over them, stalking like Grendel, and got out of his way, except for the oblivious couples who walked slowly, absorbed in themselves, and teenagers who leaned smoking against the parapets—he thought of Vivienne, Cate's little minx of a friend in Portsmouth—and watched passersby with a knowing insolence.

He wanted to pitch them all into the Tiber.

As they got to the other end of the bridge, they stepped past an old gypsy woman feigning disease with baroque excess. She lay shaking on the stones with a dirty little girl beside her, a beggar in training. A spasm of contempt went up his neck.

They waited for the traffic to thin out, crossed to Piazza Trilussa against the light, and turned down a side street. Halfway down the block, Spence stepped into a passageway. She unlocked a gate and led him up two flights of stairs to her apartment. The cat jumped down from the broad windowsill as they came in. Spence opened the shutters, and Forrest heard a fountain splashing in a courtyard outside.

"I have a card," he told her.

"That's fine," she said nervously. "If you don't mind, let me do the dialing. It will be faster."

Forrest got out his wallet and found the piece of paper with Cousin Emily Barron Hayes' number in Gallatin on it and gave it to her. She touched the keypad expertly and waited. After a few moments, she put down the receiver, her eyebrows troubled, and repeated the process. This time she handed the slip of paper back to him.

"Not in service."

"Not in service," he repeated.

"Do you have another number?"

"That's her number."

"Have you called it before?"

"Well, no, but—listen, I need to get over there. Can you help me change my flight?"

"Well, I suppose," she said. "But don't you need to know what's going on? Isn't there someone else you could call?"

"I just need to go there. I've got a bad feeling about it."

"What about your wife, Mr. Forrest? She was very upset, and it seems—"

"We came on Alitalia from New York," he interrupted, "but I need something that goes directly to Atlanta."

She stared at the floor. The cat came over and snaked between her stolid English calves.

"Mr. Forrest..."

"Okay, let me do it," he said impatiently.

"No, no, I'll check," she sighed. "You're too upset. I'll need your credit card now."

He got out his wallet and handed her the American Express card.

"I'll talk to Marisa later," he said. "I know where she'll be."

Spence glanced at him as she sat down on the couch.

"But you don't know where your daughters are? Yours from an earlier marriage, I take it?"

"Hell, no!" he shouted, and she cringed back.

"You were unfaithful to her," she said.

He stared at her—plumpish, middle-aged, English. Her spinster blood was up.

"Have you ever been married?" he asked.

"Twice," she said definitively, as though to cut off speculations about her naïveté. "So this trip was to heal things?"

"That's right."

"But you did something, I take it." Her face had a knowing worldliness that irritated him. "When you were in Viterbo."

"None of your business," he said. "If you give me back the credit card, I can make arrangements at the airport."

"I hate to see someone make a mistake it will be hard to remedy," she said, "and leaving your wife in Italy strikes me as a very large mistake. You haven't even tried to call her."

"Did you hear what she said? She said I had to go back. She doesn't want to go back home."

"So she says, Mr. Forrest. Have a little imagination." She pulled a phone book from the drawer of the end table next to her, found the Alitalia number and asked him when he was originally supposed to return. A Saturday, he didn't know the date—maybe July 26? She touched in the number, waited, and started speaking rapid Italian.

How would he get his luggage? He had to get back to the hotel and then out to Fiumicino. He'd have to get a cab. It would add up. He touched his wallet. A hundred Euros left, maybe. The thought of meeting Marisa at the hotel gave him a dark qualm: her head thrust forward, that ugliness in her face that he himself had put there.

What if he just left his luggage behind? But his passport was in the laptop bag at the hotel, and he couldn't leave his laptop in any case, not with his new book on it.

And he couldn't leave Marisa without any money.

As though they had any money. Cash advances on the credit card at a whopping interest rate, that's what they had. Which Marisa didn't know. Should he take the train to Fiumicino to save money?

He drifted over to the window and gazed out. Mopeds, horns bleating out there in the night. She would find out everything soon enough, and then it would truly be hell. Either you saw the whole summer as daring venture capitalism, as he did, or you saw it the way she would when she found out, as a rotten fabric of lies and chicanery.

Why did he even care about saving the marriage? But the thought of losing her panicked him. They were a couple, Braxton and Marisa. The occasional college girls didn't mean anything. Seriously. They were just a diversion, a spice. Insignificant. He had always thought that she would love him no matter what—not that he had wanted her to find out about these little adventures. But if she had, he always thought, she would pray for him and be there to give him grief when he came home.

But to annul him? Braxton Forrest, annulled. As though he had never owned up to his marriage or his daughters. He did not want Cate and Bernadette to be like those empty girls from broken homes who came through his classes, conditioned for the world as advertised, ripe for rote male consumption. Soulless emotions, scripted vanity, cluelessness about any real moral order. Not that he had helped them.

He pushed away an image of Natalia.

"Mr. Forrest?" called Spence. When he turned, she was holding the receiver with her hand over the mouthpiece. "They can transfer you to a nonstop Delta flight going into Atlanta, but it's going to cost you another $800. Are you willing to pay that?"

"$800! That's my only choice?"

"So it seems. I've done my best at explaining the situation. If you were getting a one-way fare for this flight at such short notice, it would cost you €1800."

"Good God. What time does it leave?"

"Tomorrow morning at 10:20. You get into Atlanta by mid-afternoon. But it's $800."

"Tell them to book it."

The absurdity of it made him lightheaded. What was $800 added to a bill he already knew he could never pay off before he died? Money had become dream-stuff. Prospero's insubstantial pageant.

He argued politics with the almost-English-speaking cab driver who kept calling him George Bush. Back at the hotel, the lobby was empty, and so was the hallway upstairs. When he opened the door to the room, there was Marisa packing her things.

"What I find incomprehensible..." she said, refusing to look at him. It was like some Doris Day movie.

"Is...?" he said sarcastically, already angry.

"Is that you actually sent your children there. Your own children."

"Our daughters, you mean?"

"You've been lying this whole time!" She turned to face him. "That number you had isn't even connected. I've been calling people for the past hour. Cousin Emily Barron Hayes. My God, you liar. Do you know where your daughters are? Have you even tried to find out?"

He saw that she obviously knew. If they were in danger, she would be panicked and not berating him.

"I give up."

Her face twisted with contempt. She pushed a nightgown into her bag, zipped it savagely, pulled it from the bed with a thump, extended the handle, pulled it to the door.

"So where are they, Marisa? Did you talk to them?"

She did not answer. She opened the door, gave him one glance, and left.

For a moment he considered the last image of her: the tight condemnation of her face, the righteousness. Then something broke. A great rage impelled him across the threshold into the hallway after her. She was already almost to the elevator. She shrank back against the wall, her hand feeling for the elevator button. Everything had a perfect, singing clarity that jumped the time to come. In a few steps he would catch her and snap her neck.

And just then an old German couple backed out of their room in front of him. He had to catch himself to keep from knocking down the old woman, who was loudly chiding her husband and who never even noticed Forrest. The man, his great knobby knees bent below the khaki shorts, scowled and adjusted his hearing aid, shaking his hand beside his head. Beyond them, the elevator door opened and Marisa made her escape.

Forrest turned and went back to the room. Rage still flickered through him like the last scraps of lightning after a storm. When had he felt anything like that? There were hot remnants of it still in his bones. A rage worthy of Achilles. Not for a very long time had he felt an emotion so absolute.

2

July 16, 2009

Above the North Atlantic, the pretty Italian woman on the aisle drank two little bottles of Merlot over a lunch of airline ravioli. When she finished and the stewardess cleared her things, she raised the armrest, wrapped a blanket around her bare shoulders, and glanced toward Forrest. There was an empty seat between them; she tucked her knees onto it and closed her eyes.

So open to his gaze. He admired her shapely bare feet and calves, the tautness of the skirt across her thighs, her hands folded childlike under her cheek, her short black hair. One ear showed a small gold hoop. A pulse beat just beneath the skin in the soft of her neck. Everything about her moved him. Who was the actress she reminded him of? The one in the Kieslowski films. Irène Jacob. God, so lovely.

He sighed and read his Mahfouz novel. After a while, his eyes lifted from the page and he gazed out the window: an ocean of gray-blue metal textured like beaten gold, a coastline. He was just reaching incuriously for the Delta magazine to look at the maps in the back when the stewardess announced that the in-flight movie was about to begin.

Would they please lower their shades? He did. He even watched the movie (some guy who turns seventeen again), until it bored him and he took off the headset, closing his eyes and drifting into brief dreams, waking when he felt his mouth fall open.

He sat up with a start. He had been dreaming about a group of women standing around a hospital bed. The in-flight movie was scrolling through endless credits. The woman in the aisle seat was gone. People began to raise the shades on their windows, so he raised the one next to him and the one just behind the seat in front of him, shielding his eyes against the light. It must be the coast of Canada down there— Nova Scotia or Newfoundland—on the great circle between Rome and Atlanta.

He was reaching for the magazine to check the map again when a man from the row in front of him reared and laid a thick, tattooed arm across the seat back, one hand open toward the forward window.

"Close!" the man demanded.

Forrest stared at him.

"*Cochon*." The man made a violent gesture over the seat back. Forrest leaned forward and pushed the man's forehead with two knuckles, feeling the tension of the thick neck. Instantly the man was trying to swing at him in the cramped space. Forrest caught his fist and squeezed it, twisting the arm. The man yelled, and whoever was next to him—child or woman—cried out, and people in other rows started up in consternation. Forrest let go. The pretty Italian woman just returning from the restroom backed into the aisle with her hand at her throat, and a stewardess hurried toward them, already calling for help.

The stewardess spoke in French too rapidly for Forrest to follow, and the man, squeezing his wrist and shoulder, responded to her in outraged grievance, gesturing at Forrest, the window. The stewardess's look turned sympathetic. Unbelievable. She nodded and spoke consolingly, not to the angry little Frenchman, but to the person hidden beside him. The two stewards also gazed down sympathetically at whoever it was and added their own comments. The stewardess patted the air calmingly. The Frenchman flipped his good hand at Forrest with dismissive contempt and disappeared back into his seat.

One steward stayed beside the people in the next row, talking with them in low tones, and the stewardess knelt beside his row, a very fair girl. Another Kieslowski type.

"I'm so sorry," she said, resting one hand on the Italian woman's knee and the other on the back of the Frenchman's seat. She looked at Forrest.

"He's traveling with his daughter," she explained in a whisper. "The girl was in an accident last week, and her mother was killed. The parents were divorced, and now he"—she gave a sideways nod—"has responsibility for the girl, and he's taking her to America. The girl hasn't slept in days. She had just fallen asleep a little while ago, and ..."

16

"I woke her up," Forrest said.

She shrugged.

"I'm sorry, but the guy just turned around," whispered Forrest, "and took a swing at me." The stewardess pursed her lips and gave a noncommittal tilt to her head. She patted the knee of his companion in the row.

"Can I bring you something? Some wine?" she asked.

"Oui, merci," the woman said. "Merlot."

French, not Italian.

"Jack Daniels," said Forrest. "How old is the girl?"

The stewardess pouted. "Twelve? Thirteen maybe."

He thought of Bernadette. She and Cate in Gallatin, where Cousin Emily Barron Hayes had turned them away like strangers, as he'd learned that morning when he found Marisa's note. His father disinherited and now his daughters unrecognized. So who had them? Marisa's refusal to tell him infuriated him all over again. She always did the phone calling, didn't she? The same way she did the speaking in Italian. He peered out the window at the dark sea and another mysterious coastline. After the stewardess brought back their wine and whiskey, the pretty French woman poured her wine and sat without speaking. He glanced at her and smiled. He admired the way she left the top three buttons of her blouse unbuttoned. He loved the clean articulation of her hand.

"Sorry for scaring you," he said. He tilted his head at the seat in front of him.

"Yes," she said, pursing her lips and glancing uneasily up the aisle.

Forrest opened his Jack Daniels, poured it over the ice, took a sip, already wanting another bottle. He stared out the window again. Stupid. What was the matter with him? He felt a touch on his arm and turned.

"What is the matter with you?" the woman asked in careful English.

"With me? Nothing."

"Yes, you are very angry, I think." She mimed an explosion by making a small gesture with her hands and raising her eyebrows.

"It's a long story," he said.

"You were very happy to hurt this man."

"I was?"

"Oh yes. You were smiling."

"Was I?"

"*Oui.* Why were you happy?"

Her irises were the color of sage. So lovely. He shrugged and smiled. She dropped her glance, but he kept looking at her downcast eyes. In a moment, she reached over to his left hand, which was lying on the seat between them, and her middle finger touched his wedding ring.

"This is why you are angry, I think."

"Maybe. Why do you say that? I'm Braxton Forrest, by the way."

She touched his proffered hand at the fingertips.

17

"I am Asia Carducci. You know our shoes?" She bent over and lifted a delicate pair of black leather shoes by the heel straps. The toes bumped against his leg when she put them on the seat for him to inspect. "Your wife would love a pair of Carduccis, *n'est-ce pas*?"

She was a Carducci? What was she doing back here in coach? Backhanded, he put three fingertips inside the toe strap and picked one up.

"Way too small for Marisa," he said.

She raised her eyebrows knowingly, as if she intuited just who Marisa was.

"Isn't Carducci an Italian name?" he asked, handing back the shoes. "Why do you have a French accent?"

She dropped the shoes, unbuckled the seatbelt, and pulled her feet up under her. Fetching her compact and lipstick from her purse, she regarded herself in the small mirror and touched up her lips. She gave a pout. Pout, touch, moue. The doubled image, the little display of narcissism. As soon as she finished, she dropped the compact back in her purse.

"You are angry with her? With Marisa?" she asked him.

"So you just ask questions, you don't answer them?"

"My father is Italian, but the headquarters are in Paris. I grew up in the Sixth Arrondissement."

"And you're going to Atlanta on business?"

"Yes. I am nervous. That is the word, *n'est-ce pas*? Nervous? *Nerveux*? It is very dangerous, the South, yes?"

"Not at all."

"The black people are angry because they were slaves? They are violent like the Muslims in the banlieues?"

"They were slaves a long time ago."

"But the white people burn crosses, *n'est-ce pas*?"

"What movies have you been watching?"

"No? It is not true?"

"I grew up in the South, and I never saw anybody burning a cross."

"Ah, you are from the South. So you defend it. Because your—how do you say it? *Ancêtres*?"

"Ancestors."

"They were in the war to keep the slaves, so you defend slavery."

Forrest stirred in his seat with irritation. "That's not all the war was about. No, I don't defend slavery. But most of the men who fought didn't own slaves."

"So you say you do not defend, but really you think slavery is good, yes? The slaves were like children? Your *grand-pere* fought to keep them from being free. Because freedom would make them unhappy?"

He shook his head wearily. Here it was, almost a century since Quentin Compson committed suicide over it. Tell about the South. On his laptop even now was the outline of a new book on evolutionary psychology and the cultural dynamics of "miscegenation," that word invented after the Civil War. He had spent most of his professional life in the North, and he hadn't missed the casual racism or the instinctive Southern condescension toward the intellectual life, but he had been careful never to lose his Southern accent, which a woman like this could never be made to understand.

"You know what?" he said. "It's a long story. You have no idea how many ambiguities I live with."

He turned and stared out the window. After a moment, he felt her hand on his arm.

"Now you are angry with me?" she said.

3

July 17, 2009

When Forrest woke from uneasy dreams of a group of large women hooded (or maybe in burqas), his head hurt, his bladder was full, and according to the clock next to him, it was 7:41 a.m. Sunlight sliced painfully through a gap in the curtains, its reflection dazzling him from a mirror across the room. The sound of traffic rose from somewhere in rushing, intermittent tides. Amid the clothes strewn on the floor, an arm of his best suit dangled from his half-unzipped suitcase.

Next to him, Marisa's head was turned away, and the sheet had ridden down almost to her hip. He leaned over to stare in bewilderment at a tattoo on the small of her back.

He sat up with a sickening lurch. The shoe heiress. He couldn't remember her name. Something Asian? Asia. Asia Carducci. A vague feeling of exposure and violation. The airplane, the rental car, the hotel, the bottle of Maker's Mark—he spotted it tipped over empty on the table near the window beside a pizza box. Atlanta. Good God. Had he ordered pizza for a shoe heiress?

He hadn't even called about the girls. How was he going to get to Gallatin?

He'd rented a car. He could drive that.

And then do what with it?

The question stuck in his head like a math problem in a feverish dream. The longer he had the car, the more it cost, and already a great whirlwind of debt howled across the Atlantic after him, a hurricane from his nightmare. He squinted around the room for his wallet, spotted it. He remembered the hotel clerk downstairs making an imprint of his American Express card, so if he left, the bill would go on the card. It was coming back to him. $460 for the night plus incidentals. Good God—and where were they? The fifty-somethingth floor of the Peachtree Plaza. But if he went downstairs with his bag and left the building, at least nobody would stop him and ask him for money.

Next to him, Asia stirred, grumbling and half-turning, throwing her right arm back toward him and exposing her right breast. In the part of her cheek next to her mouth was the imprint of a little chain she wore on her wrist. Her eyes did not open and in a moment her soft snore resumed.

What was it about her that ticked him off a little?

She had his wedding ring.

In her purse. She had actually removed it from his finger and put it in her purse like some kind of trophy. Maybe she went around seducing husbands and stealing their wedding rings. Well not his. As quietly as he had ever gotten up to leave one of his little girls when he had put her down for a nap, he edged to the side of the bed, eased off one leg, then the other, and stood tottering, six feet five inches of naked nausea.

He looked on his end table, under the bed.

Things about Asia were beginning to come back to him now. Her recherché tastes, her demands. He had a dark qualm, the sense that he had exposed things about himself he did not want known, not by anyone. Something in particular that he had told her.

He had to find her purse. Very cautiously, he lifted a towel from the end table on her side of the bed. Not there. Maybe it was in the bathroom, where he needed to go in any case. The door already stood a little open, the floor still wet from where it looked like they had splashed in the shower, the towels wadded, flung around. He closed the door and used the toilet. There were his clothes, kicked into the corner. He fished up his underwear and put it on. Some of it was coming back, the way she—but there beside the sink he saw a black leather bag.

Peering down into it, Forrest found her passport and opened it. He stared at it in confusion. Maya R. Davidson. It would expire in 2011, which meant that the photo was eight years old, probably taken in college, maybe for a semester abroad, her teeth not yet perfect. A Cuthbert, Georgia address. And here was her business card. Maya R. Davidson, Dixintel Systems.

The little liar.

The slumming Asia Carducci: excellent, disturbing. But an assistant supervisor in the service management division of Dixintel? He pulled out her wallet. Take a credit card? No. All her cash? He felt metaphysically cheated, and this was payback. Still, the little liar knew his name. He slid out three new twenties. She had been drunk enough to lose track. Probably an expense account anyway.

He folded the bills and set them down. His mouth tasted awful. He grabbed the little complementary mouthwash and swished it around in his mouth frantically, then spat it into the sink. Splashed cold water over his face, stared at himself in the mirror. Everybody said he had remarkably young skin, probably part of his mother's Scandinavian heritage, and he still had his great mane of hair. The gray blended smoothly into the blond. But for two weeks now, he'd been unable to ride his Cannondale or get to the gym and it showed. He had once made a joke about getting fat that Marisa didn't think was funny. He called it seeing the buffalo. His nipples were the eyes, his belly button in its wild swirl of hair the mouth. The bigger his stomach got, the more you could see the buffalo gazing out on his lost prairies, as mournful as that little Italian restaurateur.

All that pasta.

The shower might wake up Asia—Maya, whatever—so he ran the hot water, moderated it with a little cold, and then dipped his head in the sink and splashed it into his hair and over his face. He toweled vigorously, finger-combed it. Flipping off the light, he tiptoed back into the bedroom and rooted silently in his suitcase for a pair of jeans that he pulled on. He transferred her money into the front pocket, put on a big, loose, blue T-shirt, and eased toward the door carrying his shoes and pulling his suitcase across the rug. On the twisted sheets, Maya Davidson snored lightly in her naked abandon, still pretending to be Asia Carducci.

He ghosted into the hallway, waited for the elevator, and got into it with relief. Halfway down the elevator to the lobby, slipping his feet into the loafers, he saw the arc of unsunned skin on his ring finger and cursed.

He punched numbers ferociously, and the swooshing elevator slowed. He had to go back up there, get in quietly—but just as the doors opened he remembered putting the key to the room inside her passport on the counter beside the sink. He cursed again. A family exiting from the next elevator all looked at him.

"Hey, watch your language," the father barked. One of those Baptist military types. Forrest started to answer him, but the three little girls were gaping over their shoulders at him as their mother, with averted eyes, herded them away, bags of bagels and muffins dangling from her milky freckled hands.

The doors closed. He yielded to the long speeding whoosh that lightened his body momentarily and made his ears pop until again it slowed, slowed, stopped. Parting, the doors revealed the lobby with its sleek modern furniture. He stared, bewildered, until a Starbucks in a far corner gave him an idea. He pulled his bag over to the front desk and asked the uniformed young black man if he could leave it there for a few minutes.

"Absolutely, sir," he said, stepping out beyond the counter and wheeling the suitcase back inside to an alcove, returning with a claim check to fill out and ripping off the part for Forrest at the perforated line. Smooth. Forrest pocketed the piece of paper and headed over to the Starbucks. While he was still in line, he ordered two venti lattes from the barista and scooped up several biscotti. When the cashier announced the price—$11.71—Forrest asked her to put it on his room tab.

"Sir, I'm sorry but we're not—"

"5017," Forrest said.

"Sir, we can't put it on your room tab. We're a separate franchise. We're not owned by the hotel, so..."

"Well, I wish I'd known that," he said. "I thought I'd just have the one bill," he explained to the tanned, sixtyish woman behind him as he dug out his wallet. She raised her eyebrows and looked away.

"Let's see," Forrest said. "Do you accept euros?" He flashed a €20 bill at her. "I just got back into the country last night and I haven't had time to get to a bank."

"No, sir, look, I'm sorry, it's just—"

"How about American Express?"

"Yes, sir! No problem," she said happily, swinging aside her hanging lock of magenta hair. She accepted his Gold Card, ran it through the machine, and gave him his receipt. He lurked, checking out the lobby, until the barista, a very pale boy with a ring through one nostril, announced the two venti lattes. He asked for a tray. The two coffees sat top-heavy in the cardboard as he headed back to the welcome desks, an arc of separate stations manned by handsome multiracial young people, all of them perfectly groomed, all of them with their hands restless on the counters. He picked an Asian girl whose skin reminded him of a dogwood blossom in dark woods on a rainy April day.

"You know what?" he said to her as he set down his unsteady tray, giving her the hapless smile that sometimes worked when he had to negotiate a grade change in the registrar's office. "I left my key in the room."

"Room number?" she said.

"5017."

She punched in the numbers and asked him for a photo ID. Taking out his wallet for his driver's license, he remembered the three stolen bills in his front pocket. Stupid—he didn't have to use the card, and he could have gotten change for tips. He put them in his wallet while the girl examined his license and then gave him a try-again smile.

"Room number 5017?"

"Woops. I know it's in the fifties and I think it's 17. Can you check my name? Braxton Forrest, two r's. F-O-R-R-E-S-T."

"Yes, sir. They even put it here on your driver's license." Saucy. "Forrest," she said. "Like the Civil War general."

He mocked gaping at her.

"Honey, did you know Cousin Bedford?"

"The one who started the Ku Klux Klan?"

"The original Klan. A kinder, gentler Klan—but never mind."

She glanced up at him, amused. "What I don't understand," she said, running a plastic card through the machine, putting it in a paper holder, and jotting a number on the outside, "is why Southerners don't just get over it."

"Frankly, my dear," he said. Her eyes, a startling green, met his as he took the card. "Are you married?"

"No, sir, but I see that your wife has ordered room service. It just popped up on your bill. The big special breakfast."

"My wife?" Forrest stared at her as terrible speculations beset him.

"Yes, sir. You'd better hurry before she eats it all."

He started away, his fingers splaying to support the tray and keep the two huge coffees from tipping over.

"Sir?"

He looked back at her

"5319. I wrote it on the envelope."

He shook his head.

5319. The fifty-third floor. He waited in front of the elevator doors, head lowered and pounding. 5319. He got in, grateful to have the elevator to himself. Finally, after an ascent that weakened his knees, the doors opened and he followed the arrows directing him to a range of rooms and found 5319.

Everything—the hallway, the door—looked completely unfamiliar. It could not be the same room he had left a few minutes before. He set the tray down on the hallway carpet and extricated the plastic card from its envelope, comparing the numbers written on the outside to the number on the door. He slid the card into the slot, the green light came one, and he pushed open the door, which immediately jammed against him.

"Who's that?" a woman's voice cried.

"It's me," said Forrest hopefully.

Asia's—Maya's—face appeared suddenly in the crack of the door. She stared at Forrest, then glanced down at the Starbucks tray on the floor, and back up at him, her face softening.

"Well look at that. You brought us some coffee," she said in a soft Georgia accent. "Isn't that sweet? I thought you were gone when I didn't see your suitcase. Here." She pushed the door closed, freed it from the sliding bar, and opened the room to him. She had on a pair of jeans and a sleeveless pink top. It was dark inside, smelling of bourbon, old pizza, funk. The Asian girl downstairs must have made that comment about the room service to get rid of him.

"Do you mind if I get some light in here?" he asked, setting down the coffee on the long dresser and walking toward the curtains.

"Wait!" she protested, but he pulled them apart as though the Wizard of Oz were hiding behind them and found himself teetering with vertigo, looking fifty-three floors straight down at the streets of Atlanta.

23

He stumbled backwards onto the bed.

"I was trying to say," she said. She went over to the window and stood with her bare toes against the glass and spread out her arms against it. "This just scares me to death."

He waited for a moment before he said anything.

"Can you see Cuthbert?"

She drooped a little.

"That's not funny," she said, turning and pouting at him. "Don't pick on Cuthbert. I bet Gallatin isn't any great shakes, either." She picked up her latte and handed him his and sat beside him on the bed. On her left deltoid was a tiny butterfly tattoo he vaguely remembered.

So she knew about Gallatin. What had he told her?

"Good morning, Maya," he said.

"Hi," she said. She met his eyes over the rim of her latte. "Have we met?"

"I guess not," he said. He took a sip of the coffee through the tiny opening in the top. Still too hot.

"It's fun being somebody else," she said. "You wouldn't have treated me that-a-way if you'd-a thought I was just Maya. You wouldn't have told me those things." She touched his arm with her cup. "The thing is, it doesn't count if it's not really me, does it?" She sat silently, the two of them gazing out at the Georgia horizon.

"What do you mean by count?"

There was a terrific pounding at the door, and both of them leapt up guiltily. She fled into the bathroom, and Forrest went to see who it was.

"Room service," said a uniformed black man his age, bumping the door aside with his prim hip and swinging a huge tray into the room. He looked around, eyebrows raised, for a place to set it. Forrest swept some items of Maya's clothing from the top of the desk, and the man set it down and raised the various lids to display the eggs Benedict, the home fries, the fruit, the juices, the various breads and muffins, the butter and jams, the coffee. He unctuously presented Forrest with a bill to sign. $43.23 for breakfast with a line for the tip. Forrest noticed a gratuity included in the total.

"So it already includes a tip," he commented, writing the printed sum in his own hand and signing it. Fat chance on the additional gratuity.

"Yes, sir," said the waiter, taking the bill stiffly. "Enjoy."

When the door closed, Maya came out of the bathroom.

"You don't mind, do you? We could split the eggs Benedict."

"You have it," he said. "I'm not that hungry."

He took a plate, put a huge, crumbling blueberry muffin on it, and tried to butter some of it, sipping his latte. He swiveled in the desk chair to face Maya, who sank down into a lotus position with her bottom against the window, holding her plate on her left hand and eating the eggs Benedict.

"You were going to leave, weren't you?" she said. The light behind

24

her made it hard to see her expression. It worried him that she seemed to remember more than he did.

"Why do you say that?" he asked.

She set aside her plate and stood up in one motion. With her forefinger, she fished out his ring from the pocket of her jeans. "Because you forgot this." She leaned over him—she had already taken a shower in the few minutes he was gone—and set it on the desk beside him. Forrest stared at it but did not touch it. Already, his heart was starting to hammer.

"I bet you left your suitcase downstairs at the desk when you realized you had to come back up here," she said, cocking her head and smiling at him as she stood between his knees, lightly jostling him. "Because it's gone." Then, shyly, almost self-consciously, she reached across him again, this time for a croissant, which she dabbed with raspberry jam. She had just put a little in her mouth and was catching a flake that fell from her bottom lip when she sank onto his thigh. "You are so bad," she said.

"What do you mean?" he asked with a qualm.

"Your new book. Gam Something and Superman."

"Oh my God, did I talk about that?"

Her sage eyes examined his as she pushed some croissant in his mouth, rocking a little on his thigh. "You don't remember? The stuff about Tarzan?"

"I told you about Tarzan?"

"Oh yes you did. But you made sure I understood you meant the one in the books, not the movie versions. You said he was the purest example of the modern superman gam something. You kept asking me if I knew Tarzan thought he was the son of a great ape. You said—"

"What?"

"You kept saying," and she imitated what he must have sounded like full of Maker's Mark, "'Tarzan recapitulated cultural phylogeny.' And you told me lots of things besides that."

"Jesus, what else?"

"Well, you said you were going to write a novel about a crazy Southerner who wants the government to repay him for depriving him of the legally purchased slaves he should have inherited from his ancestors. A satire, sort of like—what was it?"

"*Dead Souls*?"

"That's it. You said this guy was going to use the Mormon genealogies to find out who the descendants of his family's slaves were and then go around trying to convince them that they belonged to him." She leaned close and brushed his lips with her fingertip. "That's nowhere near as funny as you thought it was. But I'm bad too."

"What do you mean?"

"Because I thought, you know, wouldn't it be nice if it turned out I belong to you?"

"Belong to me?"

He stared at her. The name Maya suddenly flamed with significance. "My god, are you black?"

Her face hovered close before his, her hand tracing lightly down his shirt.

"Maybe. Maybe I am."

The next time he woke up, someone had the door open to where the bar stopped it and was knocking on it very rapidly at the same time. "Senor? Senor?"

Maya silently scrambled off the bed and into the bathroom, pulling the coverlet with her. He winced and sat up.

"What is it? Who's that?"

The door shut. There was a rapid burst of Spanish, not addressed to him, and he heard someone answer down the hall, then more voices, a high-pitched gabble of alarm gathering back toward him. A terrible thought struck him and he rolled over in bed to look at the clock. It was ten minutes after noon—and when was checkout time? He hadn't even looked. Again the door cracked open. "Senor? No checkout, yes?" a woman's harsh voice said.

"Does anybody speak English?" he yelled.

The door slammed shut again.

Another $460. The sound in the hallway was a warning squall of the storm to come. Soon, gales would be howling around him. Ruin, that shipwrecked and sodden word. He didn't know where his girls were, nobody knew where he was—well, nobody except Maya and American Express. Marisa, betrayed and abandoned, was somewhere in Italy without money, as she would soon discover.

He couldn't think of what to do. He was standing in the middle of the room, completely at a loss, when there was a knock on the door, this time measured and professional.

He flipped aside the bar and realized in the last split-second as he swung open the door that he had forgotten to dress. "Oh Jesus!" cried the black woman standing there, and by reflex he immediately slammed the door shut.

"Sorry," Forrest said, opening the door a crack and peering around it.

"Mr. Forrest?" she said in a strained voice. She was heavyset, middle-aged, officious.

"Yes, ma'am."

"It's past checkout time. The housekeepers need to get in here. We're going to have to ask you to vacate it, please, or the hotel will—"

"Charge me?" Forrest demanded eagerly.

"Yes, sir."

"So they haven't automatically charged me, is that right? I mean, the next night didn't automatically go on my card at noon?"

"No, sir, but we will have to—"

"We'll be out in two minutes," he said, shutting the door again.

Five minutes later, Forrest was holding the door open for Maya, and the huddle of housekeepers with their carts and vacuums watched him from a few doors away. Maya came out into the hallway with her bag and then impulsively embraced him. There was a burst of commentary, and Maya turned to the women and said something in rapid Spanish that made them put their hands on their mouths. She started toward the elevators, pulling her bag with elegant hip-intensive hauteur. Asia again.

He followed her and smoothed his hand down her back and onto her bottom. They stepped into the elevator, where an elderly couple regarded them apprehensively. Just as the doors were closing, he cried, "Where's my ring?" and got back out. "I'll meet you in the lobby," he said over his shoulder.

The cart was in front of the room, and the door was propped open with a trashcan. He heard somebody working in the bathroom. Another housekeeper had her back to him as she vacuumed near the window. He knocked to get her attention, but she did not hear him. "Senora!" he said. He had just stepped inside when she switched off the machine and turned around, humming, and saw him. Her eyes went wide. Her hand went to her throat. She was young, a little plump, but pretty. Her tongue came out and wet her lips as she stared at him, and just then, the other woman, fortyish and shapeless, came out of the bathroom and started barking Spanish, waving the back of her hand at him. Forrest shook his head, touched his finger, and went over to the desk.

No ring.

"Where is it?" he demanded, showing them his ring finger where the ring was missing. "Where's my ring?" He tapped the top of the desk with a forefinger to show them where it had been. "My ring?" he said, turning the imaginary ring around on his finger with his fingertips.

The older woman immediately turned suspicious eyes on the younger woman, who shook her head and backed away. Her hand made a chop of denial. But the older woman shook a threatening finger at her and kept talking until the younger woman's face looked panicked and she burst into tears. The older woman fished in the pockets of the girl's apron and in the pockets of her pants and even reached down the front of her shirt. She finally turned helplessly to Forrest, her attitude suddenly humble and imploring, both her palms up.

Oh, yes, he understood her. Yes, yes. He nodded, large with compassion. He gave her a no-big-deal expression. He waved the matter off. As he was leaving, she was still pleading with him, her hands tented before her as if in prayer, but as soon as he was in the hallway, his rage kicked in. He slapped the wall, cursed savagely as he waited for the elevator, and punched the first floor button repeatedly when the elevator arrived.

Maya was waiting for him in the lobby, ten feet from the opening doors. She sat atop her bag with perfect posture, her legs crossed at the ankles, her hands folded on her lap. She stood as he came up to her. "You dumbass," she whispered, taking his hand and pressing the ring firmly into his palm. "I knew you'd forget it. Just put it on."

He did. When he retrieved his suitcase, he asked the young man to change a stolen twenty, and then gave him a couple of dollars. He started for the door with Maya clicking along beside him in her Carducci shoes, his yummy little yogi. He would go to the parking garage and get the car. Then what? The world was all before them. They would go to her place, and after a few acrobatic hours, he would drive to the Hertz lot at the airport, and she would follow him and bring him home to keep. Every morning, she would sit on the floor with her hands around a cup of coffee, wearing nothing but his T-shirt, and she would gaze at him until she couldn't stand it and she would clamber into his lap with her legs around him and kiss him and taste like raspberry.

"Holy shit," she murmured. She had taken a Blackberry out of her purse. Where did that come from? "Listen, can you run me down to our main office? It's about ten blocks from here."

"Right now?"

"Can you? I need to be there in fifteen minutes."

"You're leaving me?"

She cocked her head at him. She unzipped her suitcase and pulled out a short jacket that somehow made her look dressed for work when she put it on.

She was leaving him?

What now? He could drive to the Hertz lot at the airport, but he would have no way to get to Gallatin if he did. So what he should do is drive to Gallatin, pick up the girls, drive back to the airport, turn in the car—he wouldn't get charged that much extra for half a day—and then fly them all to Boston. American Express. Then they'd have to get from Boston to Portsmouth, but there must be a shuttle, and American Express would let him take it. They would get home, and Marisa would not be there, and what he had not told them would come out. Their mother. The threat to his job because of Natalia.

But the most immediate thing was to pick up the girls, and he didn't know where they were. He pictured himself driving around the courthouse square in Gallatin for the fourth or fifth time, passing the Confederate soldier marching northward, his rifle on his shoulder. He unconsciously slowed and stopped walking in midstride and stood transfixed in the middle of the lobby, his eyes glazed.

"What's the matter?" asked Maya, tensed to go. He could not move. "Braxton? Should I get a taxi?" She was leaning away from him toward the door. She fished a card and a pen out of her purse and jotted down a number on the back. "That's my cell," she said, handing it to him. "Call me, please. I mean it. Please. This afternoon." She came back and kissed him, then turned and fled through the doors. Within seconds, a yellow taxi had consumed her and she was gone into the flow of traffic.

Freeing the car from the garage cost him $23 of the money he had stolen from Maya. Would she figure it out? She seemed to remember other things, which worried him.

He pulled out of the garage exit, looking for I-75 South. Signs directed him to Harris Street and in a few blocks he was on the ramp and up onto the expressway, where the traffic flowed smoothly past Turner Field and then I-20 and the I-85 split toward the airport and then south. He passed the exit for I-285, then McDonough. Locust Grove. That summer right out of high school when he was a chainman on the surveying crew, they had worked on a tract of land almost this far north. He remembered going through a field of flowering grasses and wondering why his eyes were swelling shut and he couldn't breathe. It must have been August. They had to knock off early, wasn't that it?

Something like that, he thought uneasily. Maurice Woodson, Mo, who wore black T-shirts with the left sleeve folded up over his pack of Marlboros and had that oily look to his skin. They always stopped and bought a six-pack of Miller after work. Bottles with twist-off caps. Forrest remembered draining two or three of them and wheezing like he had emphysema while Mo smoked Marlboros. Was that right? Something like that. Somebody else was with them. Bertram Everett? Or was it Tony Wright?

The familiar dark qualm came. He wondered what else he had told Maya last night. His willingness to tell her things had something to do with being back in Georgia, but it was also her curiosity as Asia Carducci. Prying, teasing. She made secrets come out, ready or not. He was suddenly filled with resentment. Maya had ruined his perfectly good plan to pick up the girls, the plan he must have had, hadn't he, before he noticed her on the seat next to him in the airplane, pretending to be somebody else?

That was a sin, wasn't it? Counterfeiters of persons were far down in Hell. Dante had Myrrha socked away down there, he thought—the one who pretended to be somebody else so she could sleep with her own father.

Soon the signs started coming. Gallatin Next Five Exits. He would come in quietly, ask a few questions, pick up the girls from wherever they were. They would drive back to Atlanta.

Fly to Boston.

His first thought was to look for them at the house where he grew up, though of course they weren't there. He got off at the first exit, crossed the railroad track onto Beauregard Drive, passed the field that was supposed to have belonged to a Georgia governor, and slowed to look up at the big houses set far back from the street, the lawns shaded by tall pecan trees and oaks. The Russell place, the Morrison house, sweet palsied Mrs. Hill's white columns. On the sidewalk ahead of him to his right, a woman walked slowly, almost meditatively, on the root-buckled concrete, her left hand to her head. A big Irish Setter pulled at the leash she held in her right hand.

An odd feeling came over him. She stopped walking and he saw her speak to the dog, which immediately sat down. She turned, not really seeing what was in front of her—she was talking on a cell phone—and her eyes passed casually over him. Late thirties, quite beautiful, and she lived here, he realized, right on Beauregard Drive. But it wasn't just that. He was going so slow her eyes came back to his, and a startled, almost panicked look passed over her face.

He stopped and put down the window, and said, "Excuse me." She held her phone against her breast and leaned forward so she could see him better inside the car.

"Yes, sir?" she said.

"Is this the way to the courthouse square?"

She looked blank, as though the question confused her.

"The courthouse square?" she said in a voice that did not come from Gallatin.

"That's right."

"Well," she said, "I usually go past past the Baptist church and turn left on Jackson Street."

"Thanks," he said. He raised a hand and drove slowly toward the curve in Beauregard Drive and the house where he had grown up. As he glanced in the rearview mirror, he saw the woman looking after him. She looked terribly familiar, but how could he possibly know her?

And then there it was: the two-story white house with dark green shutters on the corner across from the First Baptist Church. He and Marisa and the girls had been here once, many years ago, so the girls could see their grandmother, but they had probably been too young to remember. It had been almost eight years since his mother died, a week to the day before 9/11. The azaleas around the front had been replaced with boxwoods, and the screen porch was glassed in, an office. He saw a middle-aged woman get up from her desk and hurry into what was once their living room. A sign out front—he slowed to read it—said Counseling Center.

T.J. Forrest, who owned several houses in the neighborhood, had let his mother live in it when Robert Forrest died, but then Harlan Connor had bought it outright when he married her and had left it to her when he died. She had left the house to Forrest, and the Baptist church had bought it for $80,000. Real estate had boomed for a while after that, and up until the crash last fall, he could have gotten half again as much. All the money had gone straight into their Portsmouth house. Not a dime of it left.

At least the church had not razed it. The lawn of St. Augustine grass looked well-kept.

That lawn had once been his battlefield with Harlan Connor. Forrest had been five years old when his mother asked him how he'd like to have a new daddy. He remembered first seeing this tall, lean, slow-talking man from out in the county, a widower with grown children who understood exactly what his mother needed and looked at Forrest with something sardonic around his mouth. Harlan Connor. Much to Forrest's amazement, his mother loved this man who not only took over his house and his mother's bed, but worse than that, told Forrest what to do. And his mother let him, even encouraged him.

A little too bookish, Connor would say to him in front of his mother. *I just need to toughen him up some.* At eight or nine years old he had to mow the grass, and Connor would stand smoking in the shade of the pecan tree like an overseer, pointing with two fingers, the cigarette between them, a half-smile on his face under the shadow of that hat he always wore. *You missed a spot.* Forrest's temper would flare up. He would yank the mower back and forth under the limbs of the fig tree, and Connor would laugh at him. On Saturdays in the summer he would take Forrest out to the farm one of his grown sons ran and make him work all day unloading feed or putting up fences and stretching barbed wire. His mother had grown up on a farm in Minnesota, and she always sided with Connor when Forrest complained about him. *He's a good man, Braxton, and he's the only father you've got. He knows how to make a man out of you.* A Connor man, maybe. It had enraged him.

By the time he was twelve, he was already strong and just at the verge of getting his growth. The work had done what Connor wanted. He could move around hundred-pound feed sacks as easily as pillows on a bed. When he went out for Pop Warner football in the seventh grade, the coaches had the boys doing blocking and tackling drills at the first practice to get them used to hitting each other. Several of the boys complained to Mr. Chambers, the head coach, that Forrest was hitting them too hard. The next day at practice, Coach Fitzgerald from the high school was standing beside Coach Chambers, watching Forrest knock the other boys backward when they tried to block him.

Forrest probably would not have hardened his heart against Connor if Mary Louise Gibson had not always been reminding him of what it meant to be a Forrest. She would be ironing the sheets on a cold winter morning, alone with him in the house, and she would tell him stories about old Mr. T.J. and mean Miss Sybil and his sweet real daddy, who was confused by being in the North, and the wicked witch Cousin Emily Barron Hayes, who had stolen everything.

31

She would tell him *It ain't right, what they done,* and how he just needed to wait for what was coming to him. *You ought to be a rich man,* she would say, looking at him through a cloud of fresh-smelling steam as she ironed the damp sheets. *These Connors, they ain't but a step up from trash. You a Forrest. That's how come Mr. Harlan ride you like he do. He know you a Forrest and he ain't nothin'. You just put up with it.* Connor had been proud of him, he knew, especially when he made All-State the first time, but they had clashed violently over Forrest's liberal ideas. *Don't you know that's what ruined your daddy?* Still, Harlan Connor had been a decent man. And yet, when he died of a heart attack the summer before Forrest's senior year, Forrest had felt only liberation. His mother had grieved for months.

You a Forrest, you hear me? Mary Louise would tell him, beaming at him on the Saturday streets of Gallatin when she saw him as a teenager. *Look at you. You strong and getting stronger. You show these ignorant folks what a Forrest is.*

4

Three decades before the Wal-Mart came to Gallatin, Rockwell's Pharmacy had been new, the way a new shirt or a new pair of shoes remains new for weeks, months—even years—until it's suddenly recognized as worn out and replaced. Back in the 1970s, when Coach Dan Fitzgerald was hardly a decade into a career that would establish unbreakable records in Georgia high school football history, Jeremiah Rockwell had abandoned his spot on the courthouse square between the Maxwell's Pool Hall, where gambling sessions went on daily in the back room, and George's Clothing, run by the only Lebanese family in Middle Georgia. Hoping to establish a new standard for his town, he had moved onto his own lot a block down Lee Street toward Interstate 75. There Jeremiah had erected a new building that embodied his dream—modern, one-story, flat-roofed, glassed all along two sides, spacious inside, with plenty of parking outside.

Because of Jeremiah's relative wealth, his urbanely witty demeanor, his good golf game, his sophisticated wife, and his phenomenally athletic son Jed, who helped win the old state championship in the history of Sybil Forrest High School, he had become a kind of patron to Coach Fitzgerald, who frequented Rockwell's Pharmacy for at least an hour or two every day in the off-season. Former players like Chick Lee could count on seeing him there, long after Jeremiah died and Jed took over the business and Wal-Mart sucked most of the business downhill to its much cheaper pharmacy. No one who had played football at Sybil Forrest, no one who cared about the greatest moment in the history of Gallatin, could betray Jed Rockwell and Dan Fitzgerald for a few lousy dollars in savings.

Halfway out the door of Rockwell's, Chick was holding his left palm toward his wife, who had lowered the passenger's window of the Navigator to do that rolling, hurry-up gesture he hated.

"Brantley, come on!" she called.

They had to pick up Alyssa from ballet in Macon, but Coach Fitzgerald—a short, thick man with broad shoulders and the remnant of a brogue—was inside at a table with Jed Rockwell telling a story about how Chick got his nickname when he first came out for football at spring practice in the ninth grade.

"He had on one of those yellow jerseys we'd make the defense wear," Coach said, enjoying himself a little too much to suit Chick. "Mike Toles came busting through the hole and ran right over him. Brantley got up and didn't know where he was. Walking in little circles like this." He stood up and imitated him. "Hell, he didn't know who he was. Making these little noises. And Buzz Dorner says, 'Here, chickie, here, chickie.' Been Chick ever since."

"Come on, Brantley!" Patricia called from the car. She had put down the window again and risked the July heat twice.

"Sit down, Chick," Jed Rockwell said. "You're letting out my air conditioning."

"Gotta go, Coach," Lee said.

"Chick Lee," said Coach, unhurried. "They even put it in the program that way. You were just glad it didn't say Brantley."

Huge, black Dutrelle Jones, the only Sybil Forrest High School graduate ever to play in the NFL, came over from the prescription counter with a small bag and traded a fist bump with Rockwell on his way to the door. "How's it going, Mr. Lee?" he rumbled at Chick.

"Can't sell a thing, Dutrelle. Thinking about giving cars away. You want one?"

"I hear you."

"You better be glad Dutrelle wasn't playing when you went out," Rockwell said. "If he'd hit you...."

"Aw now," said Dutrelle Jones, laughing and rocking Chick by the shoulder. "Y'all little white men can't help it. You mighty dressed up, ain't you?"

"Going to Atlanta tonight. Date with my wife."

Patricia called again from the Navigator.

"Watch out now," said Dutrelle.

"Shut the door!" said Rockwell.

"How come you didn't give Dutrelle a nickname, Coach?" asked Chick, waving to Patricia.

"Marvin Love called him Train Wreck. But with a name like Dutrelle, why would you need a nickname?" said Coach.

"Y'all just jealous," said Jones. Chick stood aside to let him leave and watched him walk toward his Dodge Ram. He would have sold Dutrelle an F-150 at cost just to have the only ex-NFL player in town driving it around. Rockwell waved him back in, so he stepped back inside and let the door close.

"Brantley!" he heard Patricia yell.

"Y'all know Dutrelle's in trouble," Rockwell said. "He started building all those houses and the bottom dropped out of the market. And he's got that high-maintenance Atlanta wife to keep happy."

They shook their heads.

"How Rosey Peters got his name..." Coach said.

"Rosey?" said Rockwell. "I've heard it about a million—"

"He came off the farm as fat as the Pillsbury doughboy."

"Patricia's going to kill me," Chick said. "Anybody playing golf Saturday?"

"Maybe I'll see you," Rockwell said.

Patricia's window came down again before he got to the Navigator, which was one handsome vehicle. "Brantley, I swear—you know she hates to be the last one picked up."

He noticed a smudge on the gleam of gold and polished it off with his handkerchief before he opened his door and settled into the leather seat.

"You could have waited for this until after we got her," he said, handing her a white paper bag. "What is this stuff? It's fifty bucks for the co-pay."

"It's for her complexion," she said, and her tone of voice hinted that any father who would ruin his daughter's life to save fifty dollars was beneath contempt. "And no," she said, "we couldn't wait to get it, because she's spending the night with Bridget, and we have to give her this before we drop her off. Otherwise, she could have gone home with Bridget to start with and saved us the trip. What were you doing?"

"You don't walk out on Coach Fitz when he's telling a story about you."

"The great Dan Fitzgerald," she said.

"Best coach in the history of the state," he said flatly. He put the Navigator in reverse and looked at his rear camera display to see if anything was behind him. A white Toyota Camry had nosed into the parking lot.

"Those girls are going to be spending the night with Bridget, too, just so you know," Patricia said.

"What girls?"

"The ones everybody's been so worried about. Those poor abandoned Yankee girls."

"Okay." He tried to remember what he had heard. Cump Forrest's daughters who thought they were supposed to stay with old Mrs. Hayes. Whoever was in the Camry had pulled into an empty parking spot, and Lee started to back up, glancing in his mirrors, when he saw a big man in jeans and a blue T-shirt getting out of the car and stretching, looking toward the drugstore.

"Good God Almighty," he said. He hit the brakes and put the Navigator in park. "Hold on a second," he said and got out of the car.

"Brantley!" she cried as he slammed the door.

"My God," he said to the man approaching him, still handsome and fit, still with his Viking head and that way of moving that made you think of National Geographic shows about lions. "Braxton Tecumseh Forrest. It's a good thing I saw you first. Get in the car."

"Chick," Forrest said, extending his hand. "How are you doing? What's the rush?"

"Hop in, hop in," he said, opening the back door of the Navigator. "This is my wife Patricia. Patricia, this is Braxton Forrest. The father of those poor Yankee girls."

Her mouth fell open.

Forrest had thought he could come quietly into Gallatin to retrieve his daughters, but he should have known better. It turned out he was more or less a wanted man. They drove south on U.S. 41 past small farm communities—Bunnville, Johnson's Store, Hereford—and Forrest angled forward from the plush back seat to explain to the Lees why he and Marisa had been out of touch in Italy.

"Marisa liked to stay at monasteries. We'd just show up and she'd knock on the door. Our cell phones were useless. Internet, you'd have to go to these little cafes if you could find one. I caught a plane back as soon as we got the news."

Chick's wife wanted to know when his plane had gotten in, and he told her it had been yesterday afternoon. She asked him why he hadn't come straight to Gallatin. He said he hadn't slept the night before he left Rome, so he wanted to get some rest before he came down.

"But you called somebody, I hope," she said.

"I didn't know who to call."

"Now that," said Chick, turning around in the driver's seat and looking at him for a second. "I have to tell you, Cump, that hurts a little. You know you can call me, day or night. And listen, you're staying with us while you're here. I'm not taking a 'no' on that one."

Forrest had not thought of Chick Lee in years. He supposed he should be grateful for this intervention or whatever it was, though he could do without this wife of his. He thought about the sprawling ranch-style house Chick's father had built in the piney part of Gallatin near the golf course and the town swimming pool. Mr. Lee had owned the Ford dealership out on I-75, and Chick had grown up with more money than most of them. All through school—he had been a year behind Forrest—he had been one of the smaller kids, a little soft.

It wasn't until Chick went out for football that he got any respect. Dan Fitzgerald had seen something in him—or had pretended to because he liked Mr. Lee. He toughened him up and put him at nose tackle. Chick weighed about a hundred and fifty pounds by his junior year, not much for the position even in their small-school division, but he was fast. He could twist his shoulders and fire through the gap between the center and the guard and be in the backfield before the quarterback could hand off the ball. More than once he intercepted the handoff. One of the assistant coaches found out that another high school listed him on their scouting report at one hundred ninety-five pounds. When Forrest was All-State for the third time his senior year, Chick had gone unnoticed by the newspapers, but by the next year, after a weightlifting regimen with all kinds of protein supplements, Chick really was one hundred ninety-five pounds. He was benching almost three hundred pounds, and he had kept his quickness. He made opposing centers and quarterbacks so nervous they would hurry the snap and fumble. Colleges started sending scouts to watch him play. Gallatin made it back to the quarter-finals of state that year, Chick was second-team All-State, and although the big colleges were unwilling to risk much on a player a few inches under six feet, a little college in South Carolina offered him a scholarship. He even played a season or two before Mr. Lee died of a heart attack and Chick came home to run the business.

Now he was soft again. He had on a cream-colored linen jacket over a light blue Polo shirt and dark blue slacks. Expensive cordovan loafers. He looked prosperous and groomed, with one of those stomachs a man like him would never get rid of, and he had married this woman who had convinced him she was even more upscale than his Navigator. What she actually was Forrest could sum up in one syllable.

"So where'd you stay last night?" asked Chick after a long silence.

"Last night?" His mind raced. "First place I found. A Day's Inn." Forrest wished that at least he had taken a shower that morning in his $460 room. Maya floated from his clothes like a pennant of sin.

"You must have slept awfully late," said Patricia Lee.

"Well, actually, Patricia," Forrest said, "I'm not being entirely honest. I picked up this cute little Italian shoe heiress on the flight back from Rome and we had sex all night at the Peachtree Plaza, so I kind of lost track of the time."

Chick guffawed at that and reached a fist back over his shoulder for Forrest to bump, but his wife reddened, shook her head, and stared out the window. She looked down at her watch. "Oh my god, Chick, hurry up! It's already after four and Alyssa's going to be in a tizzy."

Chick set his cruise control at seventy-five on the smooth two-lane, and they flashed past a country store that Forrest remembered from a surveying job that summer. 1969. Another qualm of dread.

They flew through Hereford and under Interstate 475.

"See, Cump, what it is," Chick said, glancing at him in the rearview mirror, slowing down as they reached the outskirts of Macon, "is it's your wife. She was so worked up, you know, when she called people? If she hadn't said she didn't know where you were. If she hadn't called so much these last couple days, I don't think it would have been in the paper, let me put it that way."

"It was in the paper?"

"Not on the front page," said Chick's wife, as though to keep him from thinking he was that important. "I thought Don handled it right."

"It was in his column," Chick said.

Leaning forward from the back seat, Forrest watched Chick's plump hand on the steering wheel.

"Who's Don?"

"Don Sutton. The publisher. He got here after you left. He writes this column about Gallatin every week in the *Record*. He mentioned your daughters."

"Mentioned them how?"

"He was praising the Baptist community," said Chick's wife. "For taking them in. Taking care of them." She sat there stiffly and her left hand with its big diamond kept clenching as though she were wadding Forrest into a spitball.

He sank back into Chick Lee's leather. The Baptist community. His house and now his daughters.

"So, if you don't mind my asking," Chick said into the rearview mirror, "did you and your wife—I mean, was there some kind of...?"

"She was put out with me."

"Put out because...?"

"Because of Cousin Emily Barron Hayes. I thought it was all set, and it turned out it wasn't."

There was a long tense silence.

"I'm sorry," said Patricia Lee, turning around in her seat to face him with her sharp black eyes and her impatient mouth, "but did you ever actually speak to Mrs. Hayes before you sent your girls down to stay with her?"

Forrest did not answer.

"I don't think so," said Patricia Lee. "Because her phone has been disconnected for two years."

"Come on, Patricia, give him a break," said Chick uncomfortably.

"I talked to your wife, Mr. Forrest. I bet that's a surprise to you, since you haven't talked to her. I told her Mrs. Hayes has a black woman who helps her, Hermia Watson, and everybody in Gallatin knows if you have any business with Mrs. Hayes—not that she'd understand it—you call Hermia."

"Okay. I never talked to her. I got letters from her."

"Do you realize that Mrs. Hayes is ninety-three years old? Did you know she was living on nothing up in that big house? Hermia Watson says she just sits all day by a window in an upstairs room looking out at the back of the property where the garden used to be, talking about people she knew when she was young. What your wife wanted to know was why Mrs. Hayes had invited your girls down to stay with her for a month. She said she had read the letters, and they were lovely. I told her Mrs. Hayes didn't know who she was half the time. I told her whoever wrote those letters, it wasn't Mrs. Hayes."

"Let's give it a rest," Chick said. "There's Alyssa."

They pulled into the parking lot of a small strip mall not far from Wesleyan College, and Forrest spotted a teenage girl with long, lovely legs standing forlornly all by herself under the awning of On Pointe Ballet in a black leotard, her blonde hair pulled back in a ponytail. As soon as she spotted the Navigator, she stamped her foot and shook both hands like claws beside her head as though she were about to go crazy.

As soon as Chick pulled up, she snatched open the right back door, flung in a bag that hit Forrest in the shoulder, got in, and slammed the door. "Oh my god! I can't believe you did this to me again. You just—" Then she saw Forrest. She cut her eyes toward her father in the front seat.

"Honey," Chick said carefully. "Alyssa, honey, this is Mr. Forrest. He's the father of the girls who—the Forrest girls who..."

She stared at Forrest with her mouth open, as though she had just found herself sitting across from Hannibal Lecter.

"You're the one?"

"I guess so," smiled Forrest.

"They think you're—Dad, how did you—"

"Alyssa!" her mother said, and the girl shivered and closed her mouth. "Here's your prescription." Her mother handed the white bag over the seat and Alyssa automatically took it, biting at her top lip and avoiding Forrest's gaze. "And that's why we're late, if you really care. It looks like you could let me know before it runs out. We'll just drive you straight to Bridget's if you have everything."

Bridget Davis, according to Chick, was the only child of the manager of the Wal-Mart that had sucked all the life out of the placid downtown Forrest remembered. Since she lived off I-75 north of Gallatin, they took the Interstate back from Macon, and Forrest tried to explain again, in ways that did not make him seem like a monster of selfishness, why he had not been in touch with his daughters. Alyssa Lee shrugged and moved her head in skeptical half-nods, but she would not look at him until he asked her if the girls were okay.

"Are they okay?" she repeated, staring at him. "You mean, are they sick?"

"I just mean, are they okay? Their spirits."

"Their spirits?" repeated Alyssa. "You mean..."

Patricia Lee sighed dramatically in the front seat. Chick nervously punched the button for the stereo system, and a Toby Keith song came on too loud.

"Dad, Jesus," complained Alyssa.

"Watch your mouth, young lady," said Patricia.

Chick turned down the radio, and Forrest gazed at this girl the age of Cate, three or four years younger than girls like Amanda and Natalia whose most intimate secrets he knew. Her just-licked lips were a little parted as she stared back at him in the effort to understand this concept he was trying to get across.

"Are they happy?" he asked

Her mouth fell open.

"You're kidding, right?"

"That bad?" he said.

"They cry, like, all the time," said Alyssa. "Their mom told them...I don't know." She chewed her lower lip and gave a half-shrug.

"Told them what?" Forrest caught Chick Lee's eye in the rearview mirror and refrained from touching the girl's hand.

"That you had gone sort of..." she said.

"*Off the rails* was how she put it to me," said Patricia Lee. "It's not an expression we use in Gallatin."

Forrest sank back in his seat. Marisa was the one off the rails.

He wondered if Maya really wanted him to call her. They flashed past all the Gallatin exits and got off on Hood Road, which used to lead to a country store and a scattering of farms. Now new developments had metastasized along it, and Chick turned into one called Tara Acres. He followed the street past huge blind houses and pulled up in a cul-de-sac in front of a place whose front entrance featured the four fake Corinthian columns of a porte cochère, ridiculously high above the brick driveway. Chick parked under it.

"I need to speak to Varina," said Patricia Lee, getting out of the car with Alyssa. Forrest watched them approach the front door. Who was it—Updike?—who had written that young women were a different species from postmenopausal ones? Alyssa and her mother waited at the door for a few seconds.

"Kind of hard to hear, isn't it?" said Chick. "What Alyssa said about your girls crying all the time."

"Yeah, except they seem to find something to cry about half the time anyway."

The front door opened, and Patricia said something and opened a hand back toward the Navigator. He saw the other woman put her fingers to her mouth and tilt her head to see past Patricia. He leaned toward the window.

"Good God, Chick, that's Tricia Honeycutt!"

"That's right, she married Judah Davis."

"But your wife used some other name."

"Varina. That's her first name. Judah makes everybody call her that."

"I heard she married some guy from out of town."

"Are you serious? You never kept up with her?"

"With Tricia? I haven't seen her in forty years."

"She came to your mother's funeral."

"I don't think so."

"She told me she did," Chick said, sounding a little hurt.

"I think I remember that now," he said, not remembering more than the faintest trace, a glance, a quick exchange maybe. "I was pretty distracted."

"Right," Chick said. "She married an insurance man named Foster a few months after graduation. They didn't make it a year." He hesitated. "She had a son. He's grown now. Lives over in Griffin and works for the State Patrol."

"I'll be damned. Sweet little Tricia. She looks pretty good."

Patricia Lee turned from the doorway, raised her eyebrows, and did a roll-down-the-window with her forefinger. Chick pressed a button and the window on the passenger side slid down.

"Hi, Varina," he said, leaning toward it.

"Hi, Chick," she called, and the rich voice thrummed through Forrest. She was shorter than Patricia. Tan and fit, she had on a white tennis outfit—a short skirt, a sleeveless top that came down in a scoop to her breasts, expensive tennis shoes. Fine-looking for a woman her age.

"Can you ask Mr. Forrest to come in, please?" said Patricia.

Forrest sighed and opened his door. As he came around the front of the Navigator, he raised his hands in a general gesture of being unready for the spotlight, and he saw that the fingers of Tricia's left hand still went to the hollow in her collarbone.

"This is Mrs. Judah Davis," Patricia said.

"Tricia, you look great," he said.

"Braxton!" She stepped past Patricia and into his arms.

"You know each other?" Patricia exclaimed, as though someone had betrayed her.

"Cump," Tricia whispered in his ear as he bent down to kiss her cheek, "what have you been doing? You smell like you've been rolling in *J'adore.*"

"*Mmm.*" Pressing her against him, he smoothed his hand down her lower back.

"You want to see your girls?"

Forrest jerked back from her.

"They're inside," she said. "Come on in."

Forrest heard teenagers in the ecstasies of reunion.

"God, Tricia," he said, "I didn't know they were—listen, let me come back, I need an hour to—Jesus, please don't tell them I'm here yet."

Then he heard Cate's voice rise sharp and clear. "My *dad?*"

No one spoke until they turned onto Hood Road and headed back toward the Interstate. Forrest sat in the back seat with his hands on his knees, staring balefully out the window. The more he thought about it, the madder he got.

"You could have given me a little warning," he said. "Why didn't you just invite the newspaper guy, what's his name. Dan? Great story, don't you think? I'm surprised he wasn't there with a cameraman."

"Come on, Cump," said Chick, shifting in his seat and glancing in the rearview mirror.

"*Abandoned Girls Berate Deadbeat Dad.* There's his headline."

Chick looked at his watch.

"Were you going somewhere?" Forrest asked. Neither of them answered. "I mean, Jesus H. Christ, Chick, a little warning, huh? What would be the harm in telling me they were there?"

"Stop the car, Brantley," said Patricia. "I'll walk back to Varina's house. I will not put up with this foul man's—this man's foul language."

"Cump, can you tone it down? I know you're upset," Chick said.

"Upset?"

"Just let me out!" said Patricia with a note of hysteria.

"Jesus, let the bitch out," said Forrest.

Chick slammed on the brakes and pulled to the side of the road. When he turned around, his face was red. "Don't call my wife a bitch," he said, his voice trembling.

"Or what, Brantley?"

"Get out of my car."

"You made me get in to start with. Take me back to my car and I'll get out."

"Apologize to my wife."

"Apologize to this bitch?" Forrest said, opening his hand toward her.

Patricia Lee fumbled at the door handle until it opened and she scrambled outside, and just then Chick's fist caught him above the temple and stunned him. He dodged a second swing and sank back into his seat, wondering at the sensation. It had been a long time since anyone had hit him. Chick was out of the car now, opening Forrest's door, still trying to get at him. He missed and punched the door frame and swore and Forrest started laughing, covering his face with his forearms as Chick climbed in and pounded at him, trying to pry his arms loose.

"Come on, Chick," he said, wheezing with laughter. "Lighten up. I'm off the rails."

"Chick!" Patricia cried. "Stop it, Chick."

"I want to clock this bastard!" Chick shouted.

Forrest laughed harder. He fought for breath.

"He really is crazy, Chick. Stop. Just look at him."

Forrest gasped and rolled over on the armrest, trying to calm down, embarrassed now that he could not stop laughing. His shoulders and arms hurt from Chick's fists. Chick slammed Forrest's door, opened the front door, knelt on his seat. "Apologize to my wife," he said, and swung the side of his fist back to catch Forrest in the jaw.

This one infuriated Forrest. When Chick drew back for another punch, Forrest caught the fist in his right hand and squeezed it, forcing the arm back, twisting it. Chick tried to resist, but after a second, he cried, "Jesus, Cump, you're going to break my arm."

"Stop hitting me."

"Okay, okay."

Forrest let go. Chick tried to flex his hand but the fingers did not seem to work. They sat panting for a moment, glaring at each other.

"Come on, Patricia," Chick said to his wife, who was staring at them from the red clay of the right-of-way. Tendrils of interested kudzu lay around her ankles.

"I'm not crazy," Forrest called to her. He flexed his jaw. "I'm just exhausted and pissed off, okay? I'm sorry."

Patricia got back in the car and closed the door. She stared straight ahead. They got on the Interstate and headed south toward Gallatin. After a moment, her shoulders begin to shake.

"I ruined my shoes," she wailed. Her handsome leopard print shoes were caked with red mud. Forrest thought wistfully of Maya's dangling Carduccis. He should call her. He would call her.

"We'll go change," Chick said.

A few minutes later, the Navigator smoothly negotiated the exit onto the main road into Gallatin, and started uphill toward Rockwell's Pharmacy and Forrest's rented car. The huge Wal-Mart loomed on the right behind a maze of filling stations and fast food restaurants.

"Would you look at that?" Forrest said contemptuously. Neither of them spoke. Chick pulled into the parking lot of Rockwell's and waited for Forrest to get out. When he did, Chick opened his door and stepped out beside him, closing the door behind him. Forrest offered his hand, but Chick did not take it.

"Listen, Chick—"

"No, you listen," Chick said, standing too close, his face red again. "Pick up your daughters and get the hell out of Gallatin."

"I will when I'm ready," Forrest said.

"Listen to me, you piece of shit," said Chick, pointing a finger in Forrest's face. "Leave Tricia alone."

"I'm sorry I called her a bitch. She was just pressing my buttons."

"I mean Tricia Davis. Tricia Honeycutt."

"What do you mean, leave her alone? I just saw her for the first time in forty years."

"I'm telling you. Leave her alone."

"Or what, Brantley?"

Chick caught his breath and almost swung on Forrest again, but he stopped himself. He got in the car, his jaw set. He backed up into an empty space, turned around, and, contrary to Forrest's expectations, did not squeal the tires on his way out of the lot.

"I'm not staying at your house?" Forrest said to the taillights.

So where was he staying?

He would have to get a room at one of the motels next to the Interstate. He got in the Camry and headed back down the hill past the Wal-Mart. He would call Tricia and figure out what to do about the girls. But no, first, before he did anything else, he wanted to call Maya. Why not? "Rolling in J'adore."

At the EconoLodge, rooms were only $50 a night. Standing in front of the pimpled clerk, he felt everything come clear. He would book a flight out of Atlanta, pick up the girls in the morning, return the rental car, and fly home tomorrow afternoon.

"You have Internet access in the rooms, don't you?"

"Yes sir. High-speed wireless."

"Do I need some kind of code or password?"

"No sir."

"Do I have to pay for local calls?"

"No sir."

He handed the clerk his American Express card, and the boy took the imprint, then activated a plastic key and told Forrest how to get to his room, which was on the back side of the motel beside the pool, away from the Interstate.

A fat woman with two fat children was splashing around in the shallow end of the pool as he rolled the suitcase to his door. The card worked on the second try, and he heaved his suitcase onto the bed, unzipped it, and rooted through clothes until he found his cell phone and charger, both of which had been useless in Italy.

As the phone started charging, he got his laptop set up on the desk, logged onto his school account, and scrolled down past dozens of messages he could not face, including one from Natalia with **B?!?!?!** in the subject line. His Gmail account was even worse. Marisa must have sent twenty messages, the most recent only hours ago. He saw that she was online right now, even though it was getting close to midnight in Italy. Worse, she could tell *he* was online. He exited quickly and opened up his American Express travel account to look for flights from Atlanta to Boston. There was a one-way nonstop on Delta at 1:55 p.m., which was a reasonable time, but the fare was $400 each. If they left on

43

Saturday, he could bring it down by about $100, but what difference did that make? He clicked on Gmail again. Sure enough, there was a fresh message from Marisa. He made his status invisible, sighed, and opened it.

Have you seen the girls?

He told her that he was in Gallatin, the girls were safe, and he was looking for ways to get back to Portsmouth. He asked her where she was and what she was doing, clicked Send, and closed the computer.

The cell phone would be charging for an hour. He could probably use it now, but he needed to clean up, so he stripped and kicked his J'adorable clothes into the corner. He had to duck to get his hair wet under the shower head, but the water was strong and hot. He stood for a long time letting it pound him, then dried off with the wash rag before he used the big towel. He hated soggy towels.

He put on some shorts and a pair of sandals, stuck the plastic key in his pocket, and went out into the hot day to sit under an umbrella beside the pool and call Maya. He punched in her number from the piece of paper she had given him. When she answered, Forrest said, "Is this Asia Carducci?" and there was a long pause. "Maya?" he said.

"You stole my money, you sick fuck."

He felt himself shrinking.

"What do you mean?"

"You took sixty dollars out of my wallet, you piece of shit." This seemed to be the description of choice. "I didn't realize you charged for your services," she said.

"That's why I called you, Maya."

"What, you want more money?"

"I called to explain. I found it in my pocket."

"Give me a break," she said. "Found it in your pocket."

"No, no, you don't understand. I stole it early this morning when I was pissed off at you for pretending to be somebody else. It was revenge for tricking me. I never expected to see you again. But then I realized I had forgotten the ring—"

"I knew it," she said.

"Wait. And when I went back up there, I met the real you, and I forgot I had the money, I swear. I found it in my pocket when I changed to get in the shower down here."

A little lie or two couldn't hurt.

"Down where? Where are you?" Her voice had softened.

"In Gallatin at the EconoLodge. Maya, when I watched you get in that taxi..."

"Really? You're telling me the truth?"

"I swear."

"Then I wish I hadn't called them."

"Called who?"

"The Gallatin police."

44

"You called them? About the sixty bucks?"

There was a long pause before she answered. "No, I told them …what you told me last night, about the girl, that black girl. Marilyn."

Forrest stood up, cold with dread. He had told her about Marilyn?

"You told them?" he said into the phone. "Why the hell did you tell them that?"

"Because you stole my money. Revenge, like you said. I thought you were—I didn't think I'd ever hear from you again. I thought you'd robbed me."

"Oh shit," Forrest murmured. "What exactly did you tell them? No, tell you what. Never mind."

"Braxton?"

He closed the phone and stared at the blue water of the swimming pool. The phone rang. He answered it wearily.

"Who has the girls?" she said. "Is it that Lee woman?"

Her voice sounded different.

"No," he said, wondering how she knew about Patricia Lee. "It's an old friend of mine, a woman I used to date."

"Well that figures," she said. "At least it's not that Lee woman. What a nightmare."

A sudden drop in his gut warned him not to say Maya's name, and an instant later the thought arrived in his brain.

"Where are you?"

"Where do you think I am, Braxton? Back in Viterbo. The only credit card I have is maxed out, and you have the American Express. How do you think I'm supposed to get back, even if I want to?"

A teenage girl in a bikini—sweet face, nice breasts—came around the corner of the motel holding the hand of a little boy. Forrest automatically deducted for the slight belly fat, the dimpling at the tops of her thighs, the slew-footed walk.

"Maybe so."

"So what are you going to do? Go back to Portsmouth? I talked to Dr. Colvert, and he told me there's some problem about a girl in one of your classes. Probably that Natalia. He doesn't think you can fight it, given your record. This new dean means business."

"I don't have a record, Marisa."

"Your reputation. He said your best option was to resign. So what are you going to do?"

Forrest could hear another call trying to get through.

"Probably go to jail."

"Go to jail? They're not going to put you in jail, Braxton. Just humiliate your family."

"Not in New Hampshire, Marisa. Right here in Gallatin. Would that make you happy?"

While she was silent, he punched Send for the other call.

"Maya?"

"I'm coming down there," she said. "I'll get this cleared up."

"No!" he shouted.

The little boy who had come around the corner with the teenage girl had been about to dive in, but now he teetered at the edge of the pool staring at Forrest, his arms flailing.

"What's the matter?" the girl cried to Forrest as she ran toward her little brother.

"Braxton?" Marisa said. Maya must have hung up.

"Piranha!" Forrest said to the teenage girl, nodding to the pool.

Brother and sister gaped at the water.

"What?" Marisa said.

"Marisa, gotta go. A little emergency," he said, closing the phone. He held it up to the girl and her brother. "I was talking to somebody else."

The girl glanced again at the water, and then both of them turned to stare at him.

"Piece of shit," he heard the girl mutter.

Back in the room he stood leaning on the desk with a feeling of impinging doom, his hands spread on either side of his unopened laptop. What had possessed him to tell a stranger—no matter how drunk he was—that he might be implicated in a murder? He pounded the desk so hard his laptop jumped, and a second later he heard the raucous TV in the next room lower its volume.

Good God. It all seemed devilishly connected, because he would never have come back to Georgia—hell, he would never have gone to Italy—if it hadn't been for those letters. Even getting caught with Natalia was because of those letters. She sprang up from his lap a second too late when the door opened and there stood Marisa with the latest one from Cousin Emily Barron Hayes.

What made Patricia Lee so sure the old lady had not written them? What did she know? It seemed very simple to him: the old witch had stolen the family fortune, she was close to death, and superstitious terror of judgment had finally moved her to remorse. If she had not written those letters, what could conceivably have moved someone else to write them? She had to have written them. He had to see her for himself and get her to admit it, which meant he'd have to drive to the other side of town, where she lived in the three-story brick house old T.J. Forrest had built, Stonewall Hill. The house Robert Forrest should have inherited. The house he should have grown up in.

Maybe he should call the woman who helped her, but he didn't have her number, and he didn't how to get it without calling Chick Lee.

Google her? What was her name? Something odd.

He put his fingertips on his laptop and suddenly remembered Maya. Was she really coming down? Surely not. He didn't have time for her now. He needed to square things with the girls. And in the meantime, he was starving. It was almost seven o'clock. The last thing he had eaten was the blueberry muffin up on the fifty-third floor of the Peachtree Plaza. If he went to the Denny's next door or the Waffle House across Lee Street, somebody might recognize him.

He put on a shirt and grabbed his keys. The teenage girl and her brother watched him as he left. A minute later, driving down the access road to the next exit, he spotted a Burger King, turned right at the stop sign, and pulled into the lot. Forrest ordered at the outdoor speaker, paid at the first window, and pulled up to the next one. The teenager handling his order was watching some girls in the parking lot and did not even look as he held the bag out. When the boy noticed it still in his hand, his eyes wandered to Forrest.

"This isn't your order?"

"I don't know," Forrest said, gazing at him, still not taking it. "I can't tell."

The boy took the bag back, opened it, looked at its contents, and checked them against the printed order hanging over his workstation.

"Two Whoppers, large fries, Diet Coke?"

"That sounds right."

The boy held the bag out again, watching Forrest, who still did not take it.

"You don't like your job?" Forrest said. "What's your name?"

The boy frowned and touched his nametag.

"That's a strange name for a white boy," Forrest said. "Jaylee."

"Naw, they screwed up my name tag. It's supposed to be Jay Lee," he said. "Two words."

"Who's your manager, Jay Lee?"

The boy ducked his head like it wasn't his night and glanced back over his shoulder at the interior of the restaurant. He said in a low voice, "Mr. Hibbs."

Forrest got out his pen and wrote "Mr. Hibbs" on the back of an envelope and showed it to the boy. "That how it's spelled?"

"Yes sir."

"You always want to make eye contact with your customer, Jay Lee. You want your customer to feel like there's been some kind of moment with you as a person, you understand? It's our view that the employees of our franchises reflect the management," Forrest said, "so I don't necessarily hold you responsible for this. But I'll be sure to bring up your name when we talk to Mr. Hibbs."

The boy's eyes had widened with alarm.

"You don't need to get on Mr. Hibbs. He's my uncle."

"Is that right? So that's how you got the job?" Forrest made a scribble

47

on his envelope.

The boy's head wryed on his neck. When he glanced to his right and patted the counter anxiously, Forrest checked his rearview mirror and saw two cars in line behind him.

"Try it again," he said. "Show me how Mr. Hibbs taught you to do it."

Jay Lee handed the bag to Forrest with a big fake smile and said, "Thank you for coming to Burger King. Have a nice night."

"Eye contact," said Forrest, pointing at his eyes. The car behind him beeped its horn.

The boy looked him in the eyes.

"Now where's my Diet Coke?" Forrest asked.

"Shit." The boy whirled around, grabbed it, and handed it out the window.

"Eye contact. Don't forget to smile. That's better. And watch your language, Jay Lee." He settled the drink in the holder, touched two fingers to his eyebrow, and pulled forward. Then he backed into a parking place facing the drive-in window. He saw Jay Lee glance over at him. For the ten minutes while Forrest ate his Whoppers and fries, the boy was a model of courteous efficiency, and Forrest suspected that after Jay Lee said something to the others inside, the whole restaurant improved its service markedly.

"And what's he then that says I play the villain?" Forrest said.

He wadded up the bags, checked his shirt and jeans for crumbs and drips, and started the car. He wished he had asked them to take out the onions. The car stank of them, but it was too hot to put the windows down.

Did he really need to go see the old lady tonight? There was a liquor store across the street. The best thing he could imagine at the moment was filling a plastic cup of motel ice with bourbon while he watched something on HBO. Take three ibuprofen, go to sleep, wake up and deal with everything tomorrow after a pot of coffee.

Tricia had said for Forrest to come back later after the girls had gotten used to the idea of his being there—or had she told him to pick them up? It was hard to remember because of Cate's fury. Maybe he should pick them up and head to Hartsfield Airport right now. Get out of town before Maya arrived or the police found him. If they were even looking for him. Maybe Maya was lying—but he didn't think so. If they went to the airport, they would have to spend the night on the floor or get still another motel room on the American Express card. Besides, what Marisa had said made it seem like a bad idea to take the girls back to Portsmouth with the Natalia matter hanging over him. So maybe he should just sit tight. He could bring them back to the EconoLodge to talk to them.

Except that Maya might show up.

Forrest pulled forward slowly. He saw Jay Lee's eyes following him from behind the glass and he touched his eyebrow again in salute. The boy lifted his fingers from the counter and said something back over his shoulder.

Teenagers loitered around their cars the way they had forty years ago, but now their eyes passed over him incuriously. He eased up to a drive-by trash can, tossed away the sack, and took a right onto Foster Drive.

On this shady stretch near Stephen Foster College, he had seen Marilyn that first night in her fishnet dress. Another wave of dread went through him. Ahead of him, a police car was coming out of the old campus loop, and Forrest watched it. When it turned left and paid no attention to him, he crossed the railroad tracks and went up the hill past derelict stores to the courthouse square. When the light turned green at the intersection of Lee and Jackson, he did not move. He watched the Confederate soldier at the corner of the courthouse square, thinking about what to do.

When his mother died, he'd thought he was through with Gallatin forever, and he hadn't even driven past Stonewall Hill. But now he made a left turn and drove down the hill to where Johnson's Mill Road split off from South Lee Street.

The old house was hardly visible. He got out by the front gate, which was padlocked shut and wreathed with poison oak, and stared through the bars at the drive that bent around to the right and followed the curve of the hill up to the six-columned front of the house. Saplings had burst up through the old pavement. Boxwood hedges that once elegantly bordered it had gone untrimmed for years, and fallen pecan limbs littered the long slope of lawn once defined by shrubs and plantings. Seed heads of Johnson grass nodded chest-high. He remembered the scatter of dogwoods in the springtime, vivid azaleas along the low stone walls that punctuated the slope and gave the house its name. Everything had disappeared behind the indiscriminate vegetation—the old iris beds, the stone steps and paths, all hidden now under this profusion of growth and decay.

He got back in the car, more shaken than he had imagined such a sight could have made him. A few hundred yards up Johnson's Mill, he pulled onto the drive that wound its way up to the back of the house. It was starting to get dark under the huge old oaks and pecan trees, but the sun still shone on the fields and ponds, bordered by woods in the distance, that made up the old estate. Though some of the outbuildings were still standing, the barn had collapsed like a horse with a broken back. Near the house itself, a work shed listed drunkenly. A dark car sat in one bay of the three-car garage that his grandfather had built eighty or ninety years before, when he was thirty years younger than Forrest was now and already a rich man. Shadows darkened the side of the house facing him, but the late sun glared off the back windows.

Before his grandmother died, she had allowed him over a few times. He remembered his hiding spot beneath a cedar on the far side of the house, the ground soft with fallen needles, where he and a little girl named Naomi had hidden together and he had found a blue robin's egg in a small pool of trapped rainwater. Another time, he had seen Cousin Emily Barron Hayes' three huge dogs scrambling after steaks on the floor. He had told the story of those dogs many times, but now the memory brought on an inexplicable qualm, as though something in it he did not remember were about to be released.

He got out and walked toward the house, shading his eyes, and suddenly the sun was gone behind some distant line of woods. He walked closer to stare up at the southern windows. High up, a white head turned. He froze. He stood still, staring, listening to the crickets begin to pulse. Somewhere, a neighbor's dog was barking.

Brrrrrrring! ... Brrrrrrring!

His phone, unbelievably loud. Forrest cursed, fumbled for the thing in his pocket, and strode back toward his car, opening it as it began to ring again.

"Hello," he said tensely.

"Braxton?" The voice had a teasing foreignness, vaguely familiar.

"Yes?"

"It's Maya."

"Maya, sweet Jesus. Where are you?"

"About five miles away." He got in the car and slammed the door. She couldn't have followed him to Gallatin. It was surreal. "Is something the matter?" she asked.

"It's—seriously, five miles away?"

"I'm just guessing. I've seen signs for Gallatin. I just passed Hood Road."

Good God, she was actually coming. Forrest started the car. "Get off at the second exit and go through the light onto the access road," he said. "The EconoLodge is just past the Shell station. You might get there before I do. I'll meet you in front."

Five minutes later, a black BMW Roadster facing outward from a parking place near the entrance flashed its lights, and he pulled into the empty space next to the driver's side. The window went down, and Maya looked at him with an enigmatic smile. She stuck her tongue out at him. He got out and went around to her car and put his hands on either side of the window. She had on white shorts and a low-cut sleeveless top. Something about her hair was different.

"Did you really call the police?" he said.

She did a little pout, a slight shrug.

"Tell me," he said.

"I was upset with you. What happened to your face? You look like somebody punched you."

He touched his temple.

"I forgot about it. What exactly did you say?"

"I just told her what you told me."

"Told who?"

"Whoever takes their calls. Some black woman."

"How did you bring it up?"

"Let's go to your room."

"Maya, come on. What did you say?" he asked.

"Maybe I should go home."

"Maybe you should," he said, standing back from her car. "Did you come to get your money back?" He fished in his pocket.

"Oh stop it!" she said. "You know what I did when I got home? I googled you. I watched that YouTube clip of you on the Charlie Rose Show."

"Which one?"

"The one predicting Obama. It was, I don't know. Amazing. I just sat there with my hand on my heart, thinking *Oh my god, I know that man.*"

"Was this after you called the police?"

"Oh, come on, Braxton. Can I please come inside?"

"I have things to do. I need to know exactly what you said."

He shook her gently as though to jostle the information loose, but it was a mistake to touch her cool shoulder. She gazed up at him. "Don't you want to drive my car?"

"I don't have time," he said. "I need to go see my daughters."

She smiled and slipped nimbly away over the gearshift console into the passenger seat. He had to bend lower to see her.

"Just show me where you picked up Marilyn the first time," she said. She patted the driver's seat. "Come on. You told me I reminded you of her. This dead girl. You told me a lot. How that first night she was wearing a white fishnet dress?"

"I told you that?"

"I'll tell you what I told the police if you show me where it was."

Forrest sighed and locked the Camry and tried to get in the BMW, but the leather seat was too far forward. He found the buttons and the seat flowed back until it reached its limit. He got in and adjusted the back and reached up to adjust the mirror. Hanging from it on a red silk cord were thirty or forty gold rings of different styles and sizes.

He turned and stared at her.

"You came back for yours," she shrugged. "That's all it takes."

He hefted the rings in his fingers. "Why do you do it?"

"I just enjoy pretending. I find out the most interesting things."

"Who are you, really?"

"You know me," she said, touching his arm. "Miss Maya from

Cuthbert. And here we are in Gallatin."

"They tell you their secrets, like I did?"

"Their wives. Their kids. Things they hardly know about themselves."

"But why not marry somebody? Why other women's husbands?"

"Because they're supposed to be like known quantities, but they haven't really been known, and so I know them. Or maybe I'm just bad. Maybe it's because of getting raped by my father's partner in the law firm when I was babysitting his kids, you think? He was married to my Sunday school teacher. I was thirteen and scared to say anything."

"Should I believe that?"

"Maybe. Or maybe I seduced him."

"So you're a serial seducer."

"I'm not a killer."

"So do you blackmail these guys?"

"Not at all. I discomfit them on occasion. Just to remind them that somebody knows them. Don't you love that word? Discomfit?"

He did not answer.

"Why don't you drive around the motel a couple of times to get used to the clutch?"

After a moment, he started the car and backed out. She leaned back against her door and watched him. He turned onto the access road and drove up to Foster Drive, where he turned past the Burger King and slowly approached the college.

The streetlights had come on. The old dormitories, their windows once warm with erotic promise, stood silent and opaque.

"Right there," he said, pointing to the sidewalk across the street from the entrance.

"Stop!" she cried.

He pulled over to the curb, alarmed. Instantly, she got out of the car. "What are you doing?" he shouted. "Come on, Maya, I'm in a hurry."

She went to the front of the car, paused to let a car pass, trailing her fingertips on the hood, then crossed the street in her sandals, imitating the way he must have described Marilyn walking, and started back down the sidewalk on the other side.

He was stirred despite himself. A pickup truck coming from town rumbled over the railroad tracks, and the driver glanced over and slowed down as he passed her. Forrest did a quick U-turn in the BMW and pulled up beside her. The other driver accelerated away.

She pretended to ignore him, her hips alive in their ancient sway of invitation.

He put down the window. "Can you get in the car?"

She lifted her chin as though he had insulted her and kept up her walk. He saw the game she wanted to play.

"Please, Marilyn?" he said.

She paused and glanced around, smoothing her hand delicately down the curve of her waist. Then she opened the door and flowed down into the seat.

"O my god!" she panted. "Did you see that guy slow down? I've never been so turned on in my whole life." She was flushed. She put her hand on his thigh. "Let's go back to the motel."

"Remember our deal. What did you tell the police?"

"Okay, okay," she said, trembling, clenching and unclenching her hands. "I got out of the meeting at four and took a taxi to my condo. My dad and my stepmother were there taking care of my dog, so I said hello to them and made up a story about last night. You probably don't remember they called me when we were up in the room. So anyway I was just getting unpacked when my dad knocked on the door and told me that Pía, my cleaning lady—she's undocumented, I have to pay her in cash—Pía was coming by in a few minutes to pick up her money. So I looked in my wallet for the cash I'd gotten out before I left, and there was sixty dollars missing and I remembered my passport sitting out on the sink and realized—I mean, I couldn't believe it. You'd robbed me, and that made me feel, my God, just this burn of humiliation. I had to borrow money from my dad to pay Pía what I owed her, and by this point I wanted to murder you. So I googled the Gallatin police to get the number and then called them up."

"What did you tell them?"

She exhaled slowly and slumped back against her door, still excited. "Okay, let me think. The black woman was on the phone, and I said, 'I want to report a possible homicide.' She asks what I mean by a 'possible homicide,' and I tell her that I met somebody who told me this story about a black woman named Marilyn Harkins who disappeared and how he thinks she was murdered. And she says, 'Who told you this?' and I said I didn't want to say, so she goes 'Unh-huh. They say why they think so?' So I told her about what you found by the river."

He could not believe he had told her so much.

"I asked her if she really wanted to know who told me the story. She sort of sighed and said, 'Go ahead.' And as soon as I said your name, I mean, she was ..."

"She was what?"

"All over it. I told her you would be in town now, because you had to find your daughters who had gotten there with nobody to meet them, and she said, 'Oh, I know about them,' and I said you would be getting to Gallatin today in a white Camry."

"Good God."

"Okay? So can we please, please go back to the motel?" she said.

5

Inside Noemi, just as the waiter was delivering the crème brûlée, the first bars of "Dixie" sounded from Chick Lee's iPhone. He grabbed it from his pocket. *Varina Davis* said the display. Tricia.

"Chick?" she said. "Have you heard anything from Braxton?"

"No," he whispered.

"Who is it?" hissed Patricia, leaning forward in her chair. Chick mouthed Varina's name at her.

"What's the matter?" asked Tricia.

"We're in a restaurant in Atlanta," Chick whispered, bending over the phone as though he were guarding a candle in the wind.

"He hasn't called me," said Tricia. "It's after nine. I've gotten his daughters calmed down enough to talk to him, and now he doesn't call."

"Sweet Jesus," Chick said.

"Go outside!" hissed Patricia.

"I'll call you right back," said Chick and ended the call. "Don't let them take this," he told Patricia, quickly scooping two spoonfuls of the crème brûlée into his mouth.

He threaded his way through the tables to the exit and stood outside the front door of the restaurant watching the downtown traffic stream past him. An old woman in rich clothes stood nearby, smoking. She made a wry face and tilted her cigarette at him.

"You too?"

Chick held the phone up by way of explanation and called her back. Tricia answered right away.

"Why doesn't he at least call? Do you think something happened to him?"

"So you don't know where he is," Chick said.

"No idea. Do you think he just left?"

"Tricia, he's a wild man. We got in a fight after we left your place."

"A fight!"

"Fists. He called Patricia a bitch."

The smoking woman raised her eyebrows at him, as though she were impressed.

After a beat, Tricia said, "Did he hurt you?"

"You mean did I hurt him?"

When she did not answer, he sighed and said, "My arm's a little sprained. I'm telling you, the man's nuts."

"What should I do?" she asked. "These girls are ... Chick, what should I do?"

"Have you called the police?"

"I'm not going to call the police!"

"Well, look," said Chick, "why don't you call the motels to see if he's there?"

"They won't tell me, will they? I don't think they're allowed to."

"No, what you do is you ask to be connected to his room, like you know he's there. Call up the Best Western and say, 'May I speak to Braxton Forrest, please?' and they'll say whatever. If he's not registered, they'll tell you."

"Okay, I'll try that. Which one do you think I should call first?"

"Something down at the Lee Street exit. The Best Western, the EconoLodge."

"Okay, if—listen, I'm sorry to disturb you. Say hello to Patricia for me."

The old woman was putting out her cigarette. "Sounds like a more exciting night than I'm having," she said, directing the last of the smoke upwards with her bottom lip. She winked at him.

Back at the table, Patricia was sipping her coffee. "What was that all about?" she asked.

"He didn't show up to see his girls."

"I don't know why they don't just lock him up."

"Look, Patricia, I'm tired of talking about him. He's all we've talked about tonight. My whole life, there he's been. Braxton Frigging Forrest— bigger, stronger, smarter, better-looking." He leaned toward her and whispered, "He even had a name for his dingaling. Cousin Bedford. We'd be in the locker room, he'd talk about what Cousin Bedford had been up to, like it was his bird dog."

"Hush!" she hissed. "You don't have to be disgusting."

"I'm just saying."

When Patricia sat there quietly for a little too long, Chick regretted having told her, because now she was thinking about it.

"And he ends up as an English teacher at some podunk college," he said. "I mean, he had scholarship offers in football and basketball. He never even liked basketball. But he said he was tired of sports after high school, and it didn't even make any difference, because he was already one of those national—what do you call those scholarships, national what?"

"National Merit? He was a National Merit Scholar?"

"Hell, yes. He could have gone to Harvard or Yale or somewhere. I think he was already accepted and everything."

"So where did he go?"

"Fucking UGA."

The woman at a nearby table glanced over at Chick, and Patricia was instantly mortified.

"Chick, are you drunk?" she asked for the other woman to overhear.

Chick poured himself another glass of wine. He and Patricia did not drink at home since they were Baptists and Patricia did not want to set a bad example for Alyssa. But nobody in Atlanta knew they were Baptists, and she would have a glass if Chick ordered a bottle. He held up the glass of whatever it was. Merlot? Something red.

"To Cousin Bedford!" he said.

Patricia blushed with such speed and power from her neck up through her cheeks to her ears and scalp that her eyes watered with humiliation. Naturally, she thought everyone else in the restaurant immediately knew what Cousin Bedford was, and the very fact that she was blushing told everybody in the restaurant (as Chick could clearly see she thought) that she also knew what Cousin Bedford was. After a few seconds, she took her purse without looking at him and started for the restroom, one hand to her temple.

Chick took a big swallow of wine and shook his head. Forrest shouldn't have called her a bitch, because it wasn't always true. On the other hand, it was true today. Braxton Forrest. He remembered the dance at the Armory in his sophomore year of high school—some kind of fake tropical thing with palm trees that the mothers spent weeks getting themselves worked up over. He, meanwhile, had spent those weeks getting worked up over calling up Tricia Honeycutt and asking her to go with him, because she was this goddess, cool and sleek as a new Mustang, and even in his own estimation he was just one of the jerk-off kings of tenth grade. But she had said yes when he finally got enough courage, and he had taken her in a brand-new Mustang from his father's lot, black as midnight. He remembered walking in, proud and humble at the same time, with Tricia Honeycutt on his arm. They had been on the dance floor, it was a slow dance, and they were both hot from the dance before, steaming a little, and he had his hand on the small of her back, and her breasts were pressed against his chest, and he could smell the perfume on her neck, where the black hair was matted down a little. His loins had started to stir, his heart had gone into a slow, blissful spin, and just then there was a tap on his shoulder.

He turned, and there was Braxton Forrest, not even looking at Chick, but smiling down at Tricia. Before he could even let her go, he felt a tremor go through her whole body, a fear and excitement. He knew, of course, knew instantly and without having to ask himself and without even feeling any resentment toward Tricia. That was that. Braxton Forrest was taller, smarter, and handsomer than he was. It was just bad luck that Forrest had noticed her while she was his date. It was like being the guy a drunk driver veers into and kills. Chance or destiny or God's providence or whatever. Forrest had a big smile with a hint of mockery in it, great teeth, one of those faces. He was just big—six-five, two hundred twenty-five pounds as a junior in high school—and he moved like a cat. Girls came to basketball games, he had heard from Graham Ashley's older sister, just to see his bare legs. He was tall enough to play forward in high school, and he could easily have switched to point guard in college. Not that he liked basketball.

Football was his game. He was quick and fluid and canny, immensely strong, a phenomenal tight end and linebacker. In a game against Hogansboro, Forrest had come off a block just as their tailback—a fast little guy—had been flashing past him, and Forrest had caught his shoulder pads behind his neck and lifted him right off the ground. Coach Fitz ran the play over and over in the film session on Sunday, because Forrest didn't throw him down, he just held him up in the air with one hand, the guy's legs kicking furiously, the pads choking him in front, until the referee blew the whistle. The kid was furious, so he went at Forrest, who picked him up again, this time by bunching his jersey in his left hand and hooking him under his shoulder pads where they crossed his chest. The referees threw flags and called offsetting penalties. It was hilarious to watch, and after he had rewound it three or four times, Coach Fitz had spat tobacco into his Styrofoam cup. "Back of his pants might be better."

Still, what got to Chick was that behind all the good looks and intelligence and power, backing them up like a gold ingot at Fort Knox used to back up the dollar, was the famous Cousin Bedford, not Chick Lee's innocent average johnson. Unfair as hell, but what were you supposed to do? Curse God and die—over your pecker? Talk about predestination. Tricia had floated away from him and into Braxton's arms as though he had never been born. He drove home alone that night. Tricia never even thought to apologize. He never held it against her, but he hated Braxton Forrest for a long time. And to think that bastard—

6

Forrest half-expected the police to be gathered around the Camry when they pulled into the EconoLodge, but the car sat undisturbed, and he drove around to the back.

"Hurry," Maya said.

As he got the key card into the slot, she pressed against him like a cat. Once the door was open, she threw her arms around his neck and wrapped her legs around his waist. He staggered forward with her sudden weight. "Call me her name again. Call me Marilyn," she whispered in his ear.

A great wave of fury rose through him. Savagely, he lifted her off him and threw her onto the bed. Her head banged hard off the headboard. This little bitch in heat with his secrets. She cowered back, terrified, holding her head, but he mastered her easily and held her down. If he could have caught Marisa in the Roman hotel, he would have lifted her by the neck, squeezing and crushing, and she would have died in his hands, dangling there like a pigeon in hawk's beak until he thought to fling her aside. Now he wanted to burst the unclean thing trapped and fluttering under the frail ribs of this little counterfeiter. She was crying out, but he did not listen. He crushed her little body in his hands. He remembered the sheer terror on Marisa's face before the old German couple came out into the hallway, and he saw with satisfaction the same look on the face of this woman, this Maya Davidson who thought she could be Marilyn.

"You want to be Marilyn?" he said to her.

She was pushing desperately against his chest.

When he let himself go in a great roar, the girl convulsed under him like a shot animal.

After a moment, he rolled away, breathless as though he had just run for miles. His lungs were hot, but his whole chest felt broken open. Cool waters bathed his heart. Closing his eyes, he drifted into a half-dream: he had been in a cave whose mouth was blocked by a huge stone, and he had pushed it aside with a violent effort that sent it bounding down a long slope toward the sea, and he was standing now on the mountainside above the orchards of olive trees and the ocean—Italy, the Tyrrhenian seacoast—and a town of red tile roofs built into the mountainside. *Goddess*, he said. Down the steep cobblestone road, he saw her, Marilyn, in her high heels, choosing her steps carefully, walking away from him, her hips in their ancient sway.

He turned his head to look at Maya. She lay still, curled on herself, her hands tendering the muscles of her arms and shoulders. The face she turned to him was empty of accusation.

"I shouldn't have come," she said in a small voice. She reached over to touch his cheek. He did not stir. "I don't know why you want to kill somebody, but don't kill me. Please don't kill me."

He did not answer.

She was still staring at him when the phone rang—not his cell phone but the motel phone. The front desk? Or the police.

It kept ringing until finally he lifted it. "Hello."

"Braxton?" A woman's voice. "It's Varina."

"Who?"

"Tricia."

"Tricia!"

"You said you were coming over." He heard her trying to control the trembling in her voice. "The girls are expecting you. I told them you were coming."

"Sweet Jesus. Give me twenty minutes."

On the bed next to him, Maya gasped alarmingly, and followed with a series of small, desperate breaths and sobs.

"Is somebody there?" Tricia asked.

"Twenty minutes," he said and hung up.

Maya sat up against the headboard. She had her hand over her heart, patting it in a faint birdlike tremor, her mouth open.

"Oh," he said. He reached over the end of the bed for his jeans, felt for his wallet, found it and opened it. "Uh-oh, I spent some of it." He held out a new twenty and a wrinkled ten. She looked at the money and then back at him. "I still owe you thirty and change," he said. When she did not take it, he put it down on the sheet beside her. She looked at it and put her hands over her face.

"O god," she gasped. Her eyes were widening with fear. She was fighting to breathe. He saw her go stiff and still. She put out a hand to touch him and it fell before reaching him. She slumped over. The breath went out of her in a long, hoarse rattle that had no sequel.

7

"Dixie" rose again from Chick's pocket, and he snatched out the phone.

Tricia. Lovely Tricia.

"You were right," she said. "He's at the EconoLodge. I think he's got some woman there. I heard her crying."

"The man never lets up, does he? Is he coming over?"

"I don't know. He said he would."

Chick drank the rest of his wine and held the empty bottle over his glass, letting it drip.

"Tricia," he said. "I love you. I've always loved you."

"Oh, Chick, you sweet man," she said. "You are so sweet."

But his heart sank, because when he looked up, his eyes watering, Patricia was standing beside the table.

His phone sang "Dixie" again at the Locust Grove exit. He grabbed at his jacket pocket. "Who is it this time?" Patricia demanded, swerving. He hated it when she drove the Navigator. Upright and tense, she gripped the wheel, wincing toward the shoulder as car after car passed her. It had taken him half an hour to calm her down in the restaurant, and she was still going at him.

Sure enough, it was Tricia's home number. Suppose she had been considering what he said, and now she was ready to leave Judah Davis and run away with him? "Dixie" started over.

"Well answer it," Patricia said.

"Varina!" he said brightly into the phone.

"Dad, it's Alyssa."

"Alyssa!" he said. "What's the matter, honey?"

"Can you come get me? Please, please, please?"

He could hardly hear her. "What's the matter? Is something wrong?"

By now, Patricia was making that impatient give-it-to-me gesture, and she veered into the breakdown lane with a sudden roar of the Pirellis. He held the phone back from her and stabbed his finger at the road.

"Drive the damn car!"

"Dad?" Alyssa was whispering. "Can you call back and say I have to leave? Say there's some kind of family emergency."

"Like what?" Chick said, his mood lightening. Picking up Alyssa would get Patricia off his case and let him see Tricia at the same time.

"I don't know!" she moaned. "Can't mom, like, get sick or something?" she hissed. "Or you forgot I had to do something early in the morning? Just get me out of here!"

"We'll be there in twenty minutes."

He slid the phone into his pocket. No way he was going to call and risk talking to Tricia.

"What was that about?" Patricia said.

"Alyssa wants us to pick her up."

"Why didn't you let me talk to her?"

"Because you're driving the car," Chick said. "Do you know how many accidents are caused by people talking on cell phones? It's as bad as drunk drivers."

"You talk on the cell phone all the time when you're driving," she said.

"That's because I know how to drive," he said. "In fact, pull off at the next exit. I don't want to show up at the Davis house with you at the wheel. It will look like I'm drunk."

"You *are* drunk."

"Not anymore. I'm fine now."

He could be drunk and watching a movie on the dashboard and still be a better driver than she was.

"The last thing we need is for you to get arrested for DUI."

"I'm fine."

Back at Noemi, needless to say, Chick had pretended to be drunker than he was. *What do you mean? You're Tricia.*

He should do it again, just to confuse her.

"Tricia, pull over."

She slapped the steering wheel. "I told you that I will not be called Tricia and I will not be called Pat," she said for about the tenth time that night. "There was somebody on that phone. I heard somebody. You were talking to somebody."

"It was Alyssa, I just said."

"I mean before, Brantley! You know what I'm talking about."

Watching Patricia handle his car was a painful thing. She had not driven until she was in her thirties. Suddenly she swerved across the next lane—immediate outraged honking from a startled van—and pointed the Navigator up the exit ramp. At the top, she lurched partway off the shoulder with the headlights jabbing unevenly into a stand of pine trees across the intersection and jammed the gear shift lever into P before the car was fully stopped. Chick's seatbelt snagged him. At least the airbags didn't deploy.

He didn't say a word. He got out of the car and walked around the back, giving it a good five feet of clearance just in case, and went up and opened the driver's door for her. When she got out, he took her elbow and walked her all the way around the back of the car through the red gleam of the taillights. He helped her into her seat as a gentleman should and left a lingering hand on her knee that made her look at him with surprise. She put her hand over his.

"Oh, Brantley," she said. "It's all because of that man. That Bedford."

8

"Any idea why she would go into cardiac arrest? Any drugs?"

Forrest shook his head.

"That's a fairly new technique you used—the hands-only."

"Just a coincidence. Somebody recently sent me a YouTube link in an email and I watched it just for the hell of it."

Maya was still unconscious. He had called 911 with one hand and knelt over her, pumping and pumping with the heel of his other hand on her sternum. The black EMS man who first entered the door found him there naked above her, pushing on her chest, her bare breasts softly shaken. Forrest had turned away to pull on his jeans while the crew gave her the shock that revived her heartbeat. When they rolled her out toward the ambulance with an IV in her arm, he stood watching as they put her in the back.

She had been dead. He had seen her die. The shock of it still numbed him.

He had actually prayed.

A police car pulled up. Out climbed a muscular boy with a buzz cut and hair so blond it looked like a white aura under the streetlights before he put on his cap. He looked around, spoke to the EMS crew, and his glance came to rest on Forrest. He came over, asked for Forrest's driver's license and took it with him as he got back in the car, where he talked on his radio. After a minute or so, he came back and pointed toward the ambulance with the pencil.

"Um, you say you knew the victim."

"Jesus, Billy, he was naked on the bed with her," said an EMS woman about his age, her mouth tense.

"Yes'm," said Billy.

"You don't remember me, do you, Braxton?"

"Sorry, it's been a long time. Diane?" he guessed.

"Kathy Kellogg," she said. The name meant nothing to him. "Kathy

Henley back then." It still meant nothing. "I was a year behind you from first grade until you graduated."

"Sure," he said, nodding. "You were in Chick Lee's class." She must have been from out in the county somewhere, one of those plain girls whose existence never quite gelled in his consciousness since they didn't live in town and he never saw them outside school.

"Billy, can I have a minute with Mr. Forrest?" she said to the policeman, and the boy raised his eyebrows and backed away.

"I don't expect you to remember me," she said. "But I remember you, and I want you to listen to me."

He nodded and she stepped closer.

"If I had to say—just looking at her—whether this girl was raped, I'd say absolutely. She's already starting to show bruising, and the contusions on the back of her thighs look nasty. You put her into cardiac arrest. You're lucky she's not dead. This time."

"What do you mean, this time?" said Forrest, and the dark qualm came.

"You know what I mean," she said. "I used to look up to you, just like everybody else did. Back then, I gave you the benefit of the doubt."

She turned and walked over to the ambulance and got in the passenger door without another look at him. The ambulance pulled out of the parking lot and headed up toward the access road, lights flashing. Inside it went lovely Maya, unconscious among strangers.

What did she mean *this time*? Kathy Kellogg, who claimed to remember him. He felt in his pocket for the keys of the Camry. The police car was not blocking it. He could go see his girls at Tricia's, and then he could get on the highway and drive somewhere, maybe back to Atlanta. Or he could go south to Florida and live in a trailer next to a fishing camp. Or he could ditch the car on a country road and head out into the woods. He saw himself loping along the edges of fields and stealing corn or cantaloupes, peering in farmhouse windows at night like Frankenstein's monster, all the dogs howling.

"So you say you knew the victim," the policeman said again, staring at the notes he had laboriously written.

"Officer…" He glanced at the nameplate on the boy's blue shirt pocket. Billy Reeves. "Officer Reeves, she's not a victim," Forrest said. "I met her in Atlanta and she came down to see me."

"Yes, sir, but this here same woman called us earlier today about you, Mr. Foster."

"Forrest."

"Sir?"

"My last name is Forrest."

"That's right," the boy said, tapping his pencil on his pad. "Anyway the victim, she told Officer Todd that you mentioned a possible homicide?" The boy tilted his head up at Forrest and a strange look came over his face. "Wait a second, you look familiar," he said.

"Forrest... Holy shit, you're the one on the Wall of Fame."

Forrest shrugged.

"You're an effing legend. Coach Fitz used to tell us stories about you. He said one time there was this big guy from another team ragging on you at football camp?"

"Maybe," Forrest said.

"Trash-talking you in the dining hall, saying he could whip you, and you took an orange out of the bowl on the table and held it up and just squushed it in your hand. Is that right?"

Forrest's head went back on his neck, as though he had just been offered a fresh garden slug in a spoon. "That's bullshit."

The boy looked deflated. "That didn't happen?"

"It was an apple. Red Delicious as I recall."

"Come on."

Forrest tilted his head and shrugged.

"No shit?" said Officer Reeves. "You did that to an *apple*?"

He held his hand out to Officer Reeves, whose eyebrows went up. He backed off, shaking his head and smiling.

"They say you never worked out, but this one time they got you in the weight room and they kept putting more and more weights on the bar until they didn't have any more, and you still benched it. Something like 450 pounds."

Forrest shrugged. "Is that a lot?"

"So he just sat there?" Reeves said. "That guy ragging on you?"

"I think he might have excused himself."

Reeves made a few whorls on his pad with his pencil, then pressed the eraser into his forehead between his eyes.

"I don't know what to do," he said, apparently unaware that he was talking out loud. He looked up at Forrest. "See, some woman in the motel called us."

"It sounded worse than it was," Forrest said.

"But you admit you were having relations with the victim?"

"I was having relations," Forrest said, resting his hand on the boy's shoulder and leaning close to him, "but I wouldn't call her a victim. Do you consider your girlfriend a victim when you have relations?"

The boy blushed like a stoplight. He looked at the ground. "Well, you called 911. I guess you could have just left if—"

A car swerved around the corner of the parking lot and headed for Forrest before hitting the brakes. Tricia got out and came at him.

"Braxton, I swear to God." She made a vague wave into the air over her shoulder.

"I was on the way, Tricia. As you can see, I had an emergency."

The back doors opened, and out came his daughters. His girls, Marisa had called them. They crept around the sides of the SUV to stand in front of him, tentative, teary, clutching their shoulders. They looked cast off, like the victims of some pogrom who had tried to escape but had been rounded up and imprisoned.

"Why's Billy Reeves here?" Tricia whispered fiercely. "What the hell did you do?"

Forrest gave a slight shake of his head.

"Girls," he said. They would not look at him. "A woman had a heart attack," he said to Tricia. "She went into cardiac arrest, and I had to give her CPR. I didn't have your number."

"So where's the ambulance?"

"It just left."

"The woman who was *in your room*?" Tricia whispered. "I *heard* her."

He nodded. Tricia swiped at her eyes and pulled forward Cate and Bernadette, who still would not look at him. The Reeves boy had the door of the police car open, and he was kneeling on the seat, talking on the radio.

"It was an emergency," Forrest said to the girls.

Cate, almost grown, already in her first beauty, stood now in the shame he had made for her. And Bernadette, little Berry, spirited and confused.

"Mr. Forrest," said Billy Reeves, approaching him. He touched his hat to the girls. "Could I speak to you?" The boy pulled Forrest aside. "I'm going to need to take you to the station," he said.

"I told you what happened. The EMS people said I saved her life."

"Well, I'm supposed to cuff you."

"What for? Let me get them away from here first. Let me talk to Tricia."

"That's your daughter?"

"No it's—look, let me talk to Mrs. Davis a minute and get the girls out of here and then you can cuff me if you have to. But it's not like I'm going to make a break for it."

The boy pressed the eraser into his forehead again.

"Tricia," Forrest called. "Can you come here a minute?"

When she came over, he said in an undertone, "I'm being arrested."

"God damn it!" she cried, and immediately covered her mouth. "What did you do?"

He asked the Reeves boy to wait and walked over to the girls. Cate looked up at him, red-eyed and resentful, and Bernadette clung to her sister.

"I'm sorry all this has happened," he said. Neither said anything. "Have you talked to your mother?"

Cate nodded.

"Is she okay?"

She shrugged.

Berry broke from Cate and punched him in the stomach as hard as she could with her small, hard fist. Unready for it, he doubled over, and had to ward off her next blows. Officer Reeves and Tricia ran over, and

Tricia, speaking in Bernadette's ear, helped pull the girl away, but his daughter's eyes blazed at him. She tried to kick him in the shins.

"Look, we'll go to Atlanta tomorrow and catch a plane and fly home," he said in a voice that sounded too high. "We'll go home." They stared at him incredulously.

"Mr. Forrest," said the Reeves boy, tilting his head toward the car.

Cate looked at the policeman and back at Forrest. Her brows contracted.

"They just want to ask me some questions," Forrest said.

"Oh my God, Dad, what did you do?" Cate said.

"It's about the woman who had the heart attack. I'll be back soon. We'll go home."

"Oh my God, it's just like Vivienne said about you and those college girls. I never thought it was true. I *defended* you."

He watched her face take in who he really was. She turned toward the car, and Tricia put her arms around her.

"I hate to do it," said Officer Reeves, and he began to clamp a handcuff on Forrest's left wrist.

"Can't you wait a fucking minute?" Forrest roared, yanking the arm from the boy's grasp. The girls' heads jerked around to look. "I just want to talk to my daughters," Forrest said, pushing the boy's chest. "Why do you have to cuff me in front of them, you dumb shit?"

The officer's eyes widened and he backed away and his hand went to his pistol.

"What, now you're going to shoot me?" Forrest shouted.

The boy moved his hand from his pistol and lifted the cuffs again. "I'm supposed to cuff you. The boss said." He had a small card in his hand. "You have the right to remain silent," he read, and while he went through the rest, Forrest let him put on the cuffs and lead him toward the police car. Tricia's car pulled away. He thought of his girls on the way back to Tricia's house. Maya unconscious in the ambulance. Marisa in Viterbo with her aunt, the emails she was probably sending him. His laptop. He thought of the books he was working on, and he stopped and turned toward Reeves.

"I need my laptop," he said.

"Your laptop?"

"It's got important work on it."

Billy Reeves pressed the eraser into his forehead.

"You won't try to escape?"

"I swear. Get out your gun and point it at me."

9

Alyssa was a sweetheart, no question about it, but she was also a pain in the butt. Having an only child was something you couldn't explain to people who had more than one. If she wanted something and you had other things to do, she took it personally. Whenever he or Patricia said they were busy, a little sob of self-pity would come into her voice, and she would say, "Well, it's not like you have a bunch of kids to worry about. It's only me." You would get the feeling that she had always wanted to be in *The Waltons or Cheaper by the Dozen*, though he didn't know how a brother or sister could have put up with her. It was odd to think about what she would have been like with sisters. Or older brothers. A little brother. Whatever.

The question was always what you would have turned out to be like, if? What if he had had brothers? What if he had been born as big and smart as Braxton Forrest? He had been an only child himself. His father had always been busy at work, his mother was more or less like Patricia, he realized, and he had grown up thinking of himself as better than everybody else and feeling sorry for himself at the same time. Alyssa probably had some of that.

But by God she could act.

"I have to go?" she whined in the foyer of the Davis house. "Why? Why do I have to go?" She stamped her foot and flung out her arms. She said they were halfway through *She's the Man*, which was, like, Shakespeare. They were going to have pizza later. She and Bridget were talking about real stuff.

"Now sugar," said Judah Davis, putting his chubby arm around Alyssa, who stood there making herself small, smiling nervously. "We'll talk some sense into your daddy here."

"Nope, gotta go," said Chick. "That SAT prep class starts at eight tomorrow morning down in Macon. Can't skip it. Good thing your mother remembered it."

"We'll get her up," said Judah Davis, squeezing her, rocking her. "I'll wake her up myself. She'll be ready when I go to work at 7:15."

"Oh, Judah," said Patricia, "that's sweet, but you know these girls will stay up half the night talking. Get your things, Alyssa."

"Mom!"

"I mean it. Right this minute."

Alyssa broke free from Judah Davis and stomped away convincingly. Davis put the stem of his pipe in his mouth and sucked noisily before getting out a lighter and directing it down into the bowl with his stubby fingers.

"Varina should be back any minute," he said. He raised his eyebrows at them and spoke around the pipe. "It's those Forrest girls. All week long, and now their daddy finally comes to town and doesn't show up to see them when he's supposed to. Did you know this Forrest fellow in school?"

"He was a grade ahead of me all the way through."

"Heard his name mentioned. Never laid eyes on him. Irresponsible from what I hear."

"That man," said Patricia, "is a monster."

Judah lowered his pipe and cocked his head. "Is that right?"

Everybody else in town knew about Tricia and Braxton, but Judah obviously had no idea. When you got to be middle-aged, you left unspoken your knowledge of what people had done when they were young. People did not say what they remembered about Tricia, and she did not say what she remembered about them. You took Judah Davis for the fat, self-important jackass he was, but you tried not to say to yourself every time you saw him, *That man has no idea.* Everybody would be too polite to bring it up to the regional manager of Wal-Mart.

What Judah Davis had needed early in life was about two years of Coach Fitzgerald. For instance, his pants. Most men would buy a waist size that rode more or less around their hips, even if their stomachs hung over a little like Chick's. But not high-water Judah. He was one of those people who needed a seatbelt extension on the plane, but instead of riding his belt low, he buckled his pants right over the fattest part of him. That must be because he had one of those butts like a couple of sofa cushions. It embarrassed you to see a butt like that on a fellow male. Back in high school, Tricia Honeycutt would have laughed at the very mention of somebody like Judah Davis, but now he and his money were a consolation prize after all her troubles, first with Forrest and then that dumb insurance man from Griffin she married, Bob Foster—not that it fooled anybody but her son.

But that was forty years ago, when she was young. The mystery was how she had consented seventeen years ago to conceive Bridget with Humpty Dumpty. Maybe he wasn't so fat then, but he was shorter than Chick, and here he was next to the portrait of hollow-cheeked Jefferson Davis. *My distinguished ancestor*, he said every time Chick came over, pointing to the president with the stem of his pipe.

Which was pure bullshit. Chick had googled Jefferson Davis. One of his daughters was the only one to get married and have children, so there were no descendants named Davis.

"Where'd y'all eat in Atlanta?" Judah was asking him, as though he were the expert on Atlanta.

"Noemi," Patricia said. "French cuisine."

"Ah—"

The outside door flew open. The two Forrest girls burst in, winced back from the adults in the foyer, and then rushed past them, their faces red with crying. They disappeared up the curving front steps. Exclamations and wails rose from the other girls upstairs. A moment later, Tricia came in and closed the front door behind her. She walked past them with hardly a glance, still in the tennis clothes she had been wearing that afternoon, and went into the family room. Curious, they drifted in after her, watching as she opened a cabinet, got out a bottle of whiskey, and poured herself half a bar glass with no ice. She sat down on the couch and looked at them.

"Help yourself," she said, tilting her head back toward the liquor cabinet.

"What in the world happened?" asked Patricia.

"Besides Braxton raping some woman with a BMW?"

"No!" Patricia cried.

"She went into cardiac arrest. The EMS people had to revive her."

Alyssa came running down the steps with her backpack, mouthing *Let's go* when she caught his eye.

"We need to let you folks get settled," Chick said.

"Chick! Wait a minute," said Tricia.

She drank off her bourbon neat and set down the glass. She crossed the room and stood close in front of him and put her hands on his elbows. She looked up into his eyes. Patricia stood five feet away, watching, her mouth open. Judah Davis held his pipe in the air, spellbound. When Tricia beckoned him with her head, Chick leaned forward and her lips went to his ear, the soft hot liquorish breath, and he felt himself helplessly stirred.

"You need to go see about him," she whispered. The words stuck together a little leaving her lips.

She stood back to see that she had struck home. She gave him a small, serious nod, and cocked her head very slightly in inquiry, holding his eyes. He nodded, and she gave his forearm a squeeze and turned away.

Judah Davis made little sucking noises on his pipe.

"Mom?" Bridget Davis called from the stairs. "Mrs. Forrest is on the phone from Italy. She wants to talk to you."

"Oh God," murmured Tricia.

When she went upstairs, Chick pushed Alyssa and Patricia toward the foyer, and they made their escape from the lurking Judah. In the car, Alyssa burst into accusations. "Where were you? Why didn't you call after I said to? God!"

"Watch your mouth," Patricia said mechanically.

"It's crazy in there," she went on. "You should hear what Bridget said."

"Like what?" Chick demanded as they pulled onto Hood Road.

"Like he sleeps with his pretty students. Like he's being fired from his college. Like he's run up huge bills."

"That man," said Patricia, "is a monster." She paused for a beat and turned toward Chick. "What did Varina say to you?"

"She's tired of Judah. She wants me to make reservations and take her to Cancun."

Alyssa burst out laughing in the backseat, which gratified Chick and hurt his feelings at the same time. Her mother turned to give her a hard look.

"Very funny," Patricia said, smoothing her skirt over her knees. "You and Varina. Ha ha."

"She hates that name," Alyssa said.

"Why do you say that?"

"She just does. Mr. Davis makes her use it."

"Well, it's her name, isn't it?"

"I guess, but Bridget says she used to be called Tricia. Right, Dad? You said that's what you always called her."

There was a long silence. He crossed the bridge and put on his blinker for the left turn onto the ramp, even though there was no one coming and no one behind them. *Ka-blink, ka-blink, ka-blink.* Lights flashed, amber and red.

"Dad?" said Alyssa. "Can you turn down the air conditioner? I'm freezing."

He reached up and adjusted the temperature up to 75. The car flowed down the ramp like a pat of melting butter. He merged effortlessly onto the Interstate. Up ahead he could see the lights of the telephone tower outside Gallatin. A few more miles. Just a few more miles.

But as they passed the first Gallatin exit, Patricia turned to look at Chick. "Well, Brantley, what did Tricia say to you?"

"She wants me to go see about Cump."

"Go see about who?"

"Forrest. At the jail. I'll drop you and Alyssa off."

"Right," she said. "Drop us off. Then you and Tricia can go to Cancun." With an ugly, jagged sound, she burst into tears.

"Oh my god, Mom!" Alyssa cried incredulously from the backseat. "He was just kidding. You know he was kidding. I mean, come on—Dad and Mrs. Davis?"

Patricia waved her off and stared out the passenger window. A minute later, though, her shoulders began to shake with laughter.

"Your dad and Varina Davis!" she said.

The two of them laughed until they wept. Finally, Alyssa shook her father merrily by the shoulder.

10

The officer who booked Forrest, LaCourvette Todd, was a short, stocky woman, maybe forty, round-faced, with a short afro and big eyes. She sat in front of an old computer at a Formica-topped desk in the middle of the room—file cabinets behind her, an overflowing metal trash can in the corner next to the bench ran along the front wall. There were two offices to his right, and Forrest could see a black officer behind the desk in the first one. The closed door of the other office had a doorplate: Jimmy Ponder, Chief of Police. As Officer Todd was typing information from Forrest's driver's license, the black man stood in the door and gave Forrest a long look. He asked Officer Todd if she needed any help.

"No, sugar, I'm fine. He's behaving himself so far."

She gave him back his driver's license to put in his wallet near his American Express card and then took his wallet with the rest of his belongings, including the keys to the rented Camry, his cell phone, and his laptop, into the office. She called Forrest sweetie when she fingerprinted him and sang "Calling for You" when she took his mug shot, humming the words she could not remember. She asked him to sit down again. "Now sweetheart," she said, "I need to ask you about a call I got this afternoon, 'cause the person who called is the same one you in here about now."

"How is she? Have you heard anything?"

"From the hospital? Not yet. Now this afternoon Miss Davidson said you told her about a woman named Marilyn Harkins who lived in Gallatin and might have been murdered?" she asked.

He hesitated. "A black girl who used to go out with white men."

"I know who Marilyn Harkins was."

"This was forty years ago," he said. "Before you were born."

"I wish that was all there was to it, sugar. Like what happened before I was born didn't count. Then I could say, now listen, just because I'm black, what's that got to do with slavery? You know what I'm saying? Why, sugar, where I go to church, the preacher even tells folks they got to be washed clean of the sin of Adam and Eve, and I didn't know either one."

"So was I arrested because of what Maya told you?"

She gazed up at him for a moment.

"No, baby, you here because when a girl says stop, you supposed to stop. That lady two doors down at the motel heard the whole thing, and she says the girl was screaming for you to stop. Billy says she's just a little bitty thing."

"So it didn't have anything to do with what I told her about Marilyn Harkins."

She frowned and pursed her lips and would not meet his eyes. "Let's get you upstairs."

On the second floor, she waited for him to use the bathroom. There was a toilet with no seat, and inside the bowl, someone's buoyant brown remnant. Various sexual drawings covered the walls, and the sharp urinous smell reminded him of grammar school, where mill boys repeating sixth grade for the third or fourth time and already destined for the penitentiary would lurk in the john to intimidate younger boys. A soggy roll of toilet paper stood on the floor. The sink was stained from constant dripping. At least there were paper towels.

"You by yourself so far," said Officer Todd when he came out. "Liable to be two or three more later. It's Friday night."

She was humming "Rock of Ages" when she locked him in the cell. She started away and then came back. "You Mrs. Inger Connor's son."

"You knew my mother?"

"My grandmama was her maid a way long time ago when you were little."

"Mary Louise? She was your grandmother?"

"Yes sir. And still is."

"She's still with us?"

"Praise God. Still has her own house."

"Still making that prime rib?"

"Everybody loves that prime rib!" she laughed. "It would trouble her to see you in here, sugar. One of her own."

"I'll go see her."

"You got to get out of here first." She reached out and patted his hand where it gripped one of the bars. "Listen, I don't believe you hurt that little girl on purpose," she said. "That's something on your heart if you did. She came down to see you, and that's asking for trouble." She paused. "But I can see why she got scared. You're a big old man."

He stood watching her as she disappeared down the stairs.

A big man. An old man.

The air was close and stuffy, and the day's heat lingered in the walls. Outside the cell, in the narrow walkway separating it from the matching cell across from it, an old window air conditioner turned itself off, groaning and gurgling, then came on again almost immediately with a rattling commotion. The vents were directed away from him. There was no chair, so he sat in the middle of a stained army cot with his back against the wall.

If he had ever been inside an actual jailhouse, he didn't remember it. Instead he remembered movies. *The Birdman of Alcatraz.* Hundreds of westerns: drunks, killers, innocent men locked up. Dozens of ways of shooting your way out or tricking the jailer out of his keys. *Sorry, Miss Todd*, he would say, touching the rim of his hat to her and giving her a wink as he left her inside the cell. *Tell Mary Louise I'll see her next time.*

He got up and gripped the bars just to see what it felt like. He imagined himself talking to Charlie Rose.

So what does freedom mean to you now, Professor Forrest?

He thought for a minute, made a mouth.

Well, Charlie, freedom for me means doing whatever I want to do on the impulse of the moment. And if something blocks me, I'm liable to explode with rage.

Charlie Rose frowned at him and tapped his eraser on the table and then pointed it at Forrest.

That sounds like a child.

71

Forrest sat back down on the cot and spread his arms. Look, I teach my classes. But I never volunteer for anything. I get myself kicked off any committee I'm appointed to.

How do you do that?

I say what I really think about required online courses on sexual harassment, or the language of assessment, or gay marriage partners on insurance policies funded by the college, or special arrangements for students with alleged disabilities.

So freedom is not being inconvenienced by what other people take seriously.

I shun the kinds of things that earn little people little honors.

What about the honors you got for your book?

Oh my God. Humiliating. Unbearable.

Really? Why's that?

Oh, you know. An honor is only as good as the person honoring you. It's hard to disguise the vast difference between what my colleagues think of me and what I know about myself.

What do you mean?

Their honors are just a way of fending off the reality of who I am.

Are you sure you want to say all this out loud on television, Prof. Forrest?

It's okay, Charlie. The only reason to play this game at all is to reveal its inadequacy.

But there you are, in a six-by-eight cell in the Gallatin County Jail.

Thank God Almighty. Free at last.

Charlie Rose turned away, and the lights dimmed. *Piece of shit,* Forrest heard him mumble.

The side of the cot was cutting into his thighs, and he tried using the lumpy pillow (no pillowcase) under his legs, but it was too thick. When he drew his feet up and tried to sit in the lotus position, the whole cot bent inward and creaked under his weight.

He stood up and stared out the window at the moths circling the streetlight above the parking lot of the old post office.

He could almost see her coming out of the shadows, the liquid sway of her hips from a night as old as Babylon or Uruk, the mesmerism of those lovely gliding near-spheres of her body caught back and barely contained by the white of the fishnet dress. The light milk chocolate of her skin, a face like the Queen of Sheba. Slowing down until the car matched her pace and she smiled, still not looking.

He took the pillow from the cot and dropped it on the floor in the corner and sat on it, resting his arms on his knees, the way Maya had done against the window of the hotel room. As though it had been waiting to see him, a huge cockroach darted into the cell, paused, darted toward Forrest, stopped, antennae waving. Forrest grunted, grabbed one of the bars, and got back up. The roach dodged this way, that way. When he moved toward it, it scurried under the pillow. Forrest kicked it aside, and then stomped the roach as it tried to escape.

He kicked at the bits of insect gore and wreckage until most of the thing was outside the bars. He already needed to urinate again, but he could wait until somebody else came upstairs. He sat back down and rocked on the pillow. He had prayed over Maya's body, her terrifying absence. Prayed, willed her life back into her, sick with fear, pumping her blood for her, the head loose on the neck against the pillow, her eyes unseeing, her arms hanging loose and dead, her breasts in a soft rhythmic wobble.

Somebody was climbing the stairs. He heard Officer Todd's merry voice, and then Chick Lee came in and walked over to the cell door.

"Cump. What the hell?"

Forrest stared at him through the bars, not getting up. "There's no place like home."

"What did you do? They're talking about rape."

"I didn't rape anybody. How did you find out I was here?"

"I was out at Tricia's house picking up Alyssa. Saw your girls."

Forrest shook his head. "They shouldn't be here. It's all because of those letters."

Chick was looking for somewhere to sit down, so he went and called down the stairs to Officer Todd, asking if she had a chair she could spare him. A few seconds later, Officer Reeves climbed the stairs and opened a folding chair for him, sliding it across the floor to him as the sound of loud voices rose from downstairs. He disappeared and Chick sat down between the cells.

"So what made you think they were real?" Chick asked Forrest.

"Why wouldn't they be? The stationery, the handwriting. And I thought the reason was pretty obvious. She doesn't have any relatives left alive, and she felt guilty about the fact that my father was disinherited, so she was looking for somebody to leave her money to."

"Mrs. Hayes? She doesn't have any money."

"Bullshit."

"You mean from Forrest Mills?"

"Of course."

"Have you seen them? All those buildings have been boarded up since the Seventies."

Reeves stuck his head back around the corner of the stairs. "Y'all got company," he said. The noise downstairs got louder. Two men cursing at each other.

"The textile business went to China a long time ago," Chick said.

"So she sold it and reinvested the money."

"If Hermia Watson hadn't started taking care of her, she'd be dead by now. She was living on cat food."

"Who is this Hermia Watson?"

A crash jerked their heads toward the stairway. Their hands cuffed behind them, two young black men burst up the stairs, cursing, slamming each other against the walls with their shoulders, butting each other, trying to cram a knee in the other's groin.

"Hey!" the Reeves boy was shouting as he tried to separate them. "Hey!"

They erupted from the top of the stairs into the space between the cells. The shorter one, broad-shouldered and bullet-headed, managed to trip the tall, skinny one, who stumbled headlong into Chick and knocked him from the chair. Officer Todd darted forward and swung her nightstick viciously up into the short one's groin as he was about to kick his rival. He sank to the floor. The older black officer pulled the tall one's arms up behind him and lifted him from the floor, opened the opposite cell, and flung him into it, where he crashed against the cot and collapsed. Reeves opened Forrest's cell and pushed the groaning short one inside, holding the door open.

"Mr. Forrest," he said. "You're free to go."

"How come *he* free to go?" shouted the black man in the other cell, instantly on his feet.

"Shut up, nigger!" yelled the man in Forrest's cell, jerking around. "It ain't none of your business *what* he do."

Chick had been knocked sprawling into the front wall. As he stood up—Forrest cringed seeing it about to happen—his forehead hit the corner of the air conditioner. He cursed and clapped his hand over the cut, but the blood welled past his hand and flowed down his forearm in a quick runnel, dripping from his elbow onto his slacks when he stumbled back and righted the chair to sit on it. Officer Todd snatched some paper towels from the bathroom to catch the blood. She got him up and led him downstairs.

The Reeves boy beckoned to Forrest.

"Come on out. I need to lock the cell," he said.

Forrest got up and left the short black man with his bloodshot eyes gripping the bars and glaring at his nemesis across the room. They were already taunting each other. Officer Reeves went over to the air conditioner and turned it off.

"What you doing?" demanded the tall one with the carefully razored haircut.

"You go on downstairs," the boy said to Forrest. "I'm right behind you." He flipped off the light. "It brings out the roaches, but it'll save the city some money."

"Come on, man!" Both men were yelling at him, but he closed the door to the upstairs so that no light from below would filter in.

"It's the only way we can get some peace and quiet," he said on the landing as he followed Forrest down.

Upstairs, the yelling intensified.

"Doesn't seem to be working," Forrest said.

"I'll go up in about ten minutes," said Officer Todd. "They generally get reasonable once it's hot enough."

She sat on the bench at the front of the room next to Chick Lee, holding a piece of ice inside a paper towel pressed against the cut on his forehead.

"The things I do for Tricia," Chick said sourly.

"So what's the story?" Forrest asked Officer Todd.

"Your young lady friend woke up and cleared you," she said.

"She's okay?"

"They're going to keep her in the hospital for observation overnight. Another thing you need to know. Your wife's been calling." She tilted her head to the open door of the office.

"Oh Lord," Forrest said, glancing at her nametag again. Her looks suddenly cohered. "Wait a minute. Something just clicked. Are you Jeff Todd's daughter?" He started to say that Jeff had been the first black player on his football team in high school and that she looked like him, but he saw her face cloud over. "Your mother is Mary Louise's daughter?"

"Was," she said.

"I'm sorry. How did she..."

"Married Jeff Todd."

Forrest waited for her to say more, but she would not look at him.

"Over here?" Forrest said and went over to the door.

The black officer picked up a piece of paper and held it toward Forrest, shaking his head.

"You mean she called here?"

"I mean to tell you. We could use that woman in the courthouse."

The paper had an airline and flight number on it.

"What's this?"

"Look to me like your come-to-Jesus," the officer said.

"Is she on this flight?"

"She says you got the American Express card." The officer handed Forrest a sack containing his wallet and his other things.

"Where's my laptop?"

The officer looked behind him and found the black laptop bag. "She says she got a rate. She says to tell you, 'Buy the ticket tonight.'"

"How did she happen to call here?"

"She said you told her you might be in jail. She don't think you doing so good."

"I'm having a fine time, Lt. Watts," Forrest said.

Watts lifted his bloodshot eyes to Forrest. He shook his head. "Get out of here, man. How old are you?"

11

Chick insisted on taking Forrest back to the motel. Officer Todd had taped a big gauze bandage on his forehead after the bleeding finally stopped, but his shirt and slacks looked grisly. Once they were in the Navigator—Chick found a towel and spread it on the seat—it was already almost midnight. Forrest groaned when Chick turned the wrong way on Lee Street toward Cousin Emily Barron Hayes' house.

"Chick, give me a break. I'm exhausted."

Chick did not speak. He took the Johnson's Mill Road fork and headed out into the country, but then the woods opened up and to Forrest's surprise a large sign announced the main entrance to Sybil Forrest High School: a long low set of new brick buildings, several large parking lots illuminated by streetlights, a track with hurdles, rows of yellow school buses. Chick turned in and drove up to the school and followed a road around its side to the back. Forrest recognized the old practice fields. The stadium loomed beyond them, now with large stands that would not shame a small college and a sign that said Fitzgerald Field.

Chick still did not speak. They eased past a field house emblazoned with a large Blue Devil. The gymnasium where they used to dress was gone, replaced by a parking lot, but the old school buildings still stood. They rolled slowly to the old entrance on Highway 41. Chick turned left toward the courthouse square and passed the filling station that Ray Ponder ran.

"How's Ray doing these days?"

"Dying of brain cancer," Chick said. "He was there the day the bus dropped off your girls. He got in touch with Hermia Watson, I think."

He eased up Main Street, a block over from where Forrest had already driven twice that night. The grammar school they attended had been condemned, but it still stood there, square and ugly, its playgrounds fenced off and posted.

"You know Fitz retired last year," Chick said as they stopped at the traffic light.

"Is that right? I haven't kept up with him."

"Somebody asked him at the banquet who the players were he remembered best. He talked some about the great ones from the other state championship team—Jed Rockwell and Dutrelle Jones and those guys. But you know who he said was the best player he ever coached? Braxton Forrest."

"Did he?" said Forrest, moved despite himself.

"He said on defense you didn't just shed blockers and make tackles. He said you did that better than just about anybody—you moved like a jungle cat—but what impressed him was you were always outsmarting the other coach, not just the other player. He said on defense you had a feel for the whole game and the intention of every play. You'd sense where the ball was going to be before the play even had time to develop. He said he never had to tell you anything twice. The only reason you didn't win state every year was the offense."

"Thank God for Graham Ashley my senior year. What happened to him?"

"He's a doctor down in Savannah."

"I thought Coach hated my guts."

"You disappointed him. But the question was who the best athlete was, so he told the truth. It pissed people off," said Chick. "If it hadn't been Coach, you see what I'm saying?"

Chick let the silence hang there, as though he expected something. He drove slowly around the courthouse square before turning to head to the motel.

"Okay, no. I don't see what you're saying."

"You had more promise than anybody we ever saw, but you were always screwing everything up. Now you come back home, it's still the same thing."

Forrest sighed. "And do but see his vice," he said. "'Tis to his virtue a just equinox, the one as long as t'other."

"What does that mean?"

"Nothing. It's just Shakespeare. So I disappointed you, too? What did you expect me to do?"

"You could have been a doctor. Run a corporation. Gone into politics—well, maybe not, the way reporters dig into your past. My God, if I'd had your—I mean, you walk out on a football scholarship and end up an English teacher? How the hell did you become an English teacher?"

He did not answer. He had to justify his life to Chick Lee? An English teacher. Frumpy women assigning sentence diagrams, fruity Mr. Hamm making them read *A Separate Peace*. How had he become an English teacher? He thought about the guilt and anguish of those nights in the dormitory in Athens that fall and winter after Marilyn's death. He rejected the football scholarship, applied his National Merit scholarship to his tuition, and lived on his summer earnings. His roommate, an economics major, quoted stock prices in his sleep. Forrest read until three or four in the morning, devouring everything recommended by the new friends he was making—smart longhaired guys from Atlanta who would proffer him a joint as they talked, a little awed to have this big ex-jock pay attention to them. He read through Hermann Hesse. *Beneath the Wheel, Steppenwolf, Siddhartha, Narcissus and Goldmund, Magister Ludi*. He had a short flirtation with Ayn Rand's fiction. He dabbled in Nietzsche and Jung. He read *The Waste Land* until its incantatory language traced itself deep in his psyche.

He wrote, too, going over and over what had happened, speculating about his family past, writing in images that he deliberately did not try to understand. At the end of his sophomore year, he first encountered the preternatural prose of Nabokov. *Lolita, Pale Fire.* By his junior year, he had read Shakespeare with his best teacher, George Montgomery. On his own, he had gone on to Faulkner, and also on his own, through dabbling in Joyce and Pound, he had come at last upon Homer. When he entered the highlands of the Iliad and then discovered the succession myth about the son of Thetis, he already had the basis for his dissertation at Yale on Achilleus, the god who was not a god, the mortal who would have overthrown the Olympians if he had been born of Zeus or Poseidon. His first book, *The Subjunctive Abyss*, was about the infinite reach of what was denied to Achilleus in advance. It gave him some reputation. He had gotten his broader fame with *The Gameme*, despite its many detractors.

"The only thing I can figure is it gives you a steady supply of college girls," Chick said.

They were riding out the old route to the city pool, past the houses of people he had known growing up.

"What are you talking about?"

"Being an English teacher."

"There are definitely college girls in college," Forrest said. "So I'm supposed to explain what exactly?"

"Where's your novel? Where's the bestseller?"

"When's the last time you read a novel?" Forrest pictured Chick with a beer in one hand, burping discreetly and fiddling with his remote in front of a big plasma TV. Chick with his Navigator and his dealership and his money and his self-importance in the Baptist church and whatever clubs he belonged to.

"Me?" He thought for a minute. "Thomas Wolfe. *The Bonfire* thing. Hated the movie."

"Tom Wolfe."

"Hey, you remind me of that guy in the book," Chick said, starting to grin. "Sherman something. The Master of the Universe guy."

"Can I get some sleep?" he asked.

Two minutes later, they were crossing the railroad tracks on the way downhill toward the Interstate, and Forrest glanced at the boxcars left on a sidetrack near the feed mill. He sat up as a memory came over him in a rush. One night he had left the car on the side of the road and he had taken Marilyn up the ladder and into a boxcar. He remembered the smell inside, oil and hay and perfume. He backed her against the wooden slats. She hiked her dress up. Lifting her, his knees suddenly buckling, both of them almost falling. The violence of him that she sweetened herself on. Her whispering to him in her strangely formal diction.

Down those side streets, hidden in the shadowy no-place between the back of the college, the Interstate, and Lee Street, was a black neighborhood. Hadn't she grown up in one of those houses? She always wanted to be let out on a dark corner or beside an empty lot, and he would drive off and see her in his rearview mirror, already back into the sway and enticement of her walk.

Where did she sleep? What kind of terrible family drove her even from childhood into her strange campaign of conquest? He must have known once. Even now he almost remembered, but things had gotten confused. He had tried to write about her in his teens, his twenties, his thirties. But for years now he had pushed the thought of her down and out of his memory.

"You know what gets me?" Chick was not done with him, but at least they were almost to the motel. "What you did to Tricia."

"Tricia? You mean tonight?"

"No, dumbass. Before you left Gallatin."

"I don't know what you're talking about."

Chick slammed the steering wheel with his palm and swerved to the right into the empty parking lot of the Piggly Wiggly where he squealed to a stop. "Get out of my car."

Chick stared at him, his pudgy right hand squeezing the gear shift knob and releasing it. A blotch of dark blood was showing in the bandage on his forehead. Forrest stared back, his hand on the door handle.

"Get out of my car," Chick said again.

"I'm happy to, Brantley." Forrest opened the door, but Chick grabbed his arm.

"What do you mean you don't know? How could you not know?"

Forrest stared at him, and Chick let go. Forrest got out of the car and retrieved his laptop from the backseat. He was halfway across the empty lot toward the EconoLodge down the hill when Chick pulled up beside him.

"Bob Foster works for the State Patrol up in Griffin. He's already a major. He turned thirty-nine on April Fool's Day."

"Who the hell is Bob Foster?"

Chick stared at him as the Navigator rolled along keeping pace. "Sweet Jesus," Chick said after a few seconds. "You're as clueless as Judah Davis."

Forrest shrugged and shook his head in irritation. "Listen, it's late. I'm tired. I don't know what you're talking about. How about I go to the motel and dream about all these little riddles?"

Chick braked the Navigator to a stop, but Forrest kept walking.

"You didn't even know?" Chick called after him.

"Know what?" Forrest shouted in a sudden rage. He whirled back toward the car, but Chick put up his window and drove away.

Forrest stood watching him disappear up the hill. Above his head, a streetlight hummed, tuning itself to the ringing in his ears.

Who the hell was Bob Foster? There were still a few cars in the big lot—an old station wagon, a pickup truck next to a clothes store beyond the Piggly Wiggly. Across Lee Street, the Wal-Mart loomed in its vast parking lot where people's houses used to be. Traffic streamed past on the Interstate, the big tractor-trailers that drove all night. When he was a boy, trains would go by in the middle of the night, four big diesel engines linked together pulling hundreds of boxcars, and the whistle would wail even at two or three in the morning to warn anyone at the crossings.

He stood swaying on his feet, looking toward Atlanta. On the access road that ran along the southbound lane of the Interstate, another motel or two lifted its sign. Clusters of filling stations followed the bend onto Lee Street, interspersed with fast food places—McDonald's, Pizza Hut, a Waffle House where he could see a few men with their elbows on the counter.

In Italy, it would already be morning. Cafes would be opening in Rome. The waiters in crisp white shirts, young and arrogant, would be making espressos and setting the potent little cups into their saucers on the shining counters with a practiced clatter. Forrest rolled his head on his neck and sighed.

He walked across the parking lot and over a grassy median past a fenced-in dumpster and angled across the back parking lot of the EconoLodge. To his surprise—he thought the management would have evicted him—his key card still worked, and his room still looked as it had when the EMS people came in to save Maya. There were the rumpled bedclothes. The ten dollar bill and the wrinkled twenty posed beside the pillow. He would see her in the morning, take her the clothes she had shed, buy her some flowers. The image of her beneath him as he kept her blood pumping stirred him now. All those Elizabethan puns about dying.

He sat on the edge of the bed to take off his shoes, thinking of her, already falling asleep. He was running naked among the cattle in some farmer's pasture, a wild man pursued by the Reeves boy. And over there, he could see her now, over there, there she was. Not Maya but Marilyn, stepping out of the garden with its tall cornstalks into the dirt road with a little skip and a shake of her head, jingling her silken necklace of rings, and in the space between setting down one bare foot and the other, that ancient rhythm of her hips began, as though she had just come walking out of Uruk.

12

July 18, 2009

At 6:30, when she heard Eumaios stirring, Hermia Watson closed her laptop. She was a little queasy from seeing all the girls thronging around her son in the pictures on Facebook, but she shouldn't have been wasting her time anyway, not with a book to write. She stretched and took her coffee cup to the kitchen. There was Eumaios, panting, waiting by the back door, and she knelt and pulled his intelligent head against her breast and looked into his unsuspicious eyes as he strained to lick her.

"You know who's in town? Do you know?"

When she stood, he drew back, dancing a little, and put a paw on the door. "You want to go out?" she said, teasing him, hand on the knob. He pawed the door again, anxious, not understanding the delay, and she thought what power she had over him. The power of teachers over small children or masters over slaves. Humiliation, control over someone else's body.

She let him out into the backyard. He ran across the deck, leapt onto the lawn, and rushed to the redwood fence between her yard and Mrs. Russell's, barking at a squirrel that scrambled along the top and then leapt for a branch of the pecan tree and disappeared in a thrashing of small branches. He toured the whole perimeter of the yard, sniffing the boxwood along the back fence. He skirted the tomatoes she'd planted—he'd better leave those alone—and stopped to sniff certain spots comprehensively. Then he marked them according to principles that eluded her. When he headed into a far corner to do his business, she turned away. She got out the Greek yogurt and put a big spoonful into her favorite bowl, adding fresh blueberries and some organic granola the Trappist monks near Atlanta made.

By now, Eumaios was pawing at the door. "What, you mean you don't know who's in town?" she asked him as he came back in. "He was right there in front of you." He wagged his tail, looking up at her, and she poured him some dry food and added liquid she had saved from a can of tuna. She ate standing while he crunched his way through his food, and when he was satisfied, she let him back out for the day. He had plenty of water in his bowl on the deck. She emptied the filter and grounds from the coffeemaker, rinsed everything, and arranged it artfully in the dishwasher.

Is this the way to the courthouse square? he had asked her. As though he were a stranger in town! As though she were a local. Braxton Forrest. Seeing him again made her feel as fluttery as a schoolgirl. She glanced at the clock and went back to the laptop in her bedroom to watch the clip from an interview in 2000 one more time.

Charlie Rose was a big man—almost six-four—but on the YouTube video, Forrest seemed much bigger, more like a retired NFL player than an academic. In that studio light, against the black background, he propped his elbows on the table where so many famous people had been, and there were those huge hands she remembered, the shoulders broad and powerful without mere massiveness—and his head, God. Like a lion's.

"There's a passage in your new book," Rose said, tapping a copy with his finger, "where you predict a black president in the near future. Really? America's ready?"

"Almost," said Forrest. "But the cultural meiotics of blackness would have to be right."

"Cultural meiotics. Explain, please."

"It's how we have to think about politics now. The old way of thinking dies hard. Everybody still pretends it's a matter of issues and policies, but for a long time, at least since television came of age in the Kennedy-Nixon debates in 1960, elections have been about the deployment of memes."

"Memes. Remind me."

"Richard Dawkins invented the word to mean a unit of cultural transmission analogous to a gene. When I use it, I'm talking about serious cultural characteristics, the kinds of markers—accent, body style, fashion, and so on—that define someone's status or social affinities. Bush and Gore might differ in their politics, for example, but as combinations of memes, they're Tweedledee and Tweedledum."

Charlie Rose smiled ambiguously.

"Now the question is what memes a black candidate would need to carry. If a black president is elected, he won't be a Republican, somebody of the Clarence Thomas stamp. He won't remind anybody of the old Civil Rights era, either. He'll probably seem tangential to the old black politics. What I picture is somebody pigmented black who isn't black in the usual American way, somebody carrying all the memes of whiteness—the accent, the physical bearing, the vocabulary. I don't think it could be a man whose ancestors were American slaves, because he would be too hard for white America to forgive."

"Forgive?" Charlie Rose said.

"Remember that line of Jack Burden's in *All the King's Men*? He says, 'Goodbye, Lois, and I forgive you for everything I did to you.' I mean forgive in that sense. A successful black candidate would have to be culturally and physically outside the heritage of American slavery—say a man whose father is an African who married an American white woman, something like that. There would be nothing America had done to him ancestrally, so to speak. So the candidate would be American and black, but his grandmother—just picture this—his grandmother would be an ordinary American white woman. But as for the candidate himself, he's what I call the gameme."

"And you say a gameme is—let me get this straight—a cultural gamete made of memes. You made up the word," said Rose, smiling and pointing his pencil at Forrest. "You're not sounding like an English teacher."

"That's right," Forrest smiled. "I made it up because I'm interested in the big epic movements in literature. A gamete is a sex cell with half the chromosomes of a somatic cell. That's how you get the unique recombinations that define us, when the sperm and the egg combine, right? So a gameme is a kind of *cultural* sex cell, a cultural whole stripped of half its content so it can be recombined with another gameme. I invented the word primarily to refer to figures in epic poetry stripped down from some cultural whole. Hector is fully Trojan, for example, but Aeneas is the already ambiguous Trojan with Troy stripped from him—he's lost his city, his wife, all the things that gave his memes their context."

"I'm not half the man I used to be," Charlie Rose said.

Forrest laughed. She loved it when he laughed like that.

"Exactly, but only if you see that by being made half, you become intensely combinational. That's what I'm thinking with this black candidate. White-born American blackness would be haploid with respect to the diploid somatic cells of American culture, so to speak: he's black—but the other half of what blackness means in America just isn't there."

"You're losing me. One more time on haploid and diploid."

Forrest leaned toward Rose, holding him in his gaze, and Hermia's heart turned as it always did when she remembered the way he had leaned toward her like that on their morning in Providence over breakfast.

"Ordinary body cells, somatic cells, are diploid." He pressed his big hands together as though he were praying. "Ordinarily, chromosomes come in pairs. Body cells have the full complement of chromosomes, forty-six in our case. But the sex cells, the sperm and the egg"—he pulled his hands apart as if by an effort and dropped his left one beneath the table—"are haploid. It's like the old story in Plato of the original people being split in half. They have half the number, so when they join with another sex cell they make up forty-six again in a new but stable combination that has never existed before. Haploids are unstable, if you see what I mean. Full of unfinished business."

Charlie Rose nodded and tilted his head.

"So let's say you get this white-born black candidate," Forrest went on. "In terms of genes, he's a stable mix, no problem. America's full of normal mixed-race people. But in terms of memes, he's a floating half, open to all kinds of recombination. He's black, but he's not. There's a kind of excitement around him that doesn't seem to have much to do with his personality—so he's like Aeneas in this respect. American blackness is the Troy he's left behind."

"Help me out on that," said Charlie Rose. "The Troy he's left behind."

"I mean that American blackness doesn't exist for him, not in a meaningful way. It's not his context, and it can never truly be his context—and yet he's black, so he's haploid, culturally unstable, needing to be recombined."

"Married, you mean?"

"Not just that. More than that. I mean that he attracts haploid cultural phenomena. He changes things. I think somebody like that could be elected, especially if other supposedly stable things were being shaken up. For example, Jimmy Carter would never have been elected in 1976 if we hadn't had the long Vietnam War debacle and then the Watergate scandal. He seemed fresh and honest—a change from the fetid political world of LBJ and Nixon that Gerald Ford inherited. Suppose something happened that made everybody weary in the same way—a long war, hard as that is to imagine, or a stock market crash. Anything that would make the race issue per se seem trivial. People would want someone who seemed to offer a new element, a change."

"Fascinating," Charlie Rose said. "But let me ask you about the biology behind your theory of the gameme. As you know, the biologist Nathan Bragg—I'm sure you've read his review essay in The New Republic—has objected that in terms of biology you're—"

She turned it off.

She might see him today. She almost certainly would see him. This very day.

Everybody up and down South Lee Street worried about Mrs. Hayes with a certain expectant keenness. They were waiting for Hermia to go in one morning and find the old woman dead. It could happen any day. In March, Mrs. Hayes had developed bronchitis and Hermia had found her wheezing beside her bed, whimpering and incontinent, unable to get up. *Aunt Ella!* Mrs. Hayes had cried in a childish voice. *Where's Aunt Ella?* Then she had looked at Hermia fearfully. *Mr. T.J. told you not to come back. You leave me alone, Pearl.* Who am I? she had asked. *Who are you? You thought I wouldn't recognize you? I know you came back for him.*

A week in the hospital that time. Ella and Pearl must have worked there when Mrs. Hayes was young. Hermia had asked LaCourvette if she knew who Aunt Ella was, or Pearl Price, but her friend had looked puzzled, almost alarmed, and changed the subject. Some of the old women at church would remember, but she hesitated to bring the matter up, unsure of the reasons for her reluctance.

She pulled up the drive and into the leaning garage with its smell of rotten wood and its floor of fine dust pitted with doodlebug holes. Two mockingbirds flashed across from the overgrown azaleas on the near side of the house and up into the big oak tree; they touched a limb like children playing tag and flashed away past the kitchen windows and out of sight. As always, she walked toward the back garden and glanced up at Mrs. Hayes' window before going in. Someday, she thought, she would see Mrs. Hayes already sitting there, and that would be that.

She unlocked the back door and stepped into the sun porch, listening as always, convinced as always that she would know if there had been some alteration in the silence. Suppose the old woman had gotten up early, disoriented? There were so many places to fall, so many odd rooms with their steps down or up.

Hearing nothing, she crossed through the sunroom into the kitchen and put down her purse before going out into the dark corridor and up the back stairs. Opening the door as quietly as she could, she peeked into Mrs. Hayes' bedroom. A slight but steady rise and fall of the sheet, a faint whistle of snoring. The hearing aids and teeth were where they were supposed to be on the bedside table. She made her way back downstairs to the kitchen, avoiding the front of the house entirely. She would have some time, so she opened the bottom drawer near the sink and put on the calico apron.

She was putting her purse in the drawer where she usually kept it when she remembered that LaCourvette had something to tell her. Just in case, she fished out her cell phone and dropped it in one of the apron pockets, anomalous as it was.

She stood at the sink and began her ritual. Every day, as she would explain to LaCourvette, she had to find some way to place the early morning back in the days of slavery the way you would place a robin's egg back in the nest, hoping your touch had not already ruined its chance to live. She would imagine being a middle-aged slave woman, ignorant but not stupid, tired but still lively. She called herself Tillie, the name of a slave she had found in the census records of the Forrest family.

It would be 1844 or so, long before Emancipation. Tillie had always been a house slave. She was Hermia's age, past most of the young foolishness of sex, too old to have young bucks or randy owners after her, and her job was to care for Old Missy. The old woman sometimes slept until nine or ten in the morning, and when she finally did wake up, it took an hour before she was ready for breakfast. Old Missy was peculiar. She'd want Tillie to take out her night soil first thing, but she didn't want her around when she was getting ready. So early morning was the time when Tillie tasted freedom.

The test was whether that freedom could be enough—not so much for Tillie as for Hermia Watson, even in imagination. Tillie would be protected by ignorance of what her life could have been; she would have her religion, such as it was, with its promise of glory-land on the other side of death. But was it enough for Hermia? If she placed herself back in the slave days, could she see even the first and simplest thing as Tillie might see it?

What if there was no way out, no thread out of the labyrinth back to her own consciousness, like being in a nightmare from which she could not awaken? She leaned forward with her hands on the kitchen counter to look through the screen at the western slope of the yard down toward the line of trees along South Lee Street. Slaves had never lived in this house, but black women, their descendants, had stood here, washing the dishes for the Forrest family. LaCourvette said that her grandmother, Mrs. Gibson, had worked here when she was young. Old Mrs. Gibson. She had seen her coming out of church on LaCourvette's arm, pushing her way along with a cane under a succession of huge, elaborate hats. LaCourvette had avoided her eyes on those occasions, which hurt Hermia's feelings a little. She had not tried to introduce herself. At some point Hermia wanted to talk to her and plumb her memories.

She walked across the kitchen, across the sun porch, and out the screen door. When she stepped out onto the stoop, she slipped off her shoes and stood barefoot on the bricks. Early sunlight filled the tops of the trees. A rooster crowed proudly somewhere in the direction of Sharp Street.

Bird too dumb to know he just some nigger's chicken.

Grit under bare feet. Tillie now, ear out for Old Missy in the house.

Hearing nothing, she tiptoe barefoot on the hard dirt under the big oak trees toward the gate to the back garden. Got to watch out for acorns cause they stick you. She open the gate quiet, quiet, and step inside. Sniff that. All that. Dew on the strawberry plants where the sun come down through the leaves. She kneel and push apart the leaves to find a strawberry and she put it in her mouth and hold it on her tongue. The other slaves be hoeing, calling out, singing up yonder in the squash plants and cucumber vines, they be stepping over cantaloupes and watermelons and men making jokes about how big the corn is, but not that big, grabbing theyselves. Beans climbing the fence near the chicken yard.

That old woman, the one they called Beulah, she watching Tillie.

You better not mess with Old Missy's berries.

Huh. Can't nobody stop me lookin'.

You aint just looking. Open yo mouf, girl.

She rolled the ripe strawberry with her tongue and bit it and her heart cried Lord Jesus! She swallowed it.

Old Missy better not see you.

Old Missy don't know nothing bout it. Aint you got business to tend to?

You my business. Old Missy know more than you think.

Hermia straightened up. Where had Beulah come from?

When nobody was there watching, Tillie would pull up weeds and just stare at them. And why? Because she loved to see how tenacious they were, how stubbornly they clung inside the earth that hid them.

Tillie be like that. All root, far as anybody know. I only lets a little bit show, a little green.

Hermia sighed. A smidgen of wonder, a shiver of happiness.

Was it foolish to imagine loving the three round leaves of a strawberry plant? Too Toni Morrison, maybe? Was it a betrayal to imagine Tillie entertaining even so small a pleasure, letting it make her want to live, free for a moment from the idea of her servitude? No, it wasn't a betrayal. Tillie had her freedoms. She had moments no one could take from her, free things that were not illusions, little beauties, a little way, like St. Therese of Lisieux. Hermia could not think of her as brutalized into a refusal of anything but the grossest animal pleasures.

She stood and brushed off her knees. The heat of the day was coming. She looked back toward the house, listening, hushing herself, just in case Mrs. Hayes was calling her. Not a sound. A great peaceful silence.

And then the sound startled her so much her hand went to her heart and she ran several steps and looked around wildly.

GLRRRRR-BRRRRRRING! GLRRRRR-BRRRRRRING!

It was unbelievably loud, completely alien to where she was, glottal, oddly slow, as though it had to overcome some impediment.

She found the phone in the pocket of her apron. She did not recognize the number.

"Hello?" she said, opening the garden gate and starting back toward the screen door. She stepped on an acorn and winced, hopping onto the other foot.

"Is this Hermia Watson?" a man said.

"This is Hermia Watson."

"Braxton Forrest."

"Oh, Professor Forrest." She felt the pulse beating in her throat.

There was a pause.

"I'm told I need to talk to you if I want to see Cousin Emily Barron Hayes."

13

Phone in hand, Forrest was standing in the parking lot of the Gallatin Hospital, not far from where Dr. Harry Lumpkin had been shot down by his nurse's jealous husband when Forrest was a freshman in high school.

"Yes, I guess we should talk," the woman was saying. If he hadn't been told she was black, he would never have guessed it from the telephone. "Mrs. Hayes gets confused very easily."

"My girls told me that Cousin Emily Barron Hayes didn't know who they were."

"That's right," said Hermia Watson. "I tried to explain it to her, but...."

"She knew who they were in those letters," said Forrest. "I wouldn't have sent my daughters down here if I hadn't believed what the letters said. I didn't have any reason not to believe them."

"I see," she said. He waited for her to make some excuse or offer some theory, but she did not. There was not the slightest tone of judgment or reproach in her voice.

"Do you think she wrote them?" he asked.

"I don't see how," she said. "But you say you got them."

"I definitely got them."

"I mean, she does have periods of lucidity, but I can't imagine her writing and addressing those letters. I'd like to see them."

"They're back in New Hampshire."

"It's not just the stationery and the envelope and—I mean, finding a stamp, getting it in the mail, all without my knowledge. She sometimes can't even find her way back to her room if she goes down the hall. You see? Not to mention her arthritis. It just seems highly unlikely to me that she wrote them, knowing her frailty as I do."

"Where are you from, Miss Watson—or Mrs. Watson? I'm not sure what to call you."

There was a slight pause. "Just Hermia is fine," she said. "I was born in Macon, but I think of myself as being from Gallatin."

"But you're not."

There was a silence on the phone.

"Hermia?" Forrest said.

"I'm not sure what you're saying."

"You're not from Gallatin, not the way LaCourvette Todd and Chick Lee are."

"Well, all right," she said, with a hint of amusement. "If you say so."

"Listen, I want to come by this afternoon. What's the chance that Cousin Emily Barron Hayes might be available?"

"Available?"

"Lucid."

"It's possible. Shall we say four o'clock?"

"I'll be there."

He closed the phone.

As soon as he did, Forrest thought about the rented Camry and his American Express card. Somehow, he had to get the Camry to Atlanta, then find a way back to Gallatin, and have some way to get around. Chick Lee! He was sure to have some kind of clunker on the lot that Forrest could borrow. He would bitch about it, but he would love having Forrest at his mercy, especially if he could put him in some worthless old car.

88

It had been at least fifteen minutes since he gave the pretty nurse Maya's purse and clothes and she'd told him to wait. He opened the hospital door into the air conditioning and walked down the hall to Maya's room, where he knocked lightly before pushing open the door.

"Maya?"

She was sitting up in bed. She looked pale and terrible. They were dark circles under her eyes.

"Don't come near me. I swear to God I'll scream."

"Come on, Maya."

"You almost killed me," she said. "Do you want to see what you did to me?" She pulled the gown down over her left shoulder. The bruises on her deltoids and triceps were dark and purplish, edged with ugly brown and yellow. "It's the same way on my legs. I can hardly move."

"But I kept you alive."

She shrugged.

"I called 911."

She turned her head and looked out the window. "I went down the tunnel and saw the light, all that stuff you read about. The near-death experience. Really strange things."

"Can I sit down?"

"Stand over there or I swear to God I'll scream."

"Miss Davidson?" said a male voice from the door of the room. Forrest looked up. Good god, it was Bill Fletcher—heavier, with jowls now, but still standing in that nervous, shambling way he had, as though there were something permanently unreliable about his ankles. He was balder and fatter, but even with his white hospital coat and his clipboard, he was still the same man. Forrest stood up smiling and walked over to shake his hand.

"I need a minute with my patient," Fletcher told him, not looking at him. "If you could wait outside."

"Bill," said Forrest. "Don't you recognize me?"

Fletcher would not look at him, so Forrest went outside and stood in the hallway until Fletcher came out and started past him.

"Jesus, Bill, what's the matter with you?"

He stopped and met Forrest's gaze. "That little girl in there is what's the matter with me," he said coldly.

Forrest had a perverse impulse to make light of it. "I just do what Cousin Bedford says."

Fletcher grimaced with disgust.

"You're fifty-eight years old, you're married, you've got two daughters in town nobody's known what to do with—"

"Doctor Fletcher," Maya said from the doorway of her room, "if you're going to release me, I'll get Braxton to drive me to my car."

She was leaning against the doorjamb in her green hospital gown with her arms crossed, forlorn. Fletcher stared at her without moving before he finally shook his head. "Pam," he said to the pretty nurse coming toward them. "Can you get the release forms, please?"

When Maya went back in the room, Fletcher tilted his head, raised his eyebrows, and regarded Forrest.

"I met her on the airplane," Forrest said.

Fletcher's black eyes, which seemed to have no irises, did not leave Forrest's.

"Does it make you feel younger or what?" he asked. "I remember when we were living in that trailer in Athens, we used to talk about Marilyn—you remember Marilyn?—and why she did what she did. I could ask the same thing about you. Except she was young and you're nearly sixty. We all get old, Cump. You can't cure it by pretending."

"I'm not pretending."

Coming back up to Fletcher, the nurse took his clipboard and put the release forms on it. He signed them and gave her the board with a nod to Maya's room. A moment later, Maya came out of the room in the clothes that Forrest had brought her, and Fletcher turned to her.

"Get those tests done. Promise me you'll do that."

"I will. Ready?" she said to Forrest.

"Let's talk some time, Bill," Forrest said, offering his hand to Fletcher, who turned away without taking it and started up the hall.

She was quiet in the car until they pulled out of the parking lot.

"I already knew I had a heart problem," she said. "Just so you know."

"Okay," he said.

"Was the doctor a friend of yours?"

"We played football together in high school. We lived together in a trailer in Athens my junior year of college."

All the way up Main Street she was quiet, staring out the window. As they turned left at the traffic light on Lee Street, she started talking without looking at him.

"I went down the tunnel toward the light that they talk about. I came into this white room. It was underground but full of sunlight, and there were bones on the floor, all kinds of bones. It smelled like the den of an animal. I could hear this clicking and tocking, and when I looked up, bones were hung up everywhere, like wind chimes. On the far side of the room these huge women were sitting there in hoods and deep purple robes. One of them motioned to me."

A shudder went up his spine as they crossed the railroad track.

"They talked to me," she said.

He waited for her to continue, but she did not.

"What did they say?"

"One of them talked. They all kept their heads lowered, and the one in the middle said something in this deep voice, very slowly. There was a door. I could see into a garden. I wanted to go inside the garden more than I've ever wanted anything, the way you want things when you're little. The one who was talking said something I couldn't understand. Another one raised her head, and I could just barely see her eyes, just for a second. My God, it was terrible."

"Terrible how?"

"I don't know how to explain it. It was like I saw all the bad things I'd ever done, even things I'd forgotten about."

"Bad things. What do you mean?"

She shook her head. They rode down the hill past the Wal-Mart in silence, and Forrest turned toward the EconoLodge and pulled into the parking lot. Her BMW sat by itself on the row, wearing its necklace of trophy rings. He parked next to it.

"Do you need to come back to the room?"

"She was talking about you," she said. "That black woman in my dream."

"Black woman?"

She opened her door. She got out of the Camry and stood uncertainly for a moment, then leaned back down to speak to him through the window.

"Did you kill Marilyn like that?"

He stared at her until she backed away. When she got in her BMW, he nodded goodbye. Both his hands were shaking when he lifted them from the steering wheel.

Did he kill Marilyn?

Maybe he got her killed. No, not like that.

But did he kill her? That was the question, and he had no way to answer it. What made it terrible was that he had forgotten so much from retelling it. All through his twenties, he had felt responsible for her death, and then—he didn't remember when exactly—he had discovered that telling Marilyn's story, always leaving out the most incriminating details, made young women open up to him. His despair about her death seemed to reveal to them, as if it were a revelation to them alone, the clue to his brooding mystery, and it moved them, it excited them: the forbidden love, the brave defiance of small-minded men, the tragic secret. That must have been why he told the woman he thought was Asia Carducci. The old ruse, long forgotten, that surfaced again when he was drunk and back in Georgia.

But what was the truth? All he remembered was the bloody dress on the tree. Had her body been thrown into the water? And who had done it? He couldn't remember where they found her. Had he seen her washed up in the river shallows with small fish nibbling at her skin? Or somewhere deep in a thicket, half-hidden by hastily piled brush?

She was talking about you. Another shudder went up his spine.

He sat for a moment collecting himself. He felt that he should say a prayer. St. Michael the something. Archbishop? Marisa said that prayer. Something about the malice and snares of the devil. Cast into Hell Satan and something.

The girls knew it. He should go out to Tricia's and check on the girls, but first he needed to get this car back to the airport.

Something definite to do. He got out and went into the EconoLodge lobby. The same boy who had been on duty the day before looked up when he heard the bell over the door. His Adam's apple bobbed up and down; his hands splayed on the counter. When Forrest asked about a shuttle, the boy nervously gave him a card for something called Azalea Middle Georgia Airport Express.

He got back in the Camry. With Maya out of the way, everything had a new clarity. All the way up I-75, he thought about what to do. He had to get another car somehow. Chick Lee was the best bet, so he'd get the shuttle driver to drop him off at the dealership. Once he was back at the motel, he'd change Natalia's grade from a sodden, toxic B to a shining A. He'd call the registrar's office and complain that she'd been given the wrong grade, and they would tell him he'd submitted it. He'd deny it. He'd say they must have made a mistake recording it. They'd say he had entered it in the online grade entry form, and he would express his astonishment, but then he would gradually soften, claiming that he had a hard time getting used to the new technology. He'd send Natalia an email apologizing for the mistake and telling her he'd just chewed out the registrar (but maybe it was his mistake). He would hope she was having a great summer. Afterward, he'd email the new dean and tell her the same thing.

That should do it.

Then he'd make an airline reservation for Marisa. As soon as he got those details taken care of, he could run out to check on the girls before he went to see Cousin Emily Barron Hayes.

Only fifty minutes after leaving the EconoLodge, Forrest pulled into the return lane for Hertz. $127.31 for two days added to his American Express card—and he had forgotten to refill the tank. The amount would show up on the next bill. He caught a Hertz bus to the main terminal, and just when he got out, an Azalea van was pulling up. Forrest ran to it and opened the passenger door.

"Going to Gallatin?"

The driver, a Taliban type, nodded and gave Forrest a peremptory get-in head move. "No bag?"

"No bags."

There was one other passenger, a man in the third row who glanced up once at Forrest and then closed his eyes. Forrest sat in the first row behind the driver and leaned up to speak to him.

"Can you drop me off at the Lee Ford dealership in Gallatin?"

The driver shook his head. "Only motel," he said. He stabbed his finger at the sign listing where the van stopped. Forrest explained to him that the Ford dealership was just off the Interstate, and after a short argument and the ten dollar bill Maya had not taken back, he got a reluctant concession.

By the time they passed Hood Road, he had a complete plan. He needed to look respectable to see his girls and Cousin Emily Barron Hayes, so when he got a car from Chick, he would go back to the motel and take a shower. He'd change into a pair of linen trousers and a good knit shirt that he could wear with his brown loafers. He'd go over to Stonewall Hill, meet Hermia Watson, and talk to the old witch who robbed his father. After he resolved the mystery of the letters, he would pick up the girls and take them back to the EconoLodge. He would leave the car there for Chick to pick up, and the three of them would catch the next shuttle back to the airport, then fly back to Boston on the first available flight.

When the van pulled up in front of the showroom of Lee Ford, Forrest handed the driver the American Express card.

"No cash?"

"I'm out."

The man sighed and pushed the button of the glove compartment, which opened with a crash. He pulled out an old manual device for credit cards and fished around until he found a triplicate form to fit into it. Even after pulling the bar repeatedly over Forrest's card, he could not get it to yield a legible imprint of the card number, so he had to trace it by hand, all the while muttering in whatever language he spoke.

"What's the holdup?" asked the other passenger sleepily, and the driver indicated Forrest with a contemptuous jerk of his head.

Finally, he turned in his seat and handed the thing to Forrest, tapping the space for him to write in the final figure. He had already filled in the cost of the trip, $45. He actually expected Forrest to tip him. Forrest wrote $45 as the total, signed it, and handed it back to him. The driver read it, slung the device onto the other seat, and waved Forrest out of the vehicle.

"I already gave you ten bucks just to stop here," Forrest said.

The man turned his head and spat out the window onto the pavement.

"Where's my credit card?" Forrest demanded.

"I give to you!"

"The hell you did." Forrest got out his wallet and showed him the empty slot. The driver looked in the old device, cursed, and then furiously shuffled all the papers and clipboards on top of the console. Still not finding it, he felt between the seats and the seat backs, bent down to look all over the floor, and finally got out and looked under the van. Finally, slapping himself with fury, he discovered it in his shirt pocket. He stared at it with loathing and handed it to Forrest with his whole body averted.

Chick Lee and his salesmen had been watching from inside the dealership.

"What was all that?" asked one of them when he came in.

"Gunga Din needs a little more belting and flaying, if you ask me. Listen, I'm wondering if you guys have a car I can use. Maybe some kind of loaner," Forrest said.

Chick glanced around at his salesmen and raised his hands at the effrontery of the question. "Call you believe this guy? *Loaners*," he said as if Forrest were a simpleton, "are for people getting their *cars fixed*."

"Somebody must have traded in something you wouldn't let anybody else drive. What about Cash for Clunkers? How about I pay you ten bucks a day for it?"

"I don't have clunkers sitting around on the lot of Lee Ford."

"Um, Mr. Lee," one of the younger salesmen said, and there was an anticipatory ripple of laughter through the showroom. "There's that Taurus."

Chick started to smile then. "There is that Taurus."

The fabric on the interior roof hung in tatters, as though the car had been used to transfer madmen with knives. The springs in the seats were shot, and Forrest was almost sitting on the floor when he left the Ford lot with all the salesmen waving at him. The air conditioner had long since expired, and the whole frame shimmied when he approached thirty-five miles per hour going down Lee Street. He parked in the back of the EconoLodge under a tree, hoping that no one would see him. After he turned it off and got out, the engine kept gulping and coming back on convulsively before it finally died with a shudder and a cloud of inky smoke. Something was dripping from the engine. The whole car ticked and hissed.

Was it worthwhile to take a shower? He would be dripping wet again by the time he got to Cousin Emily Barron Hayes' house. But he needed one now. He passed the pool, where the teenage girl from the eavesdropping family sat up and gawked at him. The maids had cleaned his room, but Forrest found a note from the manager saying that he hoped there would not be any more "disterbences." His laptop sat there like a land mine. He ignored it until after his shower. Clean, shaved, and deodorized, he sat down naked to open his Gmail.

MAKE THE RESERVATION! said the first one.

Marisa had included all the information for the flight, and all he had to do was click a link and fill in the credit card details. She would arrive—he looked more closely—next week, Tuesday, thank God, not tomorrow as he had first feared. But she was flying to Atlanta, not Boston. She was coming here.

Okay, he'd fly her to Atlanta. He smiled, made the reservation, filled in the American Express card details from memory, e-mailed her the confirmation number, and clicked a link that downloaded the information to his Outlook program. "All's well," he wrote in the body. "See you next week."

All's well. You bet. On the college e-mail account, there was a message from the new dean and one from Natalia. He opened the one from Natalia first. "I can always take it back," it said, with one of those winking icons. An instant of longing spangled through his blood. She was the daughter of a Nigerian surgeon and a blonde Ph.D. who taught at Tufts. She had an unguarded open smile, and somehow she reminded him of Alysoun in *The Miller's Tale*. She was a prymerole, a piggesnye.

The e-mail from the new dean—a woman named Jennifer Flowers who had been an administrator at Marquette—said that there had been a serious accusation by one of his students. He needed to contact her office immediately.

Instead, Forrest called Mary Locke, the registrar's secretary, and complained bitterly that one of his students had been given the wrong grade. Two minutes later, exactly according to plan, he had the registrar Alice Meunier on the phone, and he was complaining about the new system while metaphorically conking himself on the head for making a mistake with it.

"No wonder this girl was mad," he said. "She's an excellent student, and it's just very unfortunate that this happened, especially since she's being considered for a Fulbright."

It was total bullshit. Dr. Meunier murmured with polite skepticism. As soon as he got off the phone, he wrote Natalia an e-mail apologizing for the mistake in the grade. It must have been the registrar's fault, even though they said he had recorded it. What was he thinking, he almost wrote, when he said that she should have read *Moby Dick* even though she had actually been to Nantucket with her family?

It was already 3:30 when he finished writing her. He would not have time to see the girls before meeting Hermia Watson at four o'clock, he realized, but he could pick them up afterwards. Pick them up in what? He imagined driving up to Judah Davis's house in the Taurus. Maybe Tricia could bring them to the motel instead. He could say he didn't have a car. Maybe she would even drive them all to the airport.

In the meantime, he e-mailed the dean, complaining hotly about the registrar's office and the new system. He said that he had already called and chewed them out. He did not say what he knew the dean would gradually realize: Walcott College would bend over backwards to keep him there. He was the only professor on the faculty whose books had given him something of a national reputation. Like her predecessors, she would learn to accept his excuses.

It was already close to four when he stood up, so he put on his tan linen slacks and the black knit shirt; they were a little wrinkled, but the humidity would help. He wore his favorite black belt and the black loafers. As he was leaving the room, he borrowed a pillow for the seat. Halfway to the car, he stopped and went back in the room to get two towels.

14

From behind the screen door, Hermia watched the smoking car shudder and die. Forrest got out of it wiping his face with a towel, which he threw back onto the seat before looking up at the house. He was graying, definitely older, but his hair—a dirty blond—was thick, and the wave on the back of his head went into curls. He still had a muscular, supple look under the knit shirt. There was still something catlike in the way he moved, some of the heavy grace of a prowling lion, and the absence of a middle-aged belly, just a thickness, suggested gravitas rather than indulgence. My god, she thought, remembering, her heart pounding. As he approached, she opened the screen door and stepped out onto the stoop. He looked up at her and smiled with recognition.

"I'll be damned," he said. "You're Hermia Watson."

"And you're Braxton Forrest."

"When I saw you yesterday, I had the feeling I'd seen you before. How's your dog?"

"Eumaios? Oh, that's right, I was walking him. He's fine."

"You named him Eumaios?"

"I guess I associate Eumaios with dogs. Or maybe men with pigs. I hear you've been busy."

"Word has already gotten around?"

"LaCourvette Todd is a friend of mine."

"My hostess, Officer Todd."

"Speaking of which," she said, smiling at him, "won't you come in?"

"When she said that, she locked me up."

She laughed. "Well, there's no telling what's going to happen to you in this house." She held the screen door open for him with her left hand, and he brushed close to her as he stepped into the sun porch.

"I know I saw you on Beauregard Drive, but I swear, you look so familiar, it's a little uncanny." He touched her elbow lightly as he looked around. "I haven't been in this house for fifty years."

"I doubt it's changed much. I told Mrs. Hayes you were coming, but that's no guarantee of anything, of course."

"Does she remember who I am?"

"It's hard to say. She certainly remembers your father."

"She's ahead of me there."

In fact, as Hermia did not say, Mrs. Hayes remembered his father obsessively. *Aunt Ella told me when I first saw him, she said, Miss*

96

Sally, don't you mess with that boy. Oh but I did mess with him, and he was mine, don't let anybody tell you different. I don't care what they say, he was mine.

"Let's go up the back stairs," Hermia said. "I can't face the front of the house."

"What's the matter with it?"

"Oh, the dust and clutter."

"Can I just take a look?"

He pushed past her and opened the door into the dark, narrow hallway where the back stairs ascended.

"Isn't there a bathroom?" he said, feeling along the wall until he found the handle and pulled it open and felt for the light.

"I can't believe you remember it. There's a string," she said.

He found it and pulled it. An ancient bare light bulb revealed the old toilet and sink. Forrest shook his head at the sharp urinous smell and pulled the cord again. He shut the door and opened another at the end of the hallway into a small sitting room. She followed him, watching as he glanced around. Nothing had been dusted in years. The Queen Anne sofa, the frail end tables, the upright chairs with cane bottoms. She supposed she should have covered them with cloths. Forrest lifted a porcelain figurine from the built-in shelves in the corner of the room and put it back, not quite in the same spot, dusting his hands on his slacks. The tiny crescent of clean shelf beneath the little white-and-blue cat disturbed the uniformity of neglect. She had a sudden fear that he would go through the rooms touching things. The house had a complacent deadness, and he was stirring up ghosts.

"We'd better catch Mrs. Hayes while she's lucid," she said.

"The place doesn't look *that* bad," he said, opening the door into the front hallway. "It just needs cleaning up and airing out."

"She was fine a few minutes ago," she said, "but you never can tell."

Forrest paid no attention to her. A pile of old newspapers and junk mail lay under the brass mail slot in the door, and he walked past it and tried the front door, which she had never opened. He forced back the big bolts securing it and turned the great knob. The hinges creaked, the door swept an arc through the old mail, and daylight surged in. She followed him onto the buckling boards of the porch, littered with leaves. The gravel drive, pierced by saplings, bent away downhill to the left and right in a big circle. What had once been a broad lawn punctuated by stone walls, shrubs, and flower beds was now weedy and full of fallen limbs, but the contours were still intact. The clock of the courthouse rose in the distance.

"You don't come out here?" he asked her.

"I went through the front of the house once," she said, "but it was disconcerting. Like I was eavesdropping on the dead."

"So how did you happen to come here at all?" he asked. "You seem a little overqualified to be tending an old lady."

"Oh, you don't want to hear my story."

"I do," he said. "Very much."

"We'd really better catch her while she's awake."

He nodded and closed the door behind them. Dust whirled up into a sunbeam that came through the window at the landing of the broad front stairs. He started up the carpeted steps.

"She keeps the hallway door locked up there," she said.

He came back down, and she led him through the old dining room, out into the parlor, into the breakfast room, and back into the darkness of the back hallway, where they were suddenly blind. He groped in the darkness before finding her arm. She guided his hand to the banister and started up the stairs, but almost immediately, she felt his other hand on her bottom and her knees weakened.

"Professor Forrest," she said.

At the top of the stairs, where the light was brighter, she gave him a look of mock exasperation. "You're worse than I thought."

He smiled and pointed down the hall toward the room that overlooked the back garden. "I saw her last night when I came by. She was sitting at the window."

"When did you have time to come by last night?" she asked. "I thought you were busy getting arrested."

"Before that," he said.

Hermia led him down the hallway, paused at the door to knock, and opened it slightly. "Mrs. Hayes?" she called. "You have a visitor."

"Is that you?" a harsh, quavering voice answered, insistent and querulous. "I've been calling and calling."

15

The room was almost empty except for the old four-poster bed with its side table and an ornate dresser with a mirror. In a white wicker rocking chair that rested on a threadbare Persian rug in front of the window across the room, Cousin Emily Barron Hayes sat leaning forward and peering intently at something outside, mottled hands gripping the armrests.

Suddenly her head cocked. "Is somebody there? Who is it? Speak up!"

"Mrs. Hayes," said Hermia Watson, "you have a visitor."

"A visitor! I don't have time for visitors."

The old woman leaned forward, and a hooked finger of her left hand swiped at the air, as though she had just seen something unmistakable and definitive. Outside, he saw the trunk and a large limb of the oak tree framing the garden gate and a little of its sunlit tangle.

"It's Mr. Forrest. He's come to see you."

Cousin Emily Barron Hayes went still and her head twitched sideways as though she had been about to look but had stopped herself. He could see the wet gleam of the corner of her eye.

"I didn't do a thing but tell the truth."

"Mr. Forrest has come to talk to you."

"You tell him I know he's dead."

"Mrs. Hayes, it's Braxton Forrest," she said. "It's Robert Forrest's son."

At first the old woman did not respond.

"It's Braxton Forrest," Hermia repeated.

Forrest moved up in front of her.

"That one," said the old woman.

"Mrs. Hayes," said Hermia again, touching her shoulder, "this is—"

"Why can't he speak for himself?" the old woman interrupted, not looking at him. "Can't the fool talk?"

"Cousin Emily Barron," he said, "do you remember who I am?"

"Why should I remember you?" she said.

"I'm Robert Forrest's son. You remember him, don't you?"

"You're not his son," she said contemptuously, and the tone of her voice lanced open an abscess of memory. She and his grandmother had been huge and terrible figures of Forrest's childhood. He had feared them, hated them, and the old feeling flooded back.

"I am his son."

"If you were his son," she said, "I would be your mother. Do I have children? Of course not. Girl!"

"Yes ma'am?" she said.

"Get this man out of my way. Get him out of here."

But Forrest squatted down in front of the chair and startled the old woman by gripping the armrests of the chair and leaning close to her. An acrid smell came off her body. Her head went back in fright and both gnarled hands rose as she stared at him.

"Why did you write those letters?" he demanded.

"Letters?" she asked, twisting fearfully toward Hermia. "What does he want with me?"

"The letters asking me to come here. To send my daughters to stay with you."

"I didn't write any letters."

"They were in your handwriting."

"My handwriting?" She barked out a laugh and held up her trembling right hand, knotted with arthritis.

"My daughters came here because you asked them," Forrest insisted. "Then you turned them away. You claimed you didn't even remember me."

"You let them in!" she said to Hermia over her shoulder, raising a trembling hand. "You're the one that let those girls in here. Trying to cheat me."

"No, Mrs. Hayes," said Hermia, "I tried to explain that they were Mr. Forrest's daughters. They said that he received letters from you inviting them here."

The old woman gave another harsh laugh. "I remember you," she said to Forrest. "The piss-pants. Braxton. If that's not a fool's name. You broke one of my best vases running through my house. His cow of a mother sent him here to ruin my things," she said to Hermia. "*Inger*. That was her name. *Inger*, who showed up with this fool in her belly and tried to claim Robert Forrest fathered him."

That vase. Another memory. He had not known his way around the house, and he had been directed to the bathroom under the back stairway, and when he was trying to find his way back outside, he came into that room he had seen just now, where he picked up the porcelain cat. It was full of the mothers of the other children invited to an Easter egg hunt, all of them holding teacups on their knees.

In his confusion, he had turned to escape. His elbow hit a lamp. Trying to right it, he tipped over the vase on top of the bookshelf next to it, and he heard the collective gasp of the women in the room as it fell and shattered on the floor.

Over their voices came the shrill cry of Cousin Emily Barron Hayes, crying *You fool! Do you know how expensive that was?* He had stood there in his mortification. *Are you going to pay for it?*

But the old woman's voice was overwriting the memory.

"I asked him if he was going to pay for it, and he said, No ma'am, and I said Oh yes you are, and he said"—she imitated a stupid child's voice—"But I don't have any money, Cousin Emily Barron Hayes."

Look at him, she had said to the women, *look at him, this stupid child of that cow who claims she married Robert Forrest. Probably pregnant with some big Swede. She's already found herself another dirt farmer.* Mrs. Adams had said, *You don't have any call to criticize Inger, Mrs. Hayes*, and the other women had murmured their agreement. *It was just an accident*, Mrs. Adams had said. *Maybe we can take up a collection to pay for your vase.* That had amused Cousin Emily Barron Hayes. *Oh my God. Take up a collection, as if everything you had—!* She had fallen into a fit of laughter. *Get out of my house, all of you!* She had stood up, driving them away in their confusion. *Get out and get your dirty children off my lawn.*

Forrest stood now looking down at the old woman's head with its slight tremor, the hands compulsively gripping the armrests.

"Why is that fool still here?" the old woman asked Hermia, and anger streamed loose across his diaphragm like a spill of burning oil. He gripped the arms of the chair and lifted her clear of the floor, holding her at eye level. Hermia Watson gasped and backed away.

"I've come to pay," he said.

She shrank from his face, glancing down fearfully like someone caught at the top of a Ferris wheel. He turned as though he were going to throw her through the window.

"Aunt Ella!" she cried in a wheeze, her eyes wide with terror. "Aunt Ella!"

"Please, Professor Forrest, put her down!" Hermia Watson cried. "Put her down!"

When he lowered the chair to the floor, the old woman sat there with a string of drool coming from the corner of her mouth, her head wobbling on her neck.

"Mrs. Hayes?" Hermia said. "Mrs. Hayes, are you all right?"

The old woman looked at her anxiously and waved her off, trying to see past her. "Where's Aunt Ella?"

"Aunt Ella's not here, Mrs. Hayes. It's me, Hermia."

"I'll see you if you go out there tonight," she said, slitting her eyes and hooking the air with her finger. "I'll see you. Who moved my chair from the window? Move it back!"

Hermia helped get the chair back to its original position, and the old woman leaned forward as though nothing had happened. Forrest stared down at the back of her head.

He had forgotten how much he hated her. He had let himself think that remorse might move even her. But who had written the letters?

Hermia Watson beckoned him from the room. She led him back downstairs to the kitchen.

"My god," he said. "How do you put up with that old witch?"

She crossed the room to the sink and distractedly put a mug in the old porcelain basin, turned on the water, turned it back off. She faced him, bracing herself with her hands on the counter behind her.

"I shouldn't have taken you up there," she said, and when she bent her head, the light from the window touched the soft plane of her left cheek, her neck. She was just lovely, a lovely thing, deeply familiar, as though she were—and a memory broke. He did know her. Professor Forrest, she had called him. He couldn't believe it. He stepped forward and pulled her to him, but both her hands pushed against his chest.

"No, please," she said.

He wanted her body against him. It would be a kind of revenge against the old woman upstairs, a kind of redemption from memory. He put his hand in the small of her back to pull her toward him again, but she twisted gently from him, and it was like dancing: now his back was to the sink, and she stepped past the table into the center of the room, smiling, one hand held out as though to calm the beast that confronted her.

"If she didn't write those letters," Forrest said, "maybe you did."

"Me?" She looked at him calmly. "Now why would I ever do that?"

"Why did you call me Professor Forrest just now?"

She bit her lip and smiled at him, raised an eyebrow.

"What?" he said.

He waited, pregnant with recognition.

"You gave a paper on evolutionary poetics and celebrity culture. You talked about Madonna?"

"I gave that paper all over the country."

"I'd heard you first at Northwestern. I was in one of the seminars you did there not long after *The Gameme* came out. You took some of us out to the lake. We sat on the rocks and looked down the shoreline at Chicago and drank bourbon from the bottle. You talked about Homer and Tarzan and Ayn Rand. That's why I went to hear you in Providence."

He remembered a red-bearded professor of Italian, a stout old feminist who gamely negotiated the rocks, and several graduate students, including Lola Gunn, a nervous, very light-skinned black girl with generous breasts in startling contrast to her vegan skinniness. She would look at him wide-eyed and lift the bottle to her mouth and drink with a delicate wince and shudder and then smile as she looked at him.

A month or so later, just after his keynote lecture at the conference in Providence, he had felt a tap on his shoulder and he had turned and there she was. Ten minutes later they were in his room, his first betrayal of Marisa. She had been profoundly shy when he touched her—trembling, doe-like—as though theirs had been the first time a man and a woman had ventured into such intimacy. It was like a murder she had asked him to commit upon her, as though she were guiding the knife blade under her breast, watching him the whole way, wanting to let him feel the way the point pierced the outer skin first, that first little agony, then between her ribs and deeper to penetrate the wall of her heart and push through the tough tissue into the inmost chambers of her as her death poured out over him. He remembered the way her head drooped to the side like a cut flower, the way she lay as though her soul had fled from her body, not upward but downward, not to hell but to the deep shades where the ancients store curses, the recesses of the dark.

"Lola," he said.

"I used to go by Lola—short for my middle name. Dolores, which I hate. Hermia Dolores Watson. If that doesn't sound like an undertaker's daughter, I swear. I still had my married name then. For most of my twenties I was Lola Gunn. But I changed my name. I wanted to start over after a very bad marriage."

But how could this be Lola Gunn? In Gallatin? He had googled her, wondering what had happened to her, but she seemed to disappear from existence after the mid-nineties.

She lifted her face and the full recognition flooded him. He took her hands.

"Did you ever think of me?" she asked.

"I tried to find you. How in the world did you end up here? Why are you playing housemaid to Cousin Emily Barron Hayes?"

"I've been living in Atlanta trying to finish a book about women under slavery. Not exactly a history, not exactly a novel. Last Christmas, I came down to visit my mother, and when I went into town to buy a few things, I decided to go by the courthouse to look through some old deeds and wills from slave days, just to spur my imagination. So when I explained what I was working on, they sent me down the hall to the county clerk. He said if I was looking for prominent families, I should start with the Forrests, because they had owned land in the county going back to the eighteen thirties or forties. Besides, their story was the most interesting because about fifty or sixty years ago, the rightful heir had been cheated out of his inheritance by the old woman who still lived in the Forrest place. If I was interested in wills, he said, I ought to find out why Braxton Forrest wasn't living out there now instead of old Mrs. Hayes.

"So I said your name. Braxton Forrest, I said. Yes, ma'am, he said. He's some kind of teacher up in New England. Braxton Forrest, I said again. Yes, ma'am. Why? Do you know him? Oh, I said, I know who he is, and I was trying to look calm, but my heart was pounding."

Forrest pulled her against him and this time she did not resist.

"The clerk, Mr. Gordon, told me that the women at his church were worried about Mrs. Hayes, mean as she was. They were always looking for somebody to take care of her."

"So you just did it out of charity?"

"More like curiosity. When I first came in here, I expected her to yell at me like she yelled at everybody else, but she just stared at me. I swear she recognized me. You, she said. Half the time, she thinks I'm somebody else. She calls me Pearl more often than not."

"So do you feed her? Change her diaper?"

She pulled her arms down to block his hands.

"Stop that. I bring her food. I do some unpleasant things. But only because I'm playing a part. Pretending to be a slave. I guess I'm just using her, but I'm keeping her alive, too. This place is just what I need for my book. So is Mrs. Hayes."

"You said your mother lives here. What's her name? Maybe I knew her."

"Maybe. She's Adara Dernier-Jones now, but LaCourvette told me she was Marilyn something growing up."

Forrest released her.

"Marilyn?"

"Jenkins I think. Marilyn Jenkins."

"No, I didn't know anybody named Marilyn Jenkins."

"No, wait. Not Jenkins, Harkins. Marilyn Harkins."

Forrest backed against the edge of the table.

"Marilyn Harkins?"

"I'm pretty sure that's her maiden name. Isn't that silly, not to know? But she had so many names, and I never knew any grandparents. I know it wasn't Hawkins. Harkins, that's right."

Forrest was finding it difficult to breathe.

"The Marilyn Harkins I knew has been dead for forty years."

"Well, my mama's not dead," she laughed. "Lord, far from it." She reached to take his hand, but he pulled away from her.

"It must be somebody else," he said. "Somebody else named Marilyn Harkins."

"If you say so. But two women like her in the same little town! LaCourvette knows things she won't tell me, but from what she says..." She raised her eyebrows. "I guess Mama must have been something to see."

Forrest stared at her. His skin seemed to be trying to crawl from his body.

"What's the matter?" she asked.

"How old are you?"

She put her hands on her hips. "What kind of question is that?"

"I'm serious. How old are you? Exactly how old?"

"You should have carded me seventeen years ago. Okay, I'm thirty-nine. I'll be forty next May."

Forty next May. She cocked her head and suddenly he saw more than Lola Gunn.

"What's the matter?" she cried.

"Oh my god," he whispered, and his knees gave. "And you're telling me she's alive?"

"What in the world?"

"And you're her daughter?"

BOOK II
Plumb

1

As soon as he left Stonewall Hill, Forrest drove to the liquor store across from the Burger King and bought a 750ml bottle of Jack Daniels. When he came out and opened the door of the Taurus, a teenage boy leaning against a pickup truck nearby in the parking lot called "Nice car." It cracked up his friends.

Forrest sat for a moment and thought about doing something to the kid.

But he drove back to the motel and went straight to his room. The Taurus was still coughing and shuddering when he came out of his room a moment later with his plastic bucket. When he pressed the bar of the dispenser next to the drink machines, a few hollow tubes of ice fell wearily from the spout. He pressed it again, and nothing happened, so he gave the machine a quick smash with his forearm. Something inside it shrieked and gave way. Ice filled his bucket in an avalanche. It spilled over the sides and kept coming. He jiggled the dispenser bar, but more and more ice clamored out, more than it seemed possible for the machine to hold. He backed away and it kept coming. When he turned, it was already climbing around his ankles, an icy Skamandros, chasing him, clattering out, bounding across the concrete in a growing semicircle.

There was nobody else in the breezeway to see it, nobody at the pool when he turned the corner. With the bucket under his left arm, he walked toward his room and reached into his back pocket for his wallet where he kept the plastic room key. He meant to call the front desk, but inside the room, he found himself staring at the thick bulge of receipts in his wallet.

Sunlit cobblestones outside a restaurant in Siena. He had been folding a receipt and feeling a smug satisfaction about forestalling the objections of Emily Barron Hayes' Dickensian accountant. *Receipts? You bet. Here they are.* But there was never an accountant. Forrest had invented him ex nihilo, just as he had replaced the actual Cousin Emily Barron Hayes with a benignly generous queen of his imagining. He had toured Italy running up thousands of dollars of real debt on American Express and saving receipts for reimbursement by a fiction.

He plucked out the thin, compressed papers he had been sitting on for two weeks. They slipped over each other in his fingers like playing cards. He dropped them in the trash and twisted the crisp plastic on the top of the whiskey bottle and sat down on the edge of the bed.

The bed where Maya had been dead on the sheets the night before. Small, naked, unbreathing.

He had almost killed her over Marilyn.

Marilyn was alive.

Hermia Watson was Lola Gunn. Lola Gunn, his lover, was Marilyn's daughter. Marilyn's daughter had no idea that he knew Marilyn.

Also his lover.

Lola Gunn.

Dread came over him, a sense of the live past, cold-blooded and undulant and swimming toward him. He had known mother and daughter. The old biblical knowing. Lola Gunn had a reason to write those letters, which meant she had gotten inside the house that should have been his and forged the name of the woman who had dispossessed his father, all to get him here.

To get him back?

Or get back at him? Had there been something about a pregnancy? Or was that somebody else?

He stared at the bottle of Jack Daniels. He thought about Cate and Bernadette leaving with Tricia last night. Cate's dismissive accusation stung him. The least he could do was go out and pick them up and take them to dinner, but the idea of seeing them filled him with terror. Why was that? It made no sense. His sweet daughters. He called 411 and got Judah Davis's home number. He lay back on the bed after dialing the number.

"Tricia?"

"No, sir, this is Bridget? Did you want to speak to my mom?"

"Please."

"May I ask who's calling?" Good phone manners, better than Cate's or Bernadette's.

"This is Braxton Forrest."

"Oh Jesus," she said. Then he heard the rising intonation, "Mom? MOM? Their dad is on the phone."

"Braxton?" Tricia said two seconds later, then, sharply, "Hang up, Bridget." He heard the click. "Listen," she said, "I need to talk to you. Alone." Her words were a little slurred.

"Is it about the girls? I was calling to see how they're doing."

"No, it's not about the girls. It's about me. You and me."

Pretty little Tricia Honeycutt, drunk.

"That was forty years ago, Tricia."

There was a pause. "Maybe for you," she said. "Maybe it can be forty years ago for you."

"Tricia, how about right now I talk to Cate? I'll be happy to talk to you later." There was a long silence. "Tricia?"

"Just a minute," she said dully. "Let me call her."

When Cate came on the phone, she was clipped. "Hello?"

"Do you and Bernadette want to go out and get something to eat? We need to talk."

"We already ate. Mr. Davis is taking us all to a movie in Macon."

"How about breakfast tomorrow?"

"We won't get in until late tonight."

He sighed. "Lunch?"

"Dad, I just ... I just don't want to talk to you right now. I don't want to see you, okay? When's Mom coming?"

"Next week. I made the reservation this morning."

"Maybe when Mom gets here."

"Come on, Cate," he said. "I can explain what happened."

"Dad, not if..." She trailed off.

"What?"

"Never mind."

When she fell silent, he said, "I went to see Cousin Emily Barron Hayes. I'd forgotten what an old bitch she is."

"Dad, please," she said.

"She didn't write those letters."

"Well duh."

"What, you knew that?"

"You saw her. But anyway, whatever. I mean that's so over."

"It's not over. Whoever wrote them cost us a ton of money and grief. Listen, I'll call you tomorrow."

"Dad..."

"What?'

"Just wait until mom gets here."

"You're telling me not to call?" His anger flared at the realization that she thought of herself as handling him. "I was going to get us tickets to fly back to Boston tonight. Don't you want to get back home?"

"Mom said she was flying to Atlanta. We're okay. Bernadette has made some friends. Just wait for mom, okay?"

Forrest snapped his cell phone shut and stood up. He filled a plastic cup with ice and poured whiskey up to the flimsy brim and drank off half the cup. The sweet cold burn spread across his abdomen.

What was he supposed to do until Marisa arrived on Tuesday?

He felt memory pressing steadily upward. He sat back on the bed and turned on the TV with the remote. He scrolled through the channels, looking for something violent enough or sexual enough to distract him. He clicked his way through the commercials about coolness and power, the comedies with their topical jokes, the police shows with their edgy knowingness and posturing.

He turned it off. The room depressed him—his laptop sitting there on standby, one little blue light flashing with latent accusation; the cell phone prostrate, like an epileptic between seizures; the motel phone, full of innocent menace; the generic walls and chairs.

He had a pair of trunks somewhere in his suitcase. He dug through all the clothes until he found the blue bathing suit he had taken to Europe but never used. He quickly stripped off his clothes and slipped on the trunks, grabbed a towel from the bathroom, remembered to put the room key in the little mesh pocket, and headed out for one of the tables with an umbrella. The teenage girl who had been there with her brother the day before lay on the lounge chair in her bikini, one knee raised, reading a glare-blue paperback. When she turned her head languidly to see who had arrived, she sat up as though a bee had stung her. Forrest took a sip of his whiskey and set it down on the glass table top.

"And how are you, my dear?" he asked, doing his Clark Gable.

"I thought they put you in jail."

He shrugged and frowned. "I didn't like it. I found it confining."

"So is that woman okay? The one you—you know." She was a bold one, this girl.

"The one I had so much trouble keeping alive? Yes, thank you, she's fine and back at home in Atlanta."

"So are you, like, going to stay out here? I've noticed you old guys stare."

Forrest laughed. "Actually, I just came out here to think. 'When to the sessions of sweet silent thought/I summon up remembrance of things past....'"

"Whatever. Stare if you want to. It's just kind of pathetic."

"How about this?" He turned his chair to face away from her.

"I just want *you* to know *I* know you're looking."

Forrest shook his head and took another sip of his whiskey. It was doing its work.

"They say if you drink by yourself, you're an alcoholic," the girl said.

"But you're here with me, dear," he said.

A boutique in Macon. He could drive twenty miles and see the living woman whose death had shaped his life. But if he went to look for her, it meant bringing everything back up. Why not just fly back home without the girls? Back in Portsmouth, he could finish smoothing things over at the college and get back to work on his book. He could be there tomorrow. Sea breezes would be coming through his office window as he sat at his desk in the late afternoon. He would hear the cry of gulls overhead. His work would he honest and clean and good, as it was when he was young.

Marisa was coming on Tuesday. She could pick up Cate and Bernadette and hear the whole wretched story, but he would be long gone.

He got up to go to his room and make a reservation online.

"Bye-bye," said the teenage girl, giving him a wave with her fingers.

He had forgotten she was there. He stared at her in confusion. He pulled the key card out of his bathing suit and lifted it in salute as he walked toward his room.

"So you aren't going to try to rape me or anything?" she said, faking a whine.

He stopped and half-turned toward her. Who was it? Who whined like that? When the girl saw him standing there and looking indecisive, she scrambled up from her chair and fled around the corner of the motel.

Bertram Everett. And out of nowhere, the smell of the cab of the truck came back to him, the coffee and cigarettes and chewing tobacco. The spoor of memory, the way to Marilyn. The three men of the surveying crew sitting shoulder to shoulder on the vinyl bench seat of the pickup on those morning drives when their clothes were still clean.

He opened the door of his room distractedly. Inside, he paused over the laptop, his left hand resting lightly on the gray surface.

At the end of the day, the pickup would stink of sweat and the river mud caked on their boots and Mo would loose farts on them and Bertram Everett would whine.

The plastic cup in his hand was empty. Forrest dipped up enough melting ice to fill it. He would make the reservation later. He screwed the top back on the Jack Daniels, closed the door, and walked back out to the table. No sign of the girl. The shaft of the umbrella was slightly tilted, and he straightened it, pulling the metal chair around to the other side of the table so he could see the water of the pool.

He remembered how he would hold in his palm the thick swell of the heavy plumb bob—Keuffel & Esser, precisely engineered—and, sitting on the tailgate of the truck before they started into the woods, he would unscrew the top cap and run fresh white string through the hole and knot it several times and screw it back on. You needed eight or nine feet of string, and you didn't want it coming loose and getting tangled while you worked. You'd wind the string tight onto the neck of the plumb bob but leave a loop at the top and secure it with a knot that tightened hard but instantly slipped loose when you needed it.

My God, Forrest thought, do I still remember how to do it? You'd unsnap the holster and pull the plumb bob out by the loop and then yank the little tag end of string and let the weight drop slowly, dangling heavily on its white string, from the inside crease of your forefinger knuckle as it found pure gravity, the pure logic of geometry. Out in the woods, in the very middle of the heat and sweat and teeming growth, this perfectly taut, clean, white vertical.

He would peer down, holding the string steady, centering the tip over the bright head of a sixteen-penny nail. (The rolls of garish pink-orange flagging tape they'd use. They'd punch the nails through a triple fold of it to stabilize them in the dirt and make them easy to find.) He'd call *good* while Mo Woodson tuned the transit's vernier to center the upright hair of the scope onto the string. *Good* as it tapped dead center. *Good!* he'd call, *Good!* The point where the tip touched the center of the nail was the contact point of a tangential plane, the Euclidian plane of property, resting on the sphere of earth. The string made visible a line extended through that exact point from the perfect conceptual center of the perfect, gravity-heavy conceptual earth and up to his steady finger. *Good,* Mo would call back and then turn the scope toward Bertram Everett's plumb bob string at the end of the next cut line.

They would have already measured the distance to the transit's new location over the next nail. The expensive transit that screwed onto the heavy wooden tripod. Its telescope and its precise vernier and its knobs on a sliding base for leveling and centering the instrument over the nail. The crew chief would hang his plumb bob from a hook that came down from the exact center of the vernier's circle, and he had to get the transit centered, leveled, and tightened over the nail the chainmen had just measured to. It took considerable skill to master. Then he turned the angle and read degrees, minutes, and seconds, flipped the scope and doubled the angle to increase the accuracy. Somewhere in the survey he would take compass bearings to locate the lines of this property on the earth's grid. It was all about angles and bearings and distances.

The vernier was calibrated brass, he thought, but how did the plates rotate? Sort of like a slide rule, but with degrees? Nobody used them now. The surveyors he'd see now beside a highway used yellow, boxy-looking, electronic theodolites with laser technology and digital displays.

He should check online for images of the old ones. Google it. *Surveying vernier.*

He lifted the cup and ice spilled against his lips. Gone already?

But he was already remembering the chain, the hundred-foot strip of metal embossed and notched at every foot for the plumb bob string, and each end had a metal loop for leather thongs that he'd wrap tight across the thick of his hand. He doubted that anybody now even knew what measurement was in those days, foot by foot over the live earth, stump and thorn and pine straw and rock, uphill and down, felt and known, not some abstract readout. The back chainman lined up the front chainman, waving him left or right until he was in a straight line with the transit. Then he wrapped the thongs around his left hand and braced himself and kept the chain taut while the front chainman pulled, keeping the chain level, his plumb bob string steady in his right hand at the hundred-foot notch, tip of the plumb bob tapping the center of the nail below. The front man had to get the right tautness and keep the chain as perfectly horizontal as possible whether they were going uphill or downhill, and once the back chainman called *good*, the front man would let the tip of the plumb bob tease, tap, delicately drop and pierce the ground and he would keep his eye on that exact spot as he called *good* and the chain slackened. Leaning down, he'd punch the bright clean sixteen-penny nail with its collar of flagging into that exact hole, and the center of the nail head would be exactly where the plumb bob tip had made the hole.

The hard part was cutting line to clear a path through the woods, clear enough for the transit to get a shot from one point to the next and unencumbered enough for the chainmen to be able to measure it. If the terrain was fairly open, they would take machetes and trim branches here and there. But for the deep woods, each man had a bush hook: a flat steel blade twelve inches long, recurved at the end, bolted onto a handle as long as a baseball bat and thick enough to sustain the shock of cutting down trees. Every morning before they started into the woods, they'd take turns sharpening the blades, like ancient warriors going into battle. On the opened back gate of the pickup truck, one man would sit casually on the handle, bracing it under him with his hands. The broad blade projected past the end of the gate, and the one doing the sharpening leaned into it, putting pressure with the heels of his hands at each end of a big mill bastard file, fingers up to avoid getting cut if the file slipped.

Delicate wisps of steel spangling off the blade's shining edge.

Bertram Everett hated cutting line, but Forrest loved it. He could slice through a two-inch pine with one backhand. He and Mo could fell a twelve-inch pine in two minutes. Sometimes they cut line through the woods all day, up and down hills, hacking through dense thickets of vines, wading through creeks and beaver ponds, stirring up yellow jackets and wasps.

And whatever else you said about the sorry bastard, Mo Woodson was good at his job.

Good God. Mo Woodson. Cigarette dangling from his mouth, sleek tan hairless arms, hair greased back from his receding hairline, black T-shirt.

Did He who made the Lamb make thee?

Mo Woodson, with his news about Marilyn.

Forrest stood up so abruptly he had to catch himself. The lights had come on around the pool and the parking lot. The western sky still showed a dull orange at the horizon, out beyond the McDonald's and an Exxon sign so tall it must be visible halfway to Macon. The teenage girl was gone.

But she had left before, hadn't she? Had she said something when she left? He needed to eat if he was going to be drinking whiskey.

Steadying himself, he took his cup back to his room, debating whether to drive somewhere in the Taurus, or order a pizza, or walk across to one of the restaurants, maybe get a big omelet at the Waffle House, an order of hash browns. Or grits. When had he last had grits?

Standing next to the TV, he refilled his cup with ice and whiskey, sipped it, and sank down on the end of the bed, already back in the stream of remembering.

That summer Forrest graduated from high school, 1969, Brother Hendricks had put Mo in charge of the crew. Maybe it was because Mo had done time in the service. Brother, a big gregarious forester who did surveying on the side, had been a drill instructor in the Marines, and Mo had been in the Army, which had sent him to Germany and France.

"Mo," Brother would say, "you ever think what damage it did to have you over there as an exhibit of the U.S.A.?"

Mo would narrow his eyes and take a drag on his cigarette.

"You ought to ask them French whores."

He loved being crew chief. He got to say how long lunch was and when they knocked off. He got to drive the pickup truck to suit his mood, sometimes creeping along, sometimes barreling down dirt roads at seventy miles per hour. Wherever they were, he always found the nearest store with alcohol immediately after work. On weekdays he would buy a six-pack of Miller for the crew—two for each of them—and on Fridays he'd throw in a cold bottle of Boone's Farm Apple Wine. He was deceptively powerful, as Forrest had discovered arm-wrestling him. His ignorance was deep and comprehensive, but he was natively intelligent, with a sly mean humor and canny understanding of people's lower motives. If anything about his mother came up, he was helplessly maudlin. Once Forrest had seen him sob for ten minutes just thinking about her. He scorned religion because he knew preachers who were hypocrites, but he was as superstitious as Huckleberry Finn, and running the crew gave him a palette to express himself. Every time a cat — not just a black cat, any cat — crossed the road in front of the truck, he would lick his forefinger and make an X on the inside of the windshield. When it rained and the windshield got foggy from having three wet men steaming and stinking inside the closed cab, all the Xs reappeared, and the windshield looked like a little graveyard of all the bad luck Mo had warded off.

"You see that," he would say solemnly. "It's done kept us all alive. I wish to God Steve would of listened." Steve Pippin, the former crew chief, a stoical, solid little man who liked to say "Life is hard," had rashly wiped the Xs off his truck windshield with a paper towel. Three months later he and his wife had been killed when their car flipped over on a rainy night after a football game.

One Friday afternoon in late June when several days of rain early in the week had delayed a survey on the Jackson road, Brother called them into his office and told them it was supposed to be clear the next day. They had to get out there and finish the survey so he could work up the plat by Monday morning. When Mo said he didn't work on Saturday, Brother, who was generally good-natured, went red and stood over him poking him in the chest and called him a dumbass redneck who was lucky to have a job now and if he didn't show up the next morning he wouldn't have one on Monday. Mo was so mad he almost quit, but instead he bought a six-pack on the way to work the next morning and, by way of protest, insisting on driving, drank all six beers before they even got to the job site, chugging each one and slinging the glass bottle left-handed over the cab—it was like shooting birds on the wing, he said—to explode it on a highway sign. He was already drunk ten miles out of Gallatin. He reeled around the truck while Forrest and Bertram Everett got out the equipment and sharpened the bush hooks. Five minutes later, he flagged down an old black man who happened by. Half an hour later the old man showed up with a pint of clear moonshine. Before Mo passed out under a sweetgum tree, his arms flung out, his black T-shirt riding up over the whiteness of his small pot belly, he poured a little of the moonshine on the ground and said, "Watch this." He threw a match on it, and the blue flame almost set him on fire.

That morning, Forrest and Bertram Everett had in common the unconscious Mo Woodson and the imagined rage of Brother Hendricks if they showed up with nothing. They had to do the work themselves.

Forrest genially despised Everett. Four years before Forrest's state championship team, Bertram—and who the hell would name his son Bertram?—had been the quarterback of the Blue Devils. He was a legendary figure, because he had single-handedly lost the region championship in Coach Fitzgerald's first winning season. Bertram was a good athlete, but a hot dog, a gambler. Not only did he ignore the plays that the coach sent in, but he threw two interceptions, the second of which a Cherokee Indian safety named Mike Thunderbird ran back for Hogansboro's winning touchdown. After that game, Bertram always had an air of grievance. He always seemed to be whining at the fact that he had to do whatever he was doing—but whatever *you* had just done, he could have done better. Forrest had grown up in the neighborhood with him, and he could never stand him.

But here they were. They laid Mo out in the back of the pickup.

Neither one had ever run the transit, but Forrest understood better what they were doing, so Everett had to concede to let him try. That meant Bertram had to swallow his pride and tramp back and forth to give Forrest the shots so they could turn the angles. He let Forrest feel his resentment every time they used the chain—yanking it, pulling too hard. When they finished the job, Everett would not go in with him to turn in the field book to Brother.

"Where's Mo?" Brother asked, flipping open the book. "Hell, these aren't Mo's notes. Whose are they?" Forrest told him that Mo had been sick so he had turned the angles himself. "Sick my ass. You don't have to cover for that piece of shit," Brother said. "If it doesn't close, he's out of a job." When a survey closed, all the angles and distances made a single, large polygon. All the work on the ground tightened into the exact measurements and thin blue lines of a plat, as this one did. When it didn't close, the crew had to go back out and do it all over.

That survey must have closed, because Mo kept his job, and it must have been the next Monday when Forrest first heard Marilyn's name. Mo hadn't had any breakfast, and he decided he had to get a honey bun before they went to work. They were on their way out to the Ocmulgee River and the 3000-odd-acre tract they had been surveying for most of July, so he stopped at Glenn's Bait Store near Jellico and came back out with a honey bun and a large cup of coffee. He sat in the driver's seat unwrapping the sticky thing and started to apply himself to it with the kind of devotion that made Forrest a little sick to his stomach to watch.

"You want me to drive?" he asked, but Mo shook his head.

"Crew chief drives."

He ate steadily through half of it, licking his fingers, before he took a sip of coffee. "Jesus, Mo," whined Bertram Everett. "Do you have to moan when you eat it?" Mo licked his lips and wiped some of the sugar from his fingers onto his jeans.

"It's just it reminds me of Paloma," he said. He ate the other half, moaning.

As they started out of the parking lot, a black cat darted out from behind some trash cans, crossed in front of them, and sped across the parking lot onto the main road, directly into the path of a tractor-trailer. All three sets of double tires ran over it, and Mo, who had spilled coffee on his leg hitting the brakes, stared at the flattened cat with his mouth open. "Jesus God Almighty Christ, did you see that?" He shuddered and made three quick Xs on the windshield with his sugar-sticky finger. He carefully crossed the main highway and turned onto the road that led to the river.

"That what you do with Paloma?" Bertram Everett said. "Put Xs on her after you do the deed?"

Mo's eyes narrowed. He hated it when anybody besides himself mentioned his wife, especially Bertram Everett. Mo had moved to Gallatin a few years earlier and married Paloma without realizing quite what kind of history he was inheriting.

"Tell you what," Mo said. "I hope you're putting a X on that nigger gal."

"Shut the fuck up!" Everett said in a sudden rage.

"Good-looking gal," said Mo. "What's her name? Marilyn?"

Everett twisted in his seat to hit Mo, but Forrest grabbed his wrist. "He's driving the truck, dumbass."

"Let go of me."

"Fine-looking gal." Mo was enjoying himself. "Swings that sweet thing down the sidewalk every night. Come on white boys. Bertram here, he been after it three or four times now."

Everett caught Mo in the right temple with his left elbow, and the truck veered over into the path of an oncoming car that swerved away, horn blasting. Mo yanked the truck back into its lane and over onto the right shoulder and back up onto the road with Everett still trying to hit him. "You dumb son of a bitch," Mo yelled, "you can't take it if somebody gets on you."

Forrest grabbed Everett's wrists.

"I got this stupid fucker. You drive," Forrest said. Everett was squirming backward and howling, "Let me go, God damn it! Let me go!"

Forrest squeezed savagely until Everett's voice rose to a panicked squeal.

"Okay! Okay!" he shouted.

When Forrest released them, the hands flopped into Everett's lap. His fingers looked like a crushed spider.

"I can't move my hands," Everett whined after a few seconds.

"Jesus H. Christ," Mo said contemptuously.

"Take me to the hospital." Everett lifted his arms and the hands hung like a dead man's. Mo furiously pulled the truck onto a dirt road and parked and got out and walked to the other side of the road, where he lit a cigarette and looked off into row of planted pines, running one hand over his slick head. Forrest got out on the other side and urinated into the ditch. After a minute or so, he saw Everett slowly flexing the fingers and rubbing his hands over each other, gingerly touching the throttled wrists.

"You better be able to cut line," said Mo, getting back into the cab, "or I'll leave your sorry ass."

Everett said nothing.

"Let's go to work," said Forrest.

"Screw you," Bertram said, not looking at him.

"What did you say?" Forrest turned in the seat to look at him.

Mo started the truck. Bertram's mouth was pinched. He turned on the radio and punched a button but it wasn't country. After a second Mo punched another button and got Merle Haggard.

Bertram sat there rigid with hatred.

Forrest picked up the whiskey bottle and started to pour more but set it back down. Memory held him like an undertow. He should go eat—put on his clothes and walk across Lee Street and get something, but when he stood up, he tipped back onto the bed. What if he ran into somebody and he had all this liquor on his breath?

There was a Pizza Hut ad next to the TV, so he dialed the number and at first ordered a medium pepperoni and sausage, and gave them his room number, but then he changed his order to a large. It would be about half an hour, they said. After he hung up, he thought about eating a large pizza by himself and what it was going to do to him. Back then, that summer, he ate huge meals and burned it all off. If they were too far from the truck to walk back out, they would carry everything in with them—the big Igloo water jug, the box with the lunches, whatever they needed for the day—and they'd sit on logs, brushing off flies and mosquitoes, and eat the two or even three enormous sandwiches their mothers or wives had made them. That was besides the Vienna sausages, sardines, chips, cheese curls, apples, oranges, Twinkies, moon pies.

That day, the day he found out about Marilyn, they broke for lunch beside the Ocmulgee near an old, one-lane metal bridge that the new road had bypassed. The river had sunk far down in its banks since the last heavy rain in early June. He was sitting on the Igloo water jug and Mo sat on a stump. Bertram, sullen and bitter all morning, sat by himself with his legs dangling from the bank, dropping his plumb bob into the shallow water as though he were fishing. Forrest could see his lips sneering. Upstream, a moccasin lazily crossed the water.

"Wait," Forrest suddenly said to Mo. "I know who you're talking about."

The girl had been walking through town every Saturday afternoon since she first began to develop a shape. She would look at no one, as full of enticement and hauteur as a runway model. He first noticed her when he was in the ninth grade. At the time, he thought of her as a town character like deaf-and-dumb Martin Sams, who dressed up in a police uniform and gabbled incomprehensibly at strangers who stopped and asked for directions. Or like Scotchy, who delivered the *Macon Telegraph* on his antique motor scooter. But he had never mentioned her to anyone, and no one had ever mentioned her to him.

For the past year, he had thought about her as his own secret possession. He had undergone a kind of conversion the previous summer. During his junior year in high school, he had won a spot at the Governor's Honors Program, an eight-week summer school in Macon where the best students in the state studied with college professors. A few black students were mixed into the dormitories with the white ones. The boys from Atlanta schools, crackling with wit and sarcasm, mocked the racism of one boy from Clayton who wouldn't sit at the same table with a black tenor.

Forrest had his own hesitations, largely the result of growing up with Harlan Connor's conventional racism, but he did not want to be mocked as a redneck. In his history class, he read Frederick Douglass, W.E.B. Dubois, Martin Luther King. His looks and athletic prowess outweighed his small-town prejudices in the general regard, and sophisticated Atlanta girls clustered around him, eager to enlighten him. By the end of the eight weeks, his perspective had shifted so much that he considered himself the hidden protector of a girl from the black high school in Gallatin—shy Deborah Harkins, who sang soprano. After he came home that August, he scorned the racism and injustice everywhere around him.

The feeling of his difference gradually came to focus on this beautiful black girl who walked through Gallatin as though for him alone. No one else, he believed, had even noticed her, but he idealized her. He thought of himself as overcoming the vast prejudice of his upbringing simply by being attracted to her, which no other white man would be. If he only had the courage to speak to her, he would show her that he alone would dare to commit the unthinkable transgression of loving her despite her blackness.

But Mo Woodson knew her? She was just a prostitute? Bertram Everett had been with her? It made him sick to his stomach. He couldn't believe it.

"I was the one told Bertram about her," Mo said in a low voice with a sideways flick of his head. He let cigarette smoke curl thickly from his mouth. "You pull up next to her and she'll say to meet her on a side street. You pick her up, and she'll get in the back seat and duck her head to stay out of sight until you're out of town."

"How much do you have to pay her?" he said dully.

Mo drew back as if Forrest had insulted him. "She won't take no money. Don't take no money and won't go with no niggers," Mo said. "If she was to go out with niggers, wouldn't no white man pick her up."

"I don't get it."

Mo shrugged. "I ain't trying to explain it. I'm just telling you."

"You just pull up and she'll go with you if you're white?"

He flipped his cigarette in a long arc into the river and shook another Marlboro out of the pack he kept rolled up in the left sleeve of his T-shirt.

"Once you been with her," Mo said, "you won't think straight for a week."

He snapped open his Zippo and flicked it and took the first drag on his new cigarette out of the invisible flame.

"So who is she?" said Forrest.

"I just said."

"You must know where she lives, stuff like that. You've been out with her."

Mo furrowed his eyebrows. "What the hell makes you think that?"

"You just said."

"I ain't said nothing about me," he said. Bertram turned his head to look at them. Mo lowered his voice and looked Forrest in the eyes. "You think Mo Woodson would go out with a nigger? When I'm married to Paloma?"

Forrest shrugged, starting to smile despite himself.

"Get that smile off your face. You tell anybody that shit...."

"What?" Forrest said. "You're the one telling me."

"I'm just messing with you," Mo said, blowing a smoke ring into the still air, back to his usual oily aplomb. "Listen, look at Bertram over yonder. He ain't been the same. He's a piss-poor excuse for a human bean these days. He ain't made for it. It's like putting a Dodge hemi in a Volkswagen, it just shakes him to pieces."

"So you just pull up beside her."

"You don't want to get messed up with that. Town hero like you."

"So you just roll down the window and what—ask her if she needs a ride? Her name's Marilyn?"

"Marilyn Harkins," Mo said.

"Harkins?"

"You happen to run into her, ask her does she remember Otis Abernathy."

"Who's Otis Abernathy?"

"Now Otis," Mo said, blowing a series of smoke rings. "I wouldn't put it past him to pick her up. But she don't know no Mo."

Forrest woke up in the middle of the night freezing. The sheets under him were clammy, soaked through from a night sweat, and the air conditioner was turned down so low the room felt like January in New Hampshire. He was still in his bathing suit. He punched the off button, pulled on a T-shirt, wrapped himself in a blanket, and stumbled to the bathroom.

Back in bed, he lay there shivering under the covers, unable to fall back to sleep. His soul felt naked and defenseless, as though some supernatural, soul-scouring death ray had fallen upon him. He saw his own vanity and cowardice and failure without the insulation of his usual fictions. He thought for some reason about the girl he had married two years into college and divorced three years later. His rages, his injustice, his cruelty to her. He remembered the little quivering white dog she insisted on keeping in their apartment in Athens and how it would whimper and scratch to be let in. One night, in fit of temper, Forrest had jerked open the door and punted the thing off the back porch into the neighbors' hedge. His wife had run screaming after it. The dog survived and slavishly humbled himself to Forrest after that, but Melba never forgave him.

That was really me, she told him. He made her into a weepy, accusatory woman. Why had he ever thought she could heal him of Marilyn?

Finally, images began to slip and flow as he fell back to sleep. Offices somewhere underground, maybe in the underworld. Forrest had killed somebody, and then killed a witness, and he had been pretending not to know the bodies were there. Brother, who was also the president of Walcott College, called him in. *Listen, everybody knows you did it.* The women behind Brother, plump and avid, looked up from their desks to see what Forrest would say, the tips of their tongues licking their lips.

He loved the truth as much as anybody, he wanted to say, but the problem was that telling the truth would get him sent to jail. He might even be executed. So he said *I didn't do it*.

Everybody knew he was lying.

When he woke up again, daylight poured in through the gap in the curtains, and the room had gotten stuffy. He got up, ripped open one of the coffee packets and made himself a pot and stood staring at himself in the mirror. Something else nagged at him. In the dream, the underground offices were off to the left, but off to the right somewhere were the women in Maya's vision. He didn't see them, but he knew they were there. He could feel them in his marrow, a bass note beneath his hearing.

Marilyn was not dead. Not dead. She had been dead for the last forty years, and now she was alive again. It struck him as absurd to think that she was now alive and running a boutique in Macon—and that she had a daughter who could be his. There it was: the thought that he had violently beaten down the day before. Hermia Watson could be... Good god—if Marilyn was alive, she probably....

A qualm of panic and nausea came over him.

But how could Marilyn be alive? And Mo Woodson, sorry-ass Mo Woodson who had taken him out to the river that morning. If Marilyn was alive, she would be as old as he was, not eighteen and beautiful as a goddess.

Marilyn, not only alive, but fat and vulgar and nearly sixty years old.

He felt his way to the toilet and threw up.

After a long hot shower, Forrest was getting dressed when there was a knock on the door. He answered it in his boxer shorts and found the boy who had first checked him in standing there with a set of car keys in his hand.

"Mr. Lee, he brought you a different car," he said. "It's that Nissan Sentra right over there." Forrest stepped out of the room to look. The boy pressed a button on the keys and the lights flashed on a decent mid-sized green sedan. The Taurus, he saw with a strange lifting of his heart, was gone. The boy handed the keys to Forrest and gave him a nod and started back to the front office.

He wondered what kind of mercy or remorse had possessed Chick. But he was grateful, because he wanted to explore some of the old places and see what memories might surface. He finished getting dressed, adjusted the Nissan to fit him, and drove out to Foster Drive and then left to go out of town. He crossed the Interstate and headed out past a

Motel 6 and a scattering of cheap-looking houses. A few miles out of town, he came around a curve and saw a tin-roofed house at the top of a hill across a meadow, and it brought something back: the image of a black woman running frantically. Something about Tony Wright. Around the next turn, he saw looming in the distance the four towers of the power plant built in the decade after he left Gallatin for college. Every mile or so, he saw them again—immense, apocalyptic. The 3000-acre tract they had been surveying that summer had been part of the early preparations for the coal-powered Ocmulgee facility run by Southeastern Energy.

Ten miles out of Gallatin, he reached the intersection with U.S. 23, the highway that went to Macon if you turned right, to Jackson if you turned left. A new filling station gleamed soullessly where Glenn's Bait Store had been. He sat for a moment trying to remember, and then crossed the highway toward Jellico. He remembered a dirt road that ended in a clearing. There was a line they had cut along an old barbed wire fence, and it came out on the bank of the river near a big tree. The bloody dress had been nailed there, clouded with flies. The scene of Marilyn's murder.

He crossed the highway, and after a quarter-mile, he knew it wasn't the place Mo had brought him that morning. But he wanted to see the river at least. He crossed the railroad tracks and saw the new bridge ahead. There was a road to the left before he got to it, so he slowed and turned down it, nosing along. Weeds grew up through the crumbling pavement. After several hundred yards, he came to a chain-link barrier that blocked the road. An ancient brown pickup truck sat blocking one of the improvised detours where cars had gone around it.

He got out and glanced inside the truck at its gashed seats and filthy pillows and walked past it toward the river. Big green grasshoppers whirred up out of the tall weeds.

Downstream from the old bridge pilings, an old black man and a little boy were fishing from the riverbank. It had not rained lately or the water would be the muddy red-orange of Georgia clay. Now it ran a dark brown, placid and low between the banks. Sunbeams slanted through the line of trees on the eastern side, glancing off the ripples below the snags. Insects showed thick as dust motes above the water. Somewhere not too far from here, within a half-mile of this spot, he had seen the proof of Marilyn's murder, but he could not remember how to get there. Two deaths that summer had derailed his life, hers and Tony Wright's.

He had seen her dress nailed on the tree. He had seen the tracks where her body had been dragged to the river. The men who had killed her made no attempt to hide the crime. They might as well have left a burning cross.

He slapped a mosquito on his neck and walked back to the car. Memory came at him again.

The day Forrest found out who Marilyn was, Bertram had gone into

Brother's office to pick up his check, and he had told Brother he wasn't coming back on Monday.

"Not coming back?" Brother said, shooting up out of his chair. "Why the hell not?"

Bertram just shook his head and stood there rubbing his wrists. "Good luck finding somebody who can work with these assholes," he told Brother, disappearing out the door.

"You could have given me a little warning!" Brother yelled after him. He turned on Mo. "What did you do, dumbass?"

Mo told him what had happened. "Tell you the truth, Bertram never was worth a shit."

Brother shook his head. "Better than nothing. Now I'm short a chainman."

"Maybe I can find somebody better."

"Who? You got somebody else in mind?"

Mo said, "Matter of fact there's a boy been asking me. Name of Tony Wright, kid from Jackson, worked on a crew up there for six months or so with Dale Hansen. One of Paloma's nephews."

And there he was on Monday morning.

An inch under six feet, sandy-haired and handsome as a Confederate cavalry officer, he had a lean grace that made Forrest feel like a bear instead of a big cat. He was tireless cutting line, and unlike Bertram he did not resent having to do it. Rock-steady with the plumb bob and the chain, he had an unironic appetite for work. He instantly saw what was required, and his intelligence was quick and aggressive. He had standards that he simply expected you to meet if you were going to call yourself a man. The challenge of the job satisfied him like a good meal, a spirit that communicated itself even to Mo, and that first week, they did more work and took more pleasure in doing it well than they had all summer.

One day a few hundred yards upriver from the old bridge, they had been cutting through thick underbrush, and whenever they stopped, clouds of mosquitoes would settle on every exposed inch of skin. When he was trying to hold the plumb bob steady, Forrest would feel them on his cheeks, his lips, his eyelids. He watched them feeding on the backs of his hands, the webs between his fingers. It was close to noon when they came to the muddy creek that emptied into the Ocmulgee just past a large bend where a big cottonwood shaded the bank. They would have to wade the creek to keep going, but Mo hated to eat with wet feet, so they broke for lunch. The big roots of the cottonwood angled out near the bank, and Forrest sat on one across from Wright, spraying himself with Off. Mo leaned back against the trunk between them.

Downstream, boys were jumping off the old bridge into the deep part, and across the river, a crop duster swooped up over the trees and turned and dropped out of sight and then came in low, spraying pesticides ten feet or so above the rows visible through a gap.

The image came back whole: Mo unwrapping the wax paper around one of the sandwiches Paloma had made him and lifting his head at the smell of the pesticide.

"I hope that shit don't get on me."

Wright grinned. "Might kill them head lice," he said.

Forrest saw Mo decide to smile. "Before your mouth gets too smart, you might want to remember how you got this job."

"Shit, Uncle Mo," said Wright. "You were so impressed with me, Brother had to hire me."

"I just felt sorry for you," said Mo. "You can't impress me. Hell, Cump here was all-state three years in a row."

"What's that mean?" Wright asked equably.

"Come on," Mo said incredulously. "All-state. In the Atlanta Journal and Constitution. Best in the fucking state."

"Best at what?"

"Football, you dumb shit," said Mo. "I didn't know you was so ignorant. Cump won the fucking state championship for the first time in the history of the school."

"Don't mean much to me."

"You're from Jackson," Forrest said, "and you didn't play football? You look like a natural running back."

"Coach up there was always after me before I quit school, but I had to work. I didn't have time to play no games."

"You grow up on a farm?"

"Why you say that?"

"I don't know. I grew up working on one every weekend for my stepfather. Most of the farm boys played football. I just wondered why you didn't."

"Ain't none of your business, is it?"

Forrest shrugged.

"Mama didn't make no money waitressing, so I done all kinds of things. Filling station, logging, construction. I got a couple of other uncles, they get me jobs. Surveying's the best so far."

"You finally lit on the best uncle," said Mo. "Where'd you get that Firebird you're driving?"

"Sweet Holy Jesus!" Wright hissed, looking at something to Forrest's left. "Don't move."

Forrest froze. Tongue flickering, a snake slid past his left boot, paused momentarily at the yellow Igloo water cooler, and flowed toward Mo, who sat staring at it with his sandwich halfway to his mouth and his eyes huge. Wright jumped up and clapped his hands and instantly it turned, raising its head on a forearm's length of sinuous reptile muscle, ready to strike.

Forrest scrambled backward over the root. Mo was already ten feet from the tree, Paloma's lovingly-made sandwich abandoned in the dirt. But Wright stood directly in front of the snake, crouched like a tennis player waiting for the serve. He feinted to the left, and when the snake struck air, he whirled down to the right and snatched the tail and in one continuous motion cracked the long body like a bull whip.

And it was dead, just like that. Wright held it up by the tip of its tail.

"God almighty damn. That's a big old bastard," Wright said, grinning. It was at least six feet long. Forrest could see the boys on the bridge staring and pointing. "Sometimes I make their heads pop off."

"If it's one thing I hate," Mo said, "it's a fucking cottonmouth."

"You want to keep him?" asked Wright.

"Why in the hell would I want to keep him?" Mo said.

"Keep other snakes off. If you cut two pieces of skin and fit 'em inside your boots, won't no snakes bite you."

"Bullshit."

"What Dale Hansen says an old nigger taught him. You need to keep him till sundown before you skin him, because a snake won't die all the way when it's daylight, so we'd have to tote him around all afternoon. I don't mind it. They's enough skin on this snake for all three of us."

"That's the dumbassedest thing I ever heard," said Mo.

"Shame to waste a good snake."

"You can't cut line and drag around a fucking dead snake."

Wright thought for a minute. Then he loosened his belt and picked up the snake. "Look here, Uncle Mo," he said, "if you was to just wedge its head up under my belt in the back, I could tighten it up and it wouldn't get in the way. Be like a tail."

Mo got out a cigarette and lit it and pointed it at Wright with a trembling hand. "Son," he said, "I ain't touching that fucking snake."

Wright looked at Forrest.

Forrest took the snake from him, holding it behind the head, feeling the alien dead weight of it, a limbless cool heavily muscled spine. A shiver went up his own spine.

"You scared of it, too?" Wright asked.

"Turn around."

Wright turned around, and Forrest wedged it beneath Wright's loosened belt between two loops of his Levis. When Wright tightened it, the bulge of the viper's head kept it from slipping back out. Wright leapt around whooping.

"Who the hell have I hired?" Mo said.

All afternoon, Forrest would look up and see Wright cutting line, trailing a thick brown tail. When they knocked off, Wright curled the dead moccasin in the back with the equipment. But then when they stopped at Glenn's Bait Store so Mo could pick up a six-pack of Miller, Wright insisted on putting it back on and wearing it inside. Forrest was standing beside the truck when a heavy, freckled woman burst out the front door with a hand on her heart, followed by an old black man. Both of them cringed back as Wright emerged, his face innocent, holding a bag of roasted peanuts and trailing the cottonmouth.

"Are you the devil?" cried the woman.

"No, ma'am," said Wright, sweet as pie. "He's my uncle."

Something about him was off.

On the way back to Gallatin from Jellico, the cell phone trilled once. When it did not ring again, he looked at the number, not recognizing it. He was sure it was Tricia. Last night she had wanted to talk about "us." Until he had seen her on Friday in her tennis clothes, he had not thought about her for decades, any more than he had thought about Chick Lee.

Girls like Jasmine Colter and Betty Brazier, who would drive out to find him working on a fence or clearing brush on Harlan Connor's farm, had detached him early on (he was fourteen) from his virginity, but they left him awash in disgust, both with himself and with them. But Tricia was ladylike, with a charm and reserve that made him protective.

He had not been cynical then. He took her virginity behind a country Pentecostal church. He knew about the place because he and Mo and Bertram came upon it when they were surveying: the grass in the cool shade under the oak trees, the long picnic tables. He took Tricia into the church lot one moonlit Friday night. They walked into the shadows and then lay on the grass beside each other looking up at the moon and the scudding clouds. The ants did not bite them; the mosquitoes did not hover over them. There was a feeling of peace, as though it were a sacred grove. He told her he loved her and meant it. Or sincerely meant to mean it.

When she cried out in pain, a dog down the road started barking. He remembered the startled and anxious sound of it. Afterwards, Tricia wept for a long time, clinging to him as he drove her around the dark roads of the county. He held her, soothing her, telling her she would be his forever and meaning that too.

Soon it was whenever they could be together, wherever their passion peaked—usually in the car, but once in a broom closet at a party, once under the branches of a fig tree in a neighbor's back yard, once in a corn field on a hot Sunday afternoon, her bare heels digging into the loose red clay between two rows of cornstalks. She was a sweet thing.

The phone rang again.

"When did you want to have that talk?" he said warmly. There was a silence. "Who is this?" he asked.

"How's your hangover?" Good god, it was Chick Lee again. "Listen, how about coming to church with me this morning?"

For a long moment he did not say anything.

"You want me to go to the Baptist church?"

"Wait, before you say anything. Just listen to me a minute. Everybody knew about the girls showing up with nowhere to go, and now everybody's heard about that girl you brought down here from Atlanta and put in the hospital. Maybe if you go to church..."

"Give me a break, Chick."

"No, maybe it'll, you know, make things look better—like you're turning over a new leaf."

"So I'm some kind of town problem?"

"Come on, Cump. If this was Atlanta, maybe nobody would care."

"But basically you're asking me to be a hypocrite. It would just be public relations."

"No, I want you to hear the guest pastor who's coming down, Jack Boehner's teacher from Emory. He's written books on stuff you'd know about. How about it? The service is at 11 o'clock."

The car clock said 8:52.

"Is this what I owe you because you brought me a better car?"

"How about I swing by and pick you up at quarter to eleven right after my Sunday school class? I'll be out front at 10:45."

"I didn't say I'd go. I'm about to go get some breakfast."

"10:45."

All through breakfast at the Waffle House—a ham-and-cheese omelet, watery grits, wheat toast with raspberry jam—he mulled over the idea of making an appearance at the Baptist Church. The prodigal son. He imagined sitting there in the padded pews with the fat hymnals in their racks before him, all the well-dressed Baptists trying their best not to eye him, but the inevitable whispers and glances brimming up all around him. The greetings, the hymns, the sermon.

Suddenly he saw himself as a Caravaggio painting. *Braxton among the Baptists*: dim townsmen pious in their pews, the beam of light coming down at a slant to illuminate only him—his stricken, uplifted face shadowed by the hand thrust up against the blinding revelation, while in the background, the preacher lifted the Bible in his left hand.

His shoulders started shaking with laughter and the overworked waitress paused on her way down the other side of the counter, coffeepot in hand.

"You need something else, sugar?"

He shook his head, still grinning, and finished his breakfast. He left her a dollar tip from the remains of Maya's money and crossed Lee Street. Yes, Braxton Forrest stepping out onto the front steps of the church with Chick, his head lowered modestly. His old friends would come up to him. He pictured the rueful joking, the disapproving but warm-hearted wives, the teenage girls hanging back and looking at him, horrified at the stories, wincing with mercy on their coltish legs.

Why not? When his phone rang on the way across the street, he said, "Chick, you're on."

"Were you expecting Chick?"

It was Tricia. "He wants to take me to church," he said.

For a moment, she did not say anything. "Well, Cate's been asking about a Catholic church. She and Bernadette say they want to go to a Mass. They want you to take them. Their mother called about it."

Anything to irritate him.

2

It was an unusually cool morning for mid-July. Hermia sat with the windows open, holding her cell phone in case anyone wondered why she was still in her car in the parking lot of St. Matthew's AME Church. Two women she didn't know passed her. Wilson Gant, who worked at the hardware store, pulled up in front of the church. His little boy ran around the car and opened the passenger door. Old Mrs. Gant in her big hat got out laboriously, snapping at her grandson's inept attempts to help her, then limped and called and waved her way with big-hipped aplomb toward the entrance of the stolid, white-steepled building. Men in their Sunday suits slapped each other's hands and bumped fists with loose-limbed humor, laughing and pointing.

Among them, drawing their deferential greetings, came Deacon Hubbard, the three buttons of his dark blue suit sternly buttoned, his posture as perfect as an old Southern planter's.

To her dismay, LaCourvette and Mary Louise Gibson arrived at church just in time for the service. LaCourvette must have parked on the road near the entrance. Hermia did not see her in her pink suit until she was already going in the door. She barely had time to get inside and find a spot in a back pew with several old men—all of them smiling and nodding at her—before the service started.

There was always something of interest in the service. The star soprano of the choir, Miss Deborah something, whom she didn't know, was full of hauteur; then there was Deacon Hubbard's rhetorical display of public prayer or Rev. Love's dramatic reading of Scripture. Marvin K. Love III was a big man in his mid-forties whose whole being took on a sheen when he preached, regardless of how good the air conditioning was. Today he read the Gospel of John about the woman taken in adultery. He stalked back and forth behind the pulpit. The purple-robed men and women of the choir were nodding and fanning themselves in the choir loft.

What was it, he kept asking, that Jesus was writing in the sand?

"Whose sins was Jesus writing down? Because you see he was talking to the scribes and Pharisees who had brought this woman to him—and who were they but the good people like us? Here they all were, all the good people who came to church on Sunday, and what are good people but those who don't do no wrong and don't have no sins to write down?

"Like *us* brothers and sisters. Like you and me, proud that *Unh-unh, no sir, WE ain't doing nothing wrong, proud that Unh-unh, WE don't cheat and steal and run around.* So whose sins was he writing down? Not mine. Why, look here, Mr. Jesus, I'm Marvin K. Love III, the pastor of St. Matthew's AME Church! If I ain't good, who *is* good? Besides, these brothers and sisters need to think I'm righteous in your sight. I'm supposed to be a light unto their path.

"But let me tell you, brothers and sisters, when I'm standing in front of the judgment seat of the Lord God Almighty, in the sight of the All-Seeing Father, I don't believe I'm going to say, *No sir, don't say a word against Marvin K. Love III, because I am spotless as the Lamb.* I tell you what. When the light of the Most High shines on me, that ray of light that leaves no hiding place, that day that makes high noon feel like midnight, am I going to claim I have no sins? I tell you what I'm going to say, I tell you right now. I'm going to call out, *Lord have mercy on me a sinner!*"

There were calls, cries, handkerchiefs waved in the air, sobs, hallelujahs.

"So whose sins did Jesus write down? Let me look down at the ground. Why look here...those are *my* sins. Every extra little glance at some fine sister's good looks, every haughty thought. Look down at the ground. Whose sins did he write? It was yours, Sister Jones. It was yours, Brother Jenkins. It was even yours, good Deacon Hubbard."

"Amen," called the old man.

"What was Jesus asking, if it wasn't whether the good people had any right to judge other people as bad people? What did he mean to teach when he wrote in the sand? Did he mean, *Rise up O ye good people and condemn the wicked among you to everlasting fire?* Is that what he meant when He said *Judge not that ye be not judged?* When he said *Love your neighbor as yourself*, did he mean to make you feel better than your neighbor, or did he hope that you would be good enough to give your neighbor a little of the same daily mercy that lets you get by in your own sight and go on living? Listen, Jesus said *If you do it unto the least of these you do it unto me*. He raised up that poor woman, yes, that sinner, and he said to her, *Woman, where are those thine accusers? Hath no man condemned thee?* She said, *No man, Lord.* Did I read that right? It says No man. And no woman either? Ain't that what it means? And Jesus said unto her, *Neither do I condemn thee: go, and sin no more.*

"Oh the sweetness of that moment. Walking away forgiven. But brothers and sisters, then she starts to think about it, that poor woman starts to tremble. How can she sin no more if even those good people, even the scribes and Pharisees, are not without sin?"

When Hermia squirmed, the old man next to her gave her knee a fatherly pat. She smiled and tilted her head, as though Marvin K. Love III's sermon was getting to her.

But what was on her mind was Braxton Forrest's look when she said the name Marilyn Harkins. As soon as the last hymn ended and the stir of leaving began, she got up to intercept LaCourvette and Mrs. Gibson in the aisle. The old woman in her huge cream-colored hat was greeting an old friend and did not notice her, but LaCourvette lit up.

"Girl, I didn't see you!"

"I need to talk to you," Hermia said, leaning close.

"Right now? Miss Mary Louise has me lined up for her Sunday dinner."

"Will you introduce me? I need to talk to her, too."

The old woman had turned from her friend and now she bestowed her large smile on Hermia as she held out her gloved hand expectantly, her eyebrows laboring toward a recognition that eluded her.

"Miss Mary Louise," LaCourvette said a little uneasily. "This is my friend Hermia Watson."

Why was she uneasy?

"*Very* pleased to meet you," said Mrs. Gibson warmly. "Very pleased. Aren't you a pretty thing? Wasn't Rev. Love fine today? And I could hear every word of it. Why don't you come join us for dinner?" LaCourvette quailed, as though a wasp had just floated toward her, but her grandmother did not notice. "I felt good enough to cook yesterday—and it's my prime rib," Mrs. Gibson went on, touching Hermia's arm as though anybody ought to know what that meant. "I just need to warm it up. Corn on the cob. Sweet potatoes with butter. Rev. Love will be there with his wife. You come on and join us."

"Now Miss Mary Louise, Hermia might have something else she needs to do," LaCourvette said. "You know she helps Mrs. Hayes."

"Oh, I know some stories about that house!" said Mrs. Gibson. "Y'all don't know what all went on."

"I'd love to hear about it," said Hermia. "Mrs. Hayes is always talking about Aunt Ella and somebody named Pearl."

Mrs. Gibson looked up at her. Behind her grandmother, LaCourvette shook her head and held up a hand. What in the world was the matter with her? Outside, LaCourvette got Mrs. Gibson safely in the car, then came around and stood in front of Hermia.

"What's got into you?"

"Me? Why are you trying to keep me from talking to your grandmother?"

"Because maybe I know what's good for you and you don't."

"I just want to ask a few questions."

"Come on, baby, I got to get things in the oven," called Mrs. Gibson.

"Tell your friend to follow us."

"We're coming, Miss Mary Louise," said LaCourvette, but to Hermia she whispered, "You don't know what you're doing."

"Then why don't you tell me?"

"Because you don't want to know. But come on," she said irritably. "You gone follow me?"

Hermia nodded and crossed the lot to her Prius, which looked odd to her in this setting. Hybrid was right—but no use getting off on that subject.

Whatever LaCourvette wasn't telling her, it had something to do with her mother. Maybe some scandal in her past. Her friend probably thought it would devastate her. But after opening the bedroom door one day in Evanston and discovering her husband in flagrante delicto with a male graduate student, what was going to shake her now? After Daddy Loum and his night visits? The girl had no idea.

She followed the brown sedan back through town past the courthouse square and down Lee Street toward Stonewall Hill. They turned right on Sharp Street before the road split and drove into the black neighborhood, where people just getting home from church spoke to each other and lingered on their front steps and porches.

After several turns, LaCourvette pulled into the short driveway of a small, white clapboard house with holly bushes on both sides of the high front steps. Hermia parked on the street behind a white Lexus with LOVE III on the license plate. Rev. Marvin K. Love III got out of the driver's side, and his wife, a delicate woman—LaCourvette said she had "nervous problems"—got out from the other side.

"Miss Watson! I didn't know you'd be joining us!" said Rev. Love, slamming the door and coming around the car and opening his arms to embrace Hermia. He squeezed her tightly against him, and she got a strong whiff of overworked deodorant and cologne as he released her, then kissed her three times—right cheek, left cheek, right cheek. "My Ethiopian brothers taught me that," he said, laughing at her discomfiture, not letting her go.

"You better watch out, Marvin," said his wife drily. "Jesus gone have something else to write in the sand."

"Let go of that girl and come on inside. Let me get dinner heated up," Mrs. Gibson called from the front sidewalk as she limped toward the front steps. "Law, look at that, my boy didn't come to mow, I'm gone get on him tomorrow first thing."

He laughed again and gathered his wife—she looked like she would break in two if he squeezed her—and drew her toward Hermia, his arms around both their waists. "You know Lavinia, don't you?" he said. The two women smiled at each other uneasily as he pulled them into an awkward collision. His hand subtly and as if unconsciously kneaded Hermia's waist and drifted in ministerial blessing over the curve of her bottom before he released her.

No wonder his wife had nervous problems.

They stepped through the seedy grass toward the front steps.

"How in the world y'all get here before we did?" Mrs. Gibson called, not turning her head as LaCourvette helped her climb. "I didn't even see y'all leave out the church. We drove straight home, but you here before us."

"He lit out the back," said Lavinia. "Man can get away fast when he needs to."

Rev. Love threw back his head and laughed, staggering comically as though the joke had exposed everything about him. "Got all those scribes and Pharisees coming after me!" he cried, and they laughed. "No, now what it is, Miss Mary Louise," he said finally, wiping his eyes and ascending the steps, "is your prime rib can move mountains. That's what it is. It puts the spirit in me that says Make haste."

Her prime rib lived up to its reputation. Marvin K. Love III carved helping after helping, mostly for himself—tender, medium-rare, dripping with gravy—and ate as though he had been commissioned to do it. He extolled the sweet potatoes (split open, golden with butter), the green beans cooked just right with fatback and onions, the soft buttery rolls. To see the preacher with his third piece of corn, holding the thick pat of butter on the tines of his downturned fork and smoothing it melting down the cob, to see him salt and pepper it and hold up the gleaming cob with the butter-slick fingers of both hands before his powerful teeth—it was, praise God, inspirational. Lavinia picked at her small helpings, but Hermia ate with more appetite than she had felt in months, mesmerized with goodness.

When LaCourvette brought out the peach cobbler, Mrs. Gibson put her hand on Hermia's, who sat at her left, and asked her how in the world she ended up at Stonewall Hill.

"I've known Miss Emily since I was a girl, and I can't say I'd pick her to talk to every day."

"It's because of a book I'm writing," Hermia said with her mouth full, touching her lips and lowering her fork. "Miss Mary Louise, this peach cobbler is..."

"It's what they mean by hallelujah!" cried Rev. Love, shaking his head. "That's all I got to say. Hallelujah! This company of lovely sisters, this peach cobbler. Praise God for this day. Hallelujah."

Mrs. Gibson wrinkled her eyebrows at him and waved off the compliments. "A book?" she said to Hermia. "About Emily Barron Hayes? Who gone read that?"

"No, ma'am. About women under slavery."

Rev. Love pursed his lips and nodded sagely. Mrs. Gibson sat back, holding her at arm's length, staring at her.

"Women under slavery?"

"Yes, ma'am. Maybe it's silly, but I thought living in a big house like that, working as a kind of servant, would give me some insight. The

132

prominence of the Forrest family, you see? Like a plantation ..."

"I worked in that house when I was a girl," said the old woman, "and I ain't never been nobody's slave."

"Amen," said Rev. Love. "But it takes more than a proclamation to make a people free. Dr. King—"

"Hush on Dr. King and let folks talk," said Lavinia. Rev. Love made a scared face and shrugged and addressed himself to the peach cobbler.

"Mrs. Gibson," Hermia said, "just to be in that situation—having to tend someone, you see? Having someone who relies on me but also has power over me? It helps me understand the ironies of slavery a little better. I've been meaning to ask you, did you know somebody named Aunt Ella? Mrs. Hayes is always calling for Aunt Ella."

Mrs. Gibson started. "She calling for Aunt Ella?" She shook her head and started to say something but checked herself. "How did you happen to light on Miss Emily out of all the mean old white ladies in the South?"

LaCourvette pushed back her chair, excusing herself, and disappeared into the kitchen, where Hermia heard a rattling of pots and pans.

"It's because my mother lives here, Mrs. Gibson," she said. "She grew up in Gallatin."

"And who's your mama, honey?"

"Adara Dernier-Jones. She's married to Dutrelle Jones."

"Fine-looking woman!" said Rev. Love.

"Uh-oh," said Mrs. Love.

"Seen her, haven't met her," Rev. Love said, patting his wife's hand. "But my man Dutrelle! Trainwreck. When I look back, I don't think, my football team won state. I think, I was on the same team as Trainwreck Jones."

But Mrs. Gibson was staring at Hermia, holding up her left hand. After a moment, her right hand, still holding Hermia's, suddenly jerked back and moved on the table as if she were feeling for a lost key in a dark place. Her gaze went glassy and unfocused. She began to stir in her chair, her mouth open.

Rev. Love dropped his fork and started up from his chair

"LaCourvette!" he called. "Come tend to Miss Mary Louise!"

Mrs. Gibson was trying to stand up. LaCourvette appeared at the door, paused, and then went to her grandmother, shaking her head.

"Y'all better go on," she said.

"I hope she's not having a stroke," Lavinia whispered.

"Naw, just one of her spells. Y'all go on."

"We'll clean up."

"No, unh-unh, it's okay. Thank you, honey, but I'll do it later. I hate to run you off, but."

"You want me to call the ambulance?" said Rev. Love, taking a last big bite of cobbler as he stood.

"That's alright. Thank you," said LaCourvette, nodding them toward the door. "That's fine. Thank y'all for coming. I'll take care of it."

The Loves preceded her out the door, whispering their concern, and when Hermia turned to look back, LaCourvette knelt and put her arms around her grandmother and shook her head. Mrs. Gibson rocked back and forth, one hand patting the table, her eyes closed. Hermia's heart pounded painfully in her throat.

"What did I say?"

After a moment, LaCourvette looked up. "Let me get her settled and I'll call you. Okay? I don't know why I got to be the one, but I guess that's how it is."

3

The girls answered Forrest's questions in monosyllables all the way to Macon. He had planned to go somewhere and get a cup of coffee while they were in church, but they claimed to be scared of being abandoned again and insisted he go with them. He found St. Joseph's and sat in the pew beside them as they crossed themselves and knelt and stood on cue, saying the Profession of Faith and all the responses. He listened to the priest's homily, which was about the loaves and the fishes. The priest quoted St. Augustine. The multiplication of the loaves and the fishes wasn't just a miracle. It wasn't just a symbol of the Eucharist. It was also about the spiritual economy of goods that increase by being shared, like love or knowledge or light in a room full of mirrors. Forrest actually found himself interested. It was a kind of gift economy.

Cate insisted on kneeling after Mass to "make her thanksgiving," just like her mother. Bernadette knelt with her.

They said they were hungry, so he took them to a Pizza Hut for lunch. They opened up a little when he asked them how Tricia was doing. Berry wanted to know if he had really dated her in high school.

"She told you that?"

They told him she had been drinking too much since the night he got to town, but in Berry's opinion, it was because she was married to Mr. Davis, who always stood too close and kept putting his arm around Cate whenever he got the chance. Cate said she didn't want to embarrass Bridget, but Mr. Davis gave her the creeps. The girls talked about how it was too bad Bridget looked like him instead of her mother and how Bridget's haircut didn't help, because it made her face look so round. Cate hoped Alyssa was coming to the lake, because she and Berry didn't want to be the only ones in bathing suits in front of Mr. Davis.

To get to Lake Tobesofkee, he had to take I-475 south for twelve or thirteen miles. At first he missed the turn for the Davis lake house and had to backtrack. When he finally found it, a two-story clapboard house with broad open porches, shaded by pines, he pulled into the driveway and saw Judah Davis come out the door in a blue polo shirt and a pair of Bermuda shorts. A yellow belt bisected his great stomach. Hamlike calves rose to slightly concave knees, dimpled like a child's. He was pointing a camcorder at them, pipe clenched in his teeth.

"There's your boyfriend," Berry said to Cate, who hesitated to open the door.

"I hope Alyssa's here," Cate sighed, pulling the handle.

Davis recorded Cate as she opened the door. "Oh my god," she murmured.

"Bridget's been about to bust for y'all to get here," called Humpty Dumpty.

Forrest had intended to drop the girls off without stopping, but he got out of the car and walked over to Davis. Cate glanced back at him apprehensively as she passed her host and went inside. Davis lowered the camera and offered his hand casually, looking back over his shoulder and calling, "Varina, honey? Your friend Mr. Forrest is here." His head snapped around when Forrest took his hand.

"Braxton."

"Braxton," said Davis, trying to match Forrest's grip. "Pleased to meet you." He tried to release the handshake, but Forrest held on as though he had not caught the cue and took Davis's right forearm in his left hand, squeezing it.

"It's mighty nice of you to put up the girls," said Forrest. "I hope they're not too much trouble for you."

"Not at all," said Davis, chuckling and edging backward now, trying to keep up the handshake, his camcorder at shoulder level in his left hand.

"Well you let me know if they are." The squeeze of heartfelt sincerity. "Listen, what kind of camera is that?" The squeeze of alert curiosity.

"Canon Vixia. Best we carry at Wal-Mart," said Davis heartily, trying again to end the handshake.

"Cate tells me you use it a lot." The squeeze of disapprobation.

Davis's eyes flicked toward Forrest's. "Memories for Bridget," he said uneasily, standing rigid, his arm trapped.

"Bridget watches those videos?" Forrest said. The squeeze of inquisition.

"Listen, you're hurting my—"

Just then, Tricia came out of the house dressed like a girl—blue jean cutoffs, a halter top—and watched her husband try to extricate himself from Forrest's grip. She took a sip of her gin and tonic.

"You might want to put the camera away," Forrest said amiably, giving Davis's bones a last little crush before letting go, "while my girls are swimming."

Flexing his fingers sullenly, Davis gingerly put his pipe back in his mouth and avoided Forrest's eyes.

"Pleasure," he said sardonically with a glance at his wife, holding the door for her.

"Tricia, let's talk when you get a chance," Forrest said.

"Hadn't you better get back to your guest?" Tricia said.

"What guest?"

"I don't know. You always have one." She raised her eyebrows at him, lifted her drink as if toasting him, and went inside.

He drove back to town on old U.S. 41, thinking about Judah Davis. Was *he* like that? He wondered about Bill Fletcher's reaction to him. Still, there was nothing unnatural about liking pretty young women, was there? How could he help it, any more than he could help admiring a beautiful tree, or the lines of a landscape, or a great sonnet? The delight of them. A tight-jeaned walking ovule, all love-pollen and aura—the all-at-once form-and-face held out into pure visibility, a blossom of beckoning to be begotten upon. The very look was delectable. And yet if you did consume them, voilà—no harm done.

Good as new. What was the matter with that?

Unless the dean found out.

Or they were his daughters.

4

LaCourvette called just as Hermia let Eumaios in the back door.

"It's me. I'm almost to your house."

"I was just about to change," she said.

"Hold off. I'm pulling in."

Eumaios barked once when he heard a door slam and then started prancing toward the front door. Still in her pink suit from church, LaCourvette came in and knelt to pat him as she always did. Good boy! Good boy! He licked her face as though it were glazed with Mrs. Gibson's peach cobbler. Hermia stood watching with her hands on her hips until her friend stood up.

"Whoo, all I need is a man who feels that way about me," said LaCourvette.

"How's Miss Mary Louise?"

"Taking her nap. She'll be alright, but you shook her up."

"I don't know what I did. I thought about it all the way home. She asked me who my mother was, and I told her Mama was married to Dutrelle Jones."

"That's all it took," said LaCourvette.

"You want some coffee?" she said.

LaCourvette followed her into the kitchen.

"Why would that upset her?" Hermia asked over her shoulder as she filled the electric kettle.

"I'll tell you when we sit down."

"Go on and tell me now." She started the kettle and carefully measured four rounded tablespoons of Kenyan coffee into her French press. When LaCourvette did not speak, she looked around. Her friend had her arms crossed over her chest, and she was staring out the back door. Her stocky little body always looked odd in a dress.

"Are you going to tell me the big secret?"

LaCourvette turned toward her, and the expression on her face shook her. "You want to know so bad, I'll tell you."

Hermia spread her hands. "I do."

"Okay. How's this? Your mama used to be the town whore."

Hermia tilted her head. Behind her on the counter, the water in the kettle roared as it heated. The town whore. The words somehow amused her, and she smiled despite herself. She pictured a grim little puritan town, plain women all in bonnets except for the floozy Marilyn Harkins.

"You don't even care?" LaCourvette said.

"It just sounds so funny. *The town whore.* Do you mean she slept around?"

"No, baby, I mean she walked the streets at night shaking her booty and white men picked her up and took her out and did their business."

Did their business. She laughed out loud.

"It's funny to you?"

"Sort of. The way you put it."

"Well, it's not funny. She got syphilis and turned in a long list of names to the county health people, and it almost got her killed. You ask anybody if they remember Marilyn. Just say the name. She was famous. But listen, don't nobody except Miss Mary Louise and me know Dutrelle Jones's wife used to be Marilyn Harkins. Even Dutrelle don't know it."

"You're saying she was the *town whore* in Gallatin,"—another explosion of giggles—"and Dutrelle doesn't know it? Girl, that's too much."

"Baby, you better sit down and think about what I'm saying."

The kettle roared, the water came to a boil, and the automatic switch turned it off. By habit she poured the water over the coffee in the French press and set the timer on the stove for four minutes.

Her mother was the town whore? It was just ridiculous.

"The town whore. Whore, really? Is that the word?"

"You the one had to know," her friend said. "I told you I didn't want to say."

"It's just that word. I just can't get it to fit my mama."

"Well you pick one. She only went out with white men. Any white man, free of charge, like it was her honor and privilege to serve them."

"Stop it."

"You ask your professor. Braxton Forrest. He knew your mama in those days. He thought he got her killed."

"Braxton Forrest?"

"I mean knew like they say know in the Bible. You just ask him."

"Oh my God. Braxton Forrest?"
"Now. Now you hearing me."

5

There was no traffic around the square except for a few cars at the restaurant where the Gallatin County Bank had been. It was after 3:00 when he pulled into Cousin Emily Barron Hayes' driveway and saw, good lord, Maya Davidson's BMW behind Hermia's Prius in the driveway. He saw the two women in the front yard, looking toward him. Maya was holding a notebook, and she had on a dark T-shirt and white shorts. At least her bruises were covered. Hermia was in her Sunday clothes.

Dread of what he had told Maya, much less what he had done to her, came over him again. Her very presence near Marilyn Harkins' daughter alarmed him. What could she possibly be doing here? Hermia's arms were crossed tightly over her chest and she looked at the ground and shook her head when Maya said something to her. They moved slowly toward him past the overgrown azaleas and down some old stone steps on the slope toward the back driveway.

He got out of the car.

"Maya. I didn't expect to see you here."

"I bet you didn't."

Somewhere back toward town, a dog started barking so fiercely they all turned their heads. Then Maya looked back at him.

"I've been doing some research," she said.

"How are you, Hermia?"

Standing behind Maya, arms still crossed, she glanced up at him with hot eyes. Good god. He focused again on Maya, dreading what she would say.

"Doing some research," he repeated.

Up the street, the dog's barking took on a new insistence.

"Your grandfather owned this estate, so I wanted to see it," she said. "That's how I met Miss Watson. I've been asking her a few questions."

"About what?"

"About my mother," Hermia said sharply. She looked like a teenager, sullen and hurt, her mouth a little open, twisting into defiance. She turned toward the house to walk away.

"Your mother?" Maya called after her.

Hermia lifted a hand despairingly and broke into a stumbling run. She opened the back door and disappeared inside, letting it slam behind her. Up the street, the dog yelped, panicking. It was being attacked by someone or something.

"My god," said Maya, turning to look in that direction again. Its cry took on an almost human sound—high, abject, unbearable. "We should do something."

Just then, the dog's cries abruptly stopped. After a moment, the Sunday afternoon peace resumed. Very faintly, they could hear old Mrs. Hayes calling for Hermia.

"Get in the car," Forrest said.

She stared at him, her eyes widening.

"I thought she was just a caregiver," said Maya. "I told her I was supposed to meet you for an interview. I said I was a reporter doing a story on you."

"Get in the car, Maya."

"I'm sorry. I didn't expect to see you again. Why do you want me to get in the car?"

"I want to talk to you."

"Please don't kill me."

She was actually terrified.

"I'm not going to kill you."

She stared at him and then got in the car. As they drove through town, he snorted, "A reporter? Why would anybody be doing a story on me?"

"You're sort of famous. What was I supposed to say? That I was the one you sent into cardiac arrest? So I said you'd mentioned a friend of yours named Marilyn Harkins who was prominent in the African-American community."

"That's the word you used?" he said. "*Prominent?*"

"Just to see how she reacted. I couldn't understand why she was so rattled. She asked me what I'd heard, so I started giving her a few more details and asking her if she knew anything about your involvement with her, because you had said it was such an important part of your early life."

"You told her that?"

"I did. I didn't know it was her mother! How would I know that?"

"Okay, okay."

"Oh, by the way—I almost forgot. I read the review of your book by that biologist, Nathan Bragg."

He sighed. Nathan Bragg again. "I never said I was doing science."

"But I guess it's sort of a classic? 'The Wreck of the Gameme: Hucksterism and the Humanities.' He made you look like—."

"There's a story behind that, Maya. He'd been dating Marisa at Georgia before I met her."

"But the Charlie Rose—that was seriously awesome. You nailed Obama."

"It got me a second edition after the election. And another book contract. Listen," he said after a moment. "I'm sorry about the other night."

She nodded. "So can you talk about it? Can you tell me why you almost killed me?"

"About Marilyn?"

She nodded. Her arms were crossed on her chest, her hands squeezing her bruised shoulders. A silk ribbon encircled her neck. Her hoard of rings, he guessed, nestled between her breasts. This little monster he'd drawn to himself. Her expression was strange, fearfully curious, as though she needed to hear what he said, as though it would explain something to her about who she was, whoever she really was, if she was anyone. He almost pitied her.

"In the summer of 1969," he said, "I worked on a surveying crew."

6

Mo Woodson opened the driver's side door and stepped out tentatively, testing the snakeskin inside his boots. They were at the end of a logging road that took them as close as they were going to get to the line they were traversing. The river was still a quarter of a mile ahead of them across terrain that was boggy and dense with thickets, alive with mosquitos. The humidity brought out a slick of sweat on Forrest's skin as soon as the truck stopped. When they were getting out the equipment, a gust shook the trees, and Mo licked his forefinger to hold it up. "Get them bush hooks sharpened. We got to work quick. The wind's coming up out of the southwest."

Tony Wright gave Forrest a warning nudge. "What does that mean, Unca Mo?"

Mo stood there in his black T-shirt, slowly polishing his Zippo on his stomach, and regarded his wife's nephew. "What does what mean?"

"Wind coming out of the southwest."

"You watch, you'll see what it means."

"You know that weatherman down in Macon? Got that bow tie, all them charts and radar and whatnot? He needs to know about your finger."

Mo gazed at him with his yellow eyes and showed him another finger.

The thunderstorm came up before lunchtime, and they had to make a run for it back through the woods with the rain coming up fast and lightning popping down into the tops of the trees across the river. Mo had the transit wrapped in his shirt, and all of them were ducking like men being shelled. Forrest sprinted ahead with the chain, the water jug, and his bush hook, and when he was throwing them in the back of the truck, he heard Wright yelling. Fifty yards back, he saw him swiping at himself with his bush hook and running in odd stops and starts. As soon as he got into the clearing, Wright flung down the bush hook, and started brushing his pants legs frantically, yelling at Forrest, "You see any more of them on me?" He peeled off his shirt like a man trying to turn himself inside out and swatted at his pants with the cloth. "I was standing in a fucking nest! I got hung up on some barbed wire."

Mo was inside the cab unscrewing the transit from the top of the tripod, and once he got it safely in its box, he got out to stow it in the back. He saw Wright still bent over, brushing down his pants legs.

"Get in the truck, dumbass!" In a great explosion of thunder, lightning split a tree a hundred yards back down toward the river. They scrambled into the cab and Mo started down the old road as the first big drops of rain hit the windshield. Another huge clap of thunder made them all cringe. Wright was holding up a finger.

"What?" Mo said.

"Yellow jacket got him," said Forrest. Wright's face was getting blotchy, his eyes puffy; his nose was running faster than he could wipe it; his breath came in a rattle.

"Sweet Jesus," Mo said.

"Get me. Hospital!" Wright wheezed.

"Jesus God Almighty," said Mo, as though he were praying, suddenly serious. "We're ten miles from town." He hit the brakes. "You drive," he told Forrest. "Drive like hell."

They switched seats. Lightning blazed again close by, and Forrest bounced from the logging road up onto the highway in a blinding rain. He had to creep along until they got to the intersection near Glenn's Bait Store, where he turned right, the rain gradually lightening, and raced toward Gallatin. He passed a slow-moving pickup truck, horn blaring, and gunned it down a long clear stretch, seventy, eighty, ninety miles an hour, leaving the storm behind, topping a hill so fast they almost left the ground. Wright had slumped over, half-conscious, pale, breathing in great rattling gasps. "Hang in there, son," Mo said, holding Wright's forehead. "Hang in there. Jesus help me, hang in there."

When they finally got to the city limits sign, they tore past the old country church and rounded the long curve to the Interstate. Forrest leaned on the horn, flashing his bright lights. He accelerated up Foster Drive to the courthouse square, ran red lights all the way around, blasting the horn, then headed downhill on Main Street, passing the slow cars, barreling down the middle of the road and forcing the oncoming traffic aside. He slowed, turned left onto Colville Street toward the hospital—two police cars chasing him by now—and skidded to a halt outside the emergency room. Mo was already lifting Wright out of the cab and carrying him through the entrance like a sick child. "He got stung and he's allergic!" he was yelling as soon as they got inside. "He needs one of them shots!"

Nurses ran toward Wright and an orderly got him on a gurney. His breath came in a labored wheeze. Seconds later, the new doctor Forrest did not know came out with a syringe and plunged it into Wright's arm. The nurse took his blood pressure and shook her head. "It's still too low," she said. The doctor—the metal bar over his shirt pocket said Raymond Carvel, M.D.—gave Wright another shot, and they waited. After a few minutes, his breathing began to be easier, and when the nurse took another reading, she looked up and said, "Thank God."

"Too close," said Dr. Carvel. Mo and Forrest stood over Wright, who lay there pallid and unconscious, his forefinger twice its usual size, his breath still rattling in his chest. Outside, they could hear the thunder crashing. The lights flickered but stayed on.

"Good God Almighty," Mo said, smoothing his left hand over his slicked head and reaching into his pocket for a cigarette. "I like to prayed."

"How come you didn't want to drive?" Forrest asked.

Mo shook his head. He was raising his Zippo to the Winston when the nurse told him he'd have to go to the waiting room to smoke. Mo nodded and snapped the lighter two or three times.

"You go on out. We'll let you know when he wakes up," she said. She glanced at their muddy jeans, their boots. Forrest was still wearing his plumb bob holster. "Where were y'all?"

"Out on the Ocmulgee," said Mo.

Dr. Carvel gave a low whistle. "I'm surprised you got him here alive. A few more minutes, you wouldn't have."

"Braxton here broke a few laws," Mo said, not seeing the two policemen who had stepped into the room. One of them was the new black officer hired by the city.

"Braxton Forrest?" asked Dr. Carvel, looking up at him. "I've heard of you." He offered his hand and Forrest shook it.

"You were the one driving?" asked the white police officer.

"Yes sir."

"He saved this boy's life," said the doctor.

"You scared half the county to death," said the white one. "But there it is, I guess. If you saved this fellow's life."

He offered his hand, and Forrest shook it.

"Come on," groaned Wright from the bed. "Mo won't get a lick of work out of him y'all keep telling him he saved my life."

They laughed, and the doctor patted Wright on the knee and told the nurse they'd better keep him a few hours for observation.

"Hey Mo," wheezed Wright. Mo turned back. "You didn't get snakebit, did you? That skin worked."

"More of your bullshit."

"Are you going to keep this job?" the doctor asked Wright.

"Damn right."

"Then we need to get you a kit. Epinephrine and a syringe. Can you give a shot?" he asked Mo.

"Did it in the Army."

"Let's get it right now," Dr. Carvel told the nurse. "Make up a kit—epinephrine, two new syringes, alcohol swabs. How about you?" he asked Forrest. "Can you give a shot?"

Forrest said he'd never done it, and Dr. Carvel had the nurse show him how to tap the syringe, how to push the air out. "Just a quick jab like you're piercing an orange and then press the plunger slow and steady," she said.

When the men were leaving the room, Forrest was the last one out. "Hey," Wright said.

Forrest turned to him.

"You just ate that shit up," Wright said. "All you did was drive the truck. I don't owe you."

"Who said you did?" asked Forrest.

"I don't owe you a fucking thing."

The next day when they got to the office to check in with Brother before heading out to the river, Mo got out of his Cutlass with a white plastic first aid kit. He called them over and opened it on his hood to show them: Band-Aids, Merthiolate, gauze, the vial of epinephrine, two syringes, and alcohol swabs.

"Now you chirren can get cuts and scrapes, and you can get stung all you want to, you dumb shit," he said to Wright. "It looks like you would of told me you were allergic to yellow jackets. I thought I was going to have to explain to your Aunt Paloma how we killed you your second week on the job."

"Yeah," he said, "but this way you got to explain to her how hero here saved my life."

Wright stared at Forrest, and then the sides of his mouth went down and he held out his hand to shake, as if in reconciliation. As soon as he had Forrest's hand, he squeezed it, intending to make him wince, but Forrest easily matched him and casually stepped up the pressure.

"How's that finger feeling?"

"Okay," said Wright, his face flushing with rage as Forrest kept going. "Okay, asshole. Let go, let go."

"What the hell?" asked Mo, pulling their hands apart and shoving Wright away, not looking at Forrest. "What's the matter with you?"

He met Marilyn the day after Neil Armstrong and Buzz Aldrin landed on the moon—the weird hop that Armstrong took from the ladder, the gleaming white spacesuits, the strange, low-budget look of the moon itself. "That's one... small step for man [crackle], one giant leap for mankind." He'd wondered even at the time whether Armstrong muffed the line. "That's one small step for *a* man" made more sense, even though it tripped up the rhythm. Otherwise, what was the difference between man and mankind? Still, all of it had been part of the spectacular surge into the sky that began under JFK. The list of heroic names: Alan Shepard, John Glenn orbiting the earth, the fated Gus Grissom, Frank Borman reading the first chapter of Genesis that Christmas of 1968—that year of assassinations, protests, bloody riots—as the earth rose sublimely over the horizon of the moon. It had been the great drama of the age, the greatest accomplishment since Columbus: the tremendous Saturn V rocket, the gantries dropping away in the massive explosion of rocket fuel, the privileged spectators who watched the launch on Merritt Island, the horn-rimmed glamour of Mission Control in Houston.

In the truck that Monday morning, Mo had the radio turned to a country station, but the songs had been preempted by the moon landing. The network played Kennedy's speech from 1961 challenging America to land on the moon by the end of the decade, and the disc jockeys kept bragging that the United States had done it when Russia was nowhere close.

"Damn right we did it," said Mo. "Did it despite LBJ putting the niggers in our schools."

"What's that got to do with it?" Forrest said.

On the radio, Richard Nixon was talking about how proud America was of its astronauts. Mo turned it down. "You look down there at NASA. This was white people knowing how to do things. It sure as hell wasn't no Martin Luther King. It was Wiener Braun."

"Wernher von Braun," said Forrest. "Why do you have to turn landing on the moon into a race thing?"

"I'm just stating facts about who done what," said Mo. "Wiener was a Nazi but they didn't care because he was the one coming up with rockets. V-2s—if we hadn't of got Wiener first, it'd be Boris and Nikita up there on the moon planting the hammer and sickle."

"You know Hitler's mistress?" Wright said. "Wiener was her brother."

"He's Wernher von Braun," said Forrest. "She was Eva Braun, no relation." But he had once thought the same thing.

"It's just to hide it they stuck that in that von thing," Wright said.

"Bullshit."

They rode along in silence for a few minutes.

"The niggers don't believe we landed on the moon," said Wright.

Mo sighed and opened his palm like a man letting the ripe, simple truth drop into his hand. "It was on TV," he said. "It was right there in front of your fucking eyes, just like Jack Ruby shooting Oswald."

"I said niggers don't believe it."

"Yeah, but what you mean is *you* don't believe it."

Just then, a black cat dashed across the highway immediately in front of them. Mo cursed, and he was already leaning up to make an X on the windshield when a running form flashed down the red clay bank, off balance, trying to stop. He slammed on the brakes, but Forrest heard a thump against the side of the truck.

"God Almighty!" Mo yelled. He slammed on the brakes and pulled off the road, already scrambling from the cab when he threw it in neutral and pushed the parking brake. Forrest and Wright were right behind him. They found a little black boy lying curled in the ditch amid the dandelions and daisy fleabane. Mo knelt over him. "Son?" he said. "Oh Jesus Lord, wake up, son."

The little boy did not move. He could not have been more than six or seven, and he was wearing nothing but a pair of dirty briefs. Forrest stared down at him, numb, unable to connect his emotions. His head jerked up when he heard a sudden wail, a terrible sound. Up the slope to the right was a tin-roofed house, hardly more than a shack. A large black woman stood on the porch, her hand at her throat, and then she rushed down the steps. An old yellow dog loped toward them well ahead of her. He picked his way gingerly down the bank and limped over, wagging his tail. When he sniffed the boy and licked his face, the boy groaned and stirred. Mo looked up at the sky and ran his hand over his hair. The boy sat up groggily and put his arm around the dog. When he noticed the three men over him, he scrambled back, his mouth open.

"Does anything hurt you, son?" Mo asked gently. "You don't look like you're bleeding. Can you stand up?"

The boy gaped at him. By this time, the woman was running down the slope calling "Lester! Lester, oh my Jesus!"

"Your name's Lester?" Mo asked the boy.

"Yessir."

"Like the governor?" asked Forrest, but the boy looked at him blankly.

"Try to stand up," Mo said. He stood and offered his hand and the boy took it and stood up and cried out, grabbing his left hip and hopping. By the time his mother reached them, he was limping around in a circle.

"Jesus! Thank you, Jesus!" she cried, a big woman in a plain cotton dress, her massive breasts loose under the cloth. Out of breath, her face shining with tears, she flapped her left hand on her heart and kept repeating, "I thought I done lost him."

"Yessum, it was a scare," Mo said. "He come barreling down that bank. He was trying to stop but he couldn't and he just bounced off the side of the truck."

"Mama, where Midnight at? You see Midnight?" the boy said.

"Midnight!" she said, suddenly furious. "You chasing that goddamn cat? You almost get yourself killed for that cat?" She slapped him hard on the back of the head, and he let out a wail. "Get up in the house fore I tear you up." He ducked another slap and scrambled, limping, up the bank, the old dog beside him, and his mother climbed after them, still railing at him.

"Close," Wright said, when they got back in the cab.

Mo sat there with his head bent for a long time. Then he licked his finger and made nine neat Xs like a tic-tac-toe grid with no Os in the top left corner of the windshield.

"I don't believe I'd claim that one," Wright said. "Not when he could walk off."

Mo started the engine.

"Fighter pilot, he only puts up kills," Wright said.

Mo stared straight ahead. He turned the engine back off.

"'O Jesus Lord, wake up, son,'" Wright mocked.

Mo turned toward him with his yellow eyes, and Wright held his stare for a few seconds, and then looked out the window. "Saying 'yessum' to that mammy. Shit, you as bad a nigger lover as hero here."

"Paloma told me your daddy was a worthless piece of shit," said Mo. "I was hoping you didn't take after him."

"Don't talk about my daddy."

"Man was pure scum. A worthless murdering piece of shit," Mo repeated, "which is why they fried the son-of-a-bitch in the chair over at Reidsville."

The two men stared each other in the eye until finally Wright turned aside.

"Ain't we going to work?"

That night, he pulled into Tricia's driveway and she came out the door before he could go up to get her. He was driving his mother's Bonneville with the bench seats. Instead of coming over to kiss him as soon as they were out of sight of her house, she kept to her side of the car. When he tried to pull her closer, she squirmed back against the door.

"No, sir," she said, and something about the way she looked at him was suddenly cloying.

"Come on, Tricia." As they rode through town, he told her about the little boy and Tony Wright's peculiar venom. She nodded, she sympathized, but when he took her hand and tried to pull her to him, she would not relent. He asked her if she was having her period.

"No," she said. "No, I'm not having my period." She gave an enigmatic smile.

He shrugged and turned his head, annoyed at her reluctance, and just then—just as they were crossing the railroad tracks near the college—he saw Marilyn in the shadows of the sidewalk. It was just after dusk, and all he could see was the white fishnet dress she wore, like a net strained against the body of a swimming naiad the color of the water.

All he wanted at that moment was to get rid of Tricia Honeycutt.

He told her he was sorry, he was still shaken up from the accident that morning, he was going home. He stopped at her house two minutes later, walked her to the door—on fire to leave her—and remembered now the look of perplexity as he turned away.

"Braxton?" she called after him, worried now. "Braxton?"

Tricia evaporated from his mind as he sped through town toward that fishnet dress in the dark. Marilyn had not gone far. She had just reached the long curve beyond the south gate of the college when he slowed the car to match her pace and leaned toward the window. Night swallowed her skin. When she turned, her smile broke from its element of darkness.

"Need a ride?" he said, dry-mouthed.

She stopped walking and he stopped the car and she reached in to take his hand. Her smooth, dry fingers, her lovely feline face. "If you desire," she said, and it was a voice purged of black dialect, purged of the South, purged almost of America itself, full of an idea of sophistication and artifice. South American or Egyptian or Babylonian.

"I do desire," he said.

She glanced back toward town, where a pair of distant headlights had appeared. "We should meet on the side street." She pointed to the next intersection, a street between the side yards of houses facing College Drive. "Would you go around the block and come back for me there?" He nodded, and she was already walking, those hips now just for him. He went down a block and turned right, right again, his heart hammering, then right again and saw her just off the street, standing still. When he pulled up beside her, she opened the back door and got in.

"Sit in the front," he said.

"Don't be silly," she said, closing the door. She gave his neck a light stroke with the tips of her nails. "You should take me out of town."

Her perfume in the car was strong. As soon as they reached College Drive, she bent down so no one he passed could see her. Men like Mo must have taught her to do it.

"Sit up here in the front seat beside me. You don't need to hide," he said. "I believe in racial equality."

"You do?" She laughed as though he had said he believed in Santa Claus, but the sound of it was polished. She must have practiced until she sounded naturally melodious. "Otis told me to expect you."

"Who's Otis?"

"I know you work with him. I already know your name. You're famous."

Mo's pseudonym. "So did Otis tell you Bertram Everett quit?"

She laughed again from the back seat. "Poor little Bertram."

They passed the Lee Ford dealership with its bright sign, crossed the bridge over the Interstate, and left behind the shabby houses just inside the city limits. He started to say something, but before he could speak, she had already flowed over the seat back, and she sat where Tricia had been only minutes before. He pulled her to his side. She was elegant, more than unfamiliar in her blackness, almost alien, this body against his. His head was light. He had the feeling that simply by touching her he would never again find the way home to Gallatin and his mother's house. She ran a fingernail down his forearm and dropped her hand lightly to his thigh.

"Where you taking me, baby?" she whispered, and her accent had lost its polish.

7

After Forrest left with the reporter from Atlanta, Hermia stood just inside the screen door, staring out at the BMW in the driveway. The sheer insult of the little bitch. "Can I just leave my car here until we finish the interview?" she had called, and Hermia had not missed the proprietary way she touched Forrest's arm. They already had something going on. Like what he'd had going on with her mother.

Her mother, the town whore.

Maya something. Davis, maybe? Maya Davis? Maya and not Maia, because Hermia had asked how it was spelled while they were doing a tour of the grounds.

"Mama named me after Maya Angelou, can you imagine?" the girl had laughed, touching her arm. "I guess she must have felt like a caged bird, who knows? But seriously, a white girl from Cuthbert, Georgia, named after Maya Angelou!"

And now Maya's car was blocking Hermia's Prius. She would have to pull forward and saw back and forth in the space between the back stoop and the BMW and the outbuildings just to get turned around, and then she would have to inch past the insult of it just to get out and go home.

Forrest had told Maya things Hermia would never even have suspected. He thought Marilyn had been murdered, because he had seen a bloody dress he knew was hers nailed to a tree beside the river. He was

148

sure that men angry at her mother had killed her to avenge their shame and exposure.

"He's obsessed with it," Maya had said. "I mean, like there's something else going on. That's what I want to find out."

Hermia asked where she intended to publish it, and Maya said, "Publish it?"

As soon as Hermia got home, she was going to google her. There was something strange about her. She had kept touching Hermia, and it made her realize how long it had been since anybody had touched her, anybody at all, and that depressed her. Local men had swarmed around her at first, but then they'd been put off by her. Her wit came out in deadly force around the ignoramuses of Gallatin, Georgia. They tried to make conversation, but her allusions to the simplest things completely baffled them, things she thought anybody would know: if not Philip Glass, then surely, say, Anselm Kiefer.

No? Well, you've heard of William Faulkner. You haven't? Alice Walker? From Eatonton. No? Flannery O'Connor from Milledgeville? No?

They knew Otis Redding and the Allman Brothers and football. After a month (this was LaCourvette telling her), she had the reputation of an ice queen.

She sighed and went upstairs to check on Mrs. Hayes. The old woman was leaning forward, raking the air with her hand as she looked out the window.

"Can I bring you something?" Hermia asked.

"What? What?" she cried, wrenching herself around. "What do you want now?"

"Nothing, Mrs. Hayes. I'm about to go home for the day, and I'm just checking to see if you need anything before I go."

Mrs. Hayes drew back her head suspiciously. "I don't know what you think you're going to get out of me. I don't care what you do. Do what you want."

"Then I'm going home."

"Well, go home, then, if you have a home. It seems to me like you're always here pestering me."

Hermia shook her head and left the room and made her way downstairs and out to her car. One of the bad days: it was useful only in helping her feel what it would be like to endure a permanent regime of humiliation. Several months ago, it would have stung her to tears, but now it was nothing—especially next to the insult of Maya Davis's knowledge about her mother. She had known all about things that Hermia herself never even suspected until LaCourvette told her.

Davidson, not Davis. Like the department store in Macon when she was a little girl.

She got in her Prius and managed to turn it around and squeeze past the sexy little BMW. What else had Forrest told her about Marilyn

Harkins? LaCourvette said no one in town besides Miss Mary Louise recognized Adara Dernier-Jones as Marilyn Harkins. But all the old people remembered who Marilyn was. Just say the name, she said, just say *Marilyn*, and they would go still and wary.

Hermia didn't want to think about it, but she couldn't stop. Not knowing for her whole life—her whole life—who her mother actually was. She had been in Gallatin for how long and didn't know until now? Since before the election. LaCourvette had tried to tell her before. One night when they had been drinking wine on the sofa and laughing like schoolgirls, LaCourvette had gone very serious. She had pushed a bare foot into the side of Hermia's thigh. *I got something I need to tell you, baby.* About what? *About your mama, baby.* Girl, what could you possibly know about my mama? You must have been talking to Gloria Jones. *No, now listen. Gloria Jones can't stand that Dutrelle left his family to marry her. You not gone listen to me?* Have some more wine. Somebody told me your daddy is that man down at the filling station across from the high school.

That had shut her up.

But now to have it come on her all at once. She wanted to go home and not get out of bed for a week. Tell all the truth, but tell it slant? Not LaCourvette. That girl got right to it: Your mama was the town whore. It could have been eased to her, but LaCourvette resented being forced to tell her at all, so it was harsh, blazing, blinding. Like seeing Matthew Gunn in bed with that boy. Like being fourteen and standing over Daddy Loum's coffin two days after he convulsed and died on top of her, visiting what he called her "little sweetness."

She was stronger now. She could stand it. In the summer of 1969 Marilyn Harkins discovered that she had syphilis, LaCourvette had told her. The county health officials made her reveal all her sexual partners. The list ran to over 150, many of them prominent citizens of Gallatin, none of them black. She never took money, but she refused herself to no one—no one white. The irony of it, the crushing and unbearable irony, was that everyone in town knew that Braxton Forrest was her lover.

She had to tell her mother that Forrest was in town. It would mean telling her what else she knew about her.

Mama, I found out who you used to be.

What do you mean, baby? I'm your mama. I've always been who I am right now.

Even when you were Marilyn Harkins?

What would her mother say to that? She could not begin to guess. Maybe she would deny everything and turn it back on her, the way she had seen her do with complaints about Daddy Loum when she was little. Maybe she would just laugh and wave her hand and say Oh so what? All that business was all a long time ago.

She called on the way to tell her mother to expect her.

Taste was certainly not Dutrelle's forte. Her mother, who had taste, whatever else might be wrong with her, had wanted a modern home that fit the hillside above Scalp Creek, but this one was pure Dutrelle. Once he fell under her spell and left his wife for Adara Dernier, he insisted on changing her plans and building her something that spoke to his imagination of power and pride. It vaguely resembled Greek revival. Two white columns projected out over the driveway: she always thought of walrus tusks. Her mother had laughed when Hermia first mentioned it to her, but she had also said never, never to criticize the house to Dutrelle.

Adara Dernier-Jones answered the door in a white tank top, a pair of white shorts, and no shoes. She looked forty-five at most, hardly older than Hermia herself, and she held a martini as though she were celebrating her contract extension with Mephistopheles. For a woman almost sixty, she was uncanny, a little terrifying. She took a sip and gave Hermia the once-over and shook her head.

"Sugar," she said, "what man in his right mind could pass you up?" She reached out and touched Hermia's cheek. "The looks I gave you and no husband? No children? You can't be trying."

"Mama, how do you know I don't have children? Besides, I'm not trying. I'm writing a book."

"Writing a book," she said dismissively. "Come on in the house. What's on your mind tonight?"

"Braxton Forrest is in town," Hermia said.

The drink fell from her mother's hand and shattered on the pebbled surface outside the door.

She started to step backward, but Hermia grabbed her arm to keep her from cutting herself. Her mother gazed blankly down at the glass, and then turned to look over her shoulder into the house, where Hermia could hear the sounds of a baseball game. When she turned back to Hermia, her face registered each new level of speculation.

"How do you know him?" her mother asked in a small voice.

"Oh, Mama," she said, surprised by pity. "He came by Stonewall Hill yesterday to see Mrs. Hayes."

"Does he know I'm in Gallatin?"

"Yes, ma'am, but—"

Her mother reeled away from her and immediately cried out. When she lifted her foot, blood welled out and ran down the instep across the ball. Great red drops fell from her toes onto the pebbled surface. Hermia clutched at her arm.

"'S going on?" Dutrelle Jones loomed on the threshold in a bathing suit and flip-flops, his huge, heavily-muscled upper body full of tattoos and scars, a slight pot belly beginning to show. He saw the cut and picked up his wife as if she were a child.

"Damn, baby. That's bad," he said. Adara pouted up at him and nodded. "We don't want blood dripping all over your carpet, do we baby?" She shook her head like a child. He glanced at Hermia. "How 'bout some paper towels?" She started toward the kitchen. "And get some ice," he called after her.

When she came back with a roll of towels and a plastic bag of ice, Dutrelle wrapped her mother's foot and carried her down a hallway decorated with NFL photographs toward the bathroom. He set her down on the lip of the sunken tub and ran cold water over her foot. Runnels of diluted blood swirled into the drain.

"I ought to spank your fanny," he said. "Dropping that good martini I made you. You want to go to emergency?"

Her mother shook her head and leaned against him. Hermia lifted her mother's foot to set it on the ice she had wrapped in a paper towel. When she glanced up at Dutrelle, she saw his eyes assessing her. She saw the slight protrusion of his lower lip.

"Dutrelle," her mother said, "go on back to your game. My little girl can tend to me."

"You sure? Everybody says you high-maintenance."

She made a mouth, and he raised both hands and left the room. When the door clicked behind him, her mother's brow clouded. She still would not look at Hermia.

"Mama, press your foot down on it," she said. Her mother obeyed her. She had beautiful feet, and Hermia said so and squeezed her ankle before she sat back up.

"Mama," she said, not looking at her face. "I heard today about...about what you did when you were young."

Her mother moaned softly and began to rock from side to side.

"Did you do that, Mama? Go out with all those men?"

After a moment, without looking up, her mother nodded.

"My god. Oh my god. Why? Why would you do that?"

Her mother murmured something.

"What did you say?"

She went still and spoke distinctly. "I said, because I liked it."

For seconds, Hermia sat as though she had not heard. Then indignation boiled across her abdomen, just under her ribs, and she felt the heat in her neck, her ears.

"You liked it? What kind of answer is that?"

Her mother shook her head and made a small frown, as though at her daughter's disrespect. She lifted her foot from the ice and the blood dripped again.

"They could make me go to school. Deacon Ray Watts, he could make me go to church and sit there next to his fat ass on that pew," she said, "but nobody made me go out at night. That was mine. That was what I did that nobody else did."

Hermia watched her. "My god, Mama."

Her mother's head came up. "What do you know about it?" she asked bitterly. "What do you think you're so wise about?"

"I think I understand something about humiliation, mama. The kind of degradation that it must have been for you. The kind of self-loathing it must have come from."

He mother laughed. "Degradation! I'm talking about glory, baby. I'm talking about the big white men in town scared to death of me. I'm talking about famous."

"But your own people must have hated you."

"My own people? Who are my own people?"

"You know what I mean."

"You don't know nothing about it. Nothing."

Suddenly the emotion broke from Hermia. "Well, you could tell me!" she cried. "All my life you've been hiding things from me. There were all these secrets I wasn't supposed to understand. Why don't you tell me if I don't know?"

"It's too complicated to tell. There are things you just don't tell your children."

Hermia wiped her tears self-consciously, appalled at her mother's hardness.

"He thought you were dead."

"Who?"

"Braxton Forrest."

Now her mother looked up into her eyes, her face full of hurt and accusation. "How do you know what he thought?"

"I talked to him."

"You talked to him about me?" she cried. "What call did you have to do that? That man is none of your business."

"Oh, Mama," said Hermia. "He is. I'm the reason he's here."

Her mother's hand went to her heart. "What do you mean?"

"I knew him before. I wrote to him. I used to love him, back when—"

"Shut your mouth!" her mother cried, and it was a moment before Hermia even realized she had been slapped. Her mother's eyes went wide, and then she put her hand on Hermia's knee and leaned over the tub and gagged. Hermia was suddenly sobbing.

"He wants to see you, Mama. Probably tomorrow."

"O Lord Jesus! O Lord!"

The door behind them opened, and Dutrelle came back in.

"Let's go to the hospital."

"I'm alright. I'm okay."

"Y'all louder than the ballgame. What's going on?"

"Nothing, Dutrelle," her mother said.

"That's some mighty loud nothing."

"It's none of your business!" cried Hermia. "I'm talking to my mother."

Dutrelle's face went cold. His mouth tightened and he pointed his finger at Hermia. "Don't tell me my business in my own house."

"Dutrelle," said her mother.

"You listening to me, bitch?"

"Don't you call my daughter a bitch," said her mother.

"She don't tell me my business," he said. He slammed the door.

"Don't mind him," her mother said miserably. "He can't make his bank note, and they're talking about foreclosing on him."

When Hermia got up, her mother turned toward her from where she sat, trembling and hugging herself.

"What do you mean you used to love him?"

"After Matthew. He came to Northwestern, and then I went to a conference in Providence. It wasn't long, it was just—"

"You can't love him," she said, and suddenly she leaned over and vomited into the bathtub between her feet. When Hermia tried to help, her mother waved her away.

"Go on. Tell Dutrelle I need to go to the emergency room."

"I can—"

"I said go on," her mother said savagely, and Hermia burst into tears.

"I'm sorry, Mama," Hermia said from the door. "I don't know who you are."

As she stumbled away, she heard her mother calling her back. She went and stood in the doorway. Her white shorts and top speckled with blood, the woman sat there slumped forward, her arms hanging loose. She began to tip to one side.

"Dutrelle!" Hermia shouted, and her mother started and looked up at her.

"Call me tomorrow," murmured Marilyn. Then Dutrelle shouldered past Hermia and scooped her up again.

She sobbed intermittently all the way home. Whatever she had expected, it wasn't this. She had innocently let Forrest know Marilyn Harkins was her mother and that she was alive. Now he would insist on seeing her. He hadn't said he wanted to see her, but it had to happen. In the meantime, what was she going to tell him if she saw him again? And she would, she had to see him, now that he knew she was Lola Gunn, because he would know she sent the letters.

She would have to explain everything to him, the whole story, as much as she could reasonably tell. He would start grilling her. *Mother and daughter? Seriously? You're Marilyn Harkins daughter?* Well, I didn't know her name was Marilyn. And for years I thought her maiden name was Perkins. *Who was your father?* A black undertaker from

Macon. He was in his fifties when he married her. *When was that?* In 1969, I think. After she left Gallatin.

Hermia's emotions flattened and grew shy even at the prospect of telling her story. Dignified Corvell Watson—Daddy Watson—had given her life and a name, but she had always been a little scared of him. She had drawn back from his touch after a boy at school told her what he did to dead people. He was always kind to her anyway. He sat with her on the nights her mother went out on errands.

Errands.

Good god, of course.

Daddy Watson's heart attack the night of the big bus accident left her mother a young and moderately wealthy widow. She remembered her mother's barely suppressed merriment after the funeral.

"Now listen, baby," Marilyn said to Hermia's earnest young teacher, who wore big round glasses and had permanent worry-lines in her forehead. "If you ever marry an undertaker, just remember he wants you to play possum." Hermia remembered not understanding what she meant, but she remembered the words exactly, because she wanted to know what put that look, first of puzzlement, then of horrified embarrassment, on her teacher's face.

He wants you to play possum.

A chill spread through her.

Marilyn married Daddy Loum within two months and they moved to his big house in Atlanta. How did she even meet him? Number two of the first three, he was a short, powerful Senegalese man with a broad smile and a gregarious nature. A full professor of French literature at Morehouse, he enrolled Hermia in a Catholic school, where she was one of the first black students. Her stepfather's tutoring and her natural aptitude made her a star.

Tutoring in everything, except how not to lie about it after he died.

Mama, it was just a boy at school. *You are NOT ruining your life because of some boy,* her mother had said, stroking her cheek, her neck, her hair. *We all make mistakes, honey, but you don't have to ruin your life over the first one. Oh, sweetheart, sweetheart.* A week later, her mother took her to an abortion clinic. Hermia had felt cored, eradicated. Daddy Loum's death and the lies in its aftermath. She had undertaken two years of penance so harsh the nuns at her school referred her to her first psychiatrist, thinking she was anorexic.

Her mother, only in her mid-thirties at the time, remarried within months of Daddy Loum's death, this time a rich lawyer. Elton Dernier was a light-skinned man in his sixties, a friend of Atlanta's black mayor, corrupt to the bone. Hermia could still remember the glitter in his eyes when he walked his prize in her designer clothes through a ballroom. In the first two years of that marriage, Hermia was going through her problems in high school. But they never hurt her grades, and by the time she graduated, she had scholarship offers from across the country. She also had a rich trust from Daddy Loum's share of his family's surely ill-gotten wealth in Senegal. Oh yes, she still lived off the interest of Daddy Loum.

Soon she was off at Vassar, and then in graduate school at Northwestern, and when Mr. Dernier died of cancer, she had hardly known him. By then her mother was in her early forties, still beautiful.

So what possessed her to go back to Gallatin? Forrest would ask her.

Maybe she was daring anybody to recognize her? Or maybe she had her eye on Dutrelle all along.

What would she tell Braxton Forrest about Dutrelle? Mainly what LaCourvette had told her. Dutrelle Jones had been the best player on Coach Fitzgerald's second championship team. He had won a scholarship to the University of Alabama and then played for two teams in the NFL. A knee injury sent him home, but not before he had put away a good deal of money. Back in Gallatin, just turning thirty, he saw the potential for black subdivisions to the south of town. He bought land to develop and started a construction company to build the houses and named the first subdivision Gloria Estates after his mother.

But when Marilyn—she was already renaming her mother—bought land of her own on the other side of the county and contracted with Dutrelle to build her house on the slope of a rocky hill above Scalp Creek, Dutrelle's piety toward his mama vanished. Within a few weeks, he left his young wife and child for middle-aged Adara Dernier. This was all ten years in the past now, but unforgotten and unforgiven, at least by Gloria Jones.

Sometimes Hermia ran into Gloria Jones when she had Dutrelle's abandoned daughter in tow.

"Who yo mama wagging that fanny at now?" Gloria would say in the middle of the grocery aisle. "She as old as I am! I know Dutrelle must be sick to death of that expensive bitch, but he can't get shut of her. You tell her she need to set her mind on Jesus."

"Mrs. Jones," Hermia would say, "you're welcome to tell her yourself."

"I wouldn't touch my ear to a phone that had her mouth on the other end of it. Ain't nobody but Jesus can clean her up."

But Professor Forrest would not be interested in Gloria Jones. After a while he would say, *What about you?* and her heart would leap.

Me? Oh, I was a legend. Sudden mood swings, impulsive things I did. Giving myself to a perfect stranger I met on the bus, the way Marilyn might have done. Marilyn Monroe, I mean. Giving myself to you. My mother was sort of obsessed with Marilyn Monroe, and now I am too. I've read Joyce Carol Oates' *Blonde* half a dozen times, and I watch *Niagara* at least once a month.

Oh, was I ever married? Well, yes, she would sigh, don't you remember? I was married once. Or Lola was, don't you remember? I told you about Matthew. Gay Matthew? How I found out the gay the same time I found out the pregnant. What in the world did he marry me for? That was the year before you met Lola, don't you remember? He and his partner live in St. Paul now, and they adopted a little Chinese boy, which makes me more than a little queasy.

Did I—no, I never remarried.

She would tell Braxton Forrest anything he asked.

8

July 21, 1969

Out past Glenn's Bait Store and down the logging road, he navigated the ruts and saplings, the bordering pine trunks summoned from the circumambient darkness. A deer went bounding away in front of the headlights, white tail upright. When he stopped, Marilyn seemed to coalesce in his hands out of the darkness, absent to sight but startling to touch; it was like laying hold of some sleek alien whose struggle was not to escape but to extract the most precious thing from him.

She was a shape shifter, a dark Thetis, and she took him in the sheath of her so comprehensively, with such knowledge, that it seemed to pull his soul loose. He was Enkidu with the temple harlot. There was an abandon in her that at the same time felt like an ancient, exact discipline, and he was suddenly adept, like being liberated (knowing no grammar) to speak the most arcane of foreign tongues. It was unlike the ordinary fleshly relish of sex. It was liberation from all the constraints of the body, naked newness of soul, transcendence. And then as it ended there came the sudden descent back into himself, back into the car, into the smell of sex, the fact of her blackness. Their polite disentanglement. His rage of wonder.

On the drive back into Gallatin, he asked her questions and she eluded him with her answers. Yes, she had grown up in Gallatin, mostly. No, she had not been away to school. No, she would not let him take her home. She wanted to be dropped off where he had picked her up, that would be fine. He tried to kiss her, but she would not let him. Yes, she would see him again if he desired.

She got out of the car.

He did desire. When?

"When you make it possible," she said, reaching her hand back in, cool and smooth. He left her on that side street, and she was already walking away then in her fishnet, her hips already back into their rhythm of enticement, back into the soft night.

Not his at all, but any white man's—Mo Woodson's, Bertram Everett's. Anybody's.

157

† † †

July 22, 1969

The next day on the way out to the river, Mo sensed something different. "You sitting there like you just shook hands with Billy Graham."

"You mean one of them Hare Krishna hippies in Atlanta," Wright said.

"The hell do you know about Atlanta?" demanded Mo, instantly incensed.

"I been up there," Wright said.

"When?"

Wright did not answer.

"When?" Mo said, turning to look at him.

"I ain't proud of it," Wright finally said, making a mouth.

"What do you mean, you ain't proud of it? Why would you be proud of it?"

"I ain't proud of how come I went."

"Whores," Mo said.

"I didn't pay no whores," Wright said, aggrieved.

"I sure as hell didn't have to pay no whores at your age," Mo said. He got out a cigarette and lit it with his Zippo, cupping his hands over the top of the wheel. "You seen the birds and the bees going after ripe figs on a fig tree? That's how the girls were with me."

"So you was kind of pecked-looking and split open and oozy?"

"I didn't pay no whores," said Mo.

"It's a difference between paying," Wright said, "and getting paid." He squirmed to get a pouch of Red Man from his back pocket.

"Getting paid?" Mo said. "Oh my lord. So you went up to Atlanta to be a gigolo? So what, old ladies? All wrinkled and dried up—"

"I ain't said nothing about old ladies."

"So ugly ones?"

Wright did not speak for a few seconds. "I ain't proud of it. It made me sick to my stomach the first time. But them queers up in Piedmont Park will pay you good money."

"Queers?" Mo gave him one disgusted look, then flung his cigarette out the window and spat after it.

"Jesus," Forrest said, his stomach turning at the thought of it.

"You know what that makes you?" Mo demanded.

Wright looked indifferent. "What does it make me?"

"A queer," Mo said.

Wright looked at him and shrugged, then leaned his head forward and spat tobacco juice into the Styrofoam cup he held.

"Hero here's gone wish I was," he said.

158

† † †

By midmorning it was already hot. They were cutting line through a thicket where no breeze stirred, and Forrest wanted to take off his shirt but mosquitoes hovered densely around them. Wright, cautious for signs of yellow jackets or wasps, took the bright orange and white range pole twenty or thirty yards ahead of them and thrust it into the ground to give them a mark to work toward.

"Come on, dumbass, that ain't far enough," Mo called. "Back it up some more. If I keep turning these little angles and distances, it's gone mess up the survey."

"There's a stand of pine trees right here behind me," Wright called back. "But if you set up right here, you got a good long shot on the next one and we won't hardly have no line to cut."

"You can't find me a shot from where I'm set up now?"

"Not unless you want to cut down four or five twelve-inch hardwoods."

"Shit," Mo sighed. "Okay, come on back."

Wright started cutting back towards them.

"Hey Forrest," Wright said when he was fifteen or twenty feet away, still screened by the branches between them. "I heard you was dating a girl."

Forrest did not answer.

"Yeah," called Mo, "he don't date boys like you do."

"Girl named Tricia," Wright said.

"What's it to you?" Forrest answered.

"I just wanted to ask you. Is her name really Tricia Honeycunt?"

Forrest stopped cutting.

"Shut up," Mo called. "What the hell you need to start something for?"

"I knew this girl in Jackson named Mary Butt," Wright went on, "but Tricia Honeycunt beats the hell out of that. Honeycunt. Damn. It reminds me of Unca Mo's figs."

Forrest pushed his way through the thicket toward Wright. Wright was laughing, backing up, the blade of the bush hook above his shoulder like the barrel of a cocked bat.

"Seriously, big man," he said. "I just want to know is Tricia Honeycunt as good as your mama."

Forrest felt the same singing, murderous clarity he had on the football field. Wright was quick, but he saw exactly how he could feint with his bush hook to make him step back and swing, and then Forrest would dodge it, swing, and lop off his worthless head.

Crashing through the thicket, Mo burst off-balance into the cut line between them and winced from the raised bush hooks. "Come on, goddamn it," he yelled, his voice high and scared. "Come on—Jesus

Christ! Put them bush hooks down! Jesus, what's the matter with you dumbasses?"

"Tell this piece of shit to apologize," said Forrest.

Wright held his bush hook at the ready, his face wild and scared, as though he had just taken the measure of what Forrest might actually do. His tongue came out and touched his bottom lip and he shook his head.

"Naw, you won't do it, hero," he said. "You got your future, you got nigger policemen want to shake your hand." He stared at Forrest until he thought his point had sunk in, then raised his eyebrows and lowered his bush hook. Mo grabbed it from him. "You got Tricia."

Mo got in Wright's face. "Shut the fuck up," he said, poking him in the sternum with his forefinger with each word and driving him backwards.

"How come you got to be on his side?" Wright complained. "He ain't no better than us."

"Us?" Mo said.

What Forrest had was not Tricia but Marilyn Harkins. Every night after work he would go home and shower thinking about her, wondering where in town she would be, where they would go, and he would eat his supper under his mother's worried, widowed eyes. Harlan Connor, a lifelong Democrat, had died of a heart attack watching the debacle of the Democratic National Convention in Chicago the summer before.

"Are you going out to the pool tonight?" his mother would ask.

"I don't know. Just riding around."

"Who are you riding around with these days? I hope you're not getting into any mischief."

"Mama, I'm about to go to college. You won't know what I'm doing there, so why are you worried about it here?"

"Well, I know you spend your days with Maurice Woodson. I've heard things about them. You know he married Paloma Parker. Harlan had plenty to say about her. And that nephew of his. Margaret Lee told me his father was put in the electric chair for murdering his own mother to get her money."

"His own mother!"

"That's right. These are the people you're with all day. My father used to say, 'Better be alone than in bad company.'"

He would get irritated and leave the table and hurt her feelings, then have to apologize to her later, but the whole time she was talking, he would be thinking that in those five minutes, Mo Woodson or Bertram Everett or some other man might have found Marilyn, and he would have to spend all that night in a futile hunt, sour with jealousy.

She would never agree to meet him.

"It will come to pass," she told him after the second night in that impossibly formal diction, "if it is meant to be."

"But you know I'm going to be looking for you. I don't want somebody else to—"

"When you make it possible," she interrupted, touching his lips, and she was out of the car and gone.

Every night he would have to search for her again in the dark, driving down street after street until he saw the motion of her hips on the road by the old depot, or near the cord mill, or on a side street near the high school, or in the graveyard near the anonymous Confederate dead.

He would pull up beside her and say her name. Marilyn.

She would never let him kiss her, as though kissing were too personal, but on the ninth or tenth night, he made her sit in the front seat beside him, although she struggled to hide. He drove once around the courthouse square with his arm around her, not letting her duck down. At nine o'clock on a weeknight, no one saw them, but he felt her trembling next to him.

He let her out two blocks from the courthouse near his friend Bill Fletcher's house. He left his car behind the post office and walked back to meet her. Bill's father, Wendell Fletcher, had brandished a pickaxe handle as a supporter of Lester Maddox in 1966 and strutted around as the local head of the George Wallace campaign in 1968. He had stood up in the Methodist Church and defied the young, liberal minister who had been quoting St. Paul on how in Christ there was neither male nor female, neither Jew nor gentile, and therefore neither black nor white.

"Rev. Millard," Wendell Fletcher had said, playing to the congregation, "the nigras have their own church and their own ways. Everybody here knows as well as I do if they come to our services, it won't be to worship." The church voted not to admit black people if they tried to attend.

At first he thought she had left him, but then she stepped from the shadows of a magnolia across the street. He pulled her into the Fletchers' yard, running with her across the St. Augustine grass and pushing through the hedge until they stood flushed against the wall. A window unit was blasting away in one of the two lighted windows. When its thermostat turned it off, Forrest could hear the television inside, and he cautiously raised his head to look in the other window. *Laugh-In.* Wendell Fletcher sat in his armchair guffawing at Flip Wilson in a dress while Mrs. Fletcher read. Forrest pulled Marilyn to him. She was shivering.

"Please," she whispered, "this is—"

He kissed her and she twisted away from him. He held her face and kissed her again and she yielded all at once and kissed him back. He took her, kissing her, pressing her against the wall, lifting her off the ground. The air conditioner switched on and drowned her moaning. It switched off just as they sank down trembling against each other, and they heard Bill inside talking to his father. A moment later, the back screen door of the house slammed. Forrest pulled her down behind the nandinas. They heard a car door, and Bill backed out of the driveway in the family Pontiac. Forrest held Marilyn's face in his hands as they crouched there, the beautiful face illuminated by light from inside, feline with its high cheekbones and shining skin and green eyes.

"Don't go out with anybody else," he whispered. "Just with me."

"I cannot promise that," she said.

"I want to see you in the daylight."

"No."

"I don't care if somebody sees us."

She put a finger over his lips. "You don't know what will happen."

"Show me where you live."

"No."

"Where do you go during the day? What do you do?"

She shook her head, and before he could stop her, she had pulled her clothes together and fled unsteadily through the bushes and across the lawn into the street. A shadow suddenly blocked the light from the window above him. Wendell Fletcher was standing there, both hands cupped against the glass. He had to have seen her, the sway of her white miniskirt under the streetlight, her glance back, her delicate wave. Forrest heard Mrs. Fletcher say something. Mr. Fletcher answered, "Nothing."

The air conditioner kicked back on, and Forrest ran crouching along the side of the house, out the driveway, and on to his car a block away. He drove slowly up toward the courthouse square, then back down through the neighborhood.

Was she hiding from him? Had somebody else already picked her up?

He drove out through the cemetery and past the high school but did not find her. His heart burned for her.

When he could not find her the next night, he drove around Gallatin for hours. Two days later, it had become a sickness. Every thought was about Marilyn. At work, not even Wright's sarcasm could get a rise out of him. He hardly touched his supper, and whatever his mother said to him, he did not hear it. He was out of the house and in the car, crisscrossing the town.

On Sunday, the fourth night, he drove into the streets where the black people lived. Near a church where the night service had just let out, he saw a group of black girls on the corner under a street light, and he pulled over.

"Y'all know Marilyn Harkins?" he asked them.

"Whooooh!" they hooted, waving their limp hands. "Man got it bad."

He waited it out. "Have you seen her?"

"How come you need her? What's the matter with me?" one girl said, stepping out into the light with a hand on one big hip, thrusting out her

162

massive bosom. "I got a lots to love."

The other girls bent over laughing.

"Do you know where she lives?"

"Listen at him. Trying to get in her house."

"I need to see her," he said. "It's important."

"What's in yo pants think it's important," said one of them. They waved him off, but one thin, pretty girl stepped closer to the window. "She stay with her aunt," she murmured.

"Where's that?"

"Let me get in I show you."

"Come on," he said, and she started to get in the back seat while the other girls stood back in surprise. "Get in the front," he said, "so you can give me directions."

"What you want with that skinny thing?" the bosomy girl called. They drove off in a chorus of taunting.

Forrest smiled at the girl as they eased down the narrow street. "What's your name?"

"Gloria."

"So you know Marilyn? Do you go to school with her?"

"No sir." She seemed very nervous.

"You don't need to call me sir. Where do I go? Straight ahead?"

"Yes sir. Turn up here at the stop sign."

"Which way?"

Tentatively, she pointed left down a street with small, shack-like houses on one side and a raw bank of red clay on the other. An empty field overgrown by kudzu bordered the Interstate's right-of-way. He could see motel signs, the endless stream of headlights.

"That one," she told Forrest. It was a sad, unpainted place with a tin roof and a sagging porch. "That where she stay at."

Forrest stared at it in the dark. No light showed. It had obviously been abandoned for years.

"You know for sure?"

"No sir."

"I thought that's why you got in the car," he said.

The street dead-ended in a pile of junk and loose garbage with a raw, fetid smell. Forrest did a careful three-point turnaround between the two ditches. As they started back, Gloria reached over and touched his arm.

"You can do me like you do her," she said in a high voice. When Forrest did not answer, she turned her head and stared out the window.

"I need to find her," he said as they headed back toward where he had picked her up.

"Don't let me out where them girls at," she said sullenly.

"Where do you want to go?"

"Where you let her out at?"

"Wherever I pick her up. How about by the college?"

"She go up there?" she asked, incredulous.

He turned at Railroad Avenue, still looking for Marilyn. Gloria reached over and stroked his arm softly.

"What?" he said, irritated by her. "What do you want? You want me to think you're like Marilyn, just because you're black?"

She winced back and started to cry. "Lemme out."

"Here?"

"Lemme out!" she screamed, twisting toward the door. "Lemme out the goddamn car!"

He hit the brakes and she threw open the door. When she got out, he stared at her.

"What you looking at?" she screamed. "Go on! Leave out of here, motherfucker!"

"How about shutting my door?" Forrest said.

As soon as she slammed it, he hit the accelerator. At the intersection with Foster Drive, he ran the stop sign and gunned it over the railroad track. He saw Bill Fletcher in the parking lot of the Dairy Queen and thought of holding Marilyn down behind the nandinas. He burst into the lot so fast a group of girls licking ice cream cones and sucking milk shake straws scattered out of the way in a spilling panic.

"What's the matter with you?" one of them cried—he didn't remember her name, one of the girls from out in the county. "You nearly ran over us!"

"There's not a goddamn thing wrong with me," he yelled out the window.

Bill Fletcher was already on the way over, walking on his bad ankles in that strangely off-kilter, Jimmy-Stewart way he had.

"Hey, Cump, hey, man. Let's talk." He got Forrest out of the car and took him by the elbow and walked him toward his own car. "You drunk?"

"No."

"So you heard about Tricia," he said.

"Heard what about Tricia?"

Fletcher stepped away to look at his face. "And that guy you work with?"

"Who? Mo?"

"The other one. From Jackson. His wife's cousin or whatever."

"That piece of shit. What about him?"

"He's been calling her. He told her you said such nice things about her, he wanted to take her out."

"Oh for Christ's sake."

"Tricia says you haven't seen her in two weeks. She called me crying because she thinks you gave her to this guy."

"Gave her to him? Bullshit."

"She says he sounds ignorant and sleazy. So why are you letting him come on to her?"

"I'm not letting him do anything," said Forrest. "I've been busy."

"I hear you ride around by yourself every night."

"Maybe I'm looking for somebody."

"Holy shit. So it's true. I didn't believe it."

"Didn't believe what?"

"That you were looking for Marilyn Harkins."

"You know her?" He was taken aback. "Have you *seen* her?"

"Good God, Braxton," he said, his face contorting strangely. "You're giving Tricia Honeycutt away for a whore?"

Forrest pushed him backward onto the hood of his car and held him by the throat.

"Everybody's watching us," gasped Fletcher.

And just then, from the corner of his eye, he saw her—the sway and summons, the dare of her body. She was across the street, just stepping over the railroad tracks and starting down the stretch of Railroad Avenue in full view of the Dairy Queen.

He let Fletcher go. He walked back to his car and got in and started it. Everybody in the parking lot was watching him as he pulled out and followed her.

As he idled beside her, keeping pace with her, she gave her hips full play, an amazing calculus, an answer to anything straight and narrow. She pretended to take no notice of him.

"Marilyn," he called.

She did not acknowledge him.

"Get in. Go with me."

Not a glance.

But at the end of the long strip, she made a small gesture to the left toward a side street, and he pulled ahead onto it and waited until she caught up with him. She got in the front seat and slid across and put her arms around him and kissed him hungrily.

"Where've you been?" he said when they pulled apart. He kissed her eyes, her ears, the line of her jaw, the soft neck. He held her breasts, smoothed her bare waist, her thighs. "My God, where have you been? God, I've missed you. I want you. I love you."

She put her hand over his mouth. "Don't say that. And don't ask me things."

"Have you been—"

"Don't ask me anything. Take me somewhere."

"Right here."

"No, stop it. Let's go somewhere. Right now. Hurry, baby."

Two blocks later they saw the boxcar.

The next morning before they got in the truck to drive out to the job, Mo took him aside in the parking lot to talk to him. His eyelids had a thick, hooded look and he smelled of liquor. He patted his chest for his cigarettes and then realized he had on a T-shirt with the pack rolled up in his left sleeve. He got one out clumsily and lit it with the Zippo, his hand trembling.

"You mind if I ask you something?" Mo said, gazing at the ground.

"Don't you want a cup of coffee?"

"Fuck it," said Mo. He lifted his head, the bloodshot yellow eyes. "You think you can go steady with her? You planning to give her your fucking senior ring? You don't know what you're messing with," he said. "Half the men in Gallatin have had her in the backseat, and now it's like it's a dry county and there's a bootlegger you was used to getting liquor from and now he won't sell it to you."

"Sorry to disappoint you," Forrest said, his heart leaping irrationally. He started toward the truck. The idea of Mo with Marilyn sickened him. Bertram Everett. All those other men—who were they? Jaycees and Lions, Sunday school teachers, men from the mill village, farmers, the self-important officers of the Touchdown Club. In a flash of intuition, he realized that Marilyn's wave that night had not been for him but for Wendell Fletcher.

Mo caught up with him and stopped him.

"Listen," he said, putting his palm over his heart with what looked like actual anguish, "it ain't me. I got Paloma. What I'm saying is people notice you. You think in a town this small—I heard you rode around the courthouse square with her sitting beside you in the front seat."

Forrest stared at him. "Where'd you hear that?"

"Hell, Paloma told me."

Forrest felt the stirrings of dread. "I'm not ashamed of her."

"Is that right? What about your mama? She's bound to hear something about it. And that girl, Tricia."

"Tricia?" Forrest said. For half a second, he did not recognize the name.

"And what about that son-of-a-bitch?" Mo said, leaning close to him as Tony Wright pulled into the lot. "What about when psycho bastard finds out?"

July 19, 2009

Maya sat across the picnic table from Forrest in the barbecue restaurant they'd found near Jackson just before it closed. They were the last customers, and the fat proprietor—a wheezing, freckled man with his red hair in a flattop—was totaling up the day's receipts at the register with an occasional glance at them. An old black man with puffy bags under his eyes was wiping down the tables, rearranging the upright rolls of paper towels and bottles of sauce. Forrest mounded the shredded pork onto a piece of white bread, dashed it with sauce, folded it, and bit into it blissfully. He stared at Maya, savoring this home food that he really preferred to anything else, wondering how he could have let himself think this girl was a European heiress.

"Okay," he said after a minute. "But what's it to you if I was in love with her?"

She opened her mouth in exaggerated shock, a meme that must have originated in Southern California, like so many other things girls her age inherited from their teenage years. "What's it to me? Think about it, Braxton."

He tilted his head in acknowledgement. But had he been in love with Marilyn? Or was it more a matter of being obsessed, addicted, under compulsion? He remembered the absoluteness of his desire, but also his willful helplessness. The defiance in his lust.

"Did I love her? What does that even mean? If it means did I want her good without respect to my own interests, of course not. You don't want happiness for the one you're in love with unless you're what makes them happy."

He sprinkled more sauce on his barbecue and dipped the bun into the Brunswick stew.

"You folks scuse me," mumbled the black man. He bumped past them, pulled out the benches under the next table, swept out the remnants of napkins, the bits of meat and bread.

"We should get out of here," Maya said.

"Y'all take your time," called the proprietor. "It takes Uncle Billy a few minutes to clean up."

Uncle Billy muttered something to himself. They finished their food, not hurrying. Forrest took the bill up to the proprietor at the cash register, plucking a couple of toothpicks from the dispenser as he handed him the American Express card with the check.

"Sir, it's cash only," the man said with slightly ironic politeness, tapping the large sign on the front of the register that said NO CREDIT CARDS.

"Woops," Forrest said, opening his wallet and finding the remains of the thirty dollars he had tried to give back to Maya.

"Oh good," Maya said sardonically. "You have some cash." She plucked a twenty from his wallet to pay and when the man gave her the change, she took several dollars back to leave on the table for Uncle Billy.

Forrest pulled out of the gravel parking lot and headed back down the highway toward Gallatin.

"You don't want to talk about Tony Wright," she said.

"I've been trying for forty years not to think about Tony Wright."

"But you admit you loved Marilyn?"

"It's hard for me to say I loved her."

"Why? My God, you're still obsessed with her."

"I mean, because she was black."

"What does that mean?"

Exactly. What did that mean?

"When I was growing up," he said, "black children didn't go to the same schools as we did. They didn't eat in the same restaurants. They didn't worship in the same churches, drink from the same water fountains, or use the same restrooms. Gallatin closed the city pool because that way white people wouldn't have to swim in the same water. They would taint you—I mean somehow soil you—if you touched the same water they swam in, especially if they were in it for their pleasure, their unspeakable black pleasure."

"Okay, Braxton, stop."

He shook his head. It was demeaning to try to explain it. No one had dinned into her the polluting otherness of "niggers"—"Nigras," as ladies said in polite company. In those days, a Southern white man's identity stemmed from the innumerable careful ways in which he was not a nigger. Forrest remembered Harlan Connor saying that the test of a man was whether he knew how to get niggers to work. Niggers were never really adults, and it was cruel to expect them to be. They wouldn't come to work on Monday, since they were still hung over from the weekend. You needed them for various unpleasant jobs, but you spent about as much time taking care of them as getting work out of them, and you could never depend on them, because they were natural thieves and as irresponsible as children. They had violent passions that they could not control, and now nigger music was infecting everything. Connor would shake his newspaper disgustedly when The Temptations or The Supremes or James Brown came on television.

He couldn't tell her that.

"Let me put it this way. I met black students my own age for the first time the summer after my junior year in high school when I went to a state honors program. I drank from the same Coke bottle as one of them that summer. That was a big deal."

"Okay," she said, humoring him. "Why was it a big deal?"

"It was drilled into you before you could think. It was the way the world was, like gravity and Coca-Cola." When she did not answer, he said, "It's hard to get rid of. You have to love your way out of it."

"But you won't say you loved her." She gave an ironic snort and turned and looked out the window.

The white stripes on the center line of the highway flashed up at him—short, short, short—then the long strip of warning yellow as they started up a hill. The trees were barely visible now at the edges of the right-of-way. The yellow curve signs loomed incandescent out of the dark.

"I thought I was enlightened. Black teenagers showed up in Sybil Forrest High School my senior year, and I believed I thought they were equal. But the idea that they were black never once slipped my mind. I still remember their names: Terry Long, Jeff Todd, Donald Redding, Patricia Thurman."

"Not Marilyn?"

"Good God, imagine that—Marilyn Harkins in the halls of Sybil Forrest High School."

Maya glanced at him and her voice had a new interest. "So what are you saying?"

"I don't know whether I loved her apart from the fact that she was black."

"That's not how you talk about her. You talk about how beautiful she was. Like she was Marilyn Monroe and not Marilyn Harkins."

"She was beautiful." Forrest was silent for a few seconds. "I've written about all this."

"Oh boy," she said. "Did you get Tarzan into it?"

"It was about Marilyn Monroe. The movie blonde was a kind of photographic negative of the available slave, whose chattel image you could own. You could publicly acknowledge her, because she was also common property. What I said was that Marilyn Monroe was sacrificed for our desire, made into what Georges Bataille calls excess—exactly the kind of using-up-everything that had to be avoided by white male responsibility. But the prototype for what I said about Marilyn Monroe was my Marilyn. She instinctively deconstructed white self-control and Protestant rectitude. White men acted white when they made her hide in the back seat on the way out of town, but what they wanted was this erotic blackness they officially despised. She had to be a secret. But it was a secret they shared while they were hiding it from each other. Marilyn was the secret sacrament of being white."

"Stop! That is such bullshit."

"Okay. But there was more to it. She turned on its head the idea that black men really lust for white women. She desired white men. She did on purpose, on her own terms, what had been done to black women for hundreds of years. She made that history come back to life and she changed it. I still don't know how to say it. I was the only one in town who wasn't in on it. Not like that."

There was a long silence.

"Well, Braxton," she said, "*that's* because you were in love with her."

Forrest drove back into the outskirts of Gallatin, past the new motels, onto Beauregard Drive, which went to the Baptist church and the house where he grew up.

His heart hurt. God, he had been in love. He had loved her. Never in his life had he loved anybody the same way. She had ruined him, she had turned everything else that would ever happen to him into a simulacrum of her splendor, and she had sealed it by dying.

But now she was not dead. She was not dead but as old as he was. She was not dead, and he had needed her death all this time to shelter what he had felt with her. She was still living, she had always been living; she was as unfamiliar as he was with that darkness, that abyss that had taken his father, his stepfather, his mother.

"If I loved her, it was naiveté and idealism. She was beyond me. On some level, she knew exactly what she was doing, and I didn't know anything. And I started to undo her."

"What do you mean?"

He waved his hand at the street, the houses, passing his own house without telling her and wondering if his own stepfather, if Harlan Connor—

"What do you mean?" she repeated.

"She was the secret, the dark queen," he said.

"You ruined it by falling in love with her?"

"No, that's not it. Men were obsessed with her. That was supposed to happen, it had to happen, but I changed her. As though I had the right to that."

He fell silent. They drove up Johnston Street toward the courthouse square. Once he had seen her there, on that dark side street by the Methodist Church, almost not believing it—a few blocks from his house, among all the neighbors—and he had pulled her into his car. Kissed her. Kept her beside him as they drove in the fading light out Main Street, north toward a place he knew. A country church, a sacred grove.

Headlights extinguished on the moonlit dirt road, rolling quietly to a stop, opening and closing the car doors carefully, he led her out into the night. The earth springing with deep moss to hold this body that he loved. Her moaning whispers in his ear, her lips soft against the lobe. What she said electrified him, terrified him. "Take me somewhere we can be. North. Take me north." And as they lay spent, the mosquitoes plundering their young skin, the dark steeple outlined against the moonlight, she said in a shy, formal voice, "I don't wish to live without you now." And when he said nothing, she rolled against him, kneeing him, suddenly slapping his face hard, then trying to scratch him, going at his eyes, "Why did you make me love you, then? Why, motherfucker?"

9

Chick Lee did not usually go to church on Sunday night, but all day long he had felt a strange terror. He had never really thought Forrest would go to church with him, so he hadn't told Patricia anything about his plans. Nobody else had expected him either, but when he arrived and took his usual seat with his family in the pew and Forrest didn't show up, he still felt publicly humiliated, because he had let himself imagine a different scenario: he was going to be the man who got Braxton Forrest to church. He sat there not triumphant but invisibly stood up.

And the sermon had sunk in like a knife. "Any one of you who does not renounce all his possessions cannot be my disciple." What would you have without God? You owed him that first breath he gave you, and you would give it back at the end, whether you wanted to or not. And when that moment came, that last moment, would you rather have all your possessions or the knowledge that you had done what Jesus asked you?

"Any one of you who does not renounce all his possessions *cannot be* my disciple."

Chick knew it was true. But did he hate Patricia and Alyssa and his Navigator and his dealership and his pool and deck and his armchair and his home entertainment center and his Viking kitchen and his king-sized Tempur-Pedic? No he did not.

Who could be saved on those terms? A few people, maybe. Nobody he knew. The Baptists usually emphasized being a good father or mother or child, exercising strong family values, serving your community, all that—but here was the gospel plain as day: a disciple had to hate his family if they got in the way of Jesus. He had to hate anything that might hinder him from being a disciple, and if he didn't hate it and couldn't do it, how could he be saved? Chick did not have a personal relationship with Jesus Christ, as other people in the church claimed to have, but he pretended he did. He cared about it. He wished he did.

Did he care just because he was scared to go to Hell?

He imagined coming before the Judgment Seat and the Judge who saw everything—all the evasions, all the secret sins nobody else saw, all the habits of selfishness that kept him small. Did he truly love God and his neighbor? He felt the eyes of God settling upon his soul.

Not really. He felt himself squirming under the unsparing scrutiny.

His Sunday school students had turned on him that morning when he started talking about sin. Everybody nowadays emphasized God's mercy. You were supposed to keep everybody's self-esteem in good shape, as though everybody had to be self-confident and self-satisfied. Whatever happened to "Have mercy on me, a sinner"?

And suddenly he was thinking about Forrest.

The man had not even known that Tricia was pregnant, much less that the son she bore forty years ago was his. How could he not know that?

Something snagged at his memory.

The rumor about Marilyn Harkins that went through Gallatin at the beginning of his senior year. That list came out and she disappeared and some people said Forrest had killed her. Tricia had to know about Forrest's obsession with her. What was she supposed to do when the boy she loved was out with a whore every night—and not only that but acting like there was nothing wrong with it? Like this black girl was his woman?

That afternoon when Chick had picked up Alyssa from the Davis lake house, Tricia had complained bitterly about Forrest. After forty years everything he did still wounded her. She was always thinking about Forrest being with somebody else instead of her, some other woman he had chosen and not her.

And there was something else about it all that nagged at him, something he couldn't quite remember. What was it? A touch of dread, like a draft from a door opening somewhere in a dark house.

So when dark came, he told Patricia and Alyssa at supper that he was going to the evening service. Patricia drew her head back in surprise. Alyssa, both elbows on the table, told him he wouldn't like it because it was for teenagers.

"It's *Mr. Rimes*," she said, as if the name were self-explanatory.

Now he saw what she meant. The music was contemporary Christian rock played by some of the teenagers, and Rimes—twenty-something, short, athletic, balding, earnest, extroverted—gave a short talk about drinking and sex, trying to make it funny instead of preachy. Embarrassed to be there, Chick tried to escape afterward without being seen, but Rimes spotted him and called out from a group of Alyssa's friends.

"Thanks for coming, Mr. Lee. Where's Alyssa tonight?"

Chick said she was tired from swimming all afternoon with the Forrest girls. Rimes excused himself and came over to him and asked how the Forrest girls were. Chick said they seemed fine. Their father was in town.

"So I hear. Tell you the truth, that's why I'm asking," Rimes said. "Sounds like he's not helping. Anything we can do, I'll count on you to let us know."

Several of Alyssa's friends still hovered, a little too interested, and Chick suddenly wanted to save face for being there. He held up his keys and started toward the Navigator as though he were late for something, and as he left, he clapped Rimes on the shoulder and said loud enough for them to overhear, "Well, I'll say it again, I'm glad you're with us."

Rimes tilted his head and smiled uneasily.

Stupid. He drove away full of unfocused anxiety, unwilling to go home. He headed through town and down to the dealership and back up

Foster Drive toward the square. As he was crossing the railroad tracks, he saw the car he had loaned to Forrest coming slowly toward him. Chick flashed his lights and stuck his arm out the window to flag him down. They stopped by each other in the middle of the street.

"How's that Nissan holding up?" he asked when Forrest's window went down. The movie star head of graying blond hair.

"Fine. Sorry about this morning. I had to take the girls to Mass in Macon."

"That's what Tricia said." He angled his head to look around Forrest at the pretty girl beside him—short black hair, very pretty. "I'm Chick Lee," he said.

"Maya Davidson."

Chick looked toward the ground and whispered, "So your wife gets here in a couple of days?"

"So I hear," said Forrest aloud. "How's Patricia?"

"Wondering where I am." He glanced in the rearview mirror as a car came up, ready to move, but it passed him on the right. "Wasn't there a cousin of Mo Woodson's that worked with you? Good-looking, arrogant kid, always with some cheap girl. Drove a yellow '67 Firebird. I had my red Mustang fastback that year, and a couple of times he'd pull up beside me at the light on the square. Like I was going to do that. I saw him one night with Tricia Honeycutt. Didn't something happen to him that summer?"

Forrest actually looked old for a second. He glanced up the street and dropped his head back against the seat before he looked at Chick again.

"Take a ride with us. We were just talking about that summer. Do you remember Marilyn Harkins?"

Chick hesitated. "I guess."

"Everybody knew about me."

"Yeah, okay."

"Why don't you park somewhere and ride with us?"

10

Under the revolving Lee Ford sign, Forrest watched Chick park his Navigator and point his keys at it. The lights flashed and the horn honked.

"Rooster man," Maya said.

The chest and stomach, the way he walked around his car, the unconscious strut of ownership. As Chick approached them, he scrutinized the Nissan he had given Forrest to use. He opened the back door but closed it again without getting in. He opened Forrest's door.

"Come on. Drive the Navigator." He handed him the keys to the Lincoln as though he were giving away his daughter.

When he got into the other car, Chick stood outside telling him how to adjust the leather seat for his legs and get the mirrors right. Maya offered to let him sit in the front, but Chick declined.

"Never sat in the back," he said, getting in. "So Maya, how do y'all know each other?"

"We met on the airplane coming back from Rome," she explained. "Have you heard of Dixintel?"

"Sounds sort of familiar," Chick said. "Computer stuff?"

"IT—networking, data retrieval, all kinds of things. I do service management."

Forrest pulled out of the parking lot and crossed the bridge over the Interstate toward the river.

"So Chick, what are you doing out on a Sunday night?"

"I'm having an affair with my cashier in Parts."

Maya lightened and turned to look at him.

"Parts?"

"Girl named Tracie Newsome. Gives Parts a higher calling, Royce Jenkins always says. Patricia complains about men always hanging over that counter. Says it's unseemly."

"So Chick, what are you doing out on a Sunday night?" Forrest repeated.

"Listen," he said, "I ought to call Patricia. Whenever I'm late, she pretends to suspect me of running around with Tracie, which gets Alyssa laughing. Which pisses me off. Actually I'm not going to call her. In fact I'm going to turn off my phone."

Just then a doe flashed across the road ahead of the Navigator and Forrest hit the brakes, instinctively watching for another deer. A spindly fawn, pausing at first on the opposite shoulder, leapt across just ahead of them and stumbled on the clay bank to their right, gathered itself in an ungainly scramble, and disappeared into the woods. He thought about the little black boy they had hit. He would be how old now? Forty-five? A middle-aged man.

"That boy you were asking about," Forrest said as they sped up again. "His name was Tony Wright."

Chick leaned up between the seats. "Didn't something happen to him that summer?"

Forrest hesitated.

"He was allergic to yellow jackets. We were working out by the Ocmulgee, and he fell in a nest of them. Anaphylactic shock."

"Oh my god, he died?" Maya gasped. "You didn't tell me that."

"I knew it was bad," Chick said. "I'd forgotten what happened."

"So what do you know about Marilyn Harkins and me?"

Forrest glanced in the mirror when Chick did not answer.

"Just what people said," Chick said.

"I've been telling Maya about her. It's okay. What did people say?"

"That you were obsessed with her. People saw you pick her up. You didn't try to hide it. You remember Bertram Everett?"

"Bertram."

"He told Tricia about you and Marilyn. I remember how she looked. We were all out at the pool, and Bertram, that snide—"

"Is he the one who told Tony Wright?" Forrest interrupted.

"Told him...?"

"About Marilyn and me. Somebody told him."

After a moment Chick said, "What difference does it make who told him?"

Forrest glanced into the mirror and Chick met his eyes.

"What do you mean?"

"I told him. It was the night after I saw him with Tricia."

"You told him?"

"We were out at the swimming pool in the parking lot. Wright—that's his name?—gets out of his car and saunters over."

Forrest could see him insolently lifting his T-shirt to rub his stomach muscles, spitting off to the side.

"So he says, 'Hey, Mustang, you looked kind of pissed off last night.'

"So I told him, 'Yeah, I don't like seeing trash like you with Tricia Honeycutt.'

"'Say what?' he says, and before I know it he's slapped me and he's backing off, ready to fight. I missed with my first punch and Wright slapped me again. He was quick as a mongoose. Somebody, I don't remember who, grabbed me and said if it was anybody's fight, it was Cump Forrest's. Well he loved that. He said he wasn't afraid of Chump Forrest.

"'Y'all go tell Chump I got me some of that Honeycunt.' Sorry, Maya. Anyway, I swung at him again, but he was too quick for me.

"So I say, 'Cump doesn't even give a shit, you dumbass. He's off with Marilyn.'

"You could see all the air go out of him. He goes, 'Marilyn?'

"Then everybody's going, 'Jesus, you don't know Marilyn? Used to be you could ride around and pick her up on the street.'

"'Before Cump got a monopoly.'

"He's like, 'A hooker?' and Ben Cawthon goes, 'Why don't you ask your uncle?' and he say, 'My uncle?'

"And Ben says, 'Nobody knows Marilyn like old Mo. One fine colored girl.'

"'A nigger?' Wright says. 'You're talking about a nigger?'"

August 18, 1969

He got home from work and threw his sweaty clothes in the laundry bin as always. He showered, ate supper with his mother, and headed out with his tennis racket, thinking that before dark he could play Graham Ashley or whoever was out at the courts on a Monday night and then find Marilyn. As he pulled from the driveway and turned right on Beauregard Drive, Mrs. Pearsall next door was rocking on her porch with her sickly husband, and she lifted a hand at him as he passed. Across the street, Mr. Hill's grandsons and their friends were playing roll-at-the-bat on the big lawn. And then down the block he saw a white dress emerge from the shrubbery onto the sidewalk.

In his mother's neighborhood?

He drove past her without looking at her, crossed to the other side of the railroad tracks where the road dipped but the railroad tracks did not, and pulled over just out of sight of the Wallace house. In the rear view mirror he saw her break into a constricted, stumbling run in the short, tight dress.

She yanked open the back door and got in, hiding below the window line. "Who that man you working with?" she demanded.

"What happened?"

"Go on, drive. Get out of town!"

He drove up to Lee Street and turned left toward the Interstate and drove down the hill.

"That man crazy!" she sobbed. Her formal diction had disappeared. "He say he kill me. And he would, too."

"What did he do to you?"

"He say he kill me!"

Forrest drove several miles out of town, turned off on Simms Road, and found the boundary flagging of a tract they had surveyed early in the summer. A hundred feet past it was a woods road they had used. Forrest straddled the ruts in the Bonneville and stopped under an old live oak in the middle of the property where a house had once been. The sun was almost down now and he got Marilyn from the backseat. Swallows dodged above the surviving chimney.

It was the only time he had ever been with her in daylight. He saw the almost freckled look of the skin of her high cheekbones, the startling hazel of her eyes, her thin brown hands holding her face. They got out, and she stood trembling against the side of the car, wincing aside when he tried to comfort her.

Slowly he coaxed the story out of her. Wright had found out from Mo that she worked a shift at a children's clothes factory near Macon, and he had waited for her outside. He had gotten her into his car by telling her that Forrest had sent him to get her. She was embarrassed, she said, that he knew where she worked, but glad he was thinking about her, especially now. On the way back to Gallatin, he turned off and started into the country. She asked him where they were going, and he said Braxton wanted it to be a surprise. He pulled off on a country road and then into the woods, and she suspected nothing. She kept thinking he was taking her to Forrest.

When they finally stopped, he smiled at her.

She asked where Forrest was, and he said Did I say he'd be here? I just said it would be a surprise. She asked what the surprise was. He said Chump wants me to show you the real thing. She said she started getting out of the car, but he grabbed her arm and pulled her back. Don't you want me to show you? He reached under the seat and brought out a hunting knife. You want me to cut your face? He touched her with the point just under her eye. Get in the back seat or I'll drag you out of the car and cut you up before I kill you. He said again to get in the back seat and she did. I got a little message I want you to send Chump. A little disease.

When he was done, he slapped her and told her she stank. He told her she wasn't nothing but a cheap nigger whore. He made her stay in the back seat, and all the way into town he called her a field nigger and a whore. He forced her from the car in front of Forrest's house, and she was trying to get away when Forrest saw her.

She squeezed her hands, crossed her arms over herself, squeezed her shoulders. Hot as it was, she shuddered uncontrollably, and he put his arms around her. She pushed back from him.

"He said if I didn't tell you," she said, "he was gone kill me and leave me in your mother's yard. Just take me somewhere. Let's just get away from here, let's just—"

Wright would be laughing the next day. Forrest would sharpen the bush hook on the tailgate of the truck and swing it backhanded and Wright's head would roll loose in the pine straw, laughing with its eyes shut. Wright's body would still be standing there. Blood would jet up from the neck, burst after burst, and the knees would buckle with each spurt but he wouldn't fall. He would turn around, and the cottonmouth would be twisting from his belt, alive all along.

She was saying something. She moved against him, but suddenly her flesh repulsed him. She stood back, smaller, crossing her arms over her breasts.

"I have to go to the clinic," she said in her formal voice. "But if I do...."

"What?"

"They will want all the names," she said, looking away into the darkening woods. Bats were flitting now in the open spaces where the old house had been, and Forrest listened to a car on the road they had

177

turned from, dreading suddenly that they would be caught. But it passed and the sound receded into the distance.

"What do you mean?"

"What do you think?"

She swung around and slapped him. She hit his face again with her fist before he grabbed her hands and held up both wrists in his grip, her body twisting beneath them.

"You're hurting me!" she cried.

He released her, and she stood rubbing her wrists, abject. Of course they wanted all the names. Whoever might be infected had to be contacted by the county health authorities.

He imagined the news burning into the stores and churches, school offices, respectable houses and bedrooms. Married women, wondering if that sore a week ago was ... if the baby in her womb was ... And Braxton Forrest, of course, named among the others, distinguished from the others by his stupidity and shamelessness. He foresaw in vivid relief his mother's humiliation. A wave of nausea passed through him, then another, and suddenly he turned aside and vomited into the weeds.

When he stood up, Marilyn had gotten into the back seat of the car, where she sat like an effigy. Mo had tried to warn him. So had Bill Fletcher. He could take her to Macon or Atlanta—but what was the point? She would reveal the names and the news would come back to Gallatin. He was the only one who could prevent it all.

How could he stop her? Should he keep her from treatment? Or get a nurse to steal penicillin, or get that new doctor to give her a shot privately. How?

Nothing made any sense.

Unless he killed her.

The ice of its logic sobered him. He could play along with her for a day or two, telling her to wait. In the meantime, he could let it be rumored about that she had syphilis and was about to reveal the names. Tomorrow night or the next night, he would pick her up and take her to the river. He would get her out in the water and hold her until she drowned and then let the lazy currents and the big white catfish have their way with her.

Everybody would suspect him, but there would be no proof, and nobody in town would want to pursue it. He would save the town. He would be a hero.

Hero, Tony Wright would say, raising his eyebrows.

He stumbled to the car, threw open the back door, and pushed Marilyn roughly down on the seat. She twisted away and scrambled back from him, pushing her knees at him.

"No, baby, don't, don't," she whispered. "I won't tell them your name."

He heard her gasp. Too late now.

"You're my blood, you're my breath. I don't care who knows it. We're going to run off. We'll go somewhere north."

She sobbed and clung to him like a drowning child. She gave him everything he didn't know she'd been holding back.

That night she let him take her home. It was across town from where Gloria had directed him—a small, decent house in the black neighborhood off Sharp Street, just a quarter mile from Stonewall Hill. They sat outside in the driveway like any dating couple, reluctant to leave each other. Inside, he could see the flickering light of a television set. A white-headed man of huge girth carried a tray and a beer can past a window where an air conditioner hummed.

"Who's that?"

"Deacon Ray Watts," she said with contempt. "Deacon Ray. Mama Harkins passed when I was ten and I had to move in with her sister. My Aunt Tillie lives here, but she's sick, see—she..." She paused. "Uncle Ray used to like to give me a bath every night or so."

Forrest said nothing.

"Then he'd put me to bed. Oh, Uncle Ray, he used to talk real soft and tell me I ought to be glad somebody would put food and clothes on me. I ought to be nice and just do what I was told. He used to tell me I was a white man's leftover, and if I said a word to Aunt Tillie, he would do something to me and tell folks he done sent me to cousins in Texas."

Forrest stared at the window, feeling the pulse in his temple. He held her hand in the dark.

"He's scared of me now." She put her hand on his cheek and kissed him. "You must understand," she said in her formal voice.

"Understand what?"

"Why I have to go to the clinic."

"I do understand."

"It isn't just for me."

"What do you mean?"

She waited before she said, "It's our baby."

"Our baby."

In the dark, she must not have seen his face betray what he felt.

"You'll come get me after I get my shots," she told him.

"Of course," he said.

She touched his face again. "I'll let you know where I'll be. I'll send you a message. I'll let you know, baby. Because I love you."

11

July 19-20, 2009

Chick saw what Forrest was working up to, and he knew he would have to turn him in. The whole sorry episode in Gallatin's history would come back up just when it had finally been forgotten. Forty years after the fact, Braxton Forrest and Tony Wright would ruin people's lives, the way Marilyn had almost ruined his father's.

He did not believe that his father had taken Marilyn out—Mr. George W. Lee would not do that—but his name had been on her list. His father had called Chick into his office to tell him the news before he heard it from somebody else. *Listen, Brantley, if people find out about this business and want to believe the worst, they'll believe it, but I'm telling you the truth. I don't know this woman. I think one of our boys might have taken her out and used my name, or maybe there's another George Lee, but son, I would never—I would never...*

His father had wept. His noble father. Over this same whore Forrest was so smitten with.

"She was pregnant when she turned in all those names?" Maya asked him.

"So she said."

"But you thought—"

"I'm getting to that."

"Cump, I should get back to town," Chick said. "I've got our weekly sales meeting first thing tomorrow morning."

It was almost midnight, and they were fifteen miles from Gallatin, bumping down a dirt road through the woods that skirted the security fence around Plant Ocmulgee. The four huge cooling towers were brightly lit, each one four hundred feet wide at the base and over five hundred feet tall. Chick had heard so many talks at various club lunches he could rattle off statistics like a tour guide: the two chimneys of the power house were as tall as the Bank of America building in Atlanta; Ocmulgee provided power all over the Southeast; the coal came from Wyoming, and the plant went through several hundred-car trainloads every single day; the county received over $6 million a year in tax revenues from the plant, which also employed four hundred people from the county. It was the largest coal-powered plant in the Western hemisphere.

Alyssa said one of her teachers—the young biology teacher whose name he could never remember—kept telling them it led the U.S. in carbon dioxide emissions. *Do you realize what that means? Gallatin County, your county, is causing more global warming than any other single place in the country! Do you feel good about that? Shouldn't you do something?* Chick told Alyssa her teacher should go to a Lion's Club lunch sometime. Southeastern Energy had already spent more money on air-quality renovation at Plant Ocmulgee than it took to build the place to start with.

"I'm almost to where it happened," Forrest said.

"If you tell us you murdered Tony Wright, we either have to turn you in or we become accessories after the fact."

Maya turned to look at him, then at Forrest. "That's right, there's no statute of limitations."

"It's not like that," Forrest said. "Jesus, just let me talk it out."

Chick squeezed both hands into fists. "How long do you think we'll be?"

Forrest shrugged. "Half an hour? An hour?"

"Let me text Patricia."

As soon as he turned on his phone, it played the first few notes of "The Bonnie Blue Flag." Three voicemails and one text. He read the text: whr r u. Words, Patricia. Use words like an adult. He texted back: With Cump—home late, and turned it back off and slid it in his pants pocket.

"If you tell me you killed Tony Wright," Chick said, "I'm turning you in. You roped me into this."

"He roped us both in," said Maya.

"You're the one who came back down here," Forrest said to her sharply. Then he looked at Chick in the mirror. "You asked me about Tony Wright. So I'm telling you."

12

August 19, 1969

The survey along the river had not closed. It was a nightmare—this huge survey with hundreds of bearings and distances, and it didn't close. What does that mean, close? Forrest had asked at the beginning of the summer, when Mo had written something down wrong on a small survey they did. Brother told him all the math had to work. All the angles and distances had to make a closed polygon. Otherwise, it was like building a house and leaving a two-foot gap where there was supposed to be a corner. It has to close.

Brother had been poring over the pages from the field book where Mo had written his notes and he called them into the office before Wright got there. He pointed to a page where several figures had been smudged by a drop of water.

"I think this must be the problem. What'd you do, sweat on it? I made these out the best I could," he told Mo. "Read 'em out to me."

Mo squinted at the page and said some degrees, minutes, and seconds but Brother checked his figures and shook his head. "Tried those." Mo and Forrest stared down at the book, dreading the idea of having to do the whole survey over until they found the mistake. Forrest could sometimes remember where they had been for certain measurements, especially long ones, and here in Mo's distance column were three in a row over 500 feet. An image came back—a long open stretch through fields of random pine saplings and weeds along the Ocmulgee.

"That's the day that storm caught us," he said. He licked his finger and held it up. "The day Wright got stung."

"Fucking A," said Mo, touching the water spot with his forefinger. "That's what that is. The day we had to take queerbait to the hospital. We were busting it that morning before it rained. Yeah, that's the day I got home to Paloma early," he said, running a finger under the collar of his T-shirt.

Brother's lip lifted and he started to say something but stopped himself. He told them to go back and turn those three or four angles again. If they were the problem, it would save a lot of trouble.

In the parking lot behind the office, Wright got out of his car tendering his crotch and swaggered to the truck. All the way out to the river, Forrest sat next to him, waiting for him to say something. Overnight, he had thought about what to do. It had to look like an accident. At least he could do that for his mother. Best would be a backswing when they were cutting line, as though he didn't know Wright was there, maybe glance the blade off a tree. Catch him in the head or neck and say he didn't know he was so close.

They drove past Glenn's Bait Shop and back up the logging road to where they had parked on the day of the storm. It was a close, overcast morning, windless and hot. Wright got out, as casual as ever, and walked over to a pine tree and unzipped himself.

"Ow! God-amighty!" he said. "How come it stings so much coming out? Hey Uncle Mo," he said

Mo glanced up from the tailgate of the truck where he was lifting the transit carefully from its box. Wright turned around.

"What do you reckon this sore is?"

Mo slumped and his head twisted down and to the side as though he had been hit by a bullet.

"Sweet hell." He spat, his face twisting with disgust.

"Come here and look at it, Uncle Mo. I hope I ain't got the VD or something. Maybe I could hold it up and find out which way the wind's blowing. Hey, hero, how about you look at it?"

Forrest did not answer.

"Somebody told me nigger gals all have VD and it don't bother them, it's like that Typhoid Mary, but if a white man was to happen to dip in that swamp, it would eat him up. Here I just done it one time and look at me."

Forrest took a bush hook from the bed of the pickup, but Mo grabbed his forearm and looked him in the eyes.

"We just cut them lines a few weeks ago." He cocked his head at Forrest, holding his gaze, as though there were some miserable understanding between them better left unsaid, some kind of agreement. "That's a sick piece of shit," he said in a low voice. "I told you he'd find out. Don't do nothing stupid."

He screwed the transit onto the tripod and shouldered it.

"Come on queerbait. Bring the chain," he said. "We need to do them distances again."

As they were going in, Wright skirted the place on the fence where he had gotten hung up and stung, but he kept talking about how he'd heard about this nigger girl in Gallatin who would do the deed with any white man, except she'd been getting kind of picky lately.

"But you just have to know how to sweet talk them colored girls," he said.

Mo and Forrest walked toward the river not answering, not acknowledging anything Wright said. Sunken in its banks, the river flowed greenish-brown. Roots of trees elbowed out on the opposite side. A massive old black woman under a broad hat and many layers of clothes sat on an upturned bucket at the bottom of the bank, fishing with a cane pole. Mo lifted a hand to her, and she called, "How y'all?"

"You got girlfriends all over, Uncle Mo," Wright said.

They found the cut line and walked south along it toward the first point on the survey where the figures had been smudged. The clearing where the transit had been set up was still evident. Brushing aside a few leaves, they found the nail punched through its fold of orange flagging. Mo concentrated on leveling the transit with the four knobs that adjusted the base plate, watching the bubbles in the two tubular levels at right angles to each other. A yellow jacket nosed at the big end of the scope and Mo shooed it away. It flew out toward Wright in an angry arc.

"Jesus!" cried Wright, batting the air. "Watch out, god damn it."

"Where's your kit?"

"In the truck."

Mo took the cigarette from his mouth and fixed Wright with his yellow eyes.

"This is your last day, dipshit. Soon as you get your paycheck, you better start hitting up one of your other uncles about a job."

"You're firing me? What for?"

"Because I can't stand your sorry ass."

"We'll see what the boss has to say about that."

"Yeah, you explain to him how half the gas got siphoned out of the truck."

Wright stared at him.

"Maybe if you was to do your job and keep your mouth shut," Mo said. He tilted his head toward the line they had cut through the woods the month before. "Get down there and give me a backsight."

When Wright started back down the line, Forrest walked forward on the path through the field of weeds and knee-high pine saplings, found the next nail near a piece of flagging tied around a tuft of bunched weeds, and waited for Mo. His nose started to run, a sudden freshet, and he wiped it with the back of his hand. When he saw Mo lift his hands, he dropped his plumb bob over the nail and held the string waist-high—steady, steady—tapping the point on the center, and watched a drop fall from his nose onto the top of the plumb bob.

"Good!" he called, and Mo called back "Good," and Forrest saw him write down the new figures, then flip the scope and focus on Wright again. "Good," he called, and then turned back toward Forrest, who was wiping his nose again. "Good," Forrest called. Tip of the plumb bob tapping dead center. "Good." After the second foresight, Mo said, "Good. Come ahead," and Forrest started back.

"How'd it check out?" he asked as he got back to Mo, who was staring into the field book and scratching his stomach with his pencil as Wright came back up the line toward them.

"It ain't even close," said Mo. "I don't know what the hell I thought I was writing down the first time. Must have been hungover. Unless I'm on the wrong point—or somebody come out here and moved the nail. Let's get this next distance to make sure."

Forrest started the chain toward the next point while Mo detached the plumb bob from the base of the transit and dropped it in its holster. Wright came up cautiously and edged past the tripod and up the line toward Forrest.

"Where the hell are you going?" Mo said. "I just said to—"

"Fuck that," said Wright. "You see the hole where the nest is at? Right there under that sweetgum. I ain't standing here."

"The last man to join the crew," said Mo with aggrieved patience, "is back chainman."

"Hell, do it yourself," said Wright. "You already fired me."

"Soon as we get to town, you better haul your sorry ass back to Jackson," said Mo, shouldering the transit.

Wright caught up to Forrest and suddenly stopped dead, open-mouthed, staring at the ground beyond them. Forrest looked, expecting a snake, and when he did Wright snatched the dangling thongs from his hand and ran backwards ahead of him up the line, whipping the length of the chain through the weeds to frustrate Forrest's attempt to grab it. He got out his plumb bob and pretended it was his penis. "Come on, Chump. Come on, Mr. Hero with the nigger girlfriend. Get back there and hold the chain."

Forrest could hardly see for fury. Blood pounded in the veins above his temples. His eyes were starting to sting, his throat seemed to be clogged, and his breath came in a wheeze. He would kill Wright as soon as he got a chance. But he went back and pinched the string over the chain at the 100-foot notch and dropped the plumb bob to tap the nail.

Wright leaned into it, pulling tighter and tighter; Forrest knew that he was planning to let go and send him staggering back into the yellow jacket nest. "Good," he called, and dropped the chain just as Wright released it. Wright wagged his head, stuck out his lower lip, bent down, pushed a nail in the ground and started up the line through the open field, snatching the chain after him and slashing at the weeds with the thongs.

Forrest's nose was running freely, and his eyes itched like fire. Allergic to something. When he got to the nail Wright had pushed in the scuffed dirt, he stepped on the thongs vanishing past it and Wright's hand snatched back. He turned with a snarl but grinned when he saw Forrest's face.

"What's the matter with you, hero?"

"Get the fucking distance," he wheezed.

"Are you crying?"

They got through the distance in hundred-foot increments of malice. Mo had set up the transit about fifty feet into pine woods from where the field ended, and Wright threaded the chain between the legs of the tripod and pulled it tight as Forrest steadied his plumb bob over the last nail. They were in pine woods that had been harvested for pulpwood years before, and there were old stumps here and there. A scattering of sweetgums brightened the sloping ground that rose from the river. Mo was looking at his field book. "What'd you get?"

"Five thirty seven," said Forrest. Mo's head tilted. Wright read the tenths and hundredths against the transit's plumb bob string. "Point five eight," he said.

"That's two tenths shorter than the first time."

"That's this asshole pulling the chain too tight," said Forrest.

"Two tenths wouldn't throw off a survey this big. The mistake had to be that last angle. What's the matter with your voice?" He looked up at Forrest and his mouth opened. "What the hell?"

"I'm allergic to something," Forrest wheezed.

"Like maybe that ragweed you just went through?" Mo said.

"Is that ragweed?" He turned stupidly to look back. He labored to breathe. He needed to sit down. Forrest held up a hand toward Mo and started toward one of the stumps.

Wright stepped in front of him, too close. "Naw, he's crying because I fucked his n—"

Forrest instinctively drove both hands up into Wright's chest and Wright went hurtling backward onto the stump where Forrest had been headed.

The wood crumbled rottenly. Wright groaned and rolled away, and Forrest saw a wedge of intact wood at its center that had caught him in the middle of his back. Then Wright screamed, screamed again. There was a sudden sharp pain in Forrest's hand, then his cheek, and he recognized yellow jackets and turned to run, wheezing. Mo was already yelling and swatting the air on his way back toward the field.

Just inside the woods, Forrest stopped to look back. The air around the stump boiled with the furious insects. A shaft of sunlight caught them in their tight fighter arcs as they flew out of the shadows. He saw Wright struggling to move. His elbows gave way. He tilted forward, his neck bending oddly as his forehead pressed into the ground and his face turned blindly toward Forrest, embossed with convulsive yellow jackets, a shimmering golden mosaic.

Forrest stumbled out of the woods and back into the field of ragweed.

He could not breathe. He bent over, laboring, his eyes and throat squeezing shut, his lungs rattling. Where was his bush hook? Mo told him the first day he started surveying to hold onto his bush hook if he got stung, and a week later, sure enough, Forrest dropped his bush hook when he got stung. Mo lorded it over him for days. He said it was as bad as a soldier throwing away his gun. "Because where'd you drop it? Where you got stung at. And where's that? Right on top of the nest. Now you have to wait until they settle back down before you can go back and get it, which means you're liable to stir the whole nest up again and hold us up for an hour. You can run like hell—but hold onto your fucking bush hook."

Vaguely, as though in a dream, he remembered leaving his bush hook in the truck, but he had left something when he got stung. What had he left?

Great gasping wheezes brought him only a little air, and a red haze broke through his lids when he strained to open his eyes.

Wright. That's what he'd left. He had to go back and get Wright, he had to drag him out of there, and he couldn't wait for the insects to calm down.

He had to go back. He lurched toward where he thought Wright was. Something hit him in the face. Confused, he backed up and started again and found himself in a tangle of branches, pine needles pricking his face. He reeled and fell. He heard Mo crashing back through the field toward him.

"Sit up, sit up."

Mo was cursing and there were noises he did not understand. Mo said, "Hold still," and then another yellow jacket stung him high up on his arm and he started to swat at it but Mo blocked his hand.

"I'm giving you a shot, dumbass. Hold still."

Mo must have gotten confused.

"I'm not him," he tried to say, but nothing came out of his throat, and he felt Mo leading him somewhere, and he followed, stumbling, and Mo sat him down on pine straw and told him to lie back. He did, but it was terrible trying to breathe, and he sat back up, his head pounding, full of strange reveries, short dreams.

Marilyn was rising from the river in a fishnet, swimming slowly. Mo swore and said Jesus, almost whining, and told him to hold still again and he felt another shot in the other arm. This time, after a minute, he felt the constriction in his chest start to ease and blessed air flowed into his lungs and he sank back on the pine straw.

"Just lie there a minute," said Mo. "God Almighty. That first shot didn't do shit. It must of took two because you're so fucking big." Forrest heard Mo whispering with a low, steady anguish: "Jesus. Jesus, Jesus God. Oh Lord, what am I gone do? Jesus help me."

His eyes still stung, but the swelling was going down, and in a minute or two he could open one eye enough to see Mo sitting with his back to him. Two tall pines towered above them. The overcast seemed to be thinning; he could see the sun trying to get through. He took a long deep breath and a wheeze rattled through it, but he was getting enough air. He sat up. Mo was smoking a cigarette and staring down the slope at Wright, the black T-shirt riding up from his belt to show a pale swatch of skin. The kit was open beside him on the ground—the hypodermic needle, the empty vial of epinephrine, the used alcohol swab.

At the bottom of the slope, Wright lay beside the stump where he had fallen. Even from this distance Forrest could see the yellow jackets still circling the air above him. He felt no joy, no release, only a dull disbelief.

"Is he dead?" he asked.

"Oh hell yeah," Mo said. "Hell yeah." He broke into sobs, leaning his head on one hand and holding up the cigarette with the other. "Jesus, Jesus."

Forrest could not speak.

"See, Mama had a heart attack," Mo said, "and I got her in the car and I's trying to get her to the hospital. We was almost there, and I come around the corner ... and there was a train at the crossing, a fucking long train, stopped dead still. I got out and screamed at the conductor, but he didn't pay no attention to me. It would move up a little and stop, then back up and stop, and then move up a little and stop. I stood there screaming at it and waving my arms and crying and leaning in to blow the horn. Mama looked over at me, I'll never forget it. She looked over at me and said 'Maurice, can't you help me, son?' And that's the last thing she said before she died."

"We should go get him," Forrest said after a minute.

"The last thing she heard in this world was me screaming and cussing."

Forrest nodded.

Mo wiped his eyes and shook his head. "We ain't touching that boy."

"What do you mean?"

"We got to go up to Glenn's. Call the sheriff and the ambulance."

"What do we need with the sheriff?"

"I been in trouble before." Mo carefully stubbed out his cigarette and flipped the butt in a long arc down the slope. He stood up and dusted off his pants and wiped his eyes. "I ain't messing with evidence. You killed him," he said, his voice rising. "I kept you from using the bush hook, but you pushed him on that nest."

Forrest's heart went to ice. "I didn't kill him."

"I seen it happen," Mo said, his voice high and desperate. He backed away to what he thought was a safe distance.

"Jesus, Mo. I couldn't breathe. I wanted to sit down on that stump. I didn't know there was a nest in it. He got in my way, so I pushed him."

"You didn't see them yellow jackets?"

"I was going to sit on that stump. I swear to God."

"You didn't want to kill him?"

"I wanted to cut his fucking head off."

Mo stared at him and then looked at the ground and nodded and blew out a long sigh. He looked at Forrest again and then pointed at his cheek. "Got you right there. That eye's gone be swole shut."

Forrest felt the hot welt on his cheek and the other one in the webbing between the first two fingers of his right hand. Mo gave him a cigarette and he crumbled some tobacco into his palm and spit on it and daubed it on the stings.

They drove back to Glenn's Bait Store and made the calls. The ambulance arrived thirty minutes later, but they had to wait another twenty minutes for the sheriff, and then they led both vehicles down the logging road. The paramedics—two men Forrest did not recognize—asked how far away the body was and one of them swore when he found out.

Mo led the procession through the woods to Wright's body. Sheriff Binder was a lean, narrow-shouldered man. Around women, his manners were as soft and polite as a preacher's, but with men he was hard and sharp. When they got to the site, Mo pointed to Wright's body and told the others about the yellow jacket nest in the stump. The sheriff walked around the scene at a safe distance and made a few notes. He carefully stepped up to the body, shaking his head at Wright's grotesquely bloated face.

"How come he didn't run?" he asked, stepping back to Forrest and Mo. "Looks like if he was allergic he would have gotten the hell out of there."

"Well, see," Mo said unctuously, his hand trembling as he lit a cigarette and pointed it, "It must of hurt him when he fell on that stump there."

"So how come you didn't drag him the hell out of there. *You* ain't allergic, are you?"

"No, sir," Mo said. "I didn't think about it at first, I mean when you get stung you just run like hell, but then it was something about the way he was laying there..."

"You were too scared of getting stung to save a man's life?"

"No, sir, when I was in the Army, they told us not to move somebody if..."

"If what?"

"Jesus Christ!" Mo said. He suddenly gagged and bent over, then staggered sideways, bent over again and vomited. "That's how come he looked like that," he said as he stood, his face contorted. "You broke his goddamn back!" he said to Forrest, lifting his T-shirt to wipe his mouth. "He couldn't even crawl off."

"Broke his back," repeated the sheriff. He gave Forrest a glance, then pursed his mouth and stared straight ahead at Wright's body. "You boys want to get him on the stretcher?" he said to the paramedics.

The men set the stretcher down beside Wright. They were moving very cautiously and watching the stump a foot away. One got Wright under the arms, the other by the feet, and they started to lift him when the middle of his body sagged curiously and they both swore at the same time and dropped the body. "Jesus, his back's broke alright," one of them said. They quickly picked him up again and shifted him onto the stretcher and took up the handles and had just started to lift him when the one in the back yelled and dropped his end. The other one swore and they both bolted. Yellow jackets poured out of the nest, and everyone scattered up the slope as the paramedics fled toward the field.

A minute later, the sheriff, opening and closing his hand where it had been stung, came up and stood beside Forrest. Mo was sitting on a rocky ledge a few yards away, smoking and talking to himself.

"Son," Binder said quietly, "that nigger gal you been romancing went to the clinic today and gave them a whole bunch of names. They called me to come down there. My job is to see she don't get killed, and that means I need to know who might want to kill her. The nurses said the list was confidential, so I asked them how I could do my job if I didn't know who wanted to kill her. The Ham girl said she couldn't help it if I happened to see the list when they were out of the room. So they left and I saw it, you understand me? It's quite a list. That's why I was late getting here. They said she was pregnant, too, just in case you don't know. And guess who's at the top of the list? You and this dead boy right here."

"I didn't break his back," Forrest said. "I was—" He broke off. The whole story about his ragweed allergy sounded weak and ridiculous. "I hated that piece of shit," he said, "but I didn't hurt him on purpose."

"Why does Mo think you did it?"

"Wright got in my way and I pushed him, but it was an accident he fell on that stump."

For a long time, the sheriff stared down the slope at Wright's body and the two paramedics edging gradually closer to their stretcher. Then he opened his hand and showed Forrest the sting in the center of his palm.

"Got me," he said. "Hurts like hell when they nail you, don't it?" He thrust out his lower lip and glanced over at Mo, who saw him and got up and approached them. "You know he's on the list, too," the sheriff said sideways and Forrest nodded.

Mo stood there sullenly, his mouth twisting. He would not look at Forrest.

"Listen, Mo," said the sheriff. "You going to say in court that this boy broke Tony Wright's back?"

Mo shook his head.

"Then why did you tell me?"

"This here was an accident."

The sheriff waited, not satisfied.

"It's just this boy acts like he owns something he don't own," Mo said.

"What are you talking about?"

"You know what I'm talking about," Mo said to Forrest.

"If you're talking about Marilyn Harkins," said the sheriff, "I'd say a lot of men in town surveyed that particular piece of property. That's according to the list she turned in to the county health department this morning. Which includes you."

Mo's mouth fell open. "What list?"

"The men she was with. She came in with syphilis."

"She turned in my name to the county?" he asked in a high, outraged voice. "Who in the hell told her my name?" He turned accusingly on Forrest. "You done it, didn't you?" He wrenched around to look at the paramedics easing again toward Wright's body. "Her sister's boy dead and now Paloma's gone find out ... Great God Almighty, she's gone find out." He fumbled out a cigarette, and his hand was trembling so badly he could hardly hold the lighter to it.

BOOK III
Errors of Closure

Since the survey was made by a circuit from A back to A it is evident that the sum of the northings should equal the sum of the southings; also the sum of the eastings should equal the sum of the westings. In practice this is rarely attained but there is an error called the error of closure ... The error of closure is caused by errors in the measurement of the lines or in observing the angles or in both.

Mansfield Merriman and John P. Brooks, *Handbook for Surveyors*, 1906

July 20, 2009

Monday morning. It was late, almost eight o'clock. She needed to check on Mrs. Hayes. She'd hardly paid any attention to her all weekend with Forrest in town—and now these nasty revelations about her mother. LaCourvette had come over last night, feeling bad, wanting to explain more and justify herself. Hermia had said nothing about confronting her mother. Instead, she had complained about Maya, the little bitch who claimed she was a reporter. Hermia had googled her and found out she worked for a company in Atlanta called Dixintel.

Oh, her.

What, you already know her?

Girl, she's the one Braxton Forrest put in the hospital.

It was one thing after another. Her mother, then Maya Davidson. Forrest had apparently gotten drunk with Maya the first night he was in Atlanta and spilled the whole story of his involvement with Marilyn. Then Maya, trying to get him in trouble for some reason, had called to tip off the police about a "possible murder." LaCourvette had been the one who answered the phone. *And then she came down to Gallatin to sleep with him! Can you beat that? And the old man sent her into cardiac arrest! And now you telling me she's back? That is one hard-up woman!* LaCourvette had started her giggling, and the two of them had laughed until they cried. But then LaCourvette had layered in another revelation, the way she did, and again it was something that made her tremble. *I bet she don't know your mama was pregnant when she turned in those names.*

And now the urgency of her dream, if it was a dream, came back to her. There was something she needed to do. Chick Lee's name nagged at her. He had been the one who bailed out Forrest. She had a feeling that she needed to talk to him.

When she parked in front of the dealership, she could see her Prius reflected in the showroom window against the backdrop of an enormous black Ford Explorer just inside. She watched herself as she got out of the car—not too bad for almost forty.

She tried the door. Locked.

She made blinders of her hands against the glass and peered inside, but she could not see a soul, so she stepped back to check the posted hours: 9 AM to 7 PM Monday through Friday, 9 AM to 6 PM on

Saturday, closed on Sunday. Was she early? She got out her cell phone. 9:03. Well, it couldn't hurt to knock, and she tapped on the door with the edge of her phone and again peered inside. After a few seconds, a plump middle-aged woman in black pants and a bright pink V-neck tunic stepped out of a hallway on the other side of the showroom and glanced around in confusion before she saw Hermia at the door. She looked up at a big clock, made a gesture of exasperation back toward the part of the building Hermia could not see, and hurried across the showroom floor past the posing cars.

"I am so sorry," she said when she turned the lock on the door and pushed it open to let Hermia in. "The salesmen are all in a meeting and I guess they're running long, whatever they talk about. Mr. Lee was late getting here this morning, it starts at 8:00, and I tell you the truth he looked like he hadn't gotten a wink of sleep. Of course it's none of my business, I just answer the phone, or that's what they think anyway, but here it is five minutes after nine almost and a customer at the door and those men, I swanee. I don't know what that means, did you ever hear it, my daughter makes fun of me, but my mama used to say it and now I say it. My mama passed away years ago, but I still say it and every time I do I think about her and how she would get so mad at my—oh, I hear them coming out now. Belle Murray," she said.

"Hermia Watson," she replied, and saw Belle Murray's brows pinch together as they shook hands, then go up in recognition.

"You're the one that helps old Mrs. Hayes! I've heard your name but I tell you the truth I pictured you as—I don't know—but, well, you're so glamorous-looking, like, gosh, Diahann Carroll or Diana Ross. Oh, but that dates me, doesn't it? I mean now everybody's talking about Michelle Obama, but you know what I mean, you're so pretty—prettier than her if you want my opinion, she's kind of mean-looking, maybe it's just her eyes are too close together—but I'm a Republican, so. I shouldn't tell you that, you might be a Democrat and not buy a car, and I'll feel bad I couldn't just keep my opinion to myself. Listen, somebody will be here in just a minute to help you, honey," she said, looking back over her shoulder. "Don't you go away, we'll find just what you need."

"Actually," Hermia said, "I was hoping to see Mr. Lee for a few minutes."

"Oh," she said, "Mr. Lee!"

"If that won't be too much of a bother," said Hermia, giving Belle's forearm a light touch.

"Not at all!" cried Belle, and she hurried toward the opening that led, Hermia supposed, to the other areas of the dealership.

She stood for a moment amid the gleaming cars, thinking about what it must be like to work in such a place. As if to answer her, three salesmen wandered into the showroom, fidgeting with their cuffs. When they saw a customer, it surprised them. They almost looked embarrassed.

The closest one was a man in his early thirties, his black hair greased into strange upward starts and flits. His face was slightly bloated, and as he approached her, he touched the knot in his necktie and tilted his head in a way that he must have imagined was gentle and inquiring, like the Big Bad Wolf composing himself to address Little Red Riding Hood. He was about to say something when Chick Lee came hurrying around the corner and saw her.

"Royce!" he called, and he came up and grabbed both the salesman's shoulders from behind in a half-hug, knocking him awkwardly forward. "Rule number one: I get to talk to all the pretty women. Sorry, my man."

He guided poor Royce toward the other salesmen and released him.

"Have to save you from these salesmen," he said, taking Hermia's hand. "They're like starving coyotes these days. Belle said you wanted to see me."

"I hope I'm not interrupting," said Hermia.

Lee yawned, covering his mouth, and then opened his hand at the showroom empty of customers. He led her back toward a large coffee machine with several glass carafes on the warmers. "How do you like your coffee?"

"Oh, I'm okay. I've had my quota this morning."

"Not me," he said, filling a large Styrofoam cup from the freshest carafe and yawning uncontrollably. "Hard time getting out of bed this morning. Come on into my office."

The hallway, she saw, led back to the parts department and the service area. Belle sat at the desk in a foyer just off the showroom, shrugging a question at Mr. Lee as he preceded Hermia into his office.

He closed the door. A large window gave him a view of almost the whole showroom, but as soon as he seated her in one of the two leather chairs facing his desk, he adjusted the mini-blinds behind her as though the light bothered him.

"Really glad you came by," he said, sitting down and blowing on his coffee. "I've been wanting to talk to you about this mess with the Forrest girls. What I can't understand is the letters Cump says he got. But I'm sorry. What brings you here?"

"To tell you the truth," said Hermia, "I'm not sure."

Lee looked at her over the rim of his cup and lowered it unsteadily onto his desk. He really did look exhausted.

"Well," he said, "you were probably drawn here by my looks and charm, like all the other pretty women who come to see me"—another huge involuntary yawn—"first thing every Monday morning." He opened his eyes wide and took another sip of coffee. "You'll be interested in this because you got drawn into this thing with the Forrest girls—last thing you expected, I bet. But you know what I was doing last night?"

"I confess I don't, Mr. Lee," said Hermia.

"You're making fun of me. But listen, I'll tell you if you do me one favor. My *father* was Mr. Lee. Would you call me Chick? It would make me feel better this morning." He took a sip of his coffee. "Especially if I can call you Hermia."

"You may. What were you doing last night, Chick?"

"Well, Hermia, I was riding around until three in the morning with Cump Forrest and this girl from Atlanta."

Hermia started so violently that Chick spilled his coffee.

"What's the matter?"

"With that—with Maya Davidson? Doing what?"

"You know her?"

"I met her. She lied to me. So what were they talking about?"

"Well, it won't mean anything to you. It was about a woman named Marilyn Harkins and somebody who raped her while Braxton was working with him. Boy named Tony Wright."

"Oh my god."

She heard Chick say, "Hermia? Miss Watson?" He was patting her cheek with one hand and holding her wrist with the other. She raised her head, gathering herself back now, straightening herself in the chair. He hovered before her.

"Thank you," she said, and seeing his compassionate face, broke suddenly into sobs that shook her whole body. He knelt beside her and put his arm around her.

"What did I say?" he asked.

She surprised herself by turning to him and throwing her arms around him, still sobbing, grateful to have someone to hold her, and just then there was a tap and the door opened. Belle Murray stood there with her mouth open.

"I just—I just—." She was holding a box of Krispy Kreme donuts.

Chick sprang up and took the whole box from her. As he pushed Belle out the door, Hermia heard him whisper in a dead tone of voice, "It's about Braxton Forrest." Belle's head went back and her mouth opened in a knowing O, as though that name would explain anything.

Chick offered Hermia a donut, but she shook her head. She was still trembling. He sank into the other leather chair with the box in his lap and picked out a chocolate glazed one and ate it in several unconscious bites. After it disappeared, his hand hovered in midair until Hermia leaned up and plucked several tissues from the box on his desk and gave them to him. Unaware of using them, he kept his eyes on Hermia's face the whole time, as though she might do something outrageous at any moment.

"So—how to put this?—had you met Braxton before?"

"Before he came down here?"

"Right, right." His hand found another donut, this one glazed, and put it in his mouth. Flakes of sugar glistened on his lips. "I didn't know if you had met him, you know, some other time."

She knew he was trying to find out if she had had an affair with him, if she was one of his former students, one of his countless lovers, like this Maya to whom Forrest had told all the things no one had ever told her.

"Yes, I met him at Northwestern. Later I got to know him at a conference in Providence. He was famous for a while, of course," and again tears welled up in her eyes. "I read *The Gameme* in graduate school. Everybody did—it was de rigueur for a year or so, like Benedict Anderson on nationalism. I had spent some time with him, but it wasn't until much later that I found out he was from Gallatin, where my mother grew up."

"You mean—okay, so you didn't grow up here, but your mother did? That's why you came here?"

"Yes. My mother grew up here."

Chick finished his glazed donut and started on another one, a jelly one that instantly overflowed his bite and dripped something unnaturally red and gummy onto the Lee Ford logo of his white polo shirt. He stared down at it helplessly, his chin tripling, his mouth a comical frown, while he held the offending donut upright in his left hand.

"Belle!" he called. "Belle!" When Belle opened the door cautiously and peered in, he looked up at her. "Get me another shirt, okay?" Belle sighed as she closed the door again. "So you say your mother grew up here?"

"Yes, she did."

"I wonder if I knew her." He leaned up to get his coffee from his desk. "What was her name?" He sat back and took a sip. She waited until his bloodshot eyes met hers. She waited until his head cocked and his eyebrows gathered in confusion.

"Marilyn Harkins," she said.

The Styrofoam cup jumped from his hand and hit the floor beside his foot. Coffee shot up onto the leg of his khakis. The spill grew on the functional blue-green carpet. Chick winced and waved down at it confusedly, staring at Hermia. Belle came in with his new shirt—apparently one of a trove somewhere in the dealership.

"Mr. Lee, you should have stayed home in bed!" she told him. She set the shirt down on the desk and hurried out.

"My God," Chick whispered, "you're—how much—I mean, has she said—"

But then Belle was back with a handful of napkins from the coffee bar and dropped them onto the spill. She picked up the cup and threw it away. Chick's mouth hung open. Blushing as pink as her tunic, flustered by Chick's awkward show and his complete obliviousness, she knelt uncomfortably and gathered up the soaked napkins. His foot was like a piece of furniture as she daubed at his pants leg and loafer.

"Belle," Chick said, finally coming to a focus. She would not look at him. "Do I have any more meetings or appointments this morning?"

"You were going to make some calls, but they can wait," she said to the floor. "Why don't you go home before you hurt yourself?"

"Go home? God, no. What are you doing in here, anyway?" he snapped. "Can't you give us a little privacy?"

Belle stared at him and stood up stiffly and left the office.

He frowned and stretched his plump right hand over his forehead to rub both temples at once. "I'm sorry," Chick said. He did not look at her. "So Marilyn Harkins was your mother," he said, his hand dropping in the diagonal gesture a lawyer would make, underscoring a fact for the jury.

"Yes, she's my mother."

Chick glanced up, startled.

"You mean she was, don't you?"

She tilted her head. "She's been living back in Gallatin for ten years." Chick's mouth opened and closed again.

"Living in—I don't—"

"She's married to Dutrelle Jones."

"Good God!" Chick cried, leaping to his feet, his hands on the sides of his head. "That's—that's Marilyn Harkins? The same one Braxton—"

"The same one," she said dully. "She's my mother."

Chick stared at her, trying to take it all in.

"Then you must be..." he murmured. His face went very red, and he bolted from his chair and out the door into the foyer, leaving the door open. Belle sat at her desk, carefully not looking up. After a few seconds, she came into the office and took the new shirt and closed the door without glancing toward Hermia.

Hermia sat very still. She tried not to think about anything at all, to stay calm. She did one of her mindfulness exercises, concentrating on the point where the breath passed into and out of her nose. *Be. Here. Now.* It was Monday morning, she was in Lee Ford in Gallatin, Georgia. In this room, in this chair. Out of nowhere a memory came to her. She was a little girl in the back seat of Daddy Watson's Cadillac, and he was driving them from Macon up to Underground Atlanta. He was talking happily about how he never thought he'd get to listen to jazz in the same place with white people, and now Atlanta even had a black mayor.

When they got to Gallatin, he wanted to pull off to speak to Mr. Lee at Lee Ford, because he said Mr. Lee had once done him a good turn when he was traveling, and he always liked to send him business and keep in touch with him. Her mother made some protest about getting to Atlanta before the traffic got bad, but Daddy Watson pulled off anyway and parked right in front of the dealership.

"Come on, let me introduce you," he said. Her mother shrank back from him, refusing to go in. Daddy was puzzled and hurt. "I want to show you off a little."

But her mother had curled against the door, sinking out of sight, shaking her head, and the more he tried to urge her, the more desperately she refused. He even got out of the car and went around and tried to open her door, but she kept locking it. Finally, he got in, backed out of the parking space, and drove onto the Interstate. A while later she sat back up. A few miles after that, she apologized, saying she was just shy about being looked at—didn't he know the way men looked at her?

He did not say a word to her all the way to Atlanta. Hermia remembered watching the side of his head from the back seat.

†††

Chick came back in, still ashen, wearing a clean shirt, sipping a new cup of coffee, and dabbing at his mouth with a napkin. He glanced at her, but he had a hard time looking her in the eye. He sat down behind his desk.

She felt that she had to say something. "I know who my mother was. What she did. I didn't know anything about it until yesterday, when LaCourvette Todd ... enlightened me. Needless to say, it was quite a shock. Then LaCourvette also told me last night my mother had been pregnant when she left town. So I found out what I guess I really knew already, that the kind old man I thought was my father was not my father. So he must have been one of those men she went out with."

Chick's mouth opened, but he checked himself. He was still very pale.

"Why did you come here this morning?" he managed to say.

"Just a feeling I needed to talk to you. LaCourvette said you came to bail out Prof. Forrest when he was arrested. She said he had told this Maya, whoever she is, about being responsible for the possible murder of my mother. When I told him she was alive and in town, he was—I thought you might know why it shocked him, why he thought—I guess you thought it too—why everybody thought she was dead. And then when I got here, you said that he had been talking about my mother until three in the morning."

"You know your mother turned in a list of names of everybody she'd..."

"Yes. I know about it."

"Well then she disappeared. A lot of people wanted to kill her, and I'm guessing Cump thought somebody did." Chick gazed at her over his desk, nervously turning his coffee cup, and moving several things around on his desk.

Her heart was hammering wildly.

"Do you think... is he ... is he my father?"

After a moment, he shrugged and put his face in his hands.

"Does he think so?" she said.

Chick looked up without meeting her eyes. "I think he might suspect it. He's found out since he's been here that he has two more children than he thought he had."

"Two more?"

"It wasn't my idea to bail out Braxton the other night. It was Tricia Davis's."

Hermia felt the heat rising in her throat.

"Who in the world is Tricia Davis?"

"You know the Wal-Mart manager, Judah Davis?" he said. "His wife. He makes her call herself Varina, but she was always … she was always Tricia to us." To her astonishment, Chick Lee began to cry. He sat behind his desk, his shoulders shaking, and the tears brimmed from his eyes unchecked and flowed down his cheeks.

Hermia felt so faint that she leaned over and put her head between her knees, as she had been taught during a spell of fainting fits in high school. Why did she even need to hear about her outrageous father and her monstrous mother, these people who had accidentally begotten her? Her mother had spent decades foisting off Hermia's very identity on poor old Daddy Watson, long after it had begun to seem implausible to Hermia that her mother would ever have married a man so much older without some reason out of the ordinary.

And now Varina Davis? Tricia Davis. She remembered meeting her, a bright woman, petite and energetic, with an easy Southern graciousness and a big smile. It was in town one day. She remembered now—Patricia Lee, Chick's wife, had been with Varina Davis on the sidewalk outside the Left Bank Grille on the courthouse square. Hermia had talked to Patricia before about Mrs. Hayes, and Patricia had been telling Varina Davis that Hermia didn't even need the job, that she had her Ph.D. from Northwestern up near Chicago and was doing it just to help out. And partly for research, wasn't that right? Research into genealogies, like Roots?

Varina Davis—Tricia Davis—had not suspected a thing. She had tilted her head and smiled and politely feigned interest.

"This woman, this Tricia. She had his baby?" she asked, raising her head.

Chick daubed at his face with a napkin and nodded.

"When?"

"About the same time you were born."

"And he didn't know this? How could he not know it?"

"Because of your mother."

"My mother?"

Chick looked up at her. "Do you know what kind of … I mean, for a man to have his name on that list. A respectable man in this town." Chick wiped his eyes roughly. "My father's name was on that list. And do you think my father would go out with a …"

"A whore," she whispered.

"I'm sorry. Daddy denied it, of course. He swore on the Bible, and he told my mother he was sure men wouldn't give such a person their real names. He said one of his mechanics or salesmen had probably used his name. But can you imagine the—I think it brought on his first heart attack. And then Braxton. Good God. He did absolutely nothing to hide his affair, and why's that? Because he wasn't a racist like the rest of us. No, Braxton Forrest was above the stupid prejudices of the South. He thought he was a hero because he took her out, and everybody else was rednecks and bigots.

"What you need to understand is how much good will he had to use up before the town turned on him. He was the best football player in the history of the school. He took the Blue Devils to the state championship, which is about as much glory as you could get in that day and age. And he was smarter than the class nerds—you see what I'm saying? He was the town hero, almost a god, and for him to do this, to flaunt his love affair with a... I'm sorry to talk about her this way."

Hermia nodded. "He was too brave."

Chick stared at her incredulously. "Too brave? What about his mother?"

"What do you mean?"

"Daddy at least gave my mama a story to tell. Cump's mother had nothing. For years after he was gone, people blamed her for what he did. I mean, she was always sort of embarrassing Harlan Connor, even though he was proud of her, because she was too liberal for Gallatin. You know, always trying to get the women in her church group to read things that made them uncomfortable and that she didn't see anything wrong with, being from Minnesota."

"Like what?"

"I don't know. Southern writers she liked.... So it's like they held her responsible for what he did, like she'd ruined him with her notions. The women cut her dead. She didn't go to her church anymore, and for a while Mary Louise Gibson had to do her shopping for her."

"Mrs. Gibson knew her?"

"She worked there when Cump was little."

"Why didn't she just move?"

"Mrs. Connor? This was her home. The whole thing eventually died down—new people moved in, a new Methodist church split off from the old one and she started going to that one. Younger women befriended her. Even my mother eventually softened. But if Braxton was 'brave,' he should have thought about what he was doing to her. He hardly ever came home after he left for college. I don't think he even saw her but a few times in the last thirty years of her life. He was off doing other things. Off being the great Braxton Forrest."

"You sound like you hate him."

"I did for a long time. Mainly because of what he did to Tricia."

"Because you loved her."

Chick sat back as if she had struck him. After a moment he seemed to collect himself. He wiped his eyes and cheeks, glanced at his watch, and looked at her with an upward tilt of his head as though they were done and she were being dismissed—as though she were one of his employees and they had come to the end of their meeting. He put his hands on his desk as though he were about to push himself up. She did not move.

"I sent those letters," she said. "The ones he thought Mrs. Hayes wrote to him."

He sat gazing at her, puzzled, and his face changed as he took in the implications of what she was saying. Then more implications occurred to him. Finally, he tilted his head and asked, very gently, "Why would you do that to his girls?"

Now suddenly she was overcome with shame, and he saw it.

"Does he know you wrote them?" he said.

"He suspects I did," she said dully.

"Can you tell me why you did it?" He sounded too gentle, like a parent talking to a small boy who has just smothered his baby sister.

How could she even begin to explain it? She remembered sitting at the desk that January afternoon, the pen in her left hand, writing the letter that Forrest would open and read, thinking it was from Mrs. Hayes, as he was drawn into her erotic game. And later, more inexcusably, she had wanted to see what his other children were like, these unsuspecting girls. But she had been the unsuspecting one, sitting there at the old desk in Stonewall Hill. She had been the fool.

"What time do you have?" she asked, and the question startled him.

He glanced again at his watch. "Five minutes to ten."

"I'd better check on Mrs. Hayes before she gets up and hurts herself." She stood and swayed dizzily, steadying herself by touching the desk. "Thank you for your time."

He spread his hands. "You're leaving now? After saying that?"

"I'd better go."

"Hermia!" he said. He got up and intercepted her as she reached for the doorknob. "Do you want me to tell him about the letters? Is that why you told me?"

Standing so close to him, she could feel thrumming through him the anxiety that underlay his cock-of-the-walk pose as Chick Lee, owner of Lee Ford. His blue eyes—watery, bloodshot, perplexed, sincere— searched hers a little desperately, and she felt a sudden pity for him, sensing the tenor of his soul, its honesties and evasions, its deep unease in the world, its terror that he hadn't lived up to life. She put her free hand on his cheek and leaned to kiss his forehead.

"It doesn't matter," she said. "Tell him if you want to. The important thing is…"

"Is what?"

"I don't know. I don't know what the important thing is any more."

"Maybe for him to acknowledge you?"

"Acknowledge me? God, no. That would mean—"

What would it mean? She thought about her son's Facebook page, and without thinking why, she embraced Chick. After a moment of surprise, he held her, seeming shy of her breasts against him. But she let him feel her whole warmth, and when he realized she did not mind, he held her tighter, tighter still, with real need. She kissed his ear and whispered into it, "You know what? You're a sweet man," and freed herself.

When she left the office, Belle Murray sat at her keyboard like Niobe turned to stone.

2

When the phone beside Forrest's bed rang, he roused himself enough to lift the receiver and drop it back down in the cradle, sure it was Marisa. Or—almost as bad—Tricia calling to chide him. Or Maya. He had dropped her off at her car in Cousin Emily Barron's driveway at four in the morning. She was supposed to be in a meeting in Atlanta by nine, and she had to go by her apartment first. He felt vaguely responsible for her sleeplessness, her bad heart. What if, on the way to Atlanta—the phone rang again almost immediately, and he picked it up and glanced at the clock. 10:03 said the red numerals.

"Hello?" he said warily.

"Hermia wrote those letters," said a man's voice. "Your other daughter."

"Who is this?" he demanded, sitting up in the bed.

"Good God," said the man and hung up.

Chick Lee. He kept forgetting about Chick Lee.

"God damn it!" Forrest shouted. He set the receiver back in its cradle and sat there naked with his hands on his knees. Hermia wrote the letters.

But didn't he know that already?

He tried to get his mind around the idea, and instantly gave up. What day was it? He labored to remember. Monday. Tomorrow afternoon, he realized with a small shudder, Marisa would arrive and his freedom would end. Not just his freedom, but this inquiry, this *recherche du temps perdu.*

Tomorrow he would have to drive to Atlanta and pick her up. All the way down she would blister him with her righteousness, accusations building and building like a black cloudbank, interrupted by lightning protestations about how much she'd prayed about the girls and where it was and how many candles she had lit. She would insist that he drive her straight to Tricia's, and there would be a big emotional scene right in front of Tricia and her fat-assed, pipe-pointing husband, who treated Forrest like somebody's pet Burmese python. Marisa would take charge of the girls, and what would he do then? Suffer his humiliation meekly?

He pictured himself fleeing into the woods of the Appalachians like that bomber who eluded the police for five years.

He stood up, cornered. There sat his laptop, poisoned by emails he could not bear to face, his manuscript dormant and unedited on the hard drive, festering in its jargon. Forrest's next big book, the next step: the idea of miscegenation filtered through evolutionary psychology and joined to the theory of the gameme, with a long excursus on Lamarck and epigenetics and neuroplasticity and Nietzschean longing for the Übermensch. Total bullshit.

Marisa was coming. Hurricane Marisa. He had one day to find out why somebody forty years ago had deliberately made him think Marilyn was dead. Mo Woodson had been there when he found the evidence. He had to see Mo. And what about Marilyn herself?

In the bathroom, he relieved himself in pinched, nervous spurts. Should he try to see her? Maybe take Hermia Watson with him? *She's your daughter*—and who had Chick gotten that from? He hadn't said it. Even Marilyn couldn't know, not without a DNA test. Shouldn't there be an instinct about such things?

But suppose she was his daughter? And suppose he had a son somewhere. What was the name Chick had used? Bob something?

There was a knock at the door, and Forrest called "Hold on." He put on his jeans before he opened it, bare-chested, expecting the maid and half-hoping it was some pretty little Mexican like the one who had been so scared when he couldn't find his ring in Atlanta. The glare from the pool dazzled him. A woman was silhouetted against it like a doe, ready to bolt.

He shaded his eyes. "Well, good morning," Forrest said.

"Are you my father?" she asked.

He stood there stupidly, squinting and scratching his stomach. "Listen," he said. "I need a cup of coffee. Can you give me a few minutes to get dressed? I'll take you to the Waffle House."

"I have to go check on Mrs. Hayes," she said, already half-turned from him.

"Okay, can I meet you at her house, say, in an hour?"

"You won't come," she said.

"I will. I swear. I just need some coffee and breakfast. I was up very late."

"So I heard. You and that so-called reporter."

Showered and shaved, wearing the last clean shirt he had, he started out the door and then decided he'd better read Marisa's email. He opened Outlook to find the one from yesterday he'd ignored. In the first few seconds, 76 unread emails collected in the inbox that gathered his various accounts besides the one at Walcott, and the number was getting higher. He almost closed the computer out of panic, but there it was with its provocative subject line - Apologies. No doubt demanding *his*. She wanted him to go around abasing himself to all the people discommoded by his existence.

Sitting on the edge of the chair, he clicked on it.

> Dear Brae—
>
> Why? Well because I told myself we were
> making a new start, just like Rachel and
> Dan did last year, if you remember.

It wasn't even for him. She thought she was answering Brae, whoever Brae was—probably one of her friends from St. Catherine of Siena, someone in that clump of vague post-menopausal women he sometimes saw her talking to. He stood up, already feeling liberated, though with peaking curiosity, he glanced at what she'd written.

> I'd been telling myself for years that
> my patience was going to work the way St.
> Monica's did, but then there we were, in
> the middle of my Italian relatives who
> didn't know me and didn't know him, and I
> felt like a total fool.

"Oh fuck it," Forrest said. He had his hand on top of the screen to close it when his eye fell on the next line.

> But I'm the one who got to stay in
> Rome. Now that I know the girls are okay,
> I can at least enjoy it a little.
> Yesterday morning, I got away from my aunt
> and caught the train into Rome. I just
> wandered by myself. I got some lunch at a
> little restaurant near Campo de Fiori and
> then drifted over into Trastevere, away
> from all the tourist spots. I visited St.
> Cecilia's. It cost a euro to get into the
> lower church, and there wasn't a soul
> there when I went down, so I didn't feel
> self-conscious about praying in front of
> the altar sculpture of St. Cecilia. You
> can tell she was decapitated, but it's the
> hands that moved me so much, especially

the way the wrist of her left hand is
twisted over. They say her right hand has
three fingers extended for the Trinity,
and her left hand just has the forefinger
to signify God's unity. But what moves me
is she reminds me of my daughter Cate, who
chose Cecilia as her confirmation name. I
just knelt there praying. For some reason
I remembered the Seamus Heaney poem about
a little adulteress they found preserved
in the bogs. So I prayed for that girl
Natalia and thought how lost she must have
been to do what she did.

Forrest groaned, his hand again poised to close the laptop. Lost. The word stung him. He remembered the first look that had come over Natalia's face when he put his hand on the small of her back and pulled her against him. She had suddenly recognized what she was about to do for her grade, which would be terrible unless—well, unless she loved him. So she convinced herself right there on the spot that she did love him. He had watched her instantaneously create a past in which she had already fallen in love with him and had been dreaming of this very moment. And then, of course, he had taken advantage of it.

Lost? Maybe. It's the kind of thing he'd once loved to talk about with Marisa. He read the rest of the email.

When I came up from the lower church, I
wanted to walk along the Tiber and cross
over and climb to a park I love on the
Aventine, but the traffic was too much for
me. I walked up a long narrow street and
crossed the Viale Trastevere and went past
lots of shops. I sat for a long time on
the steps of the fountain outside Santa
Maria in Trastevere. A dirty man with long
blonde dreadlocks was over to my right on
the lower steps playing a lute —I swear—
just like somebody in a Frans Hals
painting. He was picking out these lovely
tunes. He had the case for his instrument
open, and people would come up and drop
euros in it. I tried to talk to him
between songs, but I think he must have
been from Eastern Europe.

After a while, I was just staring up at
the mosaics under the pediment. I felt the
oddest bliss come over me, as though I
were a peasant in the Middle Ages who had

come into Rome on a pilgrimage, but also—I
know you understand what I mean—feeling a
communion with all the dead who had ever
seen what I was seeing. That sense of a
simple, eternal *now*. It's been years since
I've felt that kind of pure wonder, but
I've had it several times lately, even
riding the train on the way in from
Viterbo this morning and seeing the farms
unfold outside the window like watercolors
in someone's sketch book, or watching the
gulls land in the Tiber and drift down on
the current and then fly upstream to do it
again.

Jesus says His eye is on the sparrow. I
think his eye might still be on us. Even
on Braxton. I fear for Braxton.

Anyway, I went inside the church, and
an old man was bustling around in that
sweet medieval gloom, and he came right up
to me. I thought he was a little crazy,
like that woman in Portsmouth who sits
down in the front of the church and sways
back and forth all through Mass. Inglese?
he asked me. I said, American, and he
said, You go a confession. Well at St.
Peter's there's always somebody available
almost anytime you go, and I'd just been
to confession there a few days before. So
I tried to tell him I just wanted to look
around and spend some time with the apse
mosaic. But no, he looked very stern.
Priest, he said. Irlandese. You go. I
shook my head and got away from him and
started down the side aisle, but then I
came to this group of old women all hooded
in their shawls, and they looked at me and
they pointed to the confessional too, one
of those old boxes where you can see the
priest through the front and there are
grates and wooden kneeling boards on the
sides. At first I shook my head at them
too, but they scowled at me and nodded at
the confessional.

The priest was watching all this. He
shrugged at me and looked bemused, so I

went over and knelt down on the side and
when he pulled back the screen inside the
grate, I whispered, "Do you speak
English?" He did. He was very Irish and
very intelligent, and after a minute,
everything came out in a rush, as though
he had lanced a wound. I hadn't realized
until then how much I'd withheld before. I
must have been there half an hour. I wish
you could know him. I feel so blessed to
have been led to him. He just happened to
be visiting Rome, a Fr. Seamus something.
    I bought a sketch pad this morning, and
I'm going to spend the rest of the
afternoon with my pencils. Pray that all
goes well before Tuesday, when I see him
again. Just a few more days of the old
country, and who knows when I'll ever get
back? I'd better get off this machine
before they charge me another two euros.
    All my love, M
    P.S. *Wink.*

All her love? He felt a twinge of jealousy. Who the hell was Brae?
And why was he subject to her criticism, as the email implied he must
have been? And what was that "wink"?

When he left the motel, it was already getting hot, so he drove the
hundred yards over to the McDonald's and decided to go inside since he
still had half an hour before Hermia would be looking for him. He
ordered two sausage biscuits with cheese, some hash browns, and a
large coffee, then swiped his American Express card on the card reader
by the counter and took his tray back to the table.

All my love. She could say that to her friends? She could, and she
meant it. He complained about Marisa, because she embarrassed him
sometimes, sometimes driving him up the wall, but she kept alive a
capacity for recognizing divine intentions and welcoming the surprising
interventions of saints and angels. She could talk heart-to-heart with the
most sophisticated academics or the simplest housemaids. It irritated
him to hear some shallow historian like Roger Carboys dismiss her
"magical thinking." Belief in God worked in adaptive terms, no question
about it. He knew too much to feel it, of course, but he admired it in
others as a genetically dormant potential being realized.

It was interesting to encounter a Marisa not armed and aiming his
infidelities back at him. *I fear for Braxton.* He remembered the day he
first took her out to lunch, long before she turned so pious. She had been
painting the hallway across from his office, reaching up with her roller,
and he had watched the soft wobble of her bottom in a glow of

entrancement. After a few minutes, he had stood in the doorway of his office.

Have you had lunch?

I'm working, she said over her shoulder, not even looking at him, as though she already knew who he was and what he looked like and what he wanted.

I know, he said, and I can't tell you how much I admire your work.

She had turned slowly to look at him. Smiling, she put her paint roller carefully back in the pan before going to wash her hands.

She was sitting across the table from him in the back of Hoagie's in Athens when he read her the passage from the *Iliad* where Athena kindles the flame above Achilles' head when he stands at the ditch and shouts. He had been writing the last chapter of *The Subjunctive Abyss*. That night, seeing her sympathy, he had told her about Gallatin.

Had he told her about Marilyn?

Of course he had told her, he realized with a slow dyspepsia of recollection. Why did he imagine he hadn't? It had already been a packaged story by his late twenties. He used the Marilyn story to impress women with his troubling, alienated angst, his solitary nobility, his heroism in love—all of it because he had endured a youthful Gehenna.

He had told her everything and she had seen through his pretensions and loved him despite it. Not only that, she had proofread the whole manuscript before he sent it off. They had surprised each other over and over with desire that did not seem to wane, and they had married in a little courthouse in South Carolina on her twenty-third birthday in 1989, the last day of June in that great year of liberations. He had been faithful to her until ... until when?

Until he turned around at the conference in Providence and saw Lola Gunn.

It was too ridiculous. She couldn't be.

He sat eating his sausage biscuit.

He glanced around for a clock and saw a stocky man with a broad snub nose and thick, hairy forearms holding a cup of coffee and staring at him, a weary strain on his face. When Forrest saw the time behind the counter and looked back at the man, he was still staring. Forrest raised his eyebrows. The man got up and walked over to him.

"You Braxton Forrest?" he asked.

"That's right."

"I've been hoping I'd run into your sorry ass," the man said. "You think you can do anything you want to, don't you, and leave other people to clean up?"

"Do I know you?" Forrest said. He stood up, looming over the man. People at the other tables turned to stare.

Instead of answering, the man swung at him and the blow glanced off the side of his head as he dodged it. The customers in line huddled back against the counter.

"Kyle! Hey, Kyle!" a woman cried.

Left-handed, Forrest grabbed the man's right wrist as he swung again and then seized him by the throat and lifted him off the floor, squeezing. The man's legs kicked at him, and he tried to pummel Forrest with his left fist, but in his rage Forrest could feel the windpipe under his grip. The man gagged, tongue protruding, both hands trying now to pry Forrest's hand from his throat. A little harder, just a little harder, and he would crush everything.

"Sir! Put him down, sir!" somebody was calling in a high terrified voice. "Hey! Hey!"

A hand was grabbing at him, and he swung around furiously. A small white woman in a McDonald's uniform cringed and backed away from him. He dropped the man who had attacked him and gave a shove that sent him backwards against a vast black teenager just coming around the condiment stand with his tray. The boy deftly shifted his food out of harm's way as he absorbed the impact. Holding his throat, the man stood bewildered for a moment, then lowered his head and stumbled from the restaurant.

Blood pounded in Forrest's temples. The other customers stared at him, food in hand. He stood like a cornered bear.

"What is this?" Forrest said to the manager. "I'm sitting here eating my breakfast and this guy comes over and attacks me."

"Yes'm, that's what happened," attested an old black man standing shakily beside a partly-finished meal at one of the other tables. "Mr. Howard he just come up to him and swing at him. I don't know what got into him."

The little manager nodded and backed away.

"So everything's okay?" she said, her palms held tensely downward at waist level. "We're okay here?"

Forrest gave a noncommittal shrug and sat back down. He'd never seen the man before. His heart kept hammering, hammering, hammering. Head low, he sipped his coffee. He could still feel the savage urge to crush the man's windpipe. He unconsciously put a bite of the sausage biscuit in his mouth. It sat on his tongue like a gobbet of corpse. He spit it onto the table, wadded up the rest of his meal disgustedly and, all eyes on him, dumped the food into the trash can on the way out, fury still circling through him like bees around a kicked hive.

Outside, he looked around, half-expecting the man to step out of a pickup with a shotgun and go for him. In the drive-through lane, a sedan edged forward, followed by a pickup, a white van, and a small yellow bus. Over toward the EconoLodge, a Wal-Mart tractor-trailer labored up the grade on Lee Street. Southbound traffic streamed by toward Florida on the Interstate. He did not see anyone getting out of a parked car, but he kept watching as he walked across the lot to his car. When he sat down in the driver's seat and started it to get the air conditioning going, he turned on the cell phone, ignoring the messages and missed calls, and pressed the Send button. He found Hermia's number. She answered right away.

"I knew you wouldn't come."

"Have you ever heard of Mo Woodson?"

"No," she said, distant and stoical.

"He's the one who first told me about your mother. Introduced me, you might say. He was there when Tony Wright died. Mo is the one who convinced me not to go the police about it when I found your mother's dress."

"I don't have the faintest idea what you're talking about."

He pinched the bridge of his nose right between his eyes. Of course she didn't.

"I'll explain it to you after I see him. Then how about ... how about you go with me to see her?" he said.

"She doesn't want to see you, Prof. Forrest. She's scared to death to see you."

"You told her I was here?"

"It seemed fair to warn her."

"Warn her?" Forrest considered the insulting implications of the word. "I have to see her. Will you go?"

"It's going to seem like I brought you."

"You did bring me." She was silent. "You wrote the letters," he said. She still did not answer. "Just go with me to see your mother. Then maybe we'll know the answer to your question." When she did not speak, he added, "Lola."

"Okay," she said weakly.

He closed the phone and started to put the car in reverse when there was a knock on his window. The man who had attacked him stood there, and Forrest stared back at him until the man made a rolling motion with his right forefinger.

"Yeah?" Forrest said as the window slid down. "What now?"

The man spat tobacco juice off to the side. "I want to explain something," he said hoarsely. "I been up all night at the hospital with an old friend of my daddy's named Ray Ponder. You know him?"

Forrest watched him closely and nodded. "He runs that filling station across from the high school."

"Ray died this morning. I been out there with Mrs. Ponder. They don't have any children left. Ray Jr. got killed in Vietnam, and they don't know what happened to their daughter. She got messed up with drugs a long time ago. After I helped Mrs. Ponder get squared away with the funeral home, I came down here to get some breakfast, and that's when I saw you."

Forrest shrugged. "Okay."

"I was at Ray's station the day the bus dropped off your daughters. Me and Ray and Jeff Todd. And you were over in Italy or whatever and your girls thought they were being picked up by a chauffeur because you told them some bullshit about how rich old Mrs. Hayes was. So Ray was the one trying to help them out, sick as he was. Old Ray, dying of cancer, losing his mind on pain pills. I saw you sitting there in front of me... "

"Okay," Forrest sighed.

"I always thought people were full of shit when they talked about you," he said, not smiling. "I won't think that now."

"What does that mean?"

"Take it how you want to."

He waited to see if Forrest would react, and when Forrest just sat there, he walked away.

❢ ❢ ❢

Back in his room, Forrest found Mo Woodson's address by looking up the Gallatin County property records online. He mapped it on Google and memorized the directions. He also found a phone number, but he didn't want to give Mo any warning.

Instead of taking the Interstate, he drove old U.S. 41 again. It paralleled the railroad that ran through little nests of Fingals and Bunns and Waldrops on the way to Hereford and Macon. New developments had cropped up all along the route. The old farms were now mere acreage, annexed as suburbs of Macon the way the land north of town was gradually becoming a suburb of Atlanta. Forty years ago, the only store in Hereford had been run by the Starkey brothers, both unmarried and more or less equally irascible. As Forrest slowed to turn, he saw that the store was still there, not boarded up, but blank and unused. Up the road a quarter-mile, a Shell station with tremendous signs attracted cars exiting the Interstate to its convenience store and barbecue.

Mo lived off a side road that was badly in need of repaving. His big aluminum mailbox had WOODSON lettered on it. He had pictured Mo in a doublewide trailer, and he was not wrong, but this one had been enhanced with a kind of foundation and firmed up almost into a real house with a porch in front and a two-car garage on the right side—both doors open, the space inside half-filled with lumber. The house sat on a piney lot on top of a ridge, and the ground fell off sharply behind it.

Forrest pulled into the asphalt driveway and parked behind a black Ford pickup with a nursery tree in the bed. A new dark-red Nissan XTerra sat beside it. When Forrest got out, an old hound roused himself from the stoop and barked once, looking back over his shoulder to see if anybody wanted him to do it again. Then he wandered out to Forrest, wagging his tail and ducking his head as if to apologize for being owned by somebody as sorry as Mo Woodson.

"Somebody there, Maureen?" a familiar voice called from the garage.

"Mo!" Forrest yelled. "Get your butt out here."

Forrest had not sufficiently imagined what he now saw. An old man shambled out of the garage and peered at him suspiciously. The oiled-looking sleekness was long gone. His last strands of hair, still slicked-back, were bone white, the skin was slack around his neck, his cheeks hung slab-like, his hands were mottled with liver spots, but something of the old lean-hipped swagger still suggested itself. After a few seconds of staring, Mo lightened and shook his head. "I will be goddamned. I will just be goddamned."

"Mo," Forrest said, "I never doubted it."

"Maureen!" he shouted. "What in the hell are you doing way out here in the woods?" he asked in a normal voice. "I thought you was a professor or some such shit. Maureen!"

"What is it, Maurice? Lunch is about ready." A small, plain-faced, busty woman in her thirties stood in the doorway. She appeared to have on one of Mo's T-shirts and nothing else. "Oh!" she cried when she saw Forrest and ducked back behind the screen.

"Want you to meet somebody. This here's Cump Forrest, used to work with me a long time ago when he was just a young buck instead of a old man."

"Hey," she said, waving her hand out the screen. "I'd come out but I'm not dressed."

"Pleased to meet you, Maureen," said Forrest. "I heard Mo had a pretty young wife, and I thought I'd come out and see if I could steal her."

"Yeah, you the first man besides me ever seen her," Mo said, shakily extracting an off-brand cigarette from his pack and firing it with his old Zippo. "I usually keep her chained up in the bedroom. You chanced on her day off, and now I got hell to pay."

"Maurice," she said plaintively, "please, honey—would you come in the house for a minute, please?"

"Be in directly."

Forrest leaned close. "Mo, I won't keep you. Three questions."

Forrest saw a flicker of fear, but Mo lifted his chin. "Shoot."

"You let her call you Maurice?"

Mo shrugged. "Maurice and Maureen. She puts it on the coffee mugs and towels and what all. She likes the sound of it."

"Second question. What happened to Paloma?"

"Paloma?" He looked stricken. "Jesus, she was—that's right, that's why we ... Hell, Cump, the cancer got her. Ate her like cotton candy, just melted her to nothing."

"I'm sorry," Forrest said.

Mo shook his head, musing. "Well, Jesus, that was a long time ago. Maureen's my third one since then."

"I'm all the way inside the kitchen," Maureen complained from the screen door, "and I can hear you using the Lord's name in vain."

"Well don't listen, sugarpie," Mo flared. He took Forrest's elbow. "Come on, walk out here to the back with me."

He dropped his cigarette on the asphalt and rocked his foot on it, then led the way around the end of the house to an unfinished deck he was building at the edge of the ridge. He set two folding chairs on the finished part. Far down the slope, a creek glimmered through the underbrush. "It's gone have a roof, a picnic table. This ridge gets breezes, but I'll screen it in if the mosquitoes get bad. Wire it, put in a big ceiling fan. Maureen's got twin boys from her first marriage, both of them over in Iraq, and it'll be nice when they visit. And when they get married and have kids, if I live that long. Meantime, I got me somewhere to drink my whiskey."

With his back to the house, he took out another cigarette and tore off the filter, his hands trembling around the lighter as he lit the ragged end.

"She don't like hearing me cough a half hour every morning, but." He inhaled and let the smoke trail out of his mouth. "Sweet Jesus that's good. So what's your third question?" he asked, his voice wary.

"How'd you get a young thing like Maureen to marry your sorry old ass?"

"You mean besides being rich and looking like Jerry Lee Lewis? I tell you one thing. Whoever come up with Viagra deserves one of them noble prizes." He sat for a minute and then extended the back of his hand toward Forrest. "Would you look at this shit?" he said, waving his cigarette over the liver spots. "And look here." He held up his right arm to make a muscle and wrinkled skin sagged loosely from his arm. "It's gone happen to you before you know it, I'm telling you. It comes on you fast. But you asked me a question. Maureen's a nurse—Monday's her day off is why she's home."

"Maurice, I smell that smoke," Maureen called. "You just had one."

"Shit," murmured Mo under his breath, blowing the smoke from the side of his mouth. "See I met her down at the hospital in Macon. She was down there when my third wife died. This was after I retired out at Plant Ocmulgee. She saw how broke up and lonesome I was, and she was friendly. She ain't getting no younger, and she ain't no beauty—probably why her first husband ran off with somebody—but she's fine for an old man like me. She's born again, a real holy woman. She felt sorry for me, you want to know the truth. Do you know that woman teaches Sunday school? She says I got a deep-down sweetness. I try to keep her fooled." He paused and looked at Forrest. "But that ain't your real question."

"I found out Saturday Marilyn Harkins is alive."

"I knew that's what you come for."

"I thought for forty years somebody had killed her."

Mo nodded. Forrest stared at the old man, who would not meet his eyes.

"Why'd you let me think that?"

"Because you were a goddamn fool." Mo tore the filter off another cigarette and lit it with the one he was still smoking. He dropped the old one into a citronella candle brimming with rainwater.

"She called my goddamn house the night after that boy got stung to death. Paloma, she'd gone over to Jackson to be with her sister, and she tried to get me to drive her, but I told her hell no, I couldn't face another goddamn thing that day, much less pretend to that boy's mama he was worth a shit. So I was setting there at the kitchen table halfway down a bottle of Jim Beam, and the phone rings. A woman says Otis, and I know it's her. I says, Jesus Christ, what if Paloma had been here and answered the phone? And she was smooth, she says, She would say nobody named Otis lives there. And then she says, You've got to help me, Mo, and I says, Why you asking me for help? Why don't you ask your boyfriend?"

August 19-20, 1969

When they got back to the office the day Tony Wright died, Brother told them to take the next day off. Forrest sat at home that night in shock. When his mother realized that he would not talk about it, she tended him like an invalid. She put lotion on his stings. She set him up in the living room with a TV tray instead of making him eat supper at the table. She brought him iced tea; she made him cheeseburgers and French fries. She sat with him while they watched the news about the aftermath of the huge rock festival at Woodstock and the search for leads about the murder of Sharon Tate. Sometimes, she would venture a question about what happened. Did the boy's mother...? But he would shake his head and say he didn't know.

They sat through reruns of *The Mod Squad* and *It Takes a Thief*. He stayed up late and watched Joe Dimaggio and Raquel Welch on Johnny Carson. When he finally went to bed, he kept going through things, over and over, until he finally fell asleep.

The phone rang the next morning before seven and woke up Forrest's mother.

"Braxton," she said, opening his door. "Can you come to the phone? It's that Maurice Woodson."

Forrest got up groggily and went to the heavy black phone in the hallway outside his mother's bedroom door. His mother hovered in her doorway, clutching her robe about her, and he shook his head at her.

"Mo?" he said.

"Bertram Everett called me drunk last night," Mo said.

"About what?"

"He said the deed was done. I asked him what deed, and he said

Marilyn, and I asked him what about her, and he told me to go out to the Swint property on the river."

His knees gave as he stood there and the hand holding the phone dropped to his side. He must have made a sound, because his mother opened her door and came back out.

"What's the matter, honey? What now?"

When he lifted the phone again, Mo was saying something. He asked him to repeat it.

"I said I'll get you in half an hour."

Mo drove Forrest in his black Cutlass out to the woods they had been surveying off Rayford Road the day Bertram Everett quit. He got out and led the way down the lines they had cut along an old fence. As they approached the river, Mo held up a hand like a squad leader on patrol. Forrest stared around dully, lifting his eyes to scan the riverbank. He thought for a split-second that he saw someone walking. But it was something white on a tree thirty yards away.

"Holy shit," Mo said beside him. Cautiously, they walked up to it. The fishnet dress had been spread on the curve of the trunk. It looked like orange flowers blossomed at the shoulders and hips, but it was 16-penny nails punched through orange flagging and nailed flush with the tree trunk. The cloth beneath the neck was stained a dull red and flies were buzzing around it.

He turned aside and vomited.

"They must of cut her and thowed her in the river naked. Lord, you can see where they drug her over."

Stupefied, Forrest glanced at the crushed grass, the collapsed section of the bank.

"And this here must be one of her sh—"

Mo was bending down to pick something up from the grass when suddenly he gave a high, feminine scream and leapt backward just as a moccasin struck the air. It regathered itself, head weaving. Wild-eyed with terror, Mo tore past him up the cut line along the fence. Caught up in the same panic, Forrest followed, crashing back through the woods as though they were being chased.

Mo flung open the door and sat panting with his forehead on the steering wheel, great convulsive shudders coursing through him. His glassy eyes passed unseeing over Forrest.

Forrest put his head in his hands. Wright yesterday, and now Marilyn, Marilyn. He imagined her terror.

After a minute of whimpering incoherently, Mo started his car.

"It's some evil coming," he said, licking his finger to make a pattern of Xs on the windshield. "God Almighty. God Almighty."

"It's already come," Forrest said.

"On me," Mo said. "It's coming on me."

Mo dropped another cigarette into the citronella candle and stood up. He put his hands in the back pockets of his jeans and stared down toward the creek, his back to Forrest. "Jesus, I leaned over to pick up that shoe, and there was that snake coming up at me. It was like that boy was—it was like it was... I never been so scared in my life." He looked back at Forrest over his shoulder. "I said that about some evil coming?"

"I remember it like it was yesterday."

Mo's head dropped and a moment later he wiped tears from his eyes. "It was Paloma. Next to my mama, she was the love of my goddamn life. Jesus. Oh, Jesus." He sat back down with his hand shading his eyes and wept dramatically.

"Maurice?" called Maureen from the window of the house. "Are y'all coming in for lunch?"

He nodded his head and raised his hand without turning toward her.

"Why did Marilyn call you?" Forrest asked.

He did not answer for a long time.

"I was always nice to her," he said at last. "She knew I liked her."

"I loved her."

"Loved her. Jesus Christ!" Mo exploded acidly. "That's why she called me. What was she supposed to do with you loving her? Did you ever think about that? Hell, no. You just loved her. Here you were the goddamn state champion town hero, in love with a nigger girl, and not even some respectable nigger girl, but the whore who just turned in the names of half the—

"Okay, Mo."

"You acted like you fucking owned her. You loved her—meaning what? I knew her better than you did. I knew where she lived, I knew what her uncle did to her, I knew where she worked, I knew she wondered who her white daddy was, all of it. You were so full of shit. You didn't love her. You were just making a point and you didn't even know it, you were so full of how everybody else was bad to the niggers. You ruined your mama's life, and you would have ruined yours and Marilyn's too. You would have tried to marry her or some dumbass thing just to make a point." He tore the filter off another cigarette and lit it.

Forrest did not answer. He had been over some of it so many times that he could not tell what he remembered and what he imagined. He stared down the slope toward the creek. But he had never gone back over the days after her death. They were cored from his memory.

Her supposed death.

Vague images came back into focus: how he quit the crew that Thursday morning. Brother argued with him, thinking it was Wright's death that had undone him. *It's not your fault that boy died. I need you on the crew. If you leave, it's just Mo. Can't you stay on a week or two until I can find somebody.* Then, when Forrest refused, Brother said, *I fought in Korea, and of anybody I've hired, I would have counted on you out on patrol. Just tell me why you're quitting.* He could not explain his reasons. *If it's that colored girl, I wouldn't have thought you'd run away from trouble, once you got yourself in it. I took you for a man of honor.* I can't tell you, Forrest said. I can't tell anybody.

The next day, trembling with self-loathing, he had packed up and left despite his mother's pleading, her climbing misery. Bill Fletcher drove him to Athens. With his summer money he stayed in a cheap motel for several weeks until the dormitory opened. He got a shot of penicillin at a clinic. When they asked how he got it, he gave them Jasmine Colter's name.

For the next four years, he went home to Gallatin for only a few days at a time. Thanksgiving, Christmas. He and his mother would sit almost unspeaking and prod their food.

He knew about the disgrace he had brought on her in the town, but he convinced himself it wasn't so bad. He rarely called. He could not remember writing, though he had found a few letters after her death. He saw no one when he did go home and heard no news about Gallatin. He got summer jobs as far away from home as he could, the first summer in Athens and the next two in Alaska at a fish-processing plant. Was it there that he had first begun to tell about Marilyn? He remembered a barmaid in Homer who had lingered to ask him if he was homesick. The feel of her thick blonde braid coming undone. Meanwhile, his life at college ran its course through the rejection of his football scholarship, his brief but memorable membership in SDS, his first marriage, his Fulbright in France—Asia Carducci had reminded him, he suddenly realized, of a French doctor's wife he had met in Rouen and wooed with his latter-day Faulknerian fable. Then graduate school at Yale, or Easy Pickings in New Haven.

Mo touched Forrest on the knee and Forrest looked up.

"What?"

"You thought you loved her, but what really happened was you got her to love you. That's what happened."

He focused on the old man in front of him.

"I see why it upset you."

"Why's that?"

"You were like her pimp."

"What's that supposed to mean?"

"You're the one who told me about her. You even told Bertram Everett about her."

Mo pursed his lips and glanced back at the house.

"You want a drink of whiskey? I got a bottle under the deck."

"No, I've got to go."

"You can't stay for lunch? You don't want to hurt Maureen's feelings."

"I just ate breakfast."

Mo raised his face to the sky and stretched his neck. "What you don't realize, it was her idea. She give me a dress she knew you'd recognize to nail up, so I done it. The people she worked with didn't know shit about Gallatin, and she had friends in Macon. I drove her down there. She knew you'd get down on yourself, hate the town, hate me, whatever, but at least you wouldn't have to pretend you loved her."

"Jesus, Mo. Give me a little credit."

"Did you ever go looking for her?"

"*I thought she was dead!*"

Mo laughed and reached over to squeeze Forrest's knee.

"You was pretty goddamn easy to fool for a guy supposed to be smart. The only thing I was scared of was you getting Hudson Binder out there, because he was gone find out it was just some ketchup on her dress and wonder what the hell I was trying to pull."

"Ketchup."

"Hey, you wanted to kill Bertram Everett, you remember that? And I told you that's what he wanted was for you to come after him." His laugh turned into a fit of coughing and he had to get up and spit into the grass. Turning back, he wiped the tears from his eyes. "I said he was gone tell the sheriff how you wanted to kill him."

Forrest watched Mo's amusement with a tight smile. "That's right. I remember you said I was the one Binder would suspect of killing Marilyn, and I believed it, especially after you put the idea in his head that I pushed Tony Wright into that stump. Besides, it would just be suspicion of murder until they did find her, and if I happened to know exactly where she'd been killed, all the suspicion would be on me. You had me set up, didn't you? You said to lay low, and we'd figure out how to play it when somebody found her body in a day or two."

Mo wheezed with laughter.

"Course, Sheriff Binder wouldn't of had any reason to suspect she was dead unless you told him, so he wouldn't of even been looking for her in the first place. The only way it would of come up is if somebody found her body in the river. Which I knew it wouldn't happen since she was alive and kicking down in Macon."

He laughed until a fit of coughing bent him over with both hands on his knees.

Forrest remembered the apocalyptic dread of those days of waiting, when he sat in the motel in Athens by the window, expecting to see a State Patrol car pull into the lot. Mo picked a shred of tobacco from his lip, noticing at last that Forrest was not laughing.

"I'm just saying. Nobody didn't find her body because she was doing just fine down there in Macon. And you didn't go looking for her."

"No I didn't, Mo," he said. "Good job. Why didn't you protect her from the people who really did want to kill her?"

"Hell, I did," Mo said hotly. "I got her out of town."

"So it was all staged just for me."

"Come on, now, don't get all mad. It was forty years ago. It was what Maureen calls a intervention. Sure you don't want some whiskey?"

Forrest stood up. "Go fuck yourself, Mo."

"Come on, don't go off like that."

As Forrest walked toward the corner of the house, he saw Maureen watching him from the window.

"I done the right thing," Mo called after him, his voice rising. "You ought to thank me for saving your ass from what you would of done."

"Jesus Christ, Mo," Forrest said, turning back to him. "For forty years I've thought I got her killed. You could at least apologize."

"She asked me to do it!" Mo cried, standing profiled against the woods on the edge of his deck, palms open. "You think about that. Here you was tangled up with the Whore of Baghdad, and she her own self asked me to cut you loose."

Halfway back to Gallatin, when the anger began to subside, Forrest started laughing. The Whore of Baghdad. He pictured Mo in bed half-listening to Maureen read to him from the Book of Revelations before turning off the lights. Where is Babylon at? Mo would ask in the dark. Honey, our Sunday School teacher said it's over there in Iraq close to Baghdad where my boys are at, Maureen would say, and as he dropped off to sleep Mo would remember snippets from the nightly news and recollect being a soldier his own self and what he done with the ladies of the night, and one thought would lead to another until finally up would come Marilyn Harkins, the Whore of Baghdad, from the deep-down sweetness of Mo Woodson.

Forrest laughed until he wheezed, laughed until his face hurt and he couldn't see for the tears. He had to pull off on the exit ramp to Rumble Road and stop the car. He got out and walked around with his hands on his hips, panting like a spent runner. A pickup coming off the Interstate onto the exit ramp slowed and the driver looked a question at him, but Forrest shook his head and waved him off. He got out his cell phone and checked the time. 1:09. Another wave of laughter shook him. He got back in the car and felt his stomach growling. He called Hermia, and she answered after three rings.

"I'm sorry I'm so late. Can I take you to lunch?" he said. When there was silence, he thought he had lost the connection, but there were odd noises—beeps and voices—in the background. "Are you there?"

"More or less," she said.

"Is something wrong?"

"Mrs. Hayes. I didn't hear anything when I first came into the house. That's about when you called. But when I went upstairs, I found her next to the window. I think she tried to open it. She'd probably been lying there since last night."

"Was she conscious?"

"I wish she hadn't been. They've got her sedated now."

"So you're at the hospital?"

"I rode with her in the ambulance. Could you pick me up?"

H

At her suggestion, Forrest took Hermia to the Left Bank Grille on the courthouse square. When he was growing up, the building had housed the Gallatin County Bank, but Hermia told him it had been bought by a couple named Ryburn who had moved down from Virginia. The pun in the restaurant's name required a vaguely Parisian atmosphere—French café chairs at glass tables, whimsical Chagall prints—but the restaurant attracted people from as far away as Macon with its upscale Southern cooking.

They found a table by the front window that overlooked the sidewalk and the courthouse square. From his angle, he could see the Confederate soldier, rifle on his shoulder, facing north at the corner of Lee and Jackson. Hermia wanted to talk before they ordered, but the Howard man had wrecked his breakfast. Forrest was starving. When a bus boy set down a complimentary basket of rolls and cornbread, he started devouring them, so she relented and they gave the waitress their orders.

"So you wrote those letters to get me down here," he said, buttering a piece of hot cornbread. "What was it? Nostalgia?"

She would not look at him. She turned her head to gaze out the window, and the skin around her eyes registered a succession of emotions. Her lips moved.

"I'm sorry?" he said, leaning forward.

"Can we not talk about that right now? Can we not?"

"Okay. But we're going to talk about it sometime. That trip to Italy, my girls stranded down here. We're going to talk about it."

"Mrs. Hayes keeps calling for somebody named Aunt Ella."

"Aunt Ella?"

"She must have been a domestic at Stonewall Hill," Hermia said. "LaCourvette knows something, but she doesn't want to tell me."

"What does that have to do with anything?

She gave a small shrug. "I think maybe a lot."

"Why are you working there? It doesn't make any sense to me."

"I'm trying to understand what you have when ..." She broke off and looked out the window.

"When what?"

"When your circumstances rob you in advance. When just being born doesn't so much let you be what you are as it shows you what you're not and never will be."

"I wrote a book about it. *The Subjunctive Abyss*. So do you mean race? That's why you're working over there, playing the housemaid?"

"Maybe."

He was still hungry when the waitress came back and set down their orders. He watched Hermia pick at a Carolina crab cake on field greens. She really was a lovely person: her elegance, her educated tastes. She was looking down at her food, not meeting his eyes. Her wrist flexed lightly as she prodded but did not pierce a bit of arugula with the tines of her fork. The idea that she was Lola Gunn, that fey, unforgettable creature—the idea that she was Marilyn Harkins' daughter—was almost too much.

No, it was too much. He took a sip of water and suddenly laughed, almost choking on the absurdity of it.

"So you actually sat somewhere and—"

He coughed again, trying to control his laughter. "You sat somewhere with an old pen and forged those letters?"

She looked up with a trembling half-smile.

"*Are* you my father?"

He was already halfway through the home-style bacon-wrapped meatloaf with mashed potatoes and gravy. He speared four or five pole beans cooked with ham hock and put them in his mouth. Forrest chewed his beans, looking at her, focusing at last on this most absurd part of the puzzle. He had already faced the probability. She was *Marilyn's* daughter, no question. She had a hint of Marilyn's high cheekbones. As he looked at her, she lifted her face uncertainly, as if she heard something faint and distant, and around her eyes and mouth, just in that moment, there was something he recognized in his girls, something he remembered seeing in his mother's oval face, a definite Scandinavian strain.

A kind of vertigo came over him. His mother. Even the color of her eyes convicted him.

When he did not answer, she raised her eyebrows. She sighed and her head sank as if she had been denied. He reached over and put his hand on hers, and she started to withdraw it, but he gripped it lightly, causing a subtle stir among the other patrons of the restaurant, all women, all pretending not to watch him.

"You have to understand something," he said. "Until Saturday, I thought your mother was dead. I hadn't heard of you until I got here and Chick Lee's wife told me. And after she told me, I thought you were a local woman helping old Cousin Emily Barron Hayes."

She turned and gazed out the window, carefully removing her hand from under his, as though its presence were an impropriety so painful that it could not be acknowledged at all. Her face remained still and listening.

"I mean, good god, Lola..."

"Don't call me Lola."

Her lips began to tremble, the more movingly the more she tried to pinch them in. Her eyes filled with tears, and she raised her face with extraordinary dignity just as they spilled over and ran down her cheeks.

"So if you are my father, what should I call you?" she said. She turned and met his gaze, wiping her eyes with her knuckles like a child. A small bitter smile played around her mouth. "Daddy Forrest? I've had so many daddies."

"So don't call me Daddy," he said.

She picked up her fork and absently flaked a bite of crab cake onto her salad. "Then what?"

He cut another bite of meat loaf with the side of his fork and dipped it in ketchup.

"Where did you get your 'Watson'?" he asked. "Hermia Watson."

"Daddy Watson was the man I thought was my father until last night. An older gentleman, very kind. An undertaker in Macon. He must have married my mother when she was pregnant with me."

Forrest nodded. Out of nowhere, he had an image of Hermia as a child in a white dress. She was standing uncertainly and holding her mother's hand in a small room full of flowers. An old man in a formal black suit came quietly through the door and greeted them, closing the door behind him. He kissed Marilyn on the cheek and whispered something—she was dressed respectably in a matching jacket and skirt—and then bent down to embrace the little girl, whose fearful eyes revealed that she always felt left out of the reality that other people inhabited.

A flash outside made him turn his head—sunlight glancing off a car door as it opened. His fork stopped in midair.

Out on the sidewalk, a beautiful black woman in a mauve jacket and skirt picked a thread from her left wrist and pointed her keys back at her car, a white Mercedes, before limping toward the restaurant door. Hermia was picking at her salad, unaware. When the woman disappeared, Forrest stared at the divider separating the dining room from the receptionist's stand. Then she was in the room. She looked Marisa's age. Her face was fuller but unwrinkled except at the corners of her eyes and a little at the neck. Gold hoop earrings inlaid with diamonds hung from her earlobes. She fussed with her purse, dropping the keys in it, and raised her eyes to scan the room, her tongue wetting her lips.

When she saw him, her mouth opened. She took a step backward.

With her eyes locked on his, she half-turned her head toward the door as though she were trying to turn away. But now Hermia followed his gaze and saw her.

"Mama," she called. She got out of her seat.

With lowered heads and sidelong glances, the women at the other tables watched their muted exchange and saw Hermia prevail. Not looking at Forrest, Marilyn limped to the table and took the chair with its back to the other tables. She sat very erect on the edge of the seat with her knees turned slightly toward the exit, not looking at him.

"Prof. Forrest," said Hermia, with a voice full of irony. "This is my mother, Mrs. Adara Dernier-Jones."

Among the perfectly polished mauve nails restively tapping the table was one with an intricate peacock design. When she started to get up, Forrest restrained her with a hand on her arm.

"Come on," he said. "Now that she's got us here."

"I am not the person you knew," she said, still not looking at him. Her voice had the old formality, but now, inhabited by decades of conscious art and the experience of wealth, it did not seem artificial.

"No you're not," he said. "You're alive."

Marilyn looked at him now, and as he met her hazel eyes, his heart yawed strangely.

"What in the world do you mean by that?" she asked, and seeing him this close, her voice softened. "Wasn't I alive then?"

Forrest felt the pulse beating in his neck. He glanced at Hermia and raised his eyebrows. He hardly registered the humiliation on her face. She excused herself and disappeared toward the restroom. Forrest took Marilyn's hand and after a moment of hesitation, she did not withdraw it. Heads leaned together at the other tables.

"I just found out Saturday," he said.

"Found out what?"

"That you're still alive."

"I don't have the faintest idea what you're talking about."

The waitress startled him, a slim white girl with nervous, freckled elbows. "Ma'am, have you had time to look at your menu?"

He withdrew his hand.

"No, but what are your specials today?" Marilyn asked, leaning back to look at her.

"We have a blackened catfish with gr—"

"That's fine, I'll take that, sweetheart."

"And anything besides water to drink?"

"Pinot grigio."

"Oh, no ma'am. We've don't serve—"

"Iced tea, then. Unsweetened."

"Yes, ma'am."

He let the waitress make her exit.

"So," he said, "when did you become—what is it? Adele?"

"Adara. I made it up. Let me look at you."

She gazed for a moment. She shook her head slightly as if to clear it and closed her eyes and let out a breath.

"I never thought this day would come," she said.

"Neither did I, needless to say."

"You're worried about my name?" She laughed and touched his forearm playfully. "When I first met Clovell Watson, it just popped out of my mouth. The lady in Macon where I stayed knew my real name, but I told Mr. Watson my name was Adara. It wasn't until years later I found out it's a real name. And do you know what it means?" She widened her eyes at him. "Virgin."

He lifted his eyebrows at this information. "So you married an undertaker."

"Seemed like a good idea," she said, "after all that business. He was as old as we are now. You never saw anybody in your life as grateful as Clovell Watson was when I married him." She gave his hand a shy touch. "I wasn't but eighteen, remember? A long time ago."

"How did you pass the blood test?"

She drew back. After a moment, she reached for her purse and started to stand. She twisted around in her chair to look at the entrance to the restaurant.

"Where did Hermia—you know she said you might try to see me, but when she called me from the hospital ..."

"I know what you did, Marilyn. Mo told me."

"What I did?"

She turned now to look at him, and at the same instant, he saw Hermia standing on the threshold. He shook his head, and just then the waitress brought the iced tea and a green salad.

"Is the other lady finished?" She gestured toward Hermia's plate. "Should I clear her place?"u

"No, she's coming back," Forrest said, and the girl glanced over at Hermia, puzzled, and answered, "Yes sir."

As soon as she left, he leaned toward Marilyn. "Why didn't you let me say goodbye? My God," he said, "for forty years—forty years—I've thought you'd been murdered."

"Murdered? What are you talking about?"

"Saturday I found out you were still alive, and today I found out you wanted me to think you were dead. My God, why? Why didn't you let me know something, even if you—"

"Murdered?"

"Mo told me. He said you gave him the dress you wore, your shoes."

"My shoes?" she repeated.

"I saw the dress. It was nailed to a tree beside the Ocmulgee and covered with blood from where they cut your throat. I saw where they'd dragged your body to the river."

She was shaking her head in disbelief, her mouth open as though her lips were shaped around some unspeakable word.

"God damn it!" he cried, slamming the table with his open hand, rattling the silverware and splashing water out of the glasses. The ladies at the other tables jolted back in their chairs, outraged. Forrest lowered his voice.

"Mo took me out there the day after Tony Wright died. I saw the little show he set up to trick me, and it worked. I was pretty stupid, but it worked. Do you have any idea...?" He glared at the women listening, who turned back to their plates. "Do you have any idea how that felt?" he whispered. "What it felt like thinking men who hated you had taken you out and raped you and cut your throat?"

She was shaking her head in denial, moaning, "No, no, no, no," and his fury rose against her, and then Hermia was back. The waitress stood paralyzed near the table with Marilyn's entrée. Despite Forrest, the ladies were staring openly, their reserve forgotten, and the owner—a tall woman with grey hair cut short and spiked—approached Forrest with a sternly tilted head.

"Please, it's okay, Mrs. Ryburn," Hermia said, half-standing to fend her off. "Just some bad news. So sorry," she said to the restaurant at large. "We'll be okay."

The waitress quickly set the plate in front of Marilyn, who ignored it, and Mrs. Ryburn went around speaking to the other patrons. But the clientele's curiosity was up.

Marilyn leaned toward him. "Mo told you I'd been murdered?"

"Forty years ago he took me to see where it happened. He told me you called him. He said it was your idea."

"Oh my God," she said, framing her face with her hands over her temples, and then covering her eyes. "Oh no. Oh my God."

"And now I know that's what you wanted. You wanted it."

"Me?" cried Marilyn in a terrible wail, and Hermia started up from her chair.

"Please!" said the owner, instantly back at their table. "I'm going to have to ask you to l—"

"*Me?* I didn't want nothing but you to come get me."

"Ma'am!" said the owner.

"Shut the fuck up!" said Marilyn, whirling to face her.

"I'm calling the police," Mrs. Ryburn said, and Hermia stepped around the table, trying to raise her mother by the arm, to move her out onto the street, anywhere, but Marilyn shook her off and leaned toward him. Forrest touched her face, transfixed by her wild grief.

"Oh my God," she kept saying. Tears spoiled the makeup on her cheeks. She took Forrest's hand with both of hers, shaking her head. "No, baby. I didn't, I didn't."

"You didn't give him the dress?"

"He was supposed to give it to *you*, so you'd believe him. So you'd have it and know it was me sent the message. That I'd given it all up for you. I didn't give him shoes. I gave him the address in Macon. I gave him the phone number."

He stared at her. "The phone number."

"So you could call me. So you could come get me."

"Come get you? You were waiting for me?"

She nodded.

"You thought I—but why didn't you just call me? My God, why did you trust Mo Woodson?"

"I thought he'd help me with you."

"Mo Woodson?"

She stared down at the table, elongating a water drop with her peacock nail. "I was so .... I thought you were so high up. Why would you give up your fine white life for me?"

"You knew I loved you. Why didn't you call me?"

"You remember how it was." Their heads were close together, their foreheads almost touching. She stared at the table, gripping his hand, the skin around her eyes trembling. "I was scared. I was just scared."

"Scared of what?"

A police car pulled up and stopped behind the parked cars outside the restaurant, lights flashing.

"Mama, come on!" Hermia said, trying to pull Marilyn away from him.

"Scared you would start thinking about it and deny me," she whispered, looking him full in the eyes. "And all this time I thought you did. All this time."

"Let's get out of here," he said, standing up and drawing her to her feet. "I'll kill that lying bastard," he whispered in her ear, murderous with rage at the thought of Mo Woodson.

Just as he said it, Officer Reeves appeared at the divider, all seriousness, with Mrs. Ryburn directing him into the room and the receptionist peeking around from behind her. Reeves' hand went to his gun when he saw Forrest. LaCourvette Todd stepped up beside Reeves and touched his arm, her eyes going from Forrest to Marilyn before she saw Hermia.

"What's the trouble?" LaCourvette asked.

"They've been disturbing my restaurant," said Mrs. Ryburn. She ran a hand into her short hair and left it there as though she were at her wits' end.

"What exactly did they do?" LaCourvette asked, turning toward her. "He's white and she's black?" LaCourvette said. "Is that disturbing your restaurant?"

"Of course not!" exclaimed Mrs. Ryburn.

"He cussed and slammed the table," a cigarette-voiced woman said. "You could of heard him over in the courthouse."

"That's exactly right," said a dignified white-haired lady at one of the other tables.

"And this one let loose a f-bomb on Mary Rose," said the earlier woman, pointing at Marilyn.

"They were having an emotional conversation that got out of hand," Mrs. Ryburn explained.

"How much do we owe you?" Marilyn asked with chilly hauteur.

"Let's just…please." Mrs. Ryburn waved everybody toward the front door.

"Could I have the check?" Forrest said. He stood at the register displaying his American Express card.

"Just go on," said Mrs. Ryburn. "Go on. Please."

"No, ma'am," he said. "I want to pay for lunch, and of course for your hospitality."

"Oh, for goodness' sake!" she cried and disappeared into the back of the restaurant. Murmurs of commiseration followed her.

"Sir," the cashier said helpfully, taking the card from his hand, "I can ring you up."

3

Chick Lee, still groggy from his nap after lunch, was waiting at the red light beside the old post office when he saw the lights of a police car flashing on Jackson Street. Across the courthouse lawn, the scene leapt into focus. Braxton Forrest was coming out of the Left Bank Grille with Hermia Watson. And next to him was the woman Chick had known as Dutrelle Jones's wife.

Marilyn Harkins.

His pulse began pounding painfully above his left temple. In the same line of sight but half a block closer, Dutrelle himself was talking over the door of his red Dodge Ram pickup in the row of parked cars on the west side of the courthouse—he hadn't even come to look at the new F-150s—and Chick saw Coach Fitzgerald on the sidewalk. As he watched, Jones glanced over at the police car and then looked again when he recognized his wife. He closed the pickup door, held up a hand to Coach, and stepped up onto the grass of the courthouse lawn. He strode diagonally across it toward them. Marilyn had her arm around Forrest's waist. She seemed to be limping.

LaCourvette Todd and the Reeves boy stood by the restaurant door talking to Mary Rose Ryburn. The car behind him honked and he glanced in his rearview mirror at a car full of teenage boys, then up at the green light. He put on his blinker. He waited as two oncoming cars passed. By now Dutrelle was up on the sidewalk and LaCourvette had both hands out toward him. Chick turned left at the light, then right at the next one, and pulled into a parking place across from the restaurant. As soon as he got out he heard the shouting.

"I said to get your hands off my wife!"

He slammed the door and started across the street when an

electrician's long van, its driver slowing to gawk at Jones and Forrest, got in Chick's way. By the time it had passed, Forrest lay sprawled backward on the sidewalk. Marilyn was kneeling beside him and glaring back over her shoulder at Jones, who stood with his arm cocked across his chest like Cassius Clay over Sonny Liston. When Chick got to them, the Reeves boy and LaCourvette Todd were backing Jones away. Jones drew back his fist, but LaCourvette whipped out her pistol with surprising authority and turned him against the wall.

"You under arrest, Dutrelle."

"You arresting me, nigger?" shouted Jones, turning back toward them, huge and threatening. Reeves backed up a step and pulled his pistol as well and pointed it at his chest. "Arrest that motherfucker trying to steal my wife!" Jones said, pointing down at Forrest. Then he noticed Hermia. "Arrest that bitch," he said. "Setting it up in my own house, right under my nose."

Chick looked at Marilyn. Good God. There she was.

"You heard me," said Jones, still talking to Hermia. "You and your girlfriend."

"Get a grip on yourself, Dutrelle," said LaCourvette.

Chick saw a line of women's faces in the window of the Left Bank—Diane Fingal, Trellis Griffin, old Mrs. Foster, some others he did not know. Mary Rose Ryburn stood in the middle of them with one hand on the top of her head and the other over her mouth.

"Sir, I'm gone need to cuff you," Reeves said. "Officer Todd, can you cover him?"

LaCourvette kept her pistol on Dutrelle while Reeves holstered his and unsnapped his handcuffs.

"You think you gone handcuff me?" Jones said, drawing himself up. "Come on and try, boy."

"Yes sir," Reeves said, looking down at the sidewalk as though he were embarrassed. But then with a swift sweep of his right leg, he hooked Jones's left leg behind the knee and shoved him while he was off balance, then snatched a flailing arm and cuffed it and somehow levered the other one down and cuffed it too and rammed Jones awkwardly into the wall. LaCourvette stood back from Reeves with her mouth open.

"Damn," she said.

"Sir," Reeves said, flushed red, "could you proceed to the vehicle, please?" Before anybody could react, Reeves had him over at the car, and Jones was ducking his head to get into the back seat, where he sat leaning forward awkwardly and glowering over at his wife.

By now Forrest was stirring on the sidewalk. Groaning, he sat up with Hermia on one side and—there she was, Marilyn Harkins, right there on the sidewalk in the middle of Gallatin—on the other side. Forrest put his hand to the back of his head. It came back gleaming with blood.

"What happened?" Chick asked Hermia, glancing as he did at

230

Marilyn, half in terror, wondering at her.

"Dutrelle attacked him," she said, shaken. "He tripped on mama's foot and hit his head on the sidewalk. Did somebody call an ambulance?" she called, raising her voice.

"I did, baby," LaCourvette answered.

"Hey Cump," Chick said, leaning over him and doing what he used to do when he helped Coach on the sideline during games. "Cump. You know where you are?"

Forrest opened his mouth and closed his eyes. He moved his head slowly as though to test it. When he opened his eyes again, he seemed to have a hard time focusing on Chick.

"Is this the promised end?" he asked.

"Do you know who I am? What day it is?"

Forrest looked up at Chick, at Hermia, at Marilyn, whose hands were trembling and whose perfume Chick could smell. "It feels like Monday," he said, slurring the words.

"Do you know what happened to you?"

His eyes had a vague, uncertain look. He shook his head and winced.

Chick patted his arm and stood up. He could hear the siren coming up Main Street from the hospital. Reeves was standing beside the police car with his legs spread and his hands crossed in front of him. Chick went up to him and cocked his head in a question.

Reeves looked at the ground. "Me and my brother watched it on YouTube. I practiced it on him a lot."

When the ambulance came, the paramedics surrounded Forrest and lifted him onto the stretcher. As they prepared to put him in the back of the ambulance, Kathy Kellogg, plump in her uniform, smiled and came over to Chick.

"You see this happen?" she asked. She had had a crush on Chick his senior year in high school. He had always thought well of her for it, even though he could not return the favor, she was so homely. Jimmy Kellogg had married her before he got himself blown up in Vietnam.

"Not all of it."

"What's Dutrelle's wife doing here?"

Chick stared over her head at Marilyn, who was limping toward the passenger side of her car with Hermia supporting her elbow. He watched her open the door and gingerly sit down and hand the keys to her daughter.

"No idea," he said.

"So Braxton's in the ambulance this time. My God," said Kathy, "it looks like after all that with Marilyn—remember that?—he would have learned his lesson." She fished a cigarette out of her uniform pocket and lit it with a little pink lighter. "There was a rumor he killed her. You ever hear that?"

Chick nodded. He wondered if Dutrelle knew who his wife really was. No, of course he didn't. Nobody knew. Everybody in town—hell, everybody in Butte, Montana—would have found out if Gloria Jones got wind of it.

"You think he did it?"

He shook his head and shrugged. The police car left, and Hermia cautiously backed Marilyn's white Mercedes out of the parking place and drove up to the green light and turned left. In the next block, the right blinker went on. Were they going to the hospital or the jail?

Kathy Kellogg blew a plume of smoke away from Chick by turning her mouth. He wondered why nurses—except she wasn't exactly a nurse—were the last people to give up smoking. Two paramedics were closing the back doors. One of them tilted his head up at Kathy.

"Gotta go take care of the hero," she said. She stepped on her cigarette and headed to the ambulance.

He hesitated on the sidewalk. His head throbbed as though he had hit the sidewalk too. Or maybe it was just the image of Hermia Watson that was throbbing. He had felt something kick in his chest when he saw her across the block, and then when he had knelt close to her over Forrest, he had felt like a teenager. He could still feel her breasts against his chest, the live curve of her back beneath his hand, the deep and unexpected need that had stirred him.

Braxton Forrest's daughter. What game was she playing? She had been the cause of all the unwanted knowledge that now burned inside Chick. Forrest's presence in town—which was all her doing—felt like the burning progress of a long movie fuse toward the depot full of dynamite, and he waited with a strange detachment, stupefied by the very idea of her.

"Chick?" Mary Rose was standing in the doorway of the Left Bank Grille. "Are you okay?"

She stepped out, hugging herself as though it were cold instead of ninety-five degrees on the Gallatin County Bank sign down the block.

"Who was that man? I mean the white man."

"That was Braxton Forrest."

"Why have I heard the name?"

"He's the one whose girls showed up in town a couple of weeks ago. What happened in there?"

"Hermia Watson brought him in. Doesn't she help that old woman—the one the girls thought they were staying with? He and Hermia were just having lunch until the other woman came in. From then on...."

"Do you know who she is?" Chick asked, as though he had no idea, feeling himself begin to blush.

"I've never seen her before. That big black man's wife, apparently."

"That's Dutrelle Jones. He played in the NFL."

"That's football?"

"Mary Rose," Chick said with mock reproach. "Listen, sorry about all the trouble."

"Well it's not your fault."

"I guess not," he said. Why did it feel like it was? "Well, I better let those girls know about their daddy. Then, if I get lucky, maybe I'll sell some cars."

4

He was a flock of birds over a field – a single, lovely, extemporaneous creature of air – like a tree whose leaves all turn their undersides at once in the wind – changing direction at some internal impulse, flying this way, upwards, and then sideways in an improvising, paradisal rearrangement of himself like the notes of music, never losing coherence, never entirely, not even when all the birds together settled back into that tree that had let them all go – all those birds in that one tree whose leaves turning upwards turned into birds when someone struck the trunk and they flew – struck with an ax, the whole trunk shuddered, struck and–

"Mr. Forrest?" Someone was shaking his arm.

He opened his eyes. He stirred and shaded his eyes against the light of the open blinds. He felt a bandage on his forehead and followed it around to a throb too tender to touch on the back of his head.

"Do you know where you are?" It was a middle-aged white nurse.

He sat up and groaned at the new pain. His nose was running and he stopped it with the sheet. Allergic to something. Ragweed flying loose, the whipping thongs at the end of the chain.

"Do you remember what happened?"

"It was an accident!" he said. "Can you make that light go away?"

She walked to the other side of the bed and adjusted the broad, louvered shades until the room was in a dim twilight. There was an empty bed between him and the hallway door, and through another open door, he could see a sink. His bladder nudged him, and he sat up to throw off the sheet, and pain drove through the back of his head like a railroad spike. He was in one of those stupid backward hospital gowns, open in the back and far too small for him. He sat pulling at the thing, the cloth straining at his shoulders, a gigantic baby.

"Now you just stay put. You got somebody needs to talk to you," the nurse simpered. "Y'all come on in," she said as though she were talking to kindergartners. "Don't be shy. Y'all come on."

Cate and Bernadette came into the room, and he yanked the sheet over himself and sat back against the pillows. Berry stayed near the door, staring at him, but Cate crossed the room and bent down and kissed his forehead. "Hi Dad."

He held a tissue to his nose.

"Hi, sweetheart."

Cate sat on the other bed, biting her lips. She had on clothes he did not recognize. Tricia. They were staying with Tricia.

"Chipmunk?" he asked Berry. After a moment, her face crumpled, and she ran to him and hugged him and fresh pain shot through his head.

"We saw her on the way in," she said. She wiped her tears on his sheet. He loved her taut little body, her thick hair and shampoo smell. She jumped up on the other bed and sat next to Cate.

"Saw who?"

"Cousin Emily Barron Hayes. She's down the hall, and that woman's with her."

"What woman?"

"The one who helps her. Miss Watson," Cate said. "She says she's coming to see you in a minute. She and her mother."

"Who's gorgeous," said Berry. "Well, I mean she is too, but her mom's like an old movie star."

"They're coming in here?"

All of them in the same room. Forrest wanted to turn over and pretend to be asleep or lie back groaning and wave them out of the room. But he sat up straighter, propping his back against the headboard with pillows and folding the top of the sheet over his lap.

"Where's Tricia?" he asked, hoping she had just dropped them off.

"She's parking the car," Cate said. "She'll be here in a second."

He closed his eyes. Oh good lord. His whole head hammered.

"Mr. Lee called and she brought us right out here," Berry said. "So somebody hit you?"

"Somebody did," he said. "Have you heard from your mother?"

"She gets in tomorrow," said Cate.

"Knock knock." Tricia stood in the doorway and crossed her arms and stared at Forrest. She looked tanned and fit in her jeans and a sleeveless button-up blouse. She walked slowly to the bed, her lips pursed. His girls were easy with her.

"Well," she said. "I guess you had it coming."

"Thanks."

"So what was this all about? Chick wasn't very coherent on the phone."

He groaned and put both hands up to his head, hoping the nurse would make them leave, but the nurse was nowhere in sight.

"Something about Dutrelle Jones?" Tricia pressed, standing over him.

"Dutrelle Jones?" Forrest said. "That's who that was? The one who played in the NFL?"

"What happened?"

"I picked up Hermia to take her to lunch. She asked her mother to join us. We were coming out of the restaurant. That's all I remember."

Tricia frowned and cocked her head.

"Chick said Dutrelle attacked you. He must have had some reason."

He was about to answer when he saw Cate and Bernadette stir. Hermia, rapping lightly on the doorjamb, stepped into the room and there with her, just behind her, in plain view of his daughters and Tricia, was Marilyn Harkins.

Smiling, Tricia stood back to let them approach. Forrest watched Marilyn (limping, leaning on Hermia) take in the situation. Her eyes lingered appreciatively on Cate, and then she gave him a glance.

"Hello, Mrs. Davis," said Hermia formally. "Hello again, girls." They all murmured their greetings. "This is my mother," she said.

"Varina Davis," said Tricia, offering her hand, which Marilyn took in silence as though it were some rare petal, turning it upward in her palm to admire it and then enclosing it with her other hand. Tricia's lips parted with surprise.

"Adara Dernier-Jones," said Marilyn. "I'm so honored to meet you."

She gazed into Tricia's eyes, and Tricia smiled, tilted her head, nodded. One beat. Two. Forrest felt his heart shaking the cloth of his hospital gown.

"Oh, Mr. Forrest," Marilyn said, turning toward him at the foot of the bed with Tricia's hand still in hers, "I couldn't be more distressed about this incident. My husband is ordinarily not so violent. It's this recession, as I was telling Hermia just yesterday. Even with Obama's new tax credit for first-time home buyers, the people in the African-American community who would be Dutrelle's usual customers just aren't buying homes."

Forrest could not fathom what she was talking about, but he shrugged and frowned as though the attack on the sidewalk were nothing.

"How are you feeling?" Hermia asked him, moving close beside his bed and lightly touching the bandages. "Does it hurt a lot? What did they say about a fracture?"

"They haven't told me a thing," said Forrest. He saw Tricia watching Hermia, her eyes tightening speculatively at the degree of her familiarity. Then Tricia's eyes went back to Marilyn with a new scrutiny. All at once, she extracted her hand.

She looked at Cate, at Bernadette, back at Hermia, and Forrest saw her head give a small, unconscious shake, rejecting what she saw. She looked back at Marilyn, who met her gaze with a small, enigmatic smile. A deep blush began to climb from Tricia's neck up through her cheeks, her ears. Her eyes were suddenly brimming.

She looked back at Hermia. Her knees gave and she gripped the foot of the bed.

"Oh no. Oh my god," she whispered, covering her mouth. She gave Forrest a searing glance as tears spilled onto her cheeks and he saw her hand clamp harder over her mouth. Her torso convulsed.

"What's wrong, Mrs. Davis?" cried Cate.

Tricia pushed past them into the bathroom and slammed the door.

They could hear her retching. All of them stood paralyzed.

"We'd better go, Mama," Hermia said to Marilyn.

Marilyn nodded. She came between the two beds, leaned down, and kissed Forrest lightly on the cheek.

"I'm so sorry about Dutrelle," she said, lingering a moment. He smelled her perfume. Behind her Cate and Bernadette watched in bewilderment. Marilyn said goodbye to each of them, taking their hands quickly, and limped from the room just behind Hermia.

"You *know* her?" Cate demanded after they left.

Tricia came out of the bathroom and rushed into the hall without a glance at him. He heard a cry. A clipboard clattered on the floor and slid past the door, and Tricia reappeared.

"Girls!" she cried, gesturing violently without raising her eyes. "Get out of there right now! Come on!"

The nurse, retrieving her clipboard, stared at him from the hallway. Bernadette rushed from the room, and Cate, her face crumpling with misery, spread her hands and said, "Dad? What's going on?"

He covered his face with one hand.

"I did know her," he said, "a long time ago."

But when he looked up, she was already gone.

5

Hermia's hands lay in her lap and she could not lift them. She stared out over the leather steering wheel at the hospital lot. Veils of heat wavered above the other cars. She was responsible for all this misery, all of it, and she still could not understand why she had done it. That one day of giddy transgression. Inauguration Day. Now everything that happened was like cutting herself when she was a teenager so she could feel the pain and see the blood she caused. Cutting deep enough into sin to feel the grainy, dense, ash-tasting absence of God she had felt after the first time with Daddy Loum.

She did not know what she was doing. What had she done to her mother? She had never seen her mother like this.

"Mama, listen," she said, and she heard her voice trembling. "Now, listen to me. Braxton Forrest is married to somebody else. He has his own life and so do you. He has those two girls. You can't just have him. It was all forty years ago."

"You saw him! That man loves me. *He thought I was dead.* All this time, he thought I was dead. I'm not dead. Baby, I'll show him I'm not dead."

"But you don't even know each other."

"Listen to me. *That's* your daddy. All the daddies you've had, and he's the real one, and I want him. He's mine and I want him. I'm sick of

236

Dutrelle. All he thinks about is money and games on TV. I know he's fooling around on me."

Hermia began to sob. She rocked back and forth in the seat with her hands over her face until finally her mother put her hand on her leg. Hermia wiped the tears from her eyes, bunched her fists, and tried to get control of herself. An elderly couple walking slowly through the lot toward the hospital gave her a worried glance, and she gave them a small smile and a wave.

She started the Mercedes and pulled out of the parking place. She should go get her car from Mrs. Hayes' house. But no, she remembered, her mother's foot was cut, and now her ankle was sore from where Forrest had tripped over it as he fell.

"Well, you're not going to like being poor."

Marilyn's whole body turned toward her. "Poor! Braxton Forrest is a famous man."

"For an academic. But you remember what Daddy Loum made. We wouldn't have had anything if he hadn't had money from his family. Prof. Forrest—"

"Your father."

"Mama, he came down here hoping he'd get some money from old Mrs. Hayes. He thought she had money."

Her mother stared at the side of her face as Hermia drove.

"Well," she said at last, turning to look out the window. "I have money of my own."

"You think Dutrelle is just going to roll over? You're talking about letting Gloria Jones off her leash. I'm talking about after she finds out her son married Marilyn Harkins."

Her mother sat frozen, as though she had not heard. Hermia turned onto Main Street and started toward town past the shaded yards, the huge old live oaks and magnolias of the big Victorian houses built early in the last century. Halfway to the courthouse square, Marilyn gave a low groan and when Hermia turned to look at her, she said, "It just broke my heart." She closed her eyes and pressed her hand over her breast.

"What are you talking about, Mama?"

"Those days when I sat there and waited, and he never called me."

"Mama, you have to realize something. You never told me a thing. Not one thing. I don't know what you're talking about."

"I remember sitting on the edge of Missy Watts' bed next to the phone and looking out the window. There was a little boy on the porch across the street. He was jumping around playing and he knocked over a fern his grandmama had on the steps. It was the way he looked over his shoulder at the screen door, scared of what was going to happen to him. It was right then—the third or fourth day. I knew right then he wasn't coming.

"I couldn't eat for a week I was so ashamed for him. That beautiful boy. That brave boy I loved. I knew it would ruin him to betray me." She broke off and with her eyes closed, lifted her face, her mouth open in suffering. "And never once to lie in bed beside him. Never in my own bed. Or any bed. Never."

"Mama, please," Hermia said.

"Just now, when we were in that room," said her mother, suddenly breaking into pained laughter. "That was the first time I ever saw him in bed—and who was there? Varina Davis! Tricia Honeycutt! Did you see her face? She like to died! Had to go throw up!" She laughed helplessly, wiping at her eyes, then glanced sharply out the window and back at Hermia, who was making a right turn at the library.

"Where you going?" she snapped.

"You can't leave your husband in jail," she said.

"I ain't studying Dutrelle."

"Mama, it wouldn't look right."

After a moment, her mother convulsed with laughter again.

"Wouldn't look right? Oh my god. Wouldn't look right!"

6

Carefully, not thinking, Forrest stared at the patterns of indentations in the textured ceiling tiles. He saw the profile of a lioness, the strong jaw, the clarity of line, but when he glanced away at a noise in the hallway and looked back, it had disappeared.

His brain doing its braining. Constellating, patterning.

Pain throbbed steadily through his cranium, but more urgent was his bladder. He hated to move, but he got up. He felt like someone balancing a narrow vase on a tray as he walked toward the bathroom, gripping the rail along the bottom of the second bed.

Dutrelle Jones. Some of it was starting to come back.

When he opened the door, he saw that Tricia had used one of the hand towels to clean up after herself and it lay accusingly on the floor beside the sink. He raised the toilet seat and hiked up the front of his gown and just as he was about to pee, he heard the nurse come in the room.

"Mr. Forrest?"

"I'm using the bathroom," he called. "Can you come back in a minute? I forgot to close the door."

"Sorry, sorry."

When he heard the door click, he let go with relief. All that iced tea and water at lunch—how long it had been? Dutrelle Jones. Wearing a suit, a huge man, bigger than Forrest, already enraged. Marilyn's husband. His stream pinched off as he remembered it.

They were outside on the sidewalk, and Marilyn had her arm around his waist, squeezing him against her in broad daylight, unwilling to let him go. He turned his head and there was Dutrelle Jones coming at him. It was like one of those train-wreck blocks downfield Coach Fitzgerald used to rewind in the Sunday film sessions—the force of it when your man is off-balance and not expecting it. Jones hit him with both hands in the chest. He might have absorbed it and stepped back, but his foot caught on something, and he fell like a tree and couldn't cushion the fall.

His hand went to the back of his head. Hermia had asked about a fracture.

"Come on," he said to Cousin Bedford. He tried to think about something else. A fountain, purling and gurgling. A river. An image came of the sluggish Ocmulgee, an old black woman standing up and staring across the river at all the shouting. Tony Wright's face covered with yellow jackets. A pang shot through his bladder. He felt the air coming through the back of his hospital gown. "Come on," he said again, shaking himself.

A hot rage at Mo Woodson, that old liar and scumbag. He thought about going out there to kill him. He imagined Maureen hiding behind the door in Mo's T-shirt, calling Mo from the garage. "Maurice, here's that man again, and now he's got him a baseball bat!" and suddenly his stream eased and he listened with satisfaction to the splashing that went on and on.

Sweet Maureen.

On his way back to the bed, the door into the hallway opened, and he turned carefully, expecting the nurse. Bill Fletcher gave him an appraising look.

"You met Dutrelle," he said.

"So they tell me."

"You want to talk about your head?"

He looked at his old friend's face and something went out of him. "What's the matter with me?"

As he got back into bed, his nose started to run again, and he grabbed a tissue from the box beside the bed.

"Did that just start?" Fletcher asked, alarmed.

"No, it's been doing this off and on since I woke up."

"That's not your nose running. That's the fluid around your brain. Cerebrospinal fluid. It's what your brain floats in, the way a baby floats in amniotic fluid."

"Brain fluid." Forrest looked at the fluid in the tissue, fighting down a mild panic. "Jesus, how does it come out my nose?"

"Down the Eustachian tube. When you hit the sidewalk, you must have fractured the occipital bone," Fletcher said, cupping his palm over the back of his own head. "With a basal skull fracture, the tissues around the brain—the meninges—can get torn and you sometimes get this leakage. When it comes out your nose, it's called rhinorrhea."

"Something you never want your rhino to have."

Fletcher smiled despite himself and shook his head.

"Seriously, Cump, if it keeps up, we'll have to get you to Macon and do a CAT scan. Let me see that."

Forrest showed him the tissue.

"No blood in it," said Fletcher. "That's good."

"So what's the treatment?"

"I didn't find the bone displaced, so I wasn't sure there was a fracture. We'll probably just wait it out and let your body heal itself. The danger is inflammation of the meninges."

"That's meningitis?"

He nodded. "Wouldn't hurt to put you on some antibiotics. The other danger is some kind of subdural bleeding that causes pressure on the cerebrum." He frowned. "But that would be tricky to diagnose."

"How so?"

"The symptoms are things like disorientation and combativeness. It's hard to tell from Braxtonitis."

It took him a second. "Screw you," he said.

"You see what I mean? Is that your brain swelling, or is it just being Cump Forrest? We're going to do the town a favor and keep you in here for the time being and observe you," Fletcher said, sitting down on the other bed. "Speaking of which, how's your friend from Atlanta?"

"Come on, Bill."

"Seriously. I'm worried about her."

"She was okay last night."

"You talked to her."

"Well, yeah." He was suddenly embarrassed. "She came back down yesterday. I swear I didn't touch her."

Fletcher stared at him. Forrest had the impression from some subtle checked impulse in his face or body that he was forcing himself not to leave. It was strange that despite the authority, the gray in his hair, the added weight, the white hospital coat with his name badge, Bill Fletcher was exactly who he had always been. Even the way his eyes shifted from Forrest to the floor reminded him of something. They were in the trailer outside Athens, and Fletcher had just come in from somewhere just as Forrest emerged from his bedroom with their roommate's girlfriend.

He had always been a disappointment to Bill Fletcher. He blew out a long breath and gingerly felt the back of his head.

"Do you want to talk about all this or not?" Fletcher said.

Forrest dropped a hand onto the sheet. "Sure," he said. "But don't you have to make rounds or something?"

"There's nobody much here except you and old Mrs. Hayes," he said. "She talks and talks, most of it about your father."

"My father?"

"Save that for later, Cump. Tell me why you're in Gallatin."

"Listen, did you know Marilyn Harkins was alive?"

Fletcher was startled.

"So you didn't know either?" Forrest asked.

"The rumor was that you'd killed her."

"That I'd killed her? Seriously?"

"She disappeared. And then you left town and never came home."

"So when we were living in the trailer and talked about her, did you think that?"

"Cump, if we had been drunk and you had confessed that you murdered her, I wouldn't have told anybody."

"That would have made you an accessory."

Fletcher shrugged and said, "I could have lived with that."

"Was your father on the list?"

Fletcher nodded. Forrest's head was pounding and he had to reach for the tissue as a new freshet came from his nose.

"When that list came out," Fletcher said, "everybody knew you'd be on it. But my daddy being on it was ... a surprise," he said mildly, but the way he said it let Forrest understand how much he had hated Marilyn Harkins. "I believed him at the time," he said. "He claimed to anybody who would listen that Marilyn had been put up to giving his name by the 'SNCC niggers' or 'the Ralph Abernathy bunch.' But the men who would ordinarily support him kept telling him to shut up, maybe because they were on the list too. My mother took a whole bottle of sleeping pills not long after that. You probably didn't know that."

Forrest shook his head without thinking and instantly regretted the movement.

"I found her in time. Mama moved into my sister's old room when she came home from the hospital. Daddy died a few months later." Bill looked up at Forrest now with a flat look in his eyes. "I wouldn't have turned you in, not if that's the only way I could help you kill her."

Forrest held the tissue to his nose. "So what did you think when you saw her?"

"Who?"

"Marilyn."

"What are you talking about?"

"Come on, Bill. She was just in here."

"Jesus Christ!" cried Fletcher, bolting to his feet. He slapped his palm on his forehead, a gesture that Forrest remembered from high school. "Jesus Christ! She's the woman married to Dutrelle Jones?"

Forrest watched him apprehensively. He had assumed—stupidly, he saw now—that people knew and did not say anything.

"Does Dutrelle know who she is?"

"Bill, look, I don't know. What's today? Monday? I found out Saturday she was alive. I thought everybody in Gallatin—"

"Knew she was Marilyn Harkins? Are you serious?"

"Sit down, Bill."

"What I want to know is what you're even doing here. Why did you come? We didn't need this."

"Sit down. It hurts my head to look up at you."

Fletcher sat down, and Forrest went over it with him. In the early spring he had received a letter at his Walcott College address signed by Emily Barron Hayes. She had expressed an interest in seeing him in the summer. It had made sense, because he thought she might feel guilty about his father's disinheritance. He had written back, describing his career, his marriage to Marisa—her art, her father's work, her Italian mother, the fact that she hadn't been back to Europe since college and that it was their twentieth anniversary. He'd like to come see her, but his mother had passed away years ago, and they were planning to go to Italy. He and Marisa would love for the girls to meet her sometime. Within the week, he received a second letter, this time at his home address. Cousin Emily Barron Hayes invited the girls down during their summer vacation. But more than that, he thought from a sentence or two in the letter that she had offered to pay for Forrest and Marisa to go to Italy.

She urged him to send the girls on the train, writing that she had always loved train travel and it would let them see the country how people used to see it. They exchanged several more letters and settled on a plan. So early in July, he put the girls on the train, he and Marisa left for Rome, and well over a week into their trip they got word that nobody had met the girls in Gallatin. Cousin Emily Barron Hayes had not written the letters, and everybody said she had lost her money long ago.

"So who wrote them?"

"Hermia Watson."

"Why would she write them?"

"I knew her before, years ago," said Forrest. "And she might be my daughter."

"Your daughter!" Fletcher exclaimed.

"Sit down."

But before he could sit back down, the pretty strawberry blonde nurse Forrest had seen with Fletcher on Friday opened the door and said that he was needed down the hall. She held the door open as Fletcher left, saying he would be back, and then she came over to Forrest.

"Oh, too bad," she said. "Somebody else got to you first." She had a clipboard in one hand and with the other she lifted a thermometer on a spiral cord toward his mouth and gestured for him to open up. With his lips around it, he winked at her and patted the bed beside him.

"You wish," she said.

When the thermometer beeped, she read it and wrote the temperature down on her chart, then leaned over him and touched the skin beneath his eyes. She had irises the color of olive leaves. His heart rose with love for her.

"There's a little bruising?" she said in an accent that was pure Gallatin. She was so close he could smell her. The swell of her uniform blouse with its pinned-on name badge. Pamela Martin, R.N. Before he knew it, he had raised his left arm and encircled her hips and tipped her toward him. Her breasts pressed against him as she pushed away, incensed, and he felt the sweet tautening curve of her bottom.

Then the clipboard slammed his head.

7

An hour after Chick called her to tell her about Forrest, Tricia called him back at his office. He listened to her gasping and crying. *And do you know who it was? Marilyn Harkins! That tramp who turned in all the names. And Hermia Watson—Chick, I couldn't believe it! I was looking at Cate and Bernadette's sister, and they didn't know it, but she did, oh yes she did.*

He was on the phone with her for half an hour, listening to her tormented tour of the summer of 1969. No, he didn't think Hermia knew Forrest was her father until today. Yes, Forrest had thought Marilyn was dead, so he obviously hadn't known about Hermia. *Well he didn't think I was dead. He just didn't care. I thought I had worked through it a long time ago, but my god, the humiliation of standing right there in front of her, realizing I was shaking hands with that ... whore who—oh my God, Chick.*

For minutes after they hung up, he sat staring at nothing. His lifelong love of Tricia Honeycutt was fading. Instead, he mused on Hermia Watson. Impossible, he told himself. Don't even think about it.

But he did think about it. There was nothing else to do. Monday afternoons were always slow.

He thought about the way she had pulled him against her, right there, right by the door, and he had felt the depth of her soft breasts against him, solid and yielding, that lovely heat.

He had to put her out of his mind.

It was 3:30. He buzzed Belle into his office and told her to call all the salesmen in. When they came, he told them to bring him their customer contacts for the past week, because he wanted to send a personal note to anybody who had dropped by. Fifteen minutes later, he was appalled to get a total of eleven names. Eleven customers in a week. No sales at all.

The implications of it—this was midsummer, when cars ought to be selling—dismayed him. Even "cash for clunkers" had petered out after that Taurus. Now, at five o'clock, everyone had fallen into the quiet of waiting out the next hour. Even the service department had a ghostly stillness.

Bill Grant had wandered out of his office. Through his blinds, Chick watched him touch the hood of the new Taurus and then walk over and stand looking out the front window. His other salesmen were probably doing the same thing Chick was—surfing the internet, the lazy bastards.

He thought about surprising Roy Doster, who was probably tilted behind his desk looking at porn. He could make a big scene: Is this what I'm paying you scumbags for? Get out there and get some customers or you're going to be out of a job. Or he could tell them all to go home, drive them out, like Jesus with the moneychangers.

Close early.

Drive past Hermia's house.

He clicked on one of the links that came up when he googled her, and there she was: Hermia Watson in a small group picture, smiling next to three other women and a tall Asian man, a backdrop of hooded figures in a desert. It was in a blog by some guy named Fareed Imroz, Literatures of Silence. What the hell did that mean? Such horseshit— Jesus should drive out the academics along with the moneychangers. Make them get real jobs. Hermia showed up as the author of several essays with long titles, and she was listed in the program for a conference about women and slavery.

There was a Marilyn Harkins on Facebook—a smiling white woman who looked like she was having a good time at a party.

Just to see, he tried Braxton Forrest.

Pages and pages of hits.

He exited his browser and stared for a minute at a very depressing Excel spreadsheet he had been ignoring. After a minute of this, he got up and opened the door. Belle Murray started—she must have dozed off at her computer. She had been cool to him since the episode with Hermia that morning, and now, without looking at him, she pushed her glasses up her nose to study a document on her desk, fingers poised on the keyboard. When he walked out into the showroom, he was surprised to see Roy Doster on one knee next to the blue Fusion hybrid, examining the window sticker.

"What do you think?" asked Chick. "Could we give it away?"

"Gas is down a dollar and half from last summer when we didn't have enough of these," Roy said, standing up. "But we ought to be doing better on F-150s. Something ought to sell."

The other salesmen were drifting out of their offices.

"Eleven customers in the last week," Chick said. "I mean we're dead in the water."

They looked at their feet. Finally, Roy Doster said, "When's our next sales event for the company?"

Chick shrugged. "Not until September. Anybody think of an excuse for a sale?" He shouldn't have to ask his salesmen, but his mind had been tangled up with what happened forty years ago instead of on selling Fords. Marilyn Harkins walking through the summer nights.

Then an idea broke over him. It was like water from a cold spring. He held a hand in the air. "Forty years ago this summer."

Furrowed eyebrows, headshakes. Foster said, "What, Vietnam?"

"No, we landed on the moon. And what else? Woodstock. You know Joni Mitchell? *We are stardust, We are golden, And we've got to get ourselves back to the garden.*" They stared at him. "That same summer, the moon landing and Woodstock. So we come up with a sale—with a prize, some kind of drawing. Lee Ford's Moon Madness and Stardust Sale."

Now they looked impressed. Where had that come from?

From his beautiful deep-breasted muse.

"Okay, how about this? You buy a car during the sale and you qualify for the drawing by making your down payment. But here's the kicker. If you win the drawing—and we need to make a big deal of it, have it filmed, let some pretty girl reach in a glass jar and fish out the name—you get the car for what it would have cost in 1969."

They stared at him.

"What if cars were like two thousand bucks?" asked Doster. "You'd have to sell ten or fifteen more cars to make up for what you're losing." He spread his hands. "Nobody's exactly breaking down the doors here."

Chick looked at the ceiling and back down at them. "How about this? The down payment for any car is the 1969 price. But if you win the drawing, the down payment buys the car. We act like we don't care about profits. We're moonstruck, we're Woodstock nation, we're high."

"Oh hell yeah," said Bill Grant.

"But most of the cars they sold then have been discontinued," said Doster doggedly. "Fairlanes, Galaxies."

"Okay, Roy, so we apply those prices to the Fusion or the new Taurus. Listen, we go for all of Middle Georgia, not just Gallatin. We buy TV ads on Channel 13, radio ads—we put up banners. The more people we get in here, the less that one car hurts us."

Bill Grant and Steve Wilkinson were with him. Even Doster looked shaken, but he said, "Those ads will cost a bundle."

"Doesn't matter," Chick said. "You have to spend money to make money. We'll get it back before we have to pay the bills."

"How about we wear Sixties clothes?" asked Grant.

Chick pictured his salesmen in bellbottoms and paisley shirts and made a face.

"I can get us some weed," offered Wilkinson.

"I bet you can," Chick said. He got out his iPhone and looked up Woodstock. Friday, August 15, to Sunday, August 17, 1969, except it spilled over into Monday, August 18. He pulled up the calendar. "My God, it's a sign! Today's July 20. It's the anniversary of the moon landing. Two weeks from today we start TV and radio ads. The sale starts Friday, August 14. We get music from all the bands that played at Woodstock. We stay open late every night. The drawing will be that Sunday night, August 16. We'll have a live band, a big party. How does that sound?"

"We're not open on Sunday," Roy Doster said.

Chick glared at him.

"Roy," he said, "we'll make an exception."

The other salesmen were pumped. In the next half hour, he divided up responsibilities, filled in Belle Murray on the calls she needed to make, and recruited Tracie Newsome to the effort. Maybe he could dress her up in some sexy Sixties clothes and have her do the drawing. But what would Patricia say about that? No, Alyssa could do the drawing. Customers liked to see the family angle. But Tracie could circulate in beads and bellbottoms, and that would sell a few pickups.

Half an hour later, the whole dealership was buzzing. It must have been visible from the street, because three customers came in just before closing.

8

Hermia left her mother (and her car) at the jail while she worked out bail for Dutrelle. Meanwhile, LaCourvette dropped Hermia off at her Prius in the hospital parking lot. She sat in her car by herself for a few minutes, thinking she should go in and check on Mrs. Hayes. But she was so drained, just so drained. *Varina Davis.* Chick must have been right about her, or why would she have acted so horrified? Her mother must have known all about her. Tricia Honeycutt, she had called her.

A wave of despair came over her. Everything she needed to know was just out of reach. People would hide the most important things from you until they died. But she understood that. Like Daddy Loum. Who would she ever tell about that?

He had taken them on vacation to St. Simons when she was eleven or twelve, and once, when her mother was taking a nap, he had taken Hermia down to the beach. They were the only black people. Daddy Loum with his little protruding stomach and his round face with the big smile that warmed you up all over and Hermia, awkward and shy about her early-developing breasts. She looked white beside him. Everybody always said she could pass, and she had chosen not to try it even then. What was the point with a daddy as black as Daddy Loum?

They walked along holding hands, and she would stop and pick up little bits of shell and driftwood. He took her down to where the waves broke up the beach, and he showed her how the little coquina clams would come tumbling in and then tilt sideways and disappear under the sand. He scooped up a handful where one had disappeared and prodded through the wet grains until he found the little striped shell smaller than his thumbnail.

"Let me see," he said, cupping his chin in his hand and grinning with his huge smile and then dipping the little thing in the incoming rush of water as she squatted beside him. "Let me see," he said thoughtfully, making a mock-serious face, and then she realized what he meant and shrieked joyfully and cried "No!" and ran down the beach spattering water in the shallows and looking over her shoulder to see if he was following her.

No, the truths you wanted to know were like those little tiny clams, exposed by accident, and when you found one it was already disappearing with only a little hole to show where it was, and if you scooped it up and teased it loose from the sand and even washed off the last grains, it would be sealed tight against you, and if you forced it open to get at it, you would kill it.

She started the car and drove home. A big red pickup truck, vaguely familiar, sat facing the wrong way in front of Mrs. Russell's house when she turned into her driveway. Maybe her grandson or nephew.

As soon as she unlocked the front door of the house, she heard Eumaios whimpering and scratching at the back door. The poor thing. He'd been outside all day with nothing to eat and she couldn't remember if she had even filled his water bowl that morning. When she unlocked the door he was all over her, jumping up, licking at her face as if he'd thought she was gone forever.

Hermia knelt and held his head with both hands, looking into his anxious, intelligent eyes.

"Stop it, now," she told him. She stroked his back, made him sit, but his front paws still tap-danced on the kitchen tiles, and as soon as she stood, he surged back up beside her. "What's the matter, Eumaios? What's wrong?" He pawed the back door, and, worried now, she looked out the window and gasped.

Dutrelle Jones sat facing her on one of the stone benches beside her small goldfish pond, his forearms on his knees. He was clenching and unclenching his fists and staring right at her. She made sure the door was locked and called LaCourvette's cell phone while she watched him.

"What's up, baby?" she answered.

"Dutrelle is in my back yard."

He could see her as she talked.

"I'll be right over."

"No, don't come now, but listen, listen. If your phone rings and you see it's me, just come right on, okay? Don't even answer it. Just come on."

"I'm coming now."

"No, hold off. It might be okay. I've got Eumaios."

When she opened the back door and stepped out onto the deck, Eumaios stayed beside her. Dutrelle had been to her house before with her mother and Eumaios knew him, but he had sensed a difference this time and he needed some cues.

"You got here before I did," Hermia called. "Where's Mama?"

He did not answer. He stood up and started walking toward her across the lawn. Eumaios dropped slightly and gave a low growl.

247

"What do you want, Dutrelle?"

Dutrelle stopped at the steps to the deck. He whistled and held out his hand, snapping his fingers, and said, "Come here, boy," to Eumaios, but the dog gave a menacing growl and tensed, ready to spring. Dutrelle's expression changed.

"What do you want, Dutrelle?"

"Your girlfriend says you brought that motherfucker to town."

"Do you mind, Dutrelle? You're not in the hood. Are you talking about Prof. Forrest?"

"I'm talking about I don't want my wife hanging all over anybody not me in the middle of town," he said, pointing his finger at her. Eumaios crouched and took two snarling steps toward him, teeth bared, and Dutrelle straightened. "Is it true? Did you get him down here?"

"I got him down here, yes."

"Why'd you want to set him up with my wife?"

"Set him up?"

"She won't even go in town when I ask her, you know that? And now you set her up with this—you hear the stories about this motherfucker? He just put a white girl in the hospital."

"Do you mind not using that language, Dutrelle?"

"They say that cracker *killed* a black girl."

"Who says that?"

"I've heard it since high school. Girl named Marilyn who turned tricks with white men and then gave the county a list. This Forrest was a KKK type, a stone cold hater."

She did not try to contain her smile.

He scowled at her. "Everybody knew he did it but they never found a body."

Now she laughed out loud.

"The fuck you laughing at?"

"A KKK type, Dutrelle? He didn't kill anybody. Least of all her."

"How do you know? How do you know, bitch?"

She paused, eager to say it, but hesitating. "Don't call me a bitch."

"How do you know?"

"Because he's my father, Dutrelle."

"Your *father*?" Dutrelle cocked his head and made a face as though she were an idiot.

But then what she meant began to sink in. He took a step backward. He lifted his face and looked at her and waved his hand as if he were brushing away flesh flies.

"That's bullshit. I used to see his picture on the Wall of Fame in the gym, you know what I'm saying? Won the state championship but then left town over this skank, they said, some whore people say he killed."

"Marilyn Harkins," she said.

"That's right," he said, his eyebrows pinching. "That's it. Marilyn Harkins."

"Dutrelle," she said. "He's my father, and I just found out."

"Bullshit. When did he ever know Adara? She told me she grew up in North Carolina and moved to Macon when she was a teenager."

"I do know how you feel, Dutrelle. I surely do. But he couldn't have killed Marilyn Harkins," she said.

"How do you know?"

She waited and then leaned toward him and said, with cold emphasis, "Because you're married to her."

He stared at her. He shook his head and stepped toward her threateningly.

She caught Eumaios by the collar as he lunged at Jones and almost yanked her off the deck. She held on and knelt beside him and whispered into his ear, smoothing his head and looking up at Dutrelle.

"Sit," she said calmly into Eumaios' ear. "Sit, boy." He sat back trembling. Dutrelle was walking in tense circles with his hand on the top of his head.

"Unh-unh. Why you want to say that about your mama? No."

"Dutrelle," she said, "Marilyn Harkins is my mother and Braxton Forrest is my father. She changed her name when she left town. She was pregnant with me. Why else do you think she would marry an old man? An undertaker."

He stopped, both hands on top of his head now, the side panels of his suit jacket lifting like sails. He stood there frozen.

"Don't nobody know that but you," he asserted at last, pointing at her, coming back to himself. But now he looked at her. "When did she tell you?"

"Dutrelle, get serious. She never told me anything."

"Who else knows?" he demanded, his voice rising.

"LaCourvette, for one."

"Your girlfriend," he sneered, as though it confirmed all his suspicions, but then he tilted his head as though he had just heard something. He closed his eyes. "Oh Lord, unh-unh. Her grandmama, old Mrs. Gibson, she tried to tell me a long time ago. She said I better find out who Adara was. Here I was about to leave my wife and child and I didn't even know who she was. I thought she was just meddling.

"But she knew, didn't she? How come she wouldn't just tell me? And now Mama gone find out," he said. "Great God, when Mama finds out—when everybody knows who that fool Dutrelle Jones married...." His eyes were wild. He stood for half a minute, paralyzed, and then broke for the side gate.

Instantly, Eumaios surged after him, pulling her off the deck and onto the grass. She hung on, pulled forward on her knees as the dog fought against the strain on his collar. Dutrelle fumbled at the latch until it opened, and Eumaios broke into a frenzy of barking as Dutrelle sprinted up the driveway to his truck. She was terrified for her mother, sick at what she had just done. She had to call LaCourvette. Eumaios was rearing and yanking her but she managed to grapple him back inside the gate and secure the latch.

"Hush now," she kept telling him. "Hush, Eumaios!" But he could not be calmed. He jumped at the gate, walked his front paws along its top, frustrated, barking madly, dancing with fury. She heard the truck screech away down the street. Old Mrs. Russell from next door—she had finally forgiven Hermia for moving into her neighborhood—appeared at the end of the driveway, peering up toward her, and the Murphy couple who always walked around the neighborhood in the late afternoon stopped with her.

Oh God, where was her phone? She had held it all through the confrontation, her thumb ready on the Send button, but she must have dropped it when Eumaios pulled her off the deck. It had to be in the grass, but where? Why hadn't she kept it mowed better? Tears blinded her. Where was it? She crawled through the grass, sweeping through it with her hand and sobbing. Eumaios came over whimpering, still excited, and licked at her salty face. Where was it?

Suddenly, it shrilled at her. She went rigid and turned toward the sound near the deck. She stood and still could not see it, but she knelt and felt for it in the weeds just beside the deck, felt farther, and found it at last a few inches under the edge. It had stopped ringing. She brushed some ants off her hand and immediately hit the Send button and held the phone to her ear without looking at the number.

"Hermia?"

It was a white man's voice.

Frantically, she cried, "Who is this?"

"It's Chick. I was just—"

"Dutrelle was here! I told him. I told him about Mama—oh God, I shouldn't have said anything! Now I'm scared he's going to—I've got to call the police."

She hung up on Chick and found LaCourvette's number and hit the Send button again. LaCourvette answered a second later. "We're coming."

"No!" cried Hermia. "He left! You've got to find him before he gets to her."

"You told him?"

"I did, it just—"

"He didn't hurt you, did he?"

"No, no, I—"

"Where would your mama be?" LaCourvette interrupted again.

"She didn't say. On the way home? I should have stayed with her!" she wailed.

"Listen, baby," LaCourvette said, "you don't think she'd go back to the hospital do you?"

"Oh god!" She pictured Mrs. Hayes lying in her hospital room, prattling about Aunt Ella while two nurses in the doorway whispered to each other about why Mrs. Dernier-Jones was in the room with Forrest. Then their heads would jerk around as Dutrelle burst into the hallway from the hospital lobby, carrying one of his big pistols. Shots, screams.

"I'm going out there," said LaCourvette.

"I'll meet you."

"No, you stay there. You don't need to be getting back in Dutrelle's way right now."

"But you'll call me—"

"I'll call you."

Eumaios was still keyed up, still barking and circling the yard and putting his paws on the gate, but now when she stood next to the back door and called him he came to her panting, wagging his tail. He ducked his head good-naturedly, as though they had done pretty well, all told. She stroked his head. "Let's feed you, okay?" He pushed against her legs, bolted past her into the kitchen, danced on the tiles as she opened the can and put it in his bowl.

She had not eaten since her half-finished salad at lunch, that disaster—what had she thought would happen? She shook her head and opened the refrigerator, looking for wine. A bottle of chardonnay with its cork swollen in the top stood tilted against the milk carton in the door. It was left from the night she and LaCourvette watched *Doubt*. It seemed like years ago. She found a wine glass and poured the wine and took a swallow. Eumaios already wanted to get back outside, so she opened the back door and stood watching him as he immediately toured the whole yard and marked it and barked a few times to let everybody know he was back. Thank God for Eumaios. Closing her eyes, she concentrated on breathing slowly through her nose, trying to clear her mind: Dutrelle's finger pointing at her, Eumaios trying to attack him.

What had she done? She put the cool glass against her temples, first right, then left. Oh God, please. Where was the cell phone now? She panicked, but there it was on the counter next to the refrigerator.

Holding it, she walked through the hallway to the living room, where she stood by the front window and looked out through the corner of the blinds. Mrs. Russell and the Murphys were gone.

Her heart labored. It was all because of that day, that one day. In a manila envelope inside the old roll-top desk that had been in the Forrest house for several generations she had found a glossy black-and-white photograph of a tall, handsome, happy man in a double-breasted suit coming up the aisle of a church with a tall blonde woman. *Robert and Inger*, it said on the back. *June 27, 1949. St. George's Methodist Church, Philadelphia, Penn.* She had been seized with excitement. Braxton Forrest's parents—and he had probably never seen the picture. She felt an intimacy with him; she could show him something about himself he didn't know; it was a way to get back close to this man who obsessed her. And in the very next pigeonhole, she had found the old stationery, a dusty box cater-cornered in one of the pigeonholes of the old desk. The printed name at the top, Emily Barron Lambert Hayes.

Mrs. Hayes had been safely in her chair, looking out over the garden and waiting for Robert Forrest, that happy man in the picture who would never come. Hermia had told her it wouldn't be long before the jonquils would be pushing up along the fence beside the woodshed. She had spoken in a calm voice, as though she were still discussing the weather, about the way they pushed up smooth and green and blind through the grains of parting soil and got free in the sunlight and broke into flower. Mrs. Hayes had gazed out with fixed eyes, her lips parted.

Hermia had wandered away smiling, as full of erotic longing as she had ever been at thirteen, when she would stand naked behind the curtains and look out at the college boys. She had left him alone for so long, just as she left her son alone. And then all at once she had weakened. She had thought Oh, why not? It was Inauguration Day. She had felt so good. So bridal. A new day in America. She had opened the windows to let in the fresh cold January air.

Suddenly her knees gave. The wine glass fell from her hand and shattered on the hardwood. She slid down the wall. Wine soaked into the Persian rug she had borrowed one night from Mrs. Hayes' front room. Glass lay glinting everywhere. Her cheek pressed the cool floor. She coveted the dangerous curved shards that looked so big, the broken stem, those brilliant jagged edges. If only she could let the dirty blood spill out of her the way she used to, but not just a bead of it, a line of it. All of it. But she could not lift her hand. She lay incandescent in the shame of what she was. She could not move at all, as though her very bones had liquefied and drained away.

9

He pushed through hanging bones. Great hooded gray figures sat hunched over something on the ground. Their shoulders dipped and swayed, as though each one were reaching for something at the urging of its appetite. They moaned in voices so low the sound seemed to come up from the very bottom of his hearing, out of the bass vibration in his marrow, then with the smooth quickness of a great cat one of them moved, not standing up, to the other side of the thing they had on the ground. A woman's bare white arm offered itself from the ground, a turning wrist and hand, as though she were lying in a bath and asking to be helped up.

One of the figures shifted its hips and leaned forward and began to devour the hand, and he saw the calm face on the ground, the neck and breasts glimmering with tesserae of gold and purple. The figures were scooping at her body with hands like children's mittens, and wherever they touched her, she was vanishing. She looked up at Forrest and lifted her eyebrows as though in mild exasperation. Her lips were moving. He saw one of her shoulders disappear, simply erased. Part of her face was swiped away, a shoulder, an eye. *Marisa?* he asked with a pang of guilt. *Maya?*

He was lying beside her, trying to keep her from vanishing. The figures loomed above him, all of them still shadowed by their hoods except for one. The ancient stony face was broad and hideous. Its eyes met his, terrible burning eyes beneath a writhing of young snakes.

Marisa? It echoed him in a mocking woman's voice. It held a handful of something like a collapsed necklace toward him. *Maya?* It mocked him. Now all the figures leaned close around him, pushing against him. They scooped at his face. They battered his delicate eggshell head.

Pain woke him. Someone was lying beside him, crowded against him and crying. Someone else was standing over him. The glare from the window blinded him, and he waved vaguely.

"Can you shut the blinds?"

"You better say your prayers," a man said.

Forrest shaded his eyes. The barrel of a pistol was six inches from his face. Dutrelle Jones stood above him. Next to him on the bed, Marilyn was reaching toward Dutrelle, imploring him. "Please don't do this. Please."

"Think you can make me your fool," Dutrelle said, almost whispering, pointing the gun at her. "Think you can lie to me."

Forrest's head hammered mercilessly.

"I never lied to you," she pleaded.

"*Never lied to me?* Everything about you was a lie. You came back here and took my family away from me and made me a fool. I loved you. I gave it all up for you. And you were a whore? You were that whore?"

"It was so *long ago*, Dutrelle. I was a different person."

His eyes, red already, suddenly brimmed with tears and the gun trembled in his hand.

"But look where you are." Jones moved the gun between Marilyn and Forrest, and the skin around his eyes tightened. "Right where you left off. It turns out this cracker didn't kill you. I'm the one Jesus saved up to kill you. Your girl found her daddy, and now she's going to lose him for good. But you first."

He thumbed back the hammer and thrust the pistol at her forehead. Forrest knocked the gun sideways just as it went off. Before Jones could recover, Marilyn was scrambling across the other bed into the hallway where nurses were screaming and shouting for help. Jones whipped the pistol back, but Forrest lunged up and caught his wrist and Jones fumbled the pistol onto the bed. Jones tried to grab it but Forrest kept him from reaching it, so Jones punched him in the side of the head with his left fist. Maddened with pain, Forrest gave Jones's wrist a savage twist that made him scream just as the police burst shouting into the room. Jones reeled backward off-balance against the other bed, spinning away, cupping his right forearm in his left hand. LaCourvette Todd had her gun leveled at Jones, who knelt on the floor cursing.

The pain was unbelievable. Gray spots blanked away part of the room. Any small movement was unbearable. He closed his eyes. Voices came to him from far away.

I ain't going to jail.

Dutrelle, please. You a hero in this town. Don't throw it all away. Just come on. We'll work it out.

I ain't going to jail.

He felt something snatch at the bed. A shot just above him, the acrid smell of smoke, people screaming. Was he—

No! Dutrelle! Put it down. Dutrelle! Don't do it!

There was another shot. Then four more shots, each one a spike, jagged and tearing. His nose was running again. His brains were running out. He kept trying to open his eyes but the gray women had their hands on him now, they were pulling him back under, tightening on him his torment of spikes and thorns.

Oh God! someone cried. Oh God!

10

Eumaios raged outside. Lying there, unable to move, Hermia waited for Dutrelle to come through the door and curse her as the filth she was and shoot her in the head. She was ready. It would be sweet to die, wouldn't it?

Wouldn't it?

He knocked at the door. Taunting her by knocking. Letting her know he was there, he was coming. She was trembling now with terror.

No, she didn't want to die. Not this way. Not at all.

He knocked again, tried the knob, and the front door opened a crack. It had come, the moment her whole life had been aimed at, and she wasn't ready. She was as terrified as she had been in Daddy Watson's kitchen. She closed her eyes, drew in on herself, whimpered, waiting for the shot, the blaze of oblivion, the terrible judgment of God. At the first footstep, she felt a hot, humiliating release on her thighs.

"Hermia?"

She looked up, startled at the voice. Mortified, she gave a cry.

"*Go away.* My God, go away."

"What happened? Are you hurt?"

"Mr. Lee, wait outside. Wait outside for me, please. Let me get changed."

When the door closed, she got up unsteadily and stepped over the glass. She could not bring anything to a focus. Eumaios was barking again, and without thinking she went to the kitchen door.

254

When she opened the back door, the dog swarmed in at her, all affection, then suddenly went still, sniffing her seriously, like a doctor examining a specimen, his nose wedging up between her legs. She pushed him away.

Nothing would settle. What was she supposed to be doing? She would have to sweep all that glass up, she should get some paper towels from the kitchen, wipe up that wine, that other. Paper towels. His claws tapping, Eumaios followed her, alert, as she took a big wad of towels with her into the living room and dropped some onto the spill of wine. The dog stepped around the glass, sniffed the wine, and then went over to the other little pool, sniffing and sniffing, fascinated, as though her whole mystery were opening to him.

"Eumaios! Move!" She thrust him away, dropped the towels, swabbing with her sandal, and picked up the paper by one edge. With the other towels, she leaned over and wiped the floor around the wine spill. Using them as a mitt, she picked up the other soaked paper and took the big wad to the kitchen and dropped it in the trashcan. She couldn't leave all that glass on the floor. She got her broom and dustpan and went back to sweep up all she could see, finding the little glints of it on the hardwood floor up under the couch, carefully brushing it out of the rug beneath her coffee table—the tiny wicked shards hidden in the weave. Otherwise, someday when she had forgotten all about them, she would cut her foot, and it would well over with thick blood like her mother's, the blood welling up red and thick and dripping from her pretty instep.

In the kitchen she emptied the dustpan, tapped it against the side of the trashcan twice, three times. Chick Lee was waiting for her, she remembered, but she had to get a shower, she felt so unclean. She stripped off her pants and underpants, pulled her shirt over her head, and unsnapped her bra, dropping everything in a pile that she gathered from the floor and stuffed into the trashcan. The tops of her bare thighs were sticky when she touched them. Wearing only her sandals, she started toward her bedroom, and just then there was a light tap on the front door, it opened a crack, and there was Chick Lee's face.

"Can you give me five minutes?" she said.

It took him a half-second to realize what he was seeing. He thumped his head on the doorjamb trying to close the door.

She saw her mother inside the yellow tape that surrounded the entrance to the hospital. Lights flashed everywhere. Several state patrolmen were conferring with Sheriff Binder. LaCourvette was talking to an older officer who looked stricken. But not her mother. She was

255

shining, curiously happy.

"Mama," Hermia called, and her mother turned, holding her hand up to the policemen. She came over to speak to her. She took Hermia's hands.

"You told Dutrelle about me," she said.

"I didn't mean to. He came over to my house. He was threatening me, he was saying—"

"It's all right. You didn't kill him."

"*Kill him?* Mama, what happened?

"Your daddy saved my life!" Marilyn said with a look so exalted it terrified Hermia. "Dutrelle had that gun right in my face about to pull the trigger, and your daddy saved my life." She shook Hermia lightly by the arm, meeting her gaze without seeing her, her eyes already cutting away, as though she were famous and the crowds were all watching her, pressing toward her.

"Mama, what happened?" Hermia said, squeezing her hands, shaking her. "What happened to Dutrelle?"

"Listen, baby. Listen." Her mother wouldn't be still. Her eyes were mad. "It's all right now. Things are back the way they're supposed to be. I'll call you later. I've got some things I need to do."

"Mama," Hermia said. But her mother had already ducked under the yellow tape. She tried to follow her, but her mother waved her off, limping away, already aiming her keys at the Mercedes.

Just as she left, a car swerved from the street into the hospital drive, careened over the curb, and sped up to the entrance. Policemen and hospital staff scattered from its path when it looked as though it would not stop, but at the last second, the driver slammed on the brakes and threw the car into park halfway onto the sidewalk. Gloria Jones leapt out and left the door hanging open, the engine running. She was already running, crying, "Where's Dutrelle? Where my baby at?" Hermia shrank back against Chick, terrified to be seen, but Gloria Jones was blind to anything but her son. She yanked through the yellow tape and pushed off the policemen and charged into the hospital.

"Dutrelle! Where my baby at? Dutrelle!"

When Chick dropped her off, Hermia started up the sidewalk to her front door, but instead of going in, she stood in the dark and watched as his car disappeared around the curve toward town. She could not calm down.

Eumaios was inside, whimpering and scratching at the door. He would protect her, but she dreaded being in the house without human company. LaCourvette was mired in police business after the shooting, and Stonewall Hill at night, unoccupied except by ghosts, would terrify her.

The glottal sound of her phone startled her. She found it in her purse, glanced at it.

"Mama?" she answered.

"Come meet me out at the house. I got to find all the papers before anybody else gets to them."

"What papers?"

"Dutrelle's. I got to open the safe, I got to make sure—" She broke off. "What's... my lord, somebody's coming up behind me."

"What is it, Mama?"

"Some fool is flashing their lights and coming right up on my bumper. They just ran right into—Oh my god, they're trying to—!"

"Who is it? Is it Gloria Jones?"

"Oh my Jesus!"

She heard a wail, a heavy thump. Something scrambled on metal. Another long terrible wail. And then the crash and the other sounds that she did not recognize but that filled her with horror. And then a ticking silence.

"Mama?" She listened, horrified.

Her knees gave and she almost fell again. She walked back and leaned against the hood of her car, found her keys, and opened the door to sit down and call 911. When a woman answered, Hermia told her there was an accident somewhere on the way to her mother's house. No, she couldn't remember the name of the road, but it was the one there, out toward Scalp Creek, out toward Jackson. When the woman asked her to be more specific, she screamed at her and hung up and found LaCourvette's number and called her.

"Baby?"

"Gloria Jones ran Mama off the road! I was on the phone with her. Call an ambulance!"

"Where you at?"

"At home. I don't know the name of the road, but she needs—I think she's—"

"Hopewell Road? You want me to get you?"

"Call an ambulance!"

"I will. I'm on my way to get you."

Eumaios was yelping by now. She got out and locked her car, feeling a twinge of nausea. When she opened the front door the dog danced around her, jumping up, licking any skin he could reach. She pushed him down and went to the kitchen to check his water bowl—the stove clock said 10:30—and tried to calm him down. She knelt and stroked his head, but just as she did, he jerked away, cocking his ears, and bolted for the front door again.

She followed him and saw LaCourvette already in the driveway. When Hermia locked the house and left him inside, he barked and whined desperately. As soon as she was in the car, LaCourvette backed out and accelerated out Beauregard Drive in the heavy police car, lights flashing.

"Did you call the ambulance?" Hermia asked.

LaCourvette nodded, but she did not look at Hermia. She slowed, crossed the tracks to the county road parallel to the Interstate, and turned on the siren to alert the oncoming cars. Within seconds, they were going eighty miles an hour down the narrow road. She turned off the siren, and it wailed, waning.

"I don't know why you told Dutrelle," LaCourvette said when it was quiet, still not looking at her.

She did not answer.

They slowed at an intersection after a mile or two, turned onto Hopewell Road, and saw the lights of the ambulance far ahead of them. LaCourvette pressed the accelerator, her jaw stiff and grim. She left the lights flashing when they parked behind the ambulance. The county sheriff, Hudson Binder Jr., arrived from the other direction just as they did. Hermia saw the Mercedes in the garish rescue lights, crushed into a big pine tree down the embankment on the left side of the road. Blue and red lights flashed everywhere, radios crackled, men shouted orders and questions.

LaCourvette got a flashlight out of the glove box and told her to stay in the car. Numb, Hermia watched her slide down the bank and approach the paramedics already working around the driver's side. She glanced in, drew back quickly, shaking her head, and climbed back up the bank, directing the flashlight beam along the shoulder. She stopped after a moment, examined something on the ground. She walked back to Hermia's side of the car and opened the door.

"Come here," she said.

"I don't want to see her. I can't look at her."

"This is something else."

Hermia got out, hugging herself as though it were cold, and followed LaCourvette along the road past men in uniforms. They were taking a stretcher from the back of the ambulance. Just off the left shoulder, a few yards from where the car must have left the road, a buck lay panting in the grass. Two of his legs were grotesquely broken, and he bled from a gash across his chest. He lifted his head with its mossy antlers, his eye liquid with pain and fear in the flashlight beam. His breath came too fast, shaking his sides as he labored to move.

"That's what I heard," Hermia said. "I heard her hit it."

"It must have made her airbag deploy too soon. How come you told me Gloria Jones ran her off the road?" she asked.

"Mama called me. She wanted me to come out to her house. But then somebody came up behind her and tried to run her off the road. I heard the whole thing. I think I heard her hit the deer. I didn't know what it was."

LaCourvette unstrapped her pistol.

"What are you doing?" Hermia said, stepping back, off-balance.

LaCourvette held the flashlight on the deer. His eye rolled wildly, the iris contracting, as he panted and struggled to move. She leaned down and put the pistol barrel to his forehead between the antlers. All Hermia could hear was the labored breathing, a thin animal scream. Then the incredibly loud report when LaCourvette pulled the trigger and the deer went terribly still.

"What the hell was that?" somebody cried.

Hermia reeled into the road.

"You got anything else I need to shoot?" LaCourvette called bitterly, and Hermia felt her knees give. She went down in the road. Her knees hit the asphalt, she felt the dirt and loose gravel grate her cheek, abrade her lips. Vehicles loomed around her, flashing lights, boots and legs running toward her.

"*You shot her?*" someone cried.

She lay there unmoving as though she were a victim being sacrificed on a platform in a huge amphitheater. Men surrounded her, looking at her, and she felt men's hands reach down to her, test her body. They pressed alcohol pads onto her raw wounds and stung her. They supported her arms, helped her up, brushed her face. Upright again, leaning on the arm of a tall man wearing some kind of uniform, she walked back to the police car and sat trembling in the front seat while the man knelt beside her, asking her questions. A paramedic cleaned her skinned knees as if she were a child.

When she said she was all right, they closed the door, and she sat there hugging herself.

She knew her mother was dead.

She did not know how long it was before LaCourvette opened the driver's side door and got in. For a long minute, she sat there rigid behind the wheel, not saying anything, staring through the windshield as the body was put into the ambulance. Finally, she started the car. She did not look at Hermia.

"I'm sorry," she said. "I'm so sorry, baby."

11

Patricia was hovering beside Chick. She kept squeezing her hands, scratching her palms, making fists so tight her knuckles popped. Now she sighed and crossed the room and sat balanced on the edge of the broad ottoman in front of Alyssa, who was curled up on the loveseat in the big Braves T-shirt she wore to bed.

There was a story about the moon landing forty years ago. Neil Armstrong, the odd weightless hop, the "one small step for [*crackle*] man." Somehow they made it feel as ancient as World War I had been to him as a boy.

Alyssa threw her head back to look at him upside down.

"Are they really going to put something on? I mean, it's just Gallatin," she said, as though the town were a village in Afghanistan so remote and insignificant that its whole population could be wiped out without drawing the attention of an Atlanta TV station.

"They'll put it on because of Dutrelle."

"It's been one thing after another ever since that Forrest man got here," Patricia said. "I knew something was going to happen."

Terrible as it was, he kept thinking about Hermia. Poised like a doe, naked as Eve. He couldn't get the image out his mind. How many times in a man's life does he see something like that? *Can you give me five minutes?* As though she'd forgotten why she was supposed to be in a hurry. Oddly unreal. Her shower took another fifteen or twenty minutes and when she finally came out in her fresh clothes and he got her into the Navigator, she asked him where they were going.

Where they were going? And only then, when he mentioned Dutrelle Jones, did she seem to come out of her spell, as though the anxiety she had misplaced somewhere had suddenly turned up panting and hungry.

On the news, there was a short clip of the Apollo 11 astronauts, now old men, with President Obama at the White House. Back in the studio, Hal Michaels straightened his notes and told his pretty black co-anchor, Renata Mitchell, that he remembered watching the moon landing. She nodded respectfully.

On cue, at a different angle, they both looked somberly at another camera.

"Police in Gallatin are still sorting out what caused a gun battle earlier tonight at the Gallatin County Hospital," Renata Mitchell said.

Alyssa sat up.

"Two people are confirmed dead," Mitchell said, "including former NFL player Dutrelle Jones and Pamela Martin, a nurse on duty at the hospital. Reporter Bill Hibbs is live on the scene in Gallatin. Bill?"

"Pamela Martin!" Patricia cried. "Oh, Chick." She leaned forward, both hands over her mouth.

Hibbs was a skinny, intense, thirtyish man who reminded him of some nervous comic actor. Hibbs had been on the way back to Atlanta from Macon when he got the call about the shootings. He was there a few minutes after Chick arrived with Hermia, and he had interviewed anybody who would talk to him.

"Renata," said Hibbs, "our sources say that Dutrelle Jones was involved in an altercation earlier today with Prof. Brantley Forrest of Amherst College in New England. Prof. Forrest, a native of Gallatin, was visiting town with his two daughters. According to witnesses, Jones attacked Forrest this afternoon outside the Left Bank Grille. I talked to the owner, Mary Rose Ryburn, about the incident." Hibbs stared at the camera, but the clip did not come on. He touched his ear, nodded distractedly, and looked down at his notes. "Prof. Forrest was coming out of the restaurant with Dutrelle Jones' wife and her daughter from a previous marriage when Mr. Jones came across the street and attacked Prof. Forrest, according to witnesses.

"Prof. Forrest suffered a skull fracture when his head hit the sidewalk. Jones was arrested for assault and released on bail earlier tonight, but he allegedly forced his way past hospital staff into Prof. Forrest's room, where he found his wife and threatened her with a handgun. I talked to Dr. William Fletcher, who was on the scene, and he said that Mr. Jones tried to shoot his wife but that Mr. Forrest managed to disarm him. When Mr. Forrest lost consciousness, Mr. Jones got the gun back and fired at the doorway where his wife was standing, but he missed her and hit the nurse, Pamela Martin. The officers on the scene shot Jones. A tragic end for a Georgia hero," he said with a rehearsed sadness. The screen filled with a photograph of Jones in his high school uniform, footage of him sacking the Georgia quarterback in his Alabama jersey, and finally Dutrelle in a Tennessee Titans uniform.

"Thanks, Bill," said Mitchell dolefully, turning to Michaels. "So sad." They shook their heads.

"In other news about the problems of the NFL," Michaels said, looking at another camera, "former Atlanta Falcons quarterback Michael Vick—still under house arrest after serving 21 months for his dog-fighting conviction—might have a new job. Gene?"

Chick raised the remote and turned off the TV. He was awash in relief. Hermia had been standing with him the whole time Hibbs interviewed him, and the last thing he needed was for Patricia to see her.

After a moment, Alyssa sighed "Wow," and rose from the couch. "Good night." She yawned and went up to her room.

"Everything I told him, he got mixed up," Chick said. "Did you hear that? *Brantley* Forrest?"

"And they certainly wouldn't hire that man at Amherst," Patricia said. "I'm just sick about Pamela Martin. She has those two little boys. Are you coming to bed?"

"I'm still too keyed up."

Patricia paused on the stairs. "Thank God Marisa Forrest is getting here tomorrow. She can take those poor girls home."

Chick asked, "Who's picking her up?"

When she didn't answer, he turned and looked at her. She started back down the stairs.

"You know what," she said. "I bet nobody even has her flight information."

"You don't think the girls have it?"

"She wouldn't expect Varina to pick her up, not with her husband in town."

"Don't you have her number in Italy?" he said, turning to look at her.

"There's a six-hour time difference. It's five-thirty in the morning over there—and she might already be on the plane."

"Okay, I'll look it up online."

"We don't even know what airline it is."

"Oh sweet hell," he said in disgust. "I'll go find out."

He heaved himself out of his chair, got his keys, and opened the door to the garage. Forrest would never remember the details, even without a head injury. He was going to have to drive to the hospital, exhausted as he was, get Forrest's room key, go down to the motel and get his laptop, and then take it back to the hospital and wait for Forrest to find the flight information. At least an hour, probably more than that.

"You know," Patricia called from the top of the stairs, "I almost wish—no, I won't say it. God forgive me. I'm sorry you have to go out, but what if her plane arrives in the morning?"

She almost wished Forrest had gotten shot instead of Dutrelle, that's what she meant. If Braxton Forrest had come home and gotten shot, it would have had a kind of roundedness to it.

He started the Navigator and backed out of the driveway.

Two hours ago Hermia Watson had sat in his car.

Back at the hospital, he pulled into the space in front of the main entrance where the news van had been. When he walked into the main hallway, two red-eyed nurses were at the nurses' station.

"Where is he?" he asked.

Betty Mullins opened her hand toward Forrest's room.

12

Any movement now was excruciating. There was an IV stand next to him, a drip of antibiotics going into the back of his left hand. Bill Fletcher had told him sometime earlier to hang on, they would be taking him to Macon for a CAT scan. Fletcher had found Forrest's cell phone and put it beside his right leg so he could answer it without having to turn and reach for it. Forrest drifted off until the phone woke him. It was Maya Davidson, of all people.

My God, I leave you alone for one day and all hell breaks loose. Listen, are you okay? They said you had a skull fracture.

I'm still alive. I had this dream about you.

No, that was Marisa. But listen, I hear you saw Marilyn. Was this Jones man her husband?

That's right.

I mean when you first started talking about it, it seemed like so long ago and you were so weird about it, and now it's all over the news...

Bill Fletcher was asking about you.

Oh. Well, I'm past all that now. And they're almost done, I think.

Who?

Those women.

What women?

The gray ones. The old ones. They wanted my necklace. You know who I'm talking about.

He must have fallen asleep again, because he was not holding the phone now. A shadow filled the doorway, a flicker in the corner of his eye, someone moving. Jones! No, Jones was dead, and he had shot the nurse when he was trying to shoot Marilyn. Her shade leaned over him now; he smelled the perfume on her neck, that sweet umbrage when he tipped her toward him. A cold draft, and there they were again, he felt them, the gray ladies, daughters of original darkness. He closed his eyes against a rising terror.

"Cump?"

He opened his eyes again. Somebody stood on his right side. He cut his eyes and could not quite see. The strain hurt his head. "Who's that?"

"Chick Lee."

"What time is it?"

"A couple of minutes to midnight."

"Stand down there so I can see you. It hurts like hell to move my head."

Chick moved around to the foot of the bed. Plump, anxious, bleary-eyed Chick.

"What are you doing here?"

"I need to know when your wife's flight gets in."

Marisa's flight. Marisa was coming. The idea flooded him with relief. But when was she coming? He could see himself naked at the laptop typing in the number from his American Express card but not paying attention to the flight time.

"I don't remember, Chick."

"How about the airline? Anything."

Was it Delta? He would be surprised if it wasn't Delta, but what if it wasn't?

"It's on my laptop."

"So I need the key to your motel room. I'll go get your laptop and bring it here."

"Look in my wallet. It should be inside my pants in the closet." Chick disappeared and came back a few seconds later holding his wallet. "It's one of those cards in the front."

"This one?"

"That looks like it. So there's internet access here?"

Chick's eyebrows went up. "Good question." He disappeared again and Forrest stared at the wall in front of him. Jones had died right there. He felt nothing for Jones. Nothing at all. Maybe it would come later. He couldn't see the bullet hole under the bracket for the television that he had seen earlier. Somebody had shot and missed, probably the Reeves boy. Not Jeff Todd's daughter, Mary Louise Gibson's granddaughter. She wouldn't miss. They must have come in to fix the hole. Spackling and paint. But hadn't the TV been on the other side of the room? Was it the same room? If they had moved him, would she find him?

Marisa was coming. An image from a dream came back to him and with it a feeling he had forgotten, something from early in his marriage, a kind of lightness: a Saturday morning, he and Marisa naked in bed after making love, early spring, the windows across from the bed open. They were sitting back against the headboard with coffee and croissants and strawberry preserves, brushing flakes of crust from the sheet, from each other's skin. Marisa's young breasts were lovely and her face full of love and sweet pleasure. A feeling of aubade or psalm. She had been such a mercy, such a mercy ... And the first time he betrayed her was with Lola Gunn.

He felt the impulse to pray. Could he pray?

"No internet," said Chick, reappearing at the foot of the bed and running a hand distractedly through his hair. "So any suggestions?" His shirttail was halfway out, his face drawn and exhausted. Forrest imagined Chick scrolling down through his emails. And what was it about telling somebody your password? Especially his. Again he remembered sitting there.

"Just open my Outlook program and check there. I downloaded the flight information onto my calendar."

"I'll call you tomorrow and let you know when she's coming." He held up the card and started to leave, speaking back over his shoulder. "Unless there's something else you need."

"I'll get somebody to pick it up tomorrow."

"Pick up what?"

"Where did she go?"

Chick came back into view. "Who?"

"I never even got to speak to her. Does Hermia know what happened?"

"Are you kidding?" Chick lifted a hand toward the television. "If you're talking about Marilyn, she told Hermia she had something to do."

Something to do? He closed his eyes, trying to figure it out, and it was on a plat and the lines kept turning into barbed wire fences and thickets of brambles. They were going to have to redo the whole survey, and it would not close unless he could admit feeling something he had tried not to feel.

But now she was leaving him, she had something to do, she was walking away from him with that sway of the hips, young again under the moon. A Firebird pulled up and she leaned over to talk to a man and he saw it was Mo Woodson and a siren was approaching from somewhere far away, growing in intensity. The sound spiked into his head. He opened his eyes. The siren faded, lights wheeled through the blinds against the walls, and the ambulance rumbled past his window.

Chick was gone. He could hear people out in the hallway, cries, bursts of lamentation. No, that had already happened. The gray women shuffled close to him, sniffed him like dogs. He felt them, large and sour as old clotted milk, but he could not turn his head to look.

Then it was later. Someone was leaning over him, holding his eyes open, first one, then the other, and shining a small painful light into each one. "Cump?" a man's voice said. Bill Fletcher. He tried to answer.

"We gave you something for pain," Fletcher said. "You were pretty loud for a while there. You probably don't remember any of it. I'm getting you down to Macon for a CAT scan." He put his hand on Forrest's shoulder.

13

All the way down the hill toward the Interstate, Chick's was the only car on the road. At the EconoLodge, he kept inserting the plastic key card, but it kept flashing red. Maybe they had thrown Forrest out. He turned it over to try another side. The light on the lock flashed green, and the door handle yielded. Stupid.

He dreaded walking into the hot and humid evidence of another male, but maids had cleaned the room, thank God, and the room had a neutralized, see-no-evil look. The laptop sat at the desk where it was supposed to be. He sat down and opened it and fiddled with the wireless mouse while the computer came out of sleep mode, then clicked the Outlook icon. Eighty-four unread emails already waited in the Inbox, and when the send/receive function began automatically, the total started ticking upward. On the calendar at the left, he saw what looked like airline information and opened it.

Yes. Marisa Forrest was flying on Alitalia from Rome to Paris. She had a two-hour layover, and then she flew on US Airways from Paris to Charlotte, then on a third flight from Charlotte to Atlanta. She arrived in Atlanta at 5:22 p.m. Right in the middle of rush hour. He found a pen and a notepad in the desk drawer and wrote down all three flight numbers.

By now the inbox had 142 emails. He was about to close the computer when it struck him that Marisa might have emailed Forrest about the trip and he clicked the inbox. He opened the latest email from Marisa and skimmed it—something about her art, her relatives, nothing about a change in plans. He was about to close the program when he saw an email with the subject line SORRY! SORRY! SORRY! from Natalia Onobanjo-Engstrom and opened it on impulse.

```
    o brax that new dean is such a bitch!
  she made threats & I didnt know what to do
  so sorry miss u
    nati
```

In the subject lines of other emails, Chick saw an ocean of trouble for Forrest. He marked the emails he had opened as unread, exited Outlook, shut down the computer, and found a beaten-up carrying case where he stowed it with its cord and mouse.

It was 1:05 according to the clock beside the bed. What if he just took a rest for a minute or two? He lay down and closed his eyes and imagined waking up there in his clothes late the next morning, disoriented and crumpled, without a toothbrush.

The first loud bars of "Dixie" heaved him upright. He found the phone in his pocket. 1:37? He had no idea where he was.

"Mr. Lee?"

"Yes?"

"LaCourvette Todd. Thank God this is your number. Listen, I hate to get you out of bed, but I'm here with Hermia, and I'm wondering if you could come over. Hold on just a second." He imagined her walking away from Hermia into another room. "Mr. Lee?" she whispered. "Her mother was killed tonight."

"Oh sweet Lord."

"I think she's suicidal. It's bad. They need me back at work, and I'm scared to leave her for a second. I don't know who else to call. Can you come? She said your name. That's why I'm calling you. I think she trusts you."

"I'm on my way," he said.

14

July 21, 2009

The television woke her. Her skirt had ridden halfway up her thighs, and she rolled away, pulling it down. Chick Lee, fully clothed, still wearing his shoes, lay turned toward her on top of the sheets, snoring lightly with his mouth open and his hands clasped under his chin like a little boy praying. She got up unsteadily, used the bathroom, splashed water on her face, and stared at herself in the mirror. Just for an instant, she saw Forrest in the shape of her forehead, and her own face felt unfamiliar, uncanny, this face she had looked at and made up all her life.

I wake and feel the fell of dark, not day.

She turned off the bathroom light and went back and lay down beside Chick and stared numbly at the news.

"Where's your wedding ring?" someone shouted. Mark Sanford, the governor of South Carolina, was being dogged by reporters about his extramarital affairs.

"What's that?" he said, as if he hadn't heard. "We all make mistakes in our life," he kept saying.

Here was one, for example: her mother was dead.

Dutrelle Jones was dead. That was another one.

Braxton Forrest had a skull fracture and might not live.

The deadly recognition that it was all her fault nosed at her again, excited, sniffing out her secrets. And there *he* was as if to remind her. On the *Today* show, Meredith Vieira was asking President Obama about criticism of the baggy jeans he had worn to throw out the first pitch at the All-Star Game last week. He grinned and defended himself. "Those jeans are comfortable, and for those of you who want your president to look great in his tight jeans, I'm sorry—I'm not the guy." A dig at George Bush, she recognized mechanically.

Other news flashed by. And then she was looking at Henry Louis Gates Jr.—Skip Gates—primly furious in a mug shot. Confronted by police while he tried to get into his own Cambridge house, he had called the white officer a racist and had put up such a fuss that he was arrested for disorderly conduct. She wondered if he remembered her. And now Al Roker was talking about the weather and the total eclipse of the sun that (sorry, folks) would not be visible anywhere in the western world, but our service men and women in Afghanistan would get to see it.

When they broke for Atlanta news, Dutrelle Jones filled the screen—Dutrelle sacking a quarterback, Dutrelle intercepting a pass and returning it for a touchdown. The reporter said Jones had been trying to shoot his wife, Adara Dernier-Jones, when he accidentally killed a white nurse and was shot by police. They showed an old file photo of her mother with Elton Dernier and Mayor Andrew Young. Gallatin police said it was just a coincidence that, half an hour later, Mrs. Dernier-Jones had died in a car crash.

"God Almighty," said Chick, sitting up in a panic. "What time is it? Good God Almighty." He gaped at Hermia in horror, scrabbled at his pocket, and came up with his iPhone. He stared at it. "She hasn't even called me?" he said, astonished. He stood up, swiping at the little display with his forefinger, then held it to his head and walked out of the bedroom.

Hermia found the remote beside the bed and turned off the television. In the silence, she could hear Chick talking earnestly. The little scandal of his staying overnight was the lightest thing on her heart. She needed to call LaCourvette, but she didn't want to. The cold way she had acted burned her now, though it had shamed her last night.

LaCourvette was the one at fault. She was the one who forced Hermia to revise everything she had ever thought about her mother. Mrs. Watson, Mrs. Loum, Mrs. Dernier, Mrs. Jones, but always Mama. Ever since LaCourvette told her, she had seen only the mask that hid Marilyn Harkins, the town whore, a monster of lust and will. A whore not from need or victimhood but choice and design. And then the last thing she had expected was what broke out of her yesterday—that terrifying love. She had been staring into the very thing that brought her into being and that made her own incest with her father—that cliché of the abused, that staple of confessional memoirs—into mere dalliance and triviality.

She thought now with a strange twisting horror of John Bell Hudson, her accidental child, the son she gave away when he was two months old and followed now on Facebook. But she had not been accidental, not for her mother. No, she had come out of that love.

And for what? To become an abyss.

"How about that?" Chick said, standing in the threshold with a light knock on the doorjamb. "Patricia didn't even know I was gone until I woke her up. I told her I fell asleep on the bed in Forrest's room when I went to pick up his laptop. That's not a lie, by the way."

"Okay," said Hermia, lifelessly. "I appreciate your coming." Her voice sounded like someone else's, alien and unused.

"Look, Hermia," he said, "are you okay?"

"Me?"

"Do you want me to call LaCourvette? Or how about you just come with me? We'll go to the hospital and check on Cump."

"Cump?"

"Forrest."

"No, you go on," she said. "You need to get to work. I guess it's better if I don't do anything. Every time I do something..." She curled up on herself, retreating again into the depths.

After a moment she felt his hand on her shoulder. He sat down beside her and touched her hair. He rocked the bed lightly, soothing her like a child, and an old, wild, secret feeling began to come over her.

"Hermia," he murmured, and the warmth rose through her. She kept crying, but self-consciously now. "Hermia, look at me." She felt his hand on her hip, rocking her gently. "Hermia, please."

15

Chick rocked her as gently as he had rocked Alyssa when she was little and could not go to sleep. Suddenly she rolled onto her back. "Daddy Loum used to do me like that," she said, wiping her eyes.

"Who's Daddy Loum?"

"He married Mama after Daddy Watson died. He used to come in and wake me up like that. He'd shake me a little and say, 'Hermia, Hermia, ma cherie amour' and when I woke up, he'd put his chin in his hand and say 'Let me see.' That was a game we played. When I was a little girl, six or seven, Daddy Loum would always say, 'Let me see,' when he was thinking about something. One time when I heard him say it I yanked my T-shirt up over my head and I said, 'See?' and he and Mama laughed till they cried. So it was a game I'd play with him even when I got older. He'd come in and wake me up and turn on the light by the bed, and he'd pretend he was thinking. He'd hold his chin like this and say, 'Let me see,' and I'd do that. He was sweet like you."

"Was he?"

"You say it," she said in a small voice.

"Say what?"

"Say 'Let me see.'"

"Let me see."

She leaned up and skinned her blouse off over her head and unsnapped her bra and stripped it off. She lay back, her breasts bare, her eyes brimming. "You know what he'd say then?"

Chick's heart labored. He gazed to the side of her, mortified, stricken with terror at her madness.

"He'd say, 'Oh my.' Just like that. 'Oh my.' And then he would always say, 'Aren't you getting to be a big girl?' He would look at me like I was the only reason God made the world. He would tell me"— she reached up and took Chick's hand and kissed his knuckles and drew his hand to her—"he would tell me I was more precious than all the gold of Ophir."

A dark giddiness overwhelmed him. The pounding in his throat made it hard to breathe. When she leaned up and put her arms around him, his hands rode of their own motion down her smooth skin to the small of her back. The heat of her heavy breasts against him, the astonishing offer of her. Her lips grazed his ear. "I ain't never know my real daddy," she said in a wondering whisper, a high, mock voice like Butterfly McQueen's.

Her real daddy? he thought stupidly. It must be some kind of game he was supposed to play. He licked his lips and tried to speak. He heard himself say, very softly, "Oh my," and as she lay back, pulling him down, he glanced incongruously at the bedside clock.

It was 8:47 on Tuesday morning. He still had his shoes on. He felt as though he had been walking all his life on the ocean floor, a dry-shod observer, admiring the green and gleaming walls of water on either side, but all this time, he had been headed to Egypt, and now the great collapsing currents swept him under.

16

At the door, she said something to him that she might regret. It was a strange, trite thing to say.

"If you ever need me, I'll be here," she said. He nodded and started to turn away and she touched his arm. "No, I mean it. You come here anytime."

He stepped back inside the house.

"Was this because of your mother?"

At first, she did not understand, but then it came burning into her. He was asking if making love to him had been a sacrifice of appeasement, if she had slept with him as a way of not feeling better than the woman whose death she caused. Had she?

He took her hands and kissed the knuckles.

"I think my father knew your mother. I think maybe he..."

She remembered her mother refusing to go inside Lee Ford.

"Oh, Chick, who knows why we do things?"

† † †

Eumaios was frantic to get out. Barefooted, she opened the door but did not go out after him. Already hot. She closed the door and looked for a moment at the bench where she had seen Dutrelle just yesterday. She half-expected to see his ghost.

He was dead. Her mother was dead. Still, her mood of the early morning had lifted a little. Chick Lee, that sweet man. It had been a long time since she had made love to anyone, but it almost seemed like the first time for Chick. Fumbling and embarrassed, he had been quick as a schoolboy, and he had lain afterward, disheveled, still almost fully clothed, his face red. He kept murmuring, "Oh my Lord, oh my sweet Lord." It could have been gratitude or remorse—she did not know. But his eyes had been full of speculation, this boy not many years from old age, still beset with his anxieties and uncertainties.

Eumaios did his business and toured the yard several times, reliving the scene of his heroics with Dutrelle. Now he suddenly stopped. His ears went up and he broke toward the gate, not barking but dancing and circling, his tail wagging furiously. It had to be LaCourvette. Then he charged to the back door, pawing it. Hermia let him in just as the doorbell rang. He skidded past her on the kitchen tiles in his haste to get to the front. LaCourvette always brought him something.

She had on her uniform. She gave Hermia an appraising look. Hermia knew her hair was a mess. She had on a T-shirt with no bra and a pair of shorts she'd fished off the closet floor.

"I came close to losing you last night, baby."

"I'm better."

"I hope I didn't mess up by asking Chick Lee over here. You're not mad at me?"

"Not about that."

LaCourvette's face went vacant. She knelt to Eumaios and held his head and let him lick her face. From her pocket she fetched a big milk bone and teased him with it. The dog sat, his brows working hopefully, and LaCourvette let him take the treat in his mouth. When she stood, she glanced at Hermia and then, getting no response, put her hand on

270

the doorknob.

"You saw me last night," she said. "I killed a man I admired my whole life! I can't sleep, I can't think."

Her eyes filled with tears and seeing her, Hermia burned with pity and stepped forward and embraced the smaller woman, cupping the back of her neck and pulling her head against her breasts.

"I know you lost your mama, baby," LaCourvette sobbed, clutching her. "I'm so sorry. I'm so sorry."

"Why did you ever tell me about her?" Hermia moaned. "Why couldn't you leave it alone? Why did I have to know? If I hadn't known—"

LaCourvette broke free. "Why did I tell you? Think about why I told you!"

Eumaios, confused and full of concern at the change of tone, whimpered and pressed anxiously against Hermia's legs, almost tripping her. Hermia put a hand on his head to calm him. Through the glass door, Hermia could see Mrs. Russell out on her sidewalk, inspecting the police car in the driveway and peering up toward the house.

She took LaCourvette's elbow and led her, wary of glass, to the sofa.

"I remember the way you looked at me after you told me."

"The way I looked at you?"

"Like you'd just given me poison and wanted to see it work."

LaCourvette tilted her head to warn her, but Hermia went on. "You remember how I was. You wanted to see me like that. You wanted me dirtied. You wanted me to know I wasn't nothing but a whore's daughter so you might—"

"What? What were you going to say?" Her friend watched her, dreading her words. Dutrelle's "girlfriend" insinuations hovered between them. "I'm the best friend you got," LaCourvette said after a moment. "Think about why I told you."

"Why? If you hadn't—"

"If I hadn't, you would have done something worse," she said.

"What could I do worse?"

"Listen!" LaCourvette said, taking her hand. "You called me up. This was back in January right after the Inauguration. You wanted to go out. You were excited, and I'd just gotten a raise. We were like a couple of teenagers. We went down to Macon to dinner."

"I remember." She drew her bare legs up on the couch next to the neatly pressed uniform trousers.

"I had chardonnay like I always do, but you started in on martinis. After you had two or three of them, I asked what in the world was up with you, and you told me you'd done something naughty."

"I told you that?"

"You told me." She leaned toward her now, taking her by the chin and forcing her to look into her eyes. "You got right in my face like this and asked me real soft did I want to arrest you? Did I want to put my mean old handcuffs on you?" Hermia pulled back from her. "So I asked you what you'd done, and you said you'd forged a letter. You said it was because of a man named Braxton Forrest. I said, Braxton Forrest! And you asked if I'd heard of him, and I said, Heard of him! My grandmama brought him up. You kept saying, You're lying! You've heard of him? You said you'd been obsessed with him for years. I asked you why, and you told me he was brilliant, but it was more than that— it was the way he looked, the way he moved. You said you loved him. You said he was your baby's daddy, and you really, really wanted him back."

Hermia sat like stone.

"I didn't say that," she answered weakly. "I wouldn't have said that."

"Oh yes you did, baby."

Hermia could hardly lift her head. "Why did you make friends with me? Because you already knew all my secrets? Because of my mother?"

"Girl, I didn't know who you were! When you came to town, I met you at church. Who wouldn't like you, you so pretty and classy? All the men, you remember? Everybody wanted to sit next to Sister Watson. About a week after that I saw you at the mall in Macon and you introduced me to your mother, you remember? Miss Mary Louise had pointed her out to me before. Your mama saw I knew who she was, and I saw you didn't. And then the night you got drunk and told me about Braxton Forrest I saw you didn't have any idea who he was, either. It scared me to death."

Hermia felt the dull thudding of her heart.

"You knew he was my father?"

"No. But what if he was? You know? I mean, light-skinned as you are. What if he was? And here you were telling me you'd already slept with him!"

"And now that he's here you told me about my mother?"

"I didn't know what else to do. You slept with him before because you didn't know he was your father, and this time you would know and you wouldn't do it."

Hermia put her face in her hands.

"Would you?" cried LaCourvette, suddenly rigid beside her.

"No! No!" Hermia said at last, looking up. "I didn't know before. But it just hurts me so much, LaCourvette! Yesterday I saw what it was he had with my mother. As soon as they saw each other, it's like I was two years old and in the way. Or like I didn't exist. But I wouldn't be here at all if she hadn't loved him so much. I've never felt love like that. I'm not ashamed to come from that."

"What about—what about your baby?"

Hermia stared at her friend. She thought of John Bell on Facebook, and the anger that flared up at the question died away.

"I haven't seen him since I gave him away. He's with a good family."

"White?"

She nodded.

"So he doesn't know who he is. He'll never know who he is."

Hermia shook her head. They sat for a while without talking.

"You know what I don't understand?" Hermia said. "I don't understand why Miss Mary Louise got so upset when she found out who I was. I mean, was it finding out my mother had a child, or was it suspecting that I was Braxton Forrest's daughter?"

LaCourvette did not answer. She stood up, squeezing her hands, and then sat back down.

"Baby, there's something I'm still not telling you."

17

Patricia was standing at the big kitchen island in her bathrobe, her hands resting on the counter tiles as though she were daydreaming, when Chick came cautiously through the door, already panicked to see her there. She looked up at him with unmistakable anguish.

"Chick," she said, and her face crumpled.

She knew. Of course she knew. Anybody driving by could have recognized his big Navigator outside Hermia's house. Some well-meaning busybody had called her.

"Chick," she said again. She had no makeup on, and she had been crying. She looked her age. "I was up half the night," she said. "When you didn't come back I knew something was wrong."

"Why didn't you call me?" he said weakly.

"Because I knew you didn't want to be out in the middle of the night. I was lying there thinking how many men would just get up and—I was thinking what a good man you are, and I'm always such a...such a bitch to you."

She came toward him and hugged him. He put his arms around her, as though to hold in his vast relief.

"No I'm not," he said. "I'm not a good man."

She hugged him tighter and looked up at him. "I was jealous of Varina Davis. You've always talked about her. But you would never, never do anything with her. I know that, Chick. I'm so sorry, honey. I'm so sorry."

He pushed Patricia gently away, because he was worried that she might smell Hermia's perfume on his shirt. Sick awareness of his adultery broke over him, a sense of sin and estrangement—the need he would have now and forever to evade the truth, to spin out small lies about his moods, his thoughts, everything. To live in a false world. He would be cut off from the source of his real life, like a branch cut off from the trunk of a tree.

He would be damned. That's what it meant to be damned.

He thought about the boys in his Sunday school class, slowly being poisoned by his hypocrisy.

"Chick," she said, clutching at him. "Chick, look at me."

He looked at her, his wife, his eyes burning, full of anguish. Long ago he had given up pretending to himself that he loved her. For years he had tolerated her out of habit, largely for Alyssa's sake, while he daydreamed about Tricia or ogled Tracie Newsome.

"Chick? I love you so much." She touched his cheek. "Can you forgive me?"

He bowed his head. The intensity of his misery made him tremble, and suddenly Patricia was sobbing, clutching at him, her face pressed blindly into Hermia's perfume. Just then Alyssa came down the stairs and into the kitchen and stood there, terrified.

He patted Patricia to break the embrace, and she turned away, hiding her face. Chick excused himself and went upstairs to their room.

His things stood in their usual places, newly alien. He felt like a ghost revisiting the house where he had once been alive. In the bathroom, he took off the clothes of his sin and pushed them into the corner. In the shower, under the copious hot water that beat against his head and neck, he resolved to call Jack Boehner and tell him to find another Sunday School teacher. How could he bear it, pretending to represent the teachings of Jesus after what he had done?

What if they found out? The secrets of all would be laid bare, the Bible said.

Or maybe he should have one last class and tell the boys about the nature of evil. For most people, he would say, it wasn't a deliberate choice to do something criminal or cruel. It was a gradual giving in to small selfishness, a dry rot in the moral structures you had to hold in place by effort and intention. Self-indulgence became second nature and it gradually distorted the shape of your life, until you were like the rich man in the parable looking at Lazarus across a great gulf.

You prayed not to be led into temptation, but after a while you didn't mean it. Suppose there was a beautiful woman lying naked beneath you, opening her arms to you ...

Desire and despair swept over him at once. He saw himself as vain and worthless, a faithless husband to a carping wife, father to a spoiled daughter. Outwardly prosperous, inwardly empty and lost. He supposed that feeling like this was the reason any man knew he needed to be saved. Jesus didn't say, Come to me all ye who have good habits and don't go dancing. He let a prostitute wash his feet with her hair. Jesus reached down into the very shit and sin of what you were.

If Chick ever went back into that class, he would tell the boys that when it came to it, you had to choose sides between God and yourself, and you had to know that in your bones, in the very core of yourself, you loved what was right and true and just, even if you were not always— maybe not ever—those things yourself. If you did not love God with your whole heart and soul and mind and strength, you had to know you could get there by at least wanting to do the right thing and trying to do it and not being too proud to ask for His help.

But what if it turned out that you weren't the rich man at all, but Lazarus? And not just the beggar, but the one in the tomb, the man helplessly dead, unable to want the least thing until something stirred in his heart and he caught his breath back in a long desperate gasp and he heard his name being called? And when he tried to get up, he had to hobble out toward daylight in his grave clothes and the stink of his own death.

18

When Forrest woke, something was jammed down his throat inflating him like a balloon, then deflating him. It overrode his instinct to breathe. His arms were bound, and he panicked, surging against whatever restrained him, unable to speak, unable to move, as though his body were no longer his own.

He rolled his eyes desperately to see where he was and find someone to help him. A white room. Figures in gray hoods sat around the walls. They lifted their slow heads. He heard a murmur of laughter. They had taken something important from him. He saw a little bald dead homunculus whose arms were bound as though he were in a straitjacket, and they were passing him around, holding him by his feet and dangling him upside down. One of them shook him like a string of Christmas bells or a child's sock full of Hershey's kisses. She set him on his feet and the little man slumped over helplessly. *What, can't stand up?* He heard another wave of laughter.

He tried to speak but the thing in his throat prevented it. It breathed him, a mechanical demon, and wild panic rose again. A woman in a white dress stood nearby with her back to him. He willed her to turn. Please help me. She turned to him. It was Marilyn in her fishnet wedding dress. Her eyes were modestly lowered. She held a bouquet of yellow roses, and as he watched, blood pulsed steadily from her cut throat onto her dress and spattered the yellow petals and gleamed on the backs of her fingers. She raised her eyes to his. *I'm not on your side, baby,* she said. *I'm on the other side.* He tried to say that he wanted to be on her side. *No,* she said. *No, baby.*

"No!" someone was shouting. "Mr. Forrest!"

He was sitting up in a tangle of tubes. His head hurt dully. Two strange nurses cowered back from him.

"Where am I?" he rasped.

"Sir, you're in Macon General Hospital," said the older one, holding out a calming hand toward him. "This is the intensive care unit. Now we need you to settle down, please."

"I'll settle down if you keep this thing out of my mouth." He had apparently broken the restraints on his arms to get the respirator out, and now held the thing toward her.

"Yes sir, we'll let the doctor know you're breathing on your own."

The other nurse, a plain woman with no figure and bitterness etched into the sides of her mouth, came around the bed and checked a tube. It apparently ran to a catheter, because he felt it in his penis. His head throbbed. He put his right hand into his hair but his fingers found nothing. With both hands he felt over his bare skull. A thick bandage covered the back of his head.

"What happened?" he said. "What day is it?"

"Tuesday afternoon," said the older nurse. "They had to do emergency surgery to relieve the pressure. You had blood clots between your skull and the brain tissues. All your personal stuff's in a bag in the closet, your ring, your wallet, everything."

Tuesday afternoon? Something about Marilyn nagged at him. Maybe if he closed his eyes. Something about picking up his laptop. He vaguely remembered giving Chick his room key. Or was it something about Marisa—but was Marisa in his motel room? There was somebody else lying dead in his bed. An Asian girl? No, Maya. Maya Cuthbert? He could not get any idea to feel right.

Then it was later. "Hey Cump," somebody was saying. "Cump, can you hear me?"

When he opened his eyes, a weary old man full of concern was leaning over him. It was Bill Fletcher.

"Bill," he said.

A different nurse marked something on a chart. A different room now.

"Can you touch your right eyebrow?" Fletcher asked. Forrest did it, and the nurse made another mark.

"I thought you were going to tell me you had to shave it off," he said. "What's she doing?"

"She's helping me with the GCS. Glasgow coma scale. I ask you to do things and check your responses. It's a test of how conscious you are."

"Can I get one for my students?" said Forrest, and his voice sounded indistinct to him, but Fletcher laughed. The nurse smiled and wrote something else down.

"How much do you remember?"

"Spotty," said Forrest. "I remember Jones." Images flickered. "I don't know."

Fletcher turned and told the nurse, "I'd say thirteen, maybe fourteen," and thanked her. When she left the room, he turned back. "You don't remember anything else?"

"Did I get up and try to go down to the emergency room?"

Fletcher nodded. "I'm sorry, Cump."

"She's dead?" Fletcher nodded again and the old dread overwhelmed him, but with a new keenness of desolation, more terrible for having seen her again. "I came down here and got her killed."

For a long time Fletcher said nothing. Forrest, closing his eyes, had almost forgotten he was there when Fletcher said, "I'm still here."

It hurt to turn his head to look at him. "Can you sit down toward the end of the bed so I can see you?"

Fletcher elevated the head of Forrest's bed and moved his chair and sat back down. "What was she doing out at the Woodson place?" he asked.

"I didn't know she went out there."

"Before she started home. She went out there, and Mo's wife ran her off."

Forrest thought about Maureen and Marilyn facing each other.

"I told her about Mo at lunch today," Forrest told him.

"Told her what?"

"That Mo convinced me she was dead."

"What do you mean convinced you?"

"He made me think she'd been killed."

Fletcher tilted his head, waiting, and Forrest felt a great weariness. When he did not go on, Fletcher said, "It was yesterday."

"It seems like it."

"No, I mean your lunch with Marilyn. That was yesterday. Today is Tuesday. Chick Lee is going to get your wife from the airport," Fletcher said. "I think he's taking your girls."

"Chick Lee," Forrest said, and he fell silent again, thinking about giving Chick the room key. He had put his laptop into the care of a Baptist who ran a Ford dealership. On the hard drive were his book and all his emails. Chick already knew more about Forrest than anybody else alive—except for Maya Davidson, who knew things he had never told anyone in Gallatin. He needed to call her and swear her to eternal silence. And why had he put himself at Chick Lee's mercy now?

Because of the flight information. He remembered telling him to use the Outlook program to keep him away from the emails, but how stupid was that? All his emails automatically went into his inbox, and all Chick would have to do was—

"Is his wife with him?" Forrest asked.

"Patricia?" Fletcher shrugged.

Forrest tried to sit up, but the pain in his head stopped him. "Do you know what they did with my cell phone?"

"It should be here." Fletcher got up and crossed the room and came back a moment later holding it toward him.

"You probably need to get back to work," said Forrest.

"I'm off today. I came down in the ambulance with you."

"I need to make a couple of calls. Can you give me a few minutes?"

"I'll be down at the nurses' station. Just buzz down there."

Forrest saw a trace of pity in his eyes.

He waited until he knew Fletcher was gone before lifting the phone to find Maya Davidson's number. The last thing he needed was her saying something else to the wrong person, and she just might. He pressed Send and waited. He pictured her at work among the lustful geeks of Dixintel who would lean from their cubicles, head after head, like the extras in a Busby Berkeley musical, to watch her as she walked away. The phone rang seven or eight times before it went into her voicemail. "Hey Maya," he said. "Can you call me as soon as you get this?" He waited a few seconds and pressed Send again. This time there was an answer on the fourth or fifth ring.

"Hello," she said tentatively.

"Maya," he said, "thanks for calling last night. I think I drifted off there at the end."

There was a pause. Then the strained voice said, "Who is this?"

"I'm sorry," he said, startled. "I must have the wrong number." But it couldn't be. It was the same one that had just gone into her voicemail.

"No," said the woman with a dogged endurance. "This is her number, but Maya ... Maya passed away."

"Oh my God." Tears sprang to his eyes and at the same time the conviction that he had already known she was dead swept over him. "Oh sweet Lord, no."

He heard her crying.

"Is this Maya's mother?"

"Yes."

"I'm a friend of hers. I'm sorry," he said. "I've been in the hospital since yesterday afternoon, and she called me last night to check on me."

There was another pause. "Who did you say this was?" she asked with a new coldness in her voice.

"My name is Braxton Forrest. I met her last week."

"Please respect our grief, whoever you are. Whatever you want."

"I just wanted to thank—"

"Maya died yesterday morning," said Mrs. Davidson. "She blacked out and ran into the side of a bridge near Locust Grove yesterday morning."

The call went dead. Was he dreaming now? He had talked to her last night. It was as real as anything else he knew was real. He could not have dreamed it. He pushed the Send button again to check the calls, scrolling down to the number he had found when he called and left the message. It was from Saturday, not from last night. He checked recent calls.

Nothing.

The sense of not possessing his own mind terrified him. Maya's last words on the phone came back to him. And he had asked who she was talking about, and she had said the old women. She knew about the old women.

His mind gave like a river bank collapsing. Maya had been drawn into Marilyn, and now both of them were dead. These women he had known. What if the old furies were still not satisfied? Suppose they were not enough, suppose the old ones had to be glutted on what was unspeakably precious to him?

Suppose they took his daughters. He remembered Cate and Berry in his hospital room, not understanding why Tricia was making them leave. He was terrified for them. Or Marisa? He thought of her airplane crossing the Atlantic. He imagined the highway Marisa and his girls would have to descend from Atlanta in Chick Lee's Navigator. They would pass Locust Grove and the very bridge where Maya Davidson had died. He wished a vague protection toward them. There was a prayer Marisa would make the girls say after the rosary. St. Michael the archangel, defend us in...in what? *Defend us in battle.* Be our protection against...Protection against something. *The malice and snares of the devil.*

19

When Eumaios nosed at her fingers, she was still sitting cross-legged on the couch in her T-shirt and shorts. She had been staring out the front window ever since LaCourvette left, replaying the conversation.

He came home on leave. Pearl was sixteen. Pretty and sassy and bright. She was Aunt Ella Parker's girl. She started coming around Stonewall Hill to help when her mama got sick.

I asked you before who Aunt Ella was, and I asked Miss Mary Louise, and neither of you would tell me.

I didn't want to get into it, baby. She was Miss Mary Louise's aunt. She cooked at the Forrest house.

So how much did your grandmother know?

Not all of it. Not all along. She didn't know about your mother all along.

What do you mean? Didn't know what about my mother?

Eumaios pushed his whole head under her left hand, and when she felt his warm tongue on her leg, she stroked him, feeling the deep central crease in his skull with her thumb. Her body felt, for an instant, oddly alien to her. This flesh, as the Bible put it. She seemed fractionally beside herself, slightly out of focus, imperfectly superimposed on her embodiment. Her ringless hands, her bare legs, the old scar from a childhood bike accident on her knee, the weight of her breasts. Knit from the first moment in her mother's womb, when the thrashing gamete of Braxton Forrest had thrust itself, tail wagging, into the egg of Marilyn Harkins.

And now her mother was dead. She lifted her palms and looked at them. She had the sense that she was just passing through this "self," this Hermia Watson. Her whole life had been like the blink of an eye, a kind of illusion, as though she had been tasked to endure the complexities of time and circumstance as part of some—what? Not a plan, exactly, but a large, unfolding, unsayable intention.

The phone startled her. She got up stiffly. She thought again that she should get rid of her landline. Eumaios trotted toward the door ahead of her, and she followed him around the corner into the kitchen. So much daylight.

It was the black funeral home director, Bertram Hubbard. The smooth low voice.

"Miss Watson, I speak for the whole community in extending to you our condolences for your loss. I know you, more than most, understand that my place is to help you through this time, just as your father would have done."

"My father?"

"Mr. Corvell Watson was a model for all of us in the profession. I wonder if I might be able to come by this morning to discuss arrangements for Mr. and Mrs. Jones?

"Mr. and Mrs. Jones?"

There was a pause.

"Am I calling at a bad time, Miss Watson?"

"No, no. I just didn't know what you meant for a second. I never thought of Dutrelle and my mother as Mr. and Mrs. Jones. I didn't realize I'd have anything to do with Dutrelle. I just..."

"Well, you see, there are a few details to attend to. You are your mother's next of kin, of course, and perhaps you and Mrs. Jones...."

"Gloria Jones killed my mother!"

There was a pause.

"Miss Watson, I'm sure we can arrange a—"

"I can't be in the same room with that woman."

Eumaios sat watching her nervously, his ears lifted, his front feet shifting. Hubbard was patient. He wanted to know if Miss Watson was aware of whether her mother had left a will or any instructions for her funeral? She told him she didn't know but she doubted it, because her mother had not been planning to be run off the road by a madwoman. Hubbard tried to soothe her. He assured her that he understood her emotions in this difficult time. Perhaps this, perhaps that—the smooth, practiced, passionless voice that came back to her from the deep past with a sense of dread. He ended by agreeing to meet her privately that afternoon at the funeral home, and she hung up trembling, her heart pounding.

She had just started to make a pot of coffee when the phone rang again.

"Yes," she said wearily, thinking it was Hubbard with some afterthought.

"Miss Watson, this is Harriet from Matthews Funeral Home. I hate to trouble you. Mr. Matthews wants you to know you have our deepest sympathy for your loss."

"Thank you," she said. "You're very kind."

She had already started to hang up when she heard the voice resume. "But Miss Watson ... Miss Watson?"

"Yes?" she said, lifting the phone to her head.

"Miss Watson, Mr. Matthews thinks you are the one best acquainted with the affairs of Mrs. Hayes, and he wanted me to ask if he could talk to you at your earliest convenience."

"What do you mean? Did Mrs. Hayes...?"

She could not stand another death. Not even this one.

"Oh, no, no, no. I'm so sorry." Harriet lowered her voice. "I told him this wasn't the best time, but he says it's urgent. Otherwise I wouldn't have bothered you."

Tears started to her eyes. She sank to the floor, her back to the counter. Eumaios came over, tentatively wagging his tail. He pushed his head into her lap, interested, and shoved his shoulder against her, and she pushed him roughly away. Harriet waited patiently for her to collect herself. After a moment, she told Harriet to go ahead. They arranged for her to meet Dillon Matthews that afternoon after she met with Mr. Hubbard. Harriet assured her again of Mr. Matthews' deepest sympathies for her loss.

When she hung up, she slumped over and lay on the kitchen tiles, curling on herself. When Eumaios tried to console her, nosing at her face, she pushed him away, but he came back, stupidly thinking she was playing.

"Go away!" she cried, slapping his face. He yelped and retreated to the corner of the room behind the kitchen table, where he watched her with lowered ears, his tongue coming out humbly to lick around his mouth, his head dropping when she glanced at him.

"Go away, goddamn it!" she shouted. She was sick of organizing her life around her dog. She got up and stalked toward him, her hand raised, and he backed tighter into his corner, tense with fear. She flung open the back door and aimed a kick at his backside as he scrambled under the kitchen table and out the opening. He leapt off the deck and then turned uncertainly, watching for any sign that she might relent. She knew he wanted to dip his head and wag his tail, all forgiveness, and come ambling back over to her, but she slammed the door.

She wept again in the shower. What was she going to do? She thought of putting a few things in her Prius and driving away toward someplace no one would ever think to look for her, somewhere south. Not Florida. South Georgia, South Alabama, somewhere she could hide away.

But she had never been able to hide, not even as a little girl when the other black children had felt a kind of awe and loathing of her white stillness. When she began to develop, she would feel the eyes of men on her, intrusive and repellent—nothing to do with who she was, just with this body they wanted to touch and push themselves into. Stupid doglike men. She turned off the water and stood trembling, hating this thing she was. She wanted not to be—not to die but not to be at all, never to have been, but she could not just turn herself off without having to die, and Lord Death, eyeing her even now, wanted her body, too. Lord Death with his shabby retainers, his soapy funeral-home euphemisms, his fluids.

She got out of the shower and toweled herself dry, avoiding the mirror. She dressed in the charcoal gray Kay Unger suit and the black Manolo Blahnik pumps her mother had bought her for her last birthday and then submitted herself to her own inspection. In the living room, she stood at the side of the picture window, gazing down Beauregard Drive toward where it bent out of sight behind the live oaks and magnolias, and called LaCourvette on her cell phone.

"I want to see Miss Mary Louise," she said when LaCourvette answered.

"Don't do that."

"I have to."

After a long pause, LaCourvette sighed. "I'll pick you up, then."

"No, I need my car. I've got a lot to do this afternoon. Just remind me where she lives, and I'll meet you there."

"You know where Mattie Walton's store is at?"

"I just know where Sharp Street is."

"Baby, it's too complicated to try to tell you. I'll swing by and you follow me."

Five minutes later the police cruiser pulled into her driveway behind the Prius. Hermia locked the front door and walked out to her car. Eumaios was whining, his paws up on the gate to the back yard. He barked once, but she ignored him. She did not look at LaCourvette either. She was opening the door and getting in when LaCourvette threw open the door of her car.

"Hey!"

Hermia sat down and closed her door, but LaCourvette came over and tapped on the window until she lowered it.

"Can we just go, please?" Hermia said.

"I don't want you bothering her if you're like this."

"I just need to talk to her."

"I told you everything she told me."

"Oh, I doubt that, LaCourvette," she said. "I really doubt that."

Mrs. Mary Louise Gibson, her big hands gnarled with arthritis, sat in her recliner in front of the television. On the side table sat a half-empty jar of dry-roasted peanuts, a square box of tissues, a worn Bible, an old-fashioned windup clock. She had the curtains closed, and the small room, cluttered with knickknacks and old photographs, was stuffy despite an old window air conditioner that shuddered as it turned on and off. Hot as it was, she had her knees covered with a knitted throw.

She smiled up at Hermia and her granddaughter in confusion. She took Hermia's hand when she came in as though they had a secret understanding, but as soon as LaCourvette turned off the television and reminded her who Hermia was, the old woman let go of Hermia's fingers and her smile faded. LaCourvette told her what Hermia wanted.

She shook her head, all the sweetness gone.

"What you doing telling her all that?"

"She needs to know, Miss Mary Louise," LaCourvette said. "You can't keep that kind of secret from somebody you care about."

"Oh, yes you can. Yes you *do*, I'm saying."

"But she needs to know who she is!"

"Don't nobody need to know they a curse!"

"What do you mean saying that?" LaCourvette demanded hotly of the old woman, who waved her hand in front of her face as though she were beset by a cloud of gnats and held it out palm upward, bending each finger as she counted.

"Her mama," she said to LaCourvette, as though Hermia were not there. "That Jones boy. That poor little nurse. My baby Braxton laid up in the hospital."

"But I never intended any of this to happen," Hermia said.

"Intended!" cried the old woman. "Girl, it's who you are. Jesus help me. Just you standing there breathing the air and being who you are. It ain't got nothing to do with what you *intended*."

"I'm not an evil woman, Mrs. Gibson."

"Miss Mary Louise," LaCourvette said, "you see this pretty woman standing in front of you? She got feelings. You can't say that to her."

"You hush. You're the one the devil's been leading by the nose."

"I just—"

"Hush your mouth! If she had some ugly mark on her face, you wouldn't make everybody look at it. You'd cover it up any way you could. Read your Bible! Adam and Eve put on fig leaves. Ain't you got sense enough to throw clothes on a ugly fact it don't help nobody to know? The more she find out, the more curse she is."

"But you told me all this, Miss Mary Louise!" LaCourvette said. "You told me yourself."

"That don't mean *you* got to tell it!" The old woman's fierceness flared up in her eyes but then suddenly faded. She sank back into her chair as if she had been struck. She laid her hand on her heart.

"Miss Mary Louise?" LaCourvette said, leaning close.

"No, you telling the truth. It's on me." Her face was ashen. The old woman waved a hand. "What call did I have to pass it on? 'The tongue is a fire, a world of iniquity.' I used to pride myself on not spreading gossip."

"Not gossip, Miss Mary Louise," said LaCourvette. "The truth. If you hadn't told me, it would have died with you."

The old woman's eyes widened.

"Oh my good Lord Jesus. That's right. Gone into the grave. Hushed up until the Last Judgment, when the sleepers awake. Pearl and Mr. Robert and Miss Inger and Miss Emily Barron and Aunt Ella and Mr. T.J. and Miss Sybil."

"Mrs. Gibson," said Hermia. The clock on the side table said ten minutes to two. "I have to go by the funeral home. I can come back for you in an hour. Will you please come with me to see my father. Please."

"Oh, Jesus come help me!" cried the old woman. "Nigger standing there in the broad daylight calling my baby father."

Hermia's whole body went hot. She could not breathe, and she turned blindly.

"Jesus help you, girl," said Mrs. Gibson. "She tell you about Pearl? She the one you favor."

"I have to go!" Hermia cried.

"Pearl Parker. Pretty as you are and nothing but trouble. I expect she guessed who her daddy was, or she wouldn't of been so sassy. Sixteen or seventeen, good-looking, sassy as a jaybird. Them light eyes. When Aunt Ella got sick during the war, Pearl come over to Stonewall Hill. Mr. Robert was home on leave. One morning Pearl was at the sink singing to herself and washing plates, and I was there in the next room polishing the silver, and I heard somebody come in the back door.

"I got up, because it might be the boy bringing groceries. I go to the door and jump back, because here come Mr. Robert, tiptoeing up behind Pearl. He didn't see me. It was warm, the window over the sink was open, the curtains was blowing, and she's over there singing some song she ain't got no business knowing, washing dishes, and the way she does it, it goes all the way down through her bottom, like she wagging her tail. Mr. Robert come across the floor barefoot. Got on them Army khakis and an old T-shirt. Tall and big-shouldered—not as tall as my baby Braxton, but a big man. He come up behind her and lean over to her ear. I'm hiding behind the doorframe watching and he says,

"'Need some help, sweet thing?'

"Pearl, she jump up and turn around and put her hand on her heart. 'Lord, you like to scared me to death, Mr. Robert!' But she was tickled. I saw her notice me, and that was all she needed. 'You can dry these here dishes,' she tells him.

"'Where's a towel?' he says.

"'Ain't no towel.' Lord, she was just grinning at him, and her tongue come teasing out over her bottom lip like this. 'Why don't you use that raggedy old shirt?' she says. 'How come these rich folks don't buy you no clothes?' She yank it aloose from his pants. She didn't have no shame, that girl.

284

"So Mr. Robert, he just skins it off over his head, and Pearl stop smiling. Just looking now, because Mr. Robert was fine. She a little worried now about me watching.

"'Why don't I use that apron, too?' he says and he reach around to yank loose the bow and pull her up close to him. She act like she trying to squirm away, but then she just go still and look up at him. 'You ain't nothing but just talk, Mr. Robert.'

"'Is that right?' he says and kisses her and I see her eyes cut over at me again. Then he reach down to squeeze her bottom and kisses her again and pulls her up against him, and he say, 'Is that right, Miss Priss?'

"She decide right then which way it was all gone go. She didn't look at me no more. She just smooths her hands down his naked back and says, 'I guess that's all the goody you got, Mr. Robert.' I remember it like it was yesterday. Where she come up with that? I guess that's all the goody you got.

"When he kiss her again, I can't stand it no more. I step out and go 'Oh!' like I had just that second come in the room. And then 'What you think you doing, girl?' I say, and she break loose, but she grinning. She know I been watching. And Mr. Robert open his mouth and I know he embarrassed, but after a second, he start whistling and drying the dishes with her apron."

"I have to go," Hermia said. Her heart was pounding painfully. She felt her way into the hallway toward the front door.

"Hermia!" LaCourvette called, following her.

The outdoor sunlight blinded her. Her foot slipped on the first step and she almost fell, but LaCourvette caught her elbow and steadied her.

"I'll get her ready," she said. "She's started talking now."

"I don't know if I can do it," Hermia said. She wiped her eyes. Several boys from the neighborhood stood astride their bicycles on the edge of the street in from of the neighbor's house, passing something between them, and they scrambled to get away as soon as they noticed LaCourvette's uniform.

"She called me a nigger," said Hermia.

"You ain't never been called that?"

"Never," she said. "Never in my whole life."

"Come break up a bar fight sometime."

She told LaCourvette she would call her from the funeral home. A neighbor stood in her threshold and then came out on her porch and picked at the dead leaves on her hanging fern to get a better look at the dressed-up woman over at Mrs. Gibson's. Hermia got in her Prius, started the car, found her way back to Sharp Street, and turned toward the funeral home.

She had lied. She had been called that name once. She was in a park, playing on the swings, and a little blonde boy was swinging beside her and telling her about his new dog. The boy's mother was watching from a bench. She smiled at Hermia. But then Marilyn came into the park and called her, standing there in the Macon daylight with her shopping bags, elegant as an orchid, and the boy's mother went stiff with disapproval. Come on, Carter! she called sharply, and the little boy dropped his feet in the scooped-out dirt and skidded to a stop at the same time Hermia did. He looked over at young Mrs. Adara Watson standing there in her heels, then back at Hermia, and he said, with a tone of wonder, as though she had just done a magic trick, *I didn't know you were a nigger.*

20

Forrest woke up drenched with sweat, terrified to move. Cautiously, he cut his eyes to see down his left side. No water moccasin. Nothing there but the railing. A cord drooped over it with a buzzer at the end. He buzzed and a nurse came and looked at his chart and injected more painkillers into the IV drip going into Forrest's right hand. His mind was not right. He felt his shaved head with his left hand and sighed and closed his eyes. When he opened them again, Bill Fletcher was leaning over him.

"How you feeling?"

His lips felt blubbery and unmanageable. "Been. Better."

"I think we've got you on the mend. How are you doing remembering things? Do you know what day it is?"

He knew that one. Tongue filled his mouth as he tried to get out the 't'.

"Tuday," Forrest managed.

"Today? Wiseass. Hard to argue with that." Fletcher patted his shoulder and told him not to try to talk. He pulled up a chair beside the bed and sat there quietly for a long time. Forrest started to close his eyes again. "I can't believe you broke Dutrelle's arm," Fletcher said, startling him back awake. "I don't see how it's even possible. They said you reached across the bed to grab him. You didn't even have any leverage on him, but you fractured Dutrelle Jones's ulna a couple of inches above his wrist. My God, Cump, he used to come in for his team physicals when he was in high school, and the boy was like Superman. His wrists were bigger than my ankles."

He remembered squeezing it as hard as he could, like the neck of a snake trying to bite him. Jones had screamed and dropped away. No one could accuse him of killing Jones. That was not on him. Not Jones.

Fletcher was saying something about how Jones had been drafted in the first round. Supposed to be another Lawrence Taylor, but something, injuries, something. Never quite lived up to expectations. Forrest blinked back awake and glanced past him at the clock on the wall. The painkiller was wearing off again. It was five minutes until two, and in a few hours Marisa's plane would be landing in Atlanta, and she would find out how much more there was that he had never told her. For the two decades before he married her, he had lived in the remnants of his guilt over Marilyn. Marisa had relieved him of that burden for a while, two years was it? Even three.

Then Lola Gunn had found him, his own daughter.

How could she be his daughter if he did not know she was his daughter? He drew back from the thought in disbelief. And Hermia Watson was Lola Gunn. After Lola Gunn, it had been that girl who looked like her. He couldn't remember her name. Marisa had discovered one of the affairs that followed. It was just after another of her miscarriages, and she already felt ill-fated. He had stood like a man being burned at the stake, immersed in the anguish he had caused. But then, not two months later, he had done the same thing again. He had just been more careful to keep it secret.

Again and again he had done it, like a shape-shifter, a beast wading back into the swamp that was his native habitat and then afterwards, resuming his human form, bringing the faint effluvium of monstrosity into the house. He knew he hurt her, but he said to himself that his desire for other women took nothing away from his love for her. Like the great chieftains and kings, he should have many wives. He was strong enough to follow the natural polygamous bent of the natural alpha male. He knew his superiority.

But why did he need her now? His whole soul longed for Marisa. The clarity of her moral nature, the simple bravery of her daily decision to follow the bidding of conscience.

Fletcher was still talking.

"I'm sorry?" Forrest said irritably. His head throbbed. "What?"

"I said we got to see greatness. I think all of us knew at the time we would never see anything like it again."

Forrest's eyebrows pinched together. His headache was burning through the painkillers, but he could speak more clearly. "I'm sorry, Bill, I'm sort of in and out. What are you talking about?"

"My God, I'm saying all this and you're not even listening."

Fletcher stood up.

"I'm sorry, Bill. Seriously, it's this stuff they give me."

Fletcher checked the chart at the foot of the bed. "Percocet," he said, and sat back down. "I'm surprised they don't have you on morphine." He sat for a minute without speaking. "I'm trying to tell you about what you meant to the town. What that game meant."

Forrest closed his eyes. Back on high school football. "Which game would that be?" he asked impassively.

"The championship against Roswell."

Despite him, old images flickered up. The smell of his shoulder pads when he lifted them over his head to settle them on his shoulders; the way the ridged pads of thick cardboard fitted into the thigh pockets of the white football pants with the elastic just below the knee; the hollow sound once you put on the helmet. He felt again the premonition before a game, like going into battle. Even now his stomach tightened.

The team had gathered behind him just inside the gym door, their cleats tapping and scraping on the concrete floor as they shuffled forward in anticipation, helmeted, armored, watching him. He suddenly raised his fist and shouted.

Blue Devils!

Blue Devils! they all shouted back.

A second time:

Blue Devils!

Blue Devils! they echoed.

And as he shouted it the third time, he raised both arms and led them sprinting down the slope onto the field, always the first of them all, always, and burst through the huge banner of the Blue Devil that the adoring cheerleaders held taut between the goalposts.

And the crowd rose and roared, BLUE! Dev-ils, BLUE! Dev-ils.

Sweet Jesus, it came back to him.

"We were up by a touchdown in the fourth quarter," Fletcher said, his eyes on Forrest's, "but Roswell had that long drive, remember? They kept running everything at Jackie Rhodes on the other side. Jackie was solid, and they couldn't break a big play, but every series they'd get two or three yards on first down, two or three on second, and then it would be third down, and they'd run a play-action pass to the tight end or one of the backs. Jackie would make the tackle, but every time they'd get just enough for a first down. Once they thought they'd switch and run it right at you. I've watched it on the film. The guard and tackle double-teamed you, but you shucked them off and swung out your arm just as the tailback started into the hole, and it looked like he'd run into a tree limb. His feet flew out from under him. *Wham!* Flat on his back."

Forrest remembered the boy's face. It had knocked the breath out of him, and he was lying there clutching the ball, his mouth a helpless O, when Forrest offered a hand to help him up.

"So they were eating up the clock, and everybody was exhausted. You had to be just as tired. You'd played both ways, every down of the game, but you kept pumping us back up in the defensive huddle, telling us this was it, this was our chance."

He was drifting off again. He saw a boy holding the ball up after he crossed the goal line, the line marked out taut and true on the field.

"They scored," he heard himself say. Where had that come from? Memories released from the networks of his neurons. He pictured the thickets and tangles of his brain, and ahead of him, with a serpent's tail, Tony Wright cutting line.

"Ed Hampton got clipped!" Fletcher said, as outraged as if it had just happened. Forrest woke back up. "You can see it plain as day on the film, but that stupid ref from Barnesville missed it. Coach Fitz was going nuts on the sideline yelling about it. But that wasn't the worst of it. You remember the onside kick?"

The ball hopping up, skittering at a slant between the two teams. One of the Blue Devil reserve guards, a big, red-faced farm boy named Hiram Hardage, saw it bouncing toward him and tried to grab it but clumsily batted it instead right into the hands of a Roswell player.

"Wasn't there a penalty?" Fletcher asked.

"I don't remember," Forrest said. "That might have been the Jackson game."

"I know Roswell had the ball at their own forty with about two minutes to go in the game. And then they started again. On first down they ran it toward Jackie. So on second down, you got us in the huddle and told Jackie to switch sides with you at the last second, right after Roswell came up to the line. So they come up and get set, and suddenly you change places, and there you are, right where they meant to run the ball at Jackie. The quarterback got so flustered he messed up the snap count and the right guard jumped offside, which put them back five yards. The next play they come up and get set and you do it again. It's too late to change the play, and you break through the line and knock that big fullback flat on his back. Six-yard loss. So now it's third and twenty-one. Do you remember all this?"

"I do now," Forrest said. The pulse in his head was starting to spike again. Just then his cell phone rang. He looked at the number and held up a hand to Fletcher, who stood up and went to the window and stared out while Forrest talked.

"Hermia," he said with a dark mix of emotions.

"Can I bring Mrs. Gibson to see you? It's very important."

Her voice was shaking. When he did not respond, she pleaded with him.

"You have to know," she told him.

"Know what?" he asked wearily.

"About your father," she said. "About Mrs. Hayes."

"When did you talk to Mary Louise?"

"Just now."

"How do you know she'll talk to me?"

"Well, if she doesn't, I'll tell you myself."

"Lola," he said. "I don't know what you want. I don't understand you. What are you talking about?"

"Please don't call me that. LaCourvette told me some of it. She knows why your father was disinherited."

"That was a long time ago, Hermia. That's got nothing to do with me anymore. Not now."

"Yes it does." He heard her breathing, almost whimpering. "Oh God. Yes it does."

"Then bring her down here," Forrest said sharply into the phone, "if you can do it without getting her killed."

He heard an intake of breath, a small moan. The line went dead.

He snapped the phone shut and pressed two fingers against the side of his head above his ear. Again it shocked him to feel the bare skin where his hair had been. He reached for the hospital call button left-handed and pressed it. Bill Fletcher had turned when the call ended. Now his brow furrowed.

"You just had the Percocet two hours ago. Is it that bad?"

Forrest nodded. The pain deepened with each pulse.

"If you want me to shut up..." Fletcher said.

"Why are you talking about football? I don't understand why you're telling me all this."

Fletcher turned his head and looked out the window. A decade from old age, Forrest judged. The same age he was. Fletcher turned back and met his eyes, lifting a hand.

"I think you forgot who you were," he said.

"Forgot who I was?" he repeated.

"You turned on yourself after the thing with Marilyn."

"Come on, Bill."

"Okay, Cump, but just listen. Yesterday, you were lying there with an epidural hematoma, for God's sake, and Dutrelle Jones was pounding on your head, and you saved her life. What you were like just started coming back to me. I remembered how you played in that game."

"The interception?"

"Not just that. It was how you were just as exhausted as the rest of us, but the rest of us were terrified that somehow we'd be the one to screw up and lose the state championship game. Not you. You loved it. You saw the whole thing. That third down play—you put a hand on Jackie's jersey and told him to fake the switch this time, just to move like he was going to switch, but to stay put. So their wide receiver brings in the play from the sideline, and Roswell comes up to the line. You and Jackie pretend to switch and the quarterback sees it right as he's taking the snap.

"He does the play fake, and when he drops back, he looks to the right, then he turns and throws it left into the flat where his coach told him to throw it, but you'd read the coach's mind. You cut in front of the tight end and caught the ball at full stride and ran it straight into the end zone before they could even react. Twenty-seven seconds left on the clock. Then we got the extra point and Jackie Rhodes made them fumble the kickoff."

Forrest nodded. Yes, he remembered that. He looked at Fletcher and waited. Fletcher raised his hands in exasperation.

"Why didn't you join the Marines or something?" Fletcher asked. "Why didn't you go to Vietnam? That's what you should have done after the thing with Marilyn. You needed to do something that would either get you killed or send you back with something else on your mind. You needed a war, I think. Like Lee or Grant or Sherman, somebody like that who was adrift before. Like that's where you would have been who you were supposed to be."

"Come on, Bill, Vietnam? Hell, I went to SDS meetings until I got mad at some self-important asshole from Atlanta and threw him across the room. Then they wanted me to run it. You remember how it was then. You didn't exactly sign up to go to Vietnam."

Fletcher shook his head. "You're not hearing me."

"*Vietnam?* Jesus."

"I'm not talking about Vietnam," Fletcher said patiently. He stood and patted Forrest on the knee. "I guess I don't know how to say it, Cump." He started to say something else but checked himself and shook his head. "Hold off for a while on the Percocet. You don't want too much in your system."

21

At the funeral home, the receptionist was as smoothly subdued and sympathetic as Missy Watts had been in Daddy Watson's funeral parlor when Hermia was a child. Mr. Hubbard came out to greet her, encompassing her hand with both of his big soft ones, gently guiding her toward another room. She felt the familiar silence overwhelm her, the floral odor tinged with a faint chemical smell.

"Would you like to view the body before we talk?" Mr. Hubbard's hand spread on the paneled brown door like a starfish. View. The word sickened her somehow, but she nodded. He pushed the door open. "I know that you have not had time to choose an appropriate coffin, Miss Watson. I have taken the liberty to use the Hosanna with the Lord's Prayer head panel. I thought it might be an elegant touch, especially with the pink interior."

And what lay there in the small chapel? What was that?

Someone's mother, some church lady, her features composed in an unrecognizable expression, the wound in her neck covered by a high collar. Where had these clothes come from? No one had asked her. Had LaCourvette gone into the house to get this suit? The face was a simulacrum of someone else—someone who could never ever have been Marilyn Harkins. Whoever lay there had not spent her youth rutting in the back seats of cars. Whoever it was had not married older men for money.

A gust of nausea went through her. She herself had come out of this body, this false thing that now lay there disguised to the world and steeped with chemicals. Hermia had been conceived when those locked hips had been all sway and heat. She had been squeezed out slick and bloody while Daddy Watson, dignified and deceived—if he was deceived—paced in the waiting room. A white curse from her mother's splitting body.

A little troublesome curse.

She put her hand out blindly to Mr. Hubbard, who turned, his face benignly composed. He stepped back from her in alarm and directed her to the restroom in the foyer behind the rows of seats.

Later, she hardly remembered what he had showed her or what she had signed. She knew little about her mother's financial affairs and nothing at all about Dutrelle Jones's. No, she did not know, oh my, how severely the recession had affected him. Her mother had mentioned it, of course. No, she had not heard of any foreclosures.

Was she aware of a will? She was not. As for the costs of the funeral—and here he had proffered a piece of paper with a large sum—she supposed it could come out of her mother's money. No, she did not have power of attorney. No, she did not have a lawyer, but she would get legal help with all these complications, yes, of course.

She sat outside in her car for five minutes before she started it. On her cell phone, she found the number that the woman from Matthews Funeral Home had called from. Why did Dillon Matthews have to talk to her today of all days? She was going to cancel. She needed to go out to the hospital and check on Mrs. Hayes, who had fallen overnight. Who knew what vitriol she might unleash on the poor nurses? At least she was used to Hermia—or Hermia was used to her.

As soon as she thought of Mrs. Hayes, she remembered the envelope. She knew exactly where it was in the big pigeonhole desk where she had found the stationery. In fact, she had first seen it, a thick business envelope, already yellowed, the very day when she wrote the first letter to her father. Mrs. Hayes had sent her to find it. Yes, that's it. Open that when I die. You'll need that. Now put it back where you found it. Maybe she would just swing by and tell Dillon Matthews she knew where to find the arrangements. His funeral home was on the way to the hospital, so she might as well get it over with.

She had met him once or twice, a plump man, probably a little younger than Forrest, but already sagging in the jowls. He wore his graying hair too long. He had that weary, knowing air of Southern men—some senator whose name she couldn't remember. The kind of man who had come to terms with his own weaknesses without illusions and who remembered everything and knew his way through great mazes of stories and details.

His arms opened wide when he came into the foyer to meet her.

"Miss Watson. I know how distressed you must be," he said, not without sympathy. He took her arm at the elbow, gently, as though he already understood her and meant to support her. He opened a hand toward the door of a room just off the foyer, where she saw papers spread out on the table. "We'll keep it short."

But she did not go in.

"Not today," she said, detaching herself and stepping backward. "I know where Mrs. Hayes' instructions are when the time comes. She left an envelope to be opened when she died."

The tip of his tongue came out and the skin around his eyes contracted.

"Tell you what," he said. He held out a hand toward the table, patting the air as though to quiet all the impatient papers. "I'll just keep everything right where it is until you get back." He glanced at his watch. "I don't mind waiting this afternoon if..."

"Mr. Matthews, she's not dead yet, is she? But my mother is." It embarrassed her to start tearing up in front of this man. "Don't you think you could have put this off a week or two?"

"I'm told she might not make it through the night," he said softly. "And I just know you're going to be a lot busier the next few days than you are today."

"Well, how thoughtful," she said, not trying to keep the sarcasm out of her voice. "But I'm *very* busy *today*. I need to check on Mrs. Hayes, and then I have to get down to Macon to see my father in the hospital."

"Is that right," he nodded. But then a puzzled expression, not entirely sincere, came over his face. "And here I thought your father was Corvell Watson. Old Mrs. Gibson, that's who told me. We were talking about you back when you started helping Mrs. Hayes, and I asked her who this pretty woman was helping Mrs. Hayes, and she told me you were Mr. Corvell Watson's daughter and I said is that right. I said my daddy thought the world of Mr. Corvell. Said he wished there were more like him. I met him once. A dignified old gentleman. He's been dead a long time, though, so that's why, you see..." He cocked his head, his eyes gleaming.

"It's my stepfather," she said, suddenly afraid.

What did he want? She looked around the foyer to see if anyone else was listening. A middle-aged woman, probably the Harriet who had called her, crossed from one room to another with a glance and a small smile.

"My mother remarried after Daddy Watson died," Hermia said.

"I see," he said. "I must have my wires crossed somewhere, because I heard she married Dutrelle Jones after her husband in Atlanta died. Some big-shot lawyer."

"That was Elton Dernier," she said. "This was another one. Well, if you'll excuse me." She started toward the door, her heart pounding absurdly.

"I be dog," said Mr. Matthews, pursuing her out the door. "But it wouldn't be that Moreland professor, because I heard he died, too. So there's another one? That's about a royal straight of daddies. And this one's in the hospital?"

"Yes sir," she said faintly as she got into her car.

"He must be down there with Cump Forrest," he said, holding the door open, his tongue wetting his lower lip.

"I'll bring those papers when the time comes," Hermia said. She pulled the door closed as he stepped back. He raised his hand to her

293

with a speculative look, not smiling.

She drove away without looking back at him. Her heart was pounding so hard she could hardly hold the wheel, and she had already driven to the courthouse square before she remembered Mrs. Hayes and what she was supposed to be doing. She went around the block past the Confederate soldier and the Left Bank and turned back toward the hospital. First she should call LaCourvette, though. There was an open parking space on the square and she pulled into it. When LaCourvette answered, Hermia did not even say hello.

"Tell her if she doesn't go with me to tell my father, I'm going to tell him myself. One way or another, he's going to know who he is. And who I am."

Mrs. Hayes lay unconscious in the hospital bed, wasted and frail. The lower half of her face was almost invisible beneath the oxygen mask. An IV ran to a withered arm. Hermia put her purse on a chair and leaned back against the windowsill, watching the old woman breathe: her lungs sounded like spider webs clotted with the remnants of little lives sucked dry. An evil old thing, dried up at last despite all her greed and sin.

The old woman's eyes opened. She looked about wildly, found Hermia, focused. A weak hand pulled away the oxygen mask and gestured for Hermia to come near. Her lips puckered as she tried to say something. Hermia leaned close.

"Priest," she said. Shocked, Hermia stood up, and Mrs. Hayes' eyes followed her like a pleading child's.

"You want a priest?" Hermia said incredulously. "A Catholic priest?"

The old woman gave a weak nod.

"In Gallatin? I think there's a minister on call, one of the Baptist or Metho—"

"A priest!" Mrs. Hayes whispered urgently.

She went down to the nurse's station and asked one of the women on duty if they had any way to get in touch with a Catholic priest, because Mrs. Hayes wanted to see one. The nurse stared at her for a moment and then consulted a list and phoned the number for her and arranged for the priest to come.

"It's a Fr. Shelton," she said after she hung up. "Retired. I didn't know they let them retire, but. He said he could be here in half an hour. He rides a Harley Davidson—with that little collar thing on! I didn't know Mrs. Hayes was a Catholic. I knew she didn't belong to one of the churches, but."

"I had no idea until just now," said Hermia.

"You're not Catholic yourself?"

She shrugged and waggled her head. If she had been anything, she would have been Catholic. She used to be Catholic, and before Daddy Loum started visiting her, she'd thought she might be like St. Thérèse and become a nun. She had loved Morning Prayer when she got to school early in those days in Atlanta, the antiphonal voices of the sisters chanting the psalms. Praise him, sun and moon; praise him, all shining stars. But the place where her faith might have been was scoured out after Daddy Loum's death, after that clinic. No penance could bring it back. For most of her life, she had felt only absence, and now Mary Louise Gibson had brought a meaning to the absence.

She was a curse.

How could a walking curse enter the kingdom of heaven?

"Matthew 23:9."

"What?" she said, startled. The nurse, lifting a clipboard, glanced up at Hermia and repeated it.

"Matthew 23:9. 'Call no man your father.' Those are the words of Jesus Christ. But the Catholics don't read the Bible." She leaned toward Hermia and raised her eyebrows significantly. "I wouldn't want one of those 'fathers' around my little boy, I tell you what," she whispered.

DORIS GIBBS, R.N. said her nametag.

"Well, thank you for calling him, Doris," Hermia said and turned away. The woman's presumption offended her.

She found Mrs. Hayes still awake.

"The priest is coming," Hermia told her.

Again the hand came up to wave her close.

"Aunt Ella," she whispered.

"Aunt Ella's dead, Mrs. Hayes."

She closed her eyes with a slight shake of her head.

"Aunt Ella told me about Mr. T.J."

"Did she tell you Robert Forrest was sleeping with Pearl Parker?"

The old woman's eyes opened, their ferocity rekindled. "Who told you that?"

"Mary Louise Gibson."

Mrs. Hayes shook her head and her face contorted with laughter. "Mary Louise never knew the half of it. Sybil suspected Aunt Ella and Mr. T.J., so he had to name that high school after her." She began to wheeze dangerously. Hermia pressed the call button and positioned the oxygen mask over her mouth again. Doris Gibbs came into the room and put a sedative into the IV. In a few minutes, the fierce eyes closed, and Hermia debated with herself about staying until the priest arrived. But she was due back at Mary Louise Gibson's house.

LaCourvette was there. She must have left and come back, because she had her own car now, not the police cruiser, and she was wearing a dress outside church for the first time Hermia could remember. She stopped Hermia at the front door, stepping outside it and closing it behind her.

"She wants me to take her," she said.

"I'll ride with you, then, if that's okay."

Hermia heard the old woman calling LaCourvette from inside the house. Her friend held out a hand to Hermia and put her head back inside the door. "What did you say, Miss Mary Louise?" She listened and excused herself to disappear into the house. She came back a moment later. "Maybe we'll see you down there later."

"She doesn't even want to ride with me?"

LaCourvette met her eyes but said nothing. Hermia turned away, mortified. She walked quickly to her car and drove off. She almost hit a boy who was dodging into the road after a puppy. She slammed on the brakes but as soon as the boy leapt out of the way, she sped past him, and someone howled something at her from one of the porches. Soon they would all hate her. They would never leave her alone now, not when they started putting it all together, like that Matthews man.

Approaching the courthouse square again, she came up behind a car whose license plate frame advertised Lee Ford, and the very idea of him made her heart leap with gratitude. Sweet Chick Lee.

22

When he heard his name called, Chick turned in his chair from his guilty daydream of Hermia Watson. Steve Wilkinson stood in the door.

"Steve," he said, pushing himself upright in his chair. "Come in."

"Hey, sorry to disturb you. Listen, I've got this idea for the TV ad."

"The TV ad." Chick stared at him.

"Yes sir. For the sale."

"Oh!" Chick said. "Right, right. I was thinking about something else. So what's your idea?"

"Okay, maybe it's cheesy, but here it is. You get a bunch of pictures of somebody about your age—I mean, maybe you want to do it yourself?—and you start with what you look like now. Then you start going backward and you're getting younger and your hair and clothes are changing, you see what I mean? And you end with what you looked like in 1969. And I'm thinking like you could have this deep voice saying back to the future or whatever and you're getting younger and younger until there you are in 1969? And here's the thing. It's not just you, but maybe a bunch of people that everybody would recognize, a different one for each ad. Maybe that old weatherman down in Macon. The oldest teachers at the high school."

The oldest teachers at the high school. *The oldest teachers at the high school were his age?*

"Absolutely," he said. "Get on it."

"Me?"

"Sure. Get people digging up pictures. Call Patricia and tell her I said to find my pictures. We need to get it done by—what's today?"

"Tuesday."

"Have the pictures by Friday so we can get them to the ad people. I'd say five different ads."

"Well, Mr. Lee, I don't—I mean, I just thought I'd run it by you, it's not like I—"

"Steve!" Chick said. He stood up and took Wilkinson by the elbow. "Don't sell yourself short. It's a terrific idea." He steered him back out the door to Belle Murray's desk. "Belle," he said, "get Steve to explain what he needs." Belle looked up at him skeptically over the rims of her glasses. "Terrific idea." He patted the salesman on the back and retreated into his office, closing the door behind him.

In a few minutes he would need to leave for Atlanta to pick up Marisa Forrest at the airport. He had to take the Forrest girls, of course. But what would they talk about all the way up there? How well he had gotten to know Hermia Watson, their half-sister, the woman who had gotten them into this mess?

Why couldn't Tricia take them up there? She had talked to Marisa many times on the phone, she already had the girls at her house, and she could just put them in her Lexus and be up there in forty-five minutes.

Tricia's home number went directly into the voice mail. When he tried her cell phone, Bridget answered, and he asked for her mother.

"She's in Pilates class."

His heart sank. "Okay, listen. I'm going to be picking up Mrs. Forrest from the airport," he said. "Can you ask the girls if they want to go?"

"Yes sir," she said, "but we're in Macon at the mall, Mr. Lee. That's why I've got my mom's phone because she said somebody might call."

"Didn't she know that their mother gets in this afternoon?"

"No sir, she said it was tomorrow."

"Seriously? The girls didn't know it was today?"

"Well, they said something, but Mom was sure it was tomorrow. Mom's been getting things mixed up lately."

"Well, it's definitely today. I'll go get her, and I should be back by 6:30 or so if the traffic's not too bad. I'll swing by your house."

"Yes sir."

Holding the phone after the call, he thought *Alyssa!* Alyssa could talk to Marisa Forrest and tell her how the girls were. He called Alyssa's cell number, and when she answered, he told her he wanted her to ride to the airport with him.

"Dad, I can't," she said. "I've got ballet. We're already on the way."

So he was going to have to drive to Atlanta by himself and pick up Marisa Forrest?

He was going to have to be the one who had to start explaining this—this—.

"Dad?"

"What?"

"I said I've got ballet."

"Okay, honey. I forgot."

He hung up the phone and stared through the window out into the showroom. After a moment, there was a knock on his door. Belle Murray opened it just a crack and stood there tense with disapproval.

"It's—"

"Knock knock," Hermia Watson said from behind her. Belle took a step aside as Hermia brushed past her and stood there in a designer suit and high heels. "Do you have a minute to help me with some personal matters?"

Belle Murray stared at him with her fingertips at her collarbone. Chick felt a deep blush reddening his ears.

"Sure, sure," he said. "Come in, Miss Watson."

23

Forrest imagined Marisa coming out into the baggage claim and being met by a stranger.

"So one more time. *Why* aren't you taking the girls?" Forrest asked groggily, holding the cell phone to his head.

"They're at the mall with Tricia," Chick said. "Tricia thought she got in tomorrow."

"So it's just you?"

"It looks like it."

"What are you going to tell her?"

"Hell, I don't know. I'll think of something."

After he closed the phone, Forrest kept thinking. Chick would have to tell her why Forrest wasn't there. *Well, he's in the hospital with a skull fracture, but don't worry, the girls are fine.* She would want to know what happened. She would ask where the girls were. Chick would face her interrogation for the whole drive back, which meant he was going to have to tell her something about Marilyn.

At least he wouldn't have to mention Hermia.

An image of Lola Gunn came back. She was standing at the window of the hotel room in Providence that first morning, turning, coming toward him, leaning forward, one knee already on the bed.

The pain in his head mounted again, and he pressed the button. A nurse came in, and he asked for more Percocet.

Later, Maya was standing in the doorway.

"You should have told me you were dead," he said.

Her eyes held his bleakly.

"So what's the story, Maya? What are you doing here now?"

But Maya was gone and the great gray ladies surrounded the other bed in his room. He heard a woman's agonized cries. The cry of a newborn. Their huge hooded shoulders shook with laughter. Call her Marilyn. *The one who spoke turned to look at him and pulled back her hood.*

It was his mother.

You just left me. Why did you leave me?

He woke up again with a start. It was almost five o'clock. Chick Lee would tell Marisa about Marilyn.

He needed to talk to Marisa. Yes, they would lie in bed with the whole day open before them, the way they had in the early days, when she was so blessedly young, just in her twenties, and she had not had Cate, and he had not betrayed her with Lola Gunn.

Just like then, they would have coffee and croissants with butter and thick raspberry jam. Flakes would fall on her bare skin, and they would talk, and he would tell her that Marilyn had come to the hospital. And why? *Just to lie next to him*, wasn't that something? Because never once in that mad month of love forty years ago had they ever been in bed together. Did she realize that? And Marisa would say, Marisa would say...

Someone was shaking his shoulder lightly.

"How you doing?" she asked him.

He stared up at her.

"Not so good. Remind me who you are," he said.

"LaCourvette Todd, Mr. Forrest. You remember me from when you were in jail."

He tried to smile. "Those were the days."

"I brought my grandmother to see you. Miss Mary Louise," she called, turning toward the doorway where Maya had been. "He's awake."

He saw her hat first, a broad white one with black edging around the brim, a crown like the Sydney Opera House, and a big black bow on one side. She was shaking her head and making the black bow tremble as she came limping in, leaning on a cane, stately as ever, dressed in a black Sunday suit.

"What they done to my baby?" she asked.

His heart flooded at the sight of her. His eyes filled with tears. After a moment he felt her hand on the side of his face. "It's all right, baby."

"Miss Mary Louise," he said at last. "I meant to come see you."

"It's all right."

"Thank you for coming," he said. He found her hand, frail now and knotty with arthritis, and brought it to his lips.

"Baby, you see if you thank me when I leave," she said kindly, touching his shaved head, his bandages. LaCourvette pushed aside the IV stand and brought over a straight-backed hospital chair for her grandmother, and the old woman sat angled toward him, her hands on the cane in front of her. LaCourvette sat at the foot of his bed.

"I got to tell you the things ain't nobody told you," said the old woman. "I want you to hear it from me, sugar. I don't want that Watson girl rattling on about what she don't understand."

"What things?"

"I saw her when she was just thirteen or fourteen," began Mary Louise Gibson, shaking her head.

"Hermia?"

Sternly the old woman lifted one hand from the cane to stop his questions.

"Saturday morning, hot summer, and here she come down the sidewalk like she was sound asleep and dreaming, like those models you see showing off clothes, not looking to the right, not looking to the left. I should have known her. It ate at me, and when I saw her the next time, I said to Mattie Jenkins—I remember right where we were in front of the bank when it was still a bank—I said, 'Who is that girl?' and Mattie told me, 'She a Harkins. She come down here from Griffin when her mama died. You remember Thelma Harkins.' So I said, 'Thelma? I thought she couldn't have no children,' and Mattie said, 'She got this one from her cousin in North Carolina. Her mama got killed and Thelma took her and brought her up. But Thelma died of the cancer two or three years ago, and Thelma's sister that married Ray Watts brought this girl to come live with her.' And I said, 'Betty Watts too sick to take care of this girl.' And then a second later I say, 'You mean this girl in that house with Ray Watts?' Mattie got on me, she said, 'He got Jesus since all that. He a deacon in the church now!' And I said, 'The devil ain't closed up shop.' I couldn't stop thinking about her, she just put me so much in mind of Pearl Parker."

Beneath the Percocet, Forrest felt the pulse in his head above his ear and he lifted his hand.

"Who's Pearl Parker," he said.

"Help me Jesus," she said.

"Miss Mary Louise," said LaCourvette, standing up, but the old woman waved her off.

"Who's Pearl Parker?" Forrest asked again, and again Mary Louise held up a hand.

"Mr. T.J. the one moved Miss Emily Barron in. Her mama was Mr. T.J.'s little sister that he loved. She died when Miss Emily Barron was born, and he got the child away from her no-count daddy. Aunt Ella was the one raised her, and Miss Emily grew up and went off to college and got married to Mr. Harold Hayes from Virginia. No, not Harold... Help me."

She held her hand out toward her granddaughter.

"Rufus," said LaCourvette.

"Mr. Rufus Hayes. When he got shot down in the war, Mr. T.J. got her to take her old rooms at Stonewall Hill. Your daddy got home from the war, and there was Emily Barron. Lord, she saw him walk in the door with his medals and she forgot all about any dead Captain Hayes. She was older than your daddy by a few years, but she was a fine-looking woman in those days. She and old Mr. T.J. thought it was just right for her to marry Mr. Robert. Your daddy wasn't studying Miss Emily Barron, though."

"His first cousin?" Forrest said.

The old woman waved it off.

"Way they figured it—I'm talking about Mr. T.J. and Miss Emily Barron—Mr. Robert and Miss Emily Barron would inherit the house and the family business together. But as soon as he got home from the war, he come straight to me when I was by myself in the kitchen. 'Mary Louise, you're looking prosperous,' he says. I remember that word. Prosperous. He says, 'I hear you got married while I was gone.' 'Yes sir,' I say, 'I got Lester Gibson to stand still long enough in front of the preacher.' He smiled at me, I can just see him leaning back against the doorjamb, got his arms crossed, smiling at me, but something different about his eyes, something he been through. I tell him he look pretty good for somebody been on all those islands I read about in the newspaper. He nod his head and then he look at me and he ain't smiling.

"He says, 'Where is she?' I turn around and get a broom or pick up a dish or something, I don't remember, but I can't stand the way he looks when he says it. 'Mary Louise,' he says, and I just stand there with my back to him. After a minute I say, 'She gone, Mr. Robert.' 'Where is she?' he says, and I say, 'You know Aunt Ella died. Mr. Clement'—this was Aunt Ella's husband, Mr. Clement Parker—'he send her up to stay with his sister in North Carolina.' Then he says, 'Where in North Carolina?' and I don't say nothing and he says, 'You better tell me, Mary Louise, because I'll find her,' so I turn around and I say, 'You don't want to be messing with Pearl, Mr. Robert. She married now.' 'Married?' 'Yes sir, she got twin babies. Born just last month.' I lied right to his face. 'She's married?' 'Yes sir,' I said. 'Happy as she can be with them babies.'

"So I knew he wasn't studying Miss Emily Barron. She flirt with him at the table, she take his arm when they went out the room, act like they got something stirring, and I don't know what all happened. But after two or three months, Mr. T.J. send your daddy up north to school with the idea that he gone come back and take over Forrest Mills."

"The Wharton School of Business," said Forrest, and her peremptory hand came up.

301

"Well, while he up there, he meet Miss Inger. Tall and blonde and from—oh Lord, where was it?"

"Minnesota."

"When Mr. Robert come back from up north with Miss Inger, I saw the whole thing. Miss Sybil—you remember Miss Sybil, don't you?'

"Vaguely."

"Mr. Robert come in the front door and there was Miss Inger with him, tall and blonde, big pretty smile, pregnant out to here with you, and he says, 'Mr. T.J., Miss Sybil, I want you to meet my wife,' and Miss Sybil said, 'Oh my lord' and run out the room and left them standing there. Mr. T.J. had his manners, and he controlled himself, but he was fit to be tied. Then Miss Emily Barron heard Mr. Robert was back and come running into the room calling 'Robert! Robert!'

"When she see him standing there with another woman about to have a baby, she stop like she run into the wall. Mr. Robert said, 'Cousin Emily Barron, let me introduce you to Inger,' and she says, 'Who is *she?*' like your mama couldn't speak English, like he done brought in a little Apache or Eskimo, and he says, 'She's my wife,' and he might as well have shot Emily Barron. '*Your wife?*' she says.

"Miss Inger kind of stepped back toward the door, because she saw she didn't know what she'd gotten into, but he put his arm around her and said, 'Inger, this is my cousin Emily Barron Hayes. Emily Barron, this is Inger Forrest, née Inger Glatt.' Miss Inger tried to smile, and she held out her hand toward Miss Emily Barron, but Miss Emily Barron didn't pay her a bit of attention. She just said, 'She can't be your wife. You're going to marry me. Isn't he, Mr. T.J.?' And Mr. T.J. said, 'Son,' and Mr. Robert said, 'Maybe you had an agreement. I didn't.' And Mr. T.J.'s face got so I thought he might have a stroke. So I come out of the dining room right then and say, 'Let me show you where you stay at, Miss Inger. This a big old house and you liable to get lost, it got so many twists and turns.' I just play the fool. 'Why you all must have met up north. I know he'd notice a pretty thing like you right off.' Just talking like that, like a fool didn't have no sense, and I got her bag to carry and told Mr. Robert to get busy and tell her about everything. I never forget the face Miss Emily Barron turned on me. Never till the day I die."

Mary Louise fell silent. Forrest had heard from his mother that the Forrest family was not happy with the marriage. He started to ask a question, but already Mary Louise's hand was rising to forestall him.

"So that's how he come back to Gallatin. Already been married for a year and ain't told nobody. He move in the house, and here was your poor mama who thought she was going to love the South, she'd read all about it, all these books. Pregnant with you, stuck in a strange house, paid no mind by Mr. T.J. and Miss Sybil and treated like trash by Miss Emily Barron. She just stayed in her room all day, and Mr. Robert he couldn't do nothing for her while he was learning how to run the mills. But she had to come out to eat now and then, and she would sit there trying to get something down in the midst of all that meanness.

"Well, old Mr. T.J. started warming to her, pretty and quiet as she was. At least she wasn't talking all the time about nothing like Miss Sybil was. One time at supper, he held up a hand and interrupted Miss Sybil who was complaining about somebody and he said, 'Now Inger, we haven't heard much from you. It must be mighty different not being in a big city like you're used to.' And she looked up, surprised he was speaking to her, and she said, 'Oh no, Mr. Forrest. I grew up on a farm in Minnesota.' Well the way she say *Minnesota* just tickle Mr. T.J., like there was a little song in it. So he got her to say it again and he ask her some more questions.

"Things ease up after that, except for Miss Emily. After a week or so, Mr. T.J. would go out on the porch to smoke after supper with Mr. Robert, and he would get your mama to go with him and tell him how her daddy built his own barn and how freezing cold it got and how they kept the stock alive. How big a moose was. She told good stories. Everything was going along. But then one summer night during dinner, I'm in the kitchen when I feel somebody grab me around the waist from behind, and I turn around, and there stands Pearl Parker.

"My heart almost stop. She say, 'Hey girl, ain't you looking fine? Lester Gibson agreeing with you. Where everybody at?' and I say, 'They eating dinner,' and she kind of smooth herself down and start through the door from the butler's pantry, and I say, 'Unh-unh, Pearl, honey. Naw, now, don't go in there, baby.' Good-looking don't say what Pearl was. She says, 'How come?' 'Cause Mr. Robert, he in there with his wife.' 'Yeah, baby, I heard he got married,' she says, 'and I got to see who.' And before I can stop her, she go sashaying right out in the dining room, and I go right behind her.

"'Well, look who's here!' says Mr. T.J. and right then I see your daddy's face change. Pearl, she just smiling, acting like everything's just fine. She says, 'How you doing, Mr. Robert? Ain't you looking good?' And Mr. Robert, he put down his fork and start to stand up. He staring at her. Pearl says, 'You keep your seat now. I just come out to say I'm back in town, and Mary Louise say to check did anybody need more beans. How you been? Is this here Mrs. Forrest? Ain't you pretty, sugar, with all that blonde hair!' And Mr. Robert says, 'How's your family? I heard you got married.' And Pearl draws back her head and says, 'Lord, I ain't married, Mr. Robert. Where you get a notion like that?' And Mr. Robert looks at me and I know how the Japanese on them islands felt. I never could get a lie to stick."

Mary Louise sat rocking on herself in the chair, her hands folded on the handle of the cane. She shook her head and sighed. The meter on the IV rack clicked steadily. Already, Forrest could feel what was coming. It was deep in his spine, gliding up toward consciousness, and he fought to keep it down. The blood was pounding in his head.

"I don't want to hear any more," he said.

303

"What's her name?" Mary Louise snapped at LaCourvette. "What's that girl's name?"

"Hermia, Miss Mary Louise. Mr. Forrest says he's tired, now. You better—"

"Better what?"

"Leave it be, Miss Mary Louise," LaCourvette said. "It's just more hurt."

"What you know about hurt? When I stand in front of God Almighty and He says, 'How come you told all them secrets?' what am I gone say? I'll say, 'Lord, I didn't want to, but I told the truth.' Once you start, you got to get to the hurt, because that's what changes you. All the way to the hurt, or it ain't no good."

"Grandmama—"

"Just hush your mouth."

She held up her hand and collected herself.

"Well, Mr. T.J. hired Pearl to take care of Miss Emily Barron. Thought maybe it would cheer her up, remind her of Aunt Ella that Emily Barron loved since she was a little girl. Course your poor mama being a Yankee didn't understand what was going on. Mr. Robert would disappear from the porch after dinner with some excuse and leave her there with Mr. T.J. all by herself. Or Miss Inger would wake up in the night and reach for him and he'd be gone.

"You could see it in her face at breakfast, when she'd look at him and he'd be just as polite, but she knew something had changed, his mind wasn't on her. Miss Emily Barron noticed it, too, jealous as she was. She was the one that caught him. She must have been sitting in her window before dark when Mr. T.J. and Miss Inger were talking out on the front porch, and she saw Mr. Robert come out the back door and walk across the backyard to the garden gate. And then a half hour later he comes back. The next night she heard him come out his room and go down the stairs, and she wait by her window and there he go again, and this time she go downstairs and out after him in the dark.

"She follow him out through the gate, creeping along, all the way to the barn. He's hurrying, he never notice her. A little light flares up in the barn, like a match, and then he's inside, and she's scared to follow him.

"She watch the next night, and there he goes, and she follow him outside to the gate. I heard it all from Pearl the next morning when she come to me scared to death. I was sick of Pearl, but Miss Emily Barron made me sick a different way. Pearl told me this time they didn't make it to the barn, Mr. Robert so crazy about her. They lying on the path through the strawberry patch, and Pearl says, 'Hush. Stop, stop. You hear somebody walking?' Then 'Baby, they somebody standing yonder. Just standing there. Oh my Lord. Say something. Is you a haint? Is that you, Mama?' and Miss Emily Barron say, 'No.'

"And Pearl don't move a muscle. After a minute, Pearl says, 'Oh my Jesus. Miss Emily Barron?' And Miss Emily Barron says, 'Yes,' like a dead woman, and Pearl says, 'What you gone do?' and she says back, 'I don't know yet.' And Mr. Robert cusses her for being meddlesome, and Miss Emily Barron says, 'Maybe I'll go tell Inger.'"

"Did she tell my mother?" he asked.

"No, baby. No, no, no. Didn't nobody tell her. I saw to that. Miss Emily Barron went straight to Mr. T.J., though, and Pearl was gone before dinner that next day."

Forrest thought now, his head pounding sickeningly, what it meant that Mary Louise was always there in his childhood, watching him.

"Gone where?"

"Back to North Carolina. But no, sir, didn't nobody say one word to Miss Inger."

He dreaded what she was going to say. He knew what it was, and it made his whole abdomen heave strangely. He wanted to escape from it, somewhere outside this bed and this body, but a great weariness held him in place.

The cell phone rang and he started wildly. He patted the bedclothes looking for it, but LaCourvette found it on the rolling tray beside a plastic pitcher of water and handed it to him.

"Braxton?"

The voice was familiar, but he could not place it. "Yes?" he said.

"I drove home from Macon just so the girls could go with him, but he had that woman with him, and I wouldn't let the girls go."

"Tricia." Pain had begun to break through the anesthetic again, a heavy, oppressive pain in his head, a deathly pain. His heart hurt with it. He felt for the call button and pressed it.

"I wouldn't let them get in the car with that bitch," she said, slurring her words. "That creepy bitch. I *know* who she is."

"Well good for you," Forrest said.

"I couldn't believe it. And Chick shows up here with her. Right at my house! You ought to thank me for not putting your girls in the same car with that—you know what? I bet she and Chick—"

"When do I get to meet my son?" he interrupted. He heard her gasp. A nurse came into the room and cocked her head at him. Forrest held up a finger to detain her until he could get off the phone. "What's his name? Robert? When do I get to meet my son?"

The phone went dead. Mary Louise Gibson, her lips set, was gazing at the floor from beneath her hat, shaking her head. LaCourvette had risen to let the nurse get by her, and now she stood looking out the window. The nurse checked his chart and the IV line.

"It's too soon to give you more Percocet, Mr. Forrest," she said. "If it's that bad, the doctor might want to switch you to something stronger."

"I want morphine."

"Can you hold on awhile?" she said. The pain that he felt now seemed comprehensive and heavy, as though gravity itself had broken through the levees of his body and flowed into every cell. He turned his hand in concession. He saw her pity. She was a young woman, maybe in her early thirties, not hardened yet.

"I'll call Dr. Rosen right now." She touched him on the shoulder as she left.

Mary Louise spoke again, as though nothing had interrupted them, and he winced back against the pillow, dreading what she would say.

"Mr. T.J. didn't speak to your daddy about it. When Miss Inger went into labor with you, he stayed with Mr. Robert in the waiting room, and he kept Miss Inger away from Miss Emily Barron's meanness when she came home from the hospital with you."

Forrest held up a hand to stop her. "I know where this is going," he said. "Please. I don't want to hear any more. I can't stand it. You're killing me."

"You got to hear it all, sugar. All the way to the hurt."

"It hurts now."

"Not like it gone hurt in a minute. When Mr. Robert told Mr. T.J. where he was going, Mr. T.J. said, 'I thought you'd be over her when you came back from the war,' and Mr. Robert said 'I'll marry her if I have to. We can live up North.' Mr. T.J. said, 'Oh for God's sake, Robert. Marry her? You're married now. You brought that girl down here; she bore your child. If you leave her I will cut you off without a penny.' And Mr. Robert said, 'I don't care what you do to me. I didn't fight that war to be told what I can't do.' And Mr. T.J. said, and I never heard his voice sound that way, he said, 'You stay away from that girl. God help me, I'll give it all to Emily Barron.' And Mr. Robert said, 'Go ahead. That can be her revenge.' And Mr. T.J. was desperate, he said, 'I'm not telling you not to see Pearl. I'm telling you a man learns to endure his own lies to protect his family.' And Mr. Robert said, 'Which family?'"

"How do you know what they said?" Forrest cried in a sudden rage.

"Because they said it right behind me when I was washing the breakfast dishes, that's how! Me standing there like they thought I was deaf," she said. "I ain't made up one thing. I wish I could forget it. When your daddy left town, Mr. T.J., he the one made something up, some story for Miss Inger, but after a month went by, your mama knew Mr. Robert wasn't coming back. I don't know when that girl was born.

"All I know is the sheriff come one morning about six months after Mr. Robert left. It was in April, right around Easter. Miss Sybil always had that Easter egg hunt out in the yard, and children from the church were running around everywhere, laughing and screaming about what they found. Miss Inger and Mr. T.J. were out on the porch in the rocking chairs watching them, and I was sitting in the porch swing nursing you from your bottle when the car pulled up. The sheriff come up the steps with his hat in his hand, and before he said a word, Mr. T.J. saw his face and put his hand over his eyes. The sheriff stood beside Mr. T.J. turning his hat. He spoke in a voice so low I couldn't hear it, but I saw Miss

Inger's face, and then Mr. T.J. rocked forward with his face in his hands, and I knew your daddy was dead."

"What about Pearl?" Forrest asked.

"Dead with him. Drove off a mountain in the fog."

"Why did my mother stay in Gallatin?"

"I told her to wait. I told her all things come to those who wait. I told her I would help her wait."

"Wait for what?" he cried.

"For Mr. T.J. to change his mind. You were right here, no matter what your daddy did. This sweet little boy. But he had running the company to worry about, and in a few years your mama met Mr. Connor and he loved her like your daddy couldn't and they got married. I was there to help you, though. Remind you who you are. And then Mr. T.J. died, and Miss Sybil died, and it was just Miss Emily Barron, and it seemed like it was all over.

"All that time went by and then—O Jesus help me!—and then one Saturday morning I see that girl coming down the sidewalk."

24

What he expected Marisa Forrest to look like, Chick could not have said. Shrewish and frumpy, he supposed. Tight, anxious, ugly with suspicion. He was surprised to see that she was taller than Patricia, almost as tall as Hermia. She had a dancer's posture, like Alyssa's teacher in Macon. Intelligent brown eyes. Her black hair, just touched with gray, was pulled back in a ponytail. Her face was longer than it was round, strong more than pretty, but she had a generous, candid expression and a large smile that suggested something more enduring than prettiness, and she did not seem defeated or embittered by being married for so long to Braxton Forrest. He liked her at once.

Puzzled at first by seeing a sign with her name on it, she listened to Chick's first hasty explanations.

"A skull fracture!" she said, coming to a dead stop in the flow of traffic toward the baggage carousel. "How did that happen? Oh my Lord. Is he okay, is he...?"

"He's conscious now. Doing better, I think. He hit the back of his head on the sidewalk," Chick said, cupping the back of his head.

"And the girls are with him?"

"Not yet. We'll pick them up and you can all go together."

She did not seem to hear their names when he and Hermia said them. She seemed to think he and Hermia were acquaintances of Forrest's drafted to pick her up, not parties to her story. He collected Marisa's baggage for her and got it to the Navigator in the parking garage. Quiet and a little remote, she sat in the front seat as they left the airport. After they merged onto the rush-hour traffic on I-285, she turned to him wearily.

"I'm sorry you had to get me at rush hour. It was the best flight I could find."

"I'm just happy you're here," Chick said.

She gazed out the window, then recollected herself and turned back toward him, as though she were just sorting out the fact of his presence.

"Tell me your name again, I'm so sorry."

"Chick Lee. You've talked to my wife."

She looked puzzled, then sharpened and reached over to touch his arm and said, almost sympathetically, "Oh, your wife is Patricia? She called you something else."

"Brantley?"

"That's it."

"Chick's been my nickname for so long I don't answer to my real name."

"And you have a daughter who knows my girls?"

"That's right," he said. "My daughter is Alyssa."

"And there's a Bridget?"

"Yes, Bridget Davis, where your girls are staying."

She nodded. She was quiet for a moment. "Your wife told me that Mrs. Hayes couldn't have written those letters," she said.

Chick tilted his head noncommittally.

"That's such a puzzle," she said. After a moment, she touched his arm again. "How in the world did Braxton hit his head on the sidewalk? You said the *back* of his head?"

"He was in—how would you put it?" he asked, glancing up at the mirror and Hermia's face.

"He had just had lunch with my mother and me," Hermia explained, leaning forward between the seats. "And we were all on the sidewalk outside the restaurant when my mother's husband attacked him."

"Your mother's husband? Your stepfather?"

"I never thought of him that way," said Hermia. "He wasn't much older than I am. He saw Prof. Forrest with my mother and something set him off."

"I don't understand."

"Dutrelle just attacked him, and he tripped over my mother's ankle. He fell backward and his head hit the concrete," Hermia said.

"Tell me your name again, dear."

"Hermia Watson, Mrs. Forrest." And then, after a moment, "I work with Mrs. Hayes."

"Oh, of course!" Marisa put a hand over her forehead in embarrassment. "I'm so tired, I just didn't take it in the first time. So you were there when the girls showed up?"

"Yes, ma'am."

"Well you'll have to tell me that story sometime. But I don't understand why your mother's husband would attack Braxton unless..." When Hermia did not reply, Marisa asked, "Was your mother a... friend of Braxton's?"

"Yes ma'am," Hermia said in a small voice.

Marisa turned and gazed out the window. Chick glanced at the mirror and then back at Marisa. She was struggling to keep her eyes open.

"The controls are down on the side. Tilt the seat back and take a nap," he told her.

"Thank you. These seats are so comfortable." The seat tilted back a little and she closed her eyes. "I'm sorry I'm so..." Her head rolled to the side, her mouth slightly open.

Chick glanced in the mirror again. Hermia had her eyes closed, too, and she was rocking her head on the seat back.

He still wasn't sure why she'd wanted to come with him, but all the way up she'd complained about LaCourvette, her best friend in town, and how she'd been kept in the dark her whole life about the most important things. How Mrs. Gibson had been rude to her. Something about a woman named Pearl at Stonewall Hill. She was upset at how Dillon Matthews was harassing her about Mrs. Hayes. Chick was the only good thing in her life right now, she told him.

"Shit!" he said, seeing the big signs over the highway. He had to swerve over two lanes to make it to the exit onto I-75 South. An old Pontiac Bonneville with all the windows open honked furiously and as Chick pulled away to the right, a long, bare, tattooed arm stretched out the driver's side to give him the finger.

"I'm so sorry," Marisa said, starting awake and sitting up. "I want to meet your mother."

Neither Chick nor Hermia could answer.

"Did I say something wrong?"

"Hermia's mother..." Chick said.

"She passed last night," Hermia said and broke into quiet sobs.

"Oh no!" Marisa cried, and then a terrible suspicion seemed to stiffen her. She began shaking her head. "Braxton had something to do with it?"

"A lot has happened," Chick said.

"Oh my god!" Marisa shrank back against the door. "She was with Braxton? And her husband shot her?"

"No," Chick said. "He didn't shoot her. Cump got the gun away from him. We'll get this straightened out later, okay? It's a complicated story. May I call you Marisa?"

Marisa framed her face in both hands. "What did Braxton do?"

"It's my fault!" cried Hermia. "I told Dutrelle."

"Told him what?" Marisa twisted around to look at her.

For a long time, Hermia could not speak. At last, in a tiny voice, she said, "That he's my father."

Marisa stared at her, taking in her face. Chick kept his eyes on the traffic.

"Your father," Marisa said.

"Yes ma'am."

Marisa turned back to the front and stared out through the windshield.

"My husband has embarrassed me before, but I have to say, this is—I don't remember him ever mentioning you. I think I'd remember that."

"He didn't know about me."

"You must be almost as old as I am," Marisa said, turning again to face her. "How old are you?"

"Thirty-nine."

"And you're Braxton's daughter?

"He thought her mother was dead," Chick said.

"But you just told me she *is* dead."

"He never suspected I was his daughter when—" Hermia broke off with a small throttled noise.

Marisa turned to face her.

"When what? Did you know him before?"

"I met him when I was a graduate student."

"What do you mean, he never suspected you were his daughter?"

When Hermia did not answer, Marisa straightened out in her seat and put her face in her hands. Chick was concentrating on the road, trying to stay out of the conversation, but he started violently when Marisa suddenly dropped her hands.

"Oh my God! You're Marilyn Harkins' daughter!"

In the rearview mirror he saw Hermia's stricken look. She said something very softly.

"Pardon me?" Marisa said.

"I said I didn't know you knew about my mother."

"Oh yes."

"Everybody but me. Everybody knew but me," she said bitterly.

There was a long silence. Chick braked as the traffic slowed; he put on his blinker, pulled into the next lane, and when it slowed too, pulled back to the right. He adjusted the temperature and touched the GPS screen as though he needed directions. They passed a sign for the Locust Grove exit. Marisa stared out through the side window. Hermia was crying quietly in the back seat. Chick's heart hurt for her.

"So you wrote those letters?" said Marisa.

"Yes ma'am." She sounded like a schoolgirl chided for messy handwriting.

"Why did you ask us to send down our daughters? It's as bad as kidnapping them. Why did you do that?"

Another hesitation.

"I wanted to see them. His other children."

"But you just said you didn't know you were his daughter."

Hermia did not answer. After a moment, Marisa sighed and crossed her arms over her chest. They rode in a frozen silence. They passed the Jackson exit. Soon they would be at Hood Road and the turn for Tricia's house.

"Miss Watson," Marisa said over her shoulder.

"Yes ma'am," replied Hermia.

"What did you *do* when the girls showed up in Gallatin with nowhere to go?"

Hermia was silent again.

"A slave doesn't have agency, Mrs. Forrest," Hermia said. "It's not up to her what happens."

Again, Marisa turned to look at her.

"Are you a slave?" she asked without inflection. Somehow, it was the coldest sarcasm Chick had ever heard. "Did a slave write those letters?"

"No, but you see the reason I was with Mrs. Hayes—you have to understand, I wouldn't have let anything bad happen to the girls," Hermia said.

"So you just let things take their course."

Chick glanced into the rearview mirror and saw the tears on Hermia's cheeks.

"There didn't seem to be a good time to tell the truth." Her voice now was flat and dull.

"It's dangerous stuff, isn't it?" Marisa said. "Especially once you try to keep it in the dark."

25

"Well, look who's here!"

Forrest opened his eyes. Was it Mary Louise? Dark dread overwhelmed him as what she had said came back to him.

No, it was another nurse. She came into view, thumped the IV a couple of times with her middle finger, patted his left knee, and leaned over to adjust his catheter, jiggling the line that ran into his penis.

"I know you'll be glad to get that thing out," she said. He almost recognized her. "Last time Maurice was in the hospital, he said the worst thing about it was having something stuck up in there."

He closed his eyes. He was dreaming, hallucinating.

It could not be Maureen Woodson.

"When I came in and saw you, I said to myself, 'Unh-unh. Well the Lord's got something in mind. Twice in two days.' I bet you're surprised to see me."

"Where's Mary Louise?" he mumbled.

"Tell you the truth, I needed to get out of the house, and I was supposed to be on duty anyway, so I got Maurice to drive me down here cause I was too shaky to drive myself, and I just couldn't stand being at home after I found out what happened to that lady, it gets me so upset." She had her hand on his arm. He opened his eyes and looked at her. "I'll get it out if you want me to. Do you think you can get up and go by yourself?"

She was talking about his catheter.

"Go ahead," he murmured.

She pulled the curtain on its metal railing around Forrest's bed, pushed aside the sheet, took Forrest in her left hand, and deftly slid the catheter tube out of his penis. She gave his penis a little pat before she put the sheet back, and then rested her hand on it.

"There's men come in here that aren't circumcised," she said confidentially, "and every time I see one it just makes me a little sick." She held up a hand of warning. "I know what you're gone say, you being a professor and all. St. Paul and the Gentiles. Maurice went over every word of it, believe you me, after I told him he needed to be circumcised.

"What I told Maurice, I said now look at the situation. Suppose you're a revival preacher like Billy Graham and you go to a new town to get everybody to convert. They're all filled with the Spirit and ready to give their lives to Jesus, and then you say, 'But men, there's some bad news comes with the good news.' You see what I'm saying? You don't want to go in talking about the Spirit and then—well, you see what I mean? That's not how you build up a congregation, you see what I'm saying?"

She looked so sincere he nodded despite himself.

"You remember that story in Genesis when those boys rape Dinah? Jacob's sons get them to be Jews and then circumcise them and then while they're lying around moaning and groaning they go back and kill them? You imagine if St. Paul had to go around circumcising all his converts is all I'm saying. Everybody laid up for days moaning and groaning. But on the other hand," she said, "when I see one of these with all that extra skin on it..." She made a snipping motion over the sheet, "I can understand why God would want—I mean, it's just cleaner-looking, for one thing. If you do it when a boy's just a few days old, it don't bother him. I saw a rabbi come in here one time and do it with a stone! A sharp stone—can you beat that? The thing is, it's the mark of the covenant from generation unto generation."

She pulled the blanket back over him. "So I finally got Maurice to be circumcised. But I had another reason. You know why?" She tilted her head and raised her eyebrows at him.

He wondered if this was how she taught Sunday School.

"You ever notice Abraham couldn't get Sarah pregnant before he was circumcised?"

"I never did," Forrest admitted.

"Well Stephen talks about it in Acts. You need to pay better attention to your Bible." She thumped him with the backs of her knuckles. "And you know what else?" He shook his head. "Maurice, he's younger than Abraham was." She stood back and nodded at him significantly. Then in a different voice, she said, "You want me to help you get to the bathroom?"

He took her up on it. He lifted his head carefully and sat up while she lowered the bar on the left side of his bed. She swung his legs around on the bed and he lowered them to the floor, leaning on her shoulder with his right hand and holding the upright pole of the IV stand with his left. She put her arm around his waist and helped him to his feet. "Gracious, you're so big. Are you okay? Sometimes people get dizzy they stand up the first time."

He felt wobbly and nauseous. "A little shaky."

She helped him to the door, opened it, and raised the seat of the toilet. "It's gone sting cause that catheter makes it all raw in there. You want to sit down?"

"Hell no."

"I tell Maurice if he says that word in jest he might end up there in earnest. Now listen, Mr. Forrest, if you want me to stay in here with you and help, I will," she said, looking up at him. "It won't embarrass me one bit."

"I'll be okay."

When she closed the door, he stood there holding himself and trying not to think. At last a little urine came out, and it stung so much he was surprised not to see blood dripping into the bowl. Finally a burning flow came, and he remembered thinking of Maureen just yesterday. It seemed impossible. In fact, everything for the past two days seemed impossible. He dropped the hospital gown that was bunched up in his left hand and stood dizzily for a few seconds hanging onto the IV pole, still feeling the burn. He closed his eyes.

When he opened the door again, he half-expected to find the room empty, but there was Maureen, and right beside her was Mo Woodson leaning on a cane and looking at Forrest with a hangdog expression.

"Mo Woodson," said Forrest. "You're a lucky man."

Maureen made a wry face and flapped a hand at him. She thought he was talking about her, and so did Mo.

"Ain't she something," he said, squeezing her around her waist.

"Yeah, and you're lucky to be alive," Forrest said.

"You don't look too good yourself, bubba. You just need you a couple of bolts in your neck and you could be in the movies."

"Marilyn said you were supposed to give me her number in Macon."

Mo's face changed. "You told her what I said?"

"You're damned right. For forty years, she thought I was too scared to come to Macon for her. If Dutrelle Jones hadn't put me in the hospital, I would've come for you yesterday."

"You the one got a dead man on his conscience," Mo said.

"Who? Dutrelle Jones?"

"You know damned well who. Tony Wright that you threw in a yellow jacket nest and broke his back."

Maureen broke from the room and he heard her running down the hall, calling.

"Bullshit," Forrest said. "Forty years, Mo."

"Here you are almost a old man, and you still ain't learned diddly. You don't know a friend when you see one. You was stupid enough back then to go after her, and I knew it. I was doing you a good deed. You would of run off with a..." Mo's whole body twisted with scorn. "Jesus, I must have had her twenty times, and I wasn't the only one. I'm talking about *after* she married that undertaker, too. Changed her name, but she didn't change. You're telling me you're mad you didn't get to marry her, hero?"

Details stood out with perfect clarity: the hairs in Mo's nostrils, the fleck of dried mucus in the corner of his eye, the pouting tension of his lower lip. Another nurse had stopped in the hallway outside the room with Maureen beside her, and Forrest saw her touch her collarbone and say, "Call security."

Forrest noticed Maya Davidson watching from the hallway, too, and it puzzled him. Something about it seemed off. She held up his wedding ring between her finger and thumb and put it in her mouth, and he was about to call her when Maureen, trembling with dramatic dismay, rushed back into the room and got between Forrest and Mo, and again he moved her out of the way and started toward Mo.

"Touch my wife one more time," Mo said, raising his cane.

"Touch her? She was just in here handling my pecker and giving me a Sunday School lesson."

Maureen gasped, and Mo's face went deadly.

"Maurice," she said, "I had to get out the catheter, he was—"

"You're telling me it's the truth?"

She put her hands over her ears.

"Now you listen to me, Maurice!" she said, holding out her hands toward him. "I was just telling Mr. Forrest about your operation and how we want us a little Isaac. I'm not embarrassed about it and you shouldn't be either. I don't care what anybody—"

The cane glanced off the side of her head and whipped out across her shoulder. She cowered down in shock, whimpering and holding her ear. Mo raised the cane again, and this time Forrest caught his forearm as it descended. The cane flipped crazily across the room, and Mo gave a high, feminine scream as he slumped to the floor. His right arm hung limp from the shoulder. He screamed again, less forcefully, and as Forrest watched, the eyes wandered strangely out of alignment, as though the eyeballs, weighted differently, had come loose in their sockets. The left side of Mo's face spasmed, and his mouth opened in an ugly rictus.

"Oh my Jesus," Maureen whimpered, stooping over him. "Oh Lord

Jesus! Help!" she cried toward the open door. "Help!"

The other nurse and two big orderlies burst into the room just before a uniformed security guard.

"He's had a stroke!" cried Maureen, still holding her ear.

"Get him down to ER!" cried the other nurse, and one of the orderlies ran back out the door as the other stooped over him.

He looked up. "What's the matter with his arm?"

Maureen glanced fearfully at Forrest.

"He was hitting Maureen," said Forrest.

The nurse opened her mouth in disbelief. "Maurice hit you? Sweet Maurice?"

Maureen nodded and began to cry. The orderly appeared with a gurney, and the two men lifted Mo onto it and started to wheel him into the hallway. Maureen did not look at Forrest as she followed them out.

The other nurse was still in the room with him. Forrest saw her as she picked up the cane from the floor. Blood pounded in his head.

"He was beating her," he said.

"He's always been sweet as pie before."

"I've known Mo a lot longer than you have. Sweet's not the word that comes to mind."

"You want to get back in the bed, Mr. Forrest?"

He looked at the bed, dreading it. He had the impulse to push past the nurse into the hall, escape the building, get out into the open air. But he got back in the bed and the nurse put something in his IV. He closed his eyes, and they were all back in the room. Mo was back on the floor.

"What's the matter with his arm?"

When the orderly took the arm to lift him onto the gurney, the whole thing slid loose from the sleeve and coiled on the floor. It flexed strangely, writhed down its length, and flowed into the hallway dragging the fingers. He could hear an outbreak of screams and shouts.

26

"Chick Lee just called and they're almost here," said Mrs. Davis from the door of Bridget's room. "Y'all come on down." She started away and then came back. "It's not just your mom, by the way," she said. "He's got that woman with him."

Cate nodded and called Bernadette, who was still in the bathroom. She paused to glance at herself in the mirror. Her mother would not recognize the shorts and the sleeveless top that Mrs. Davis had bought her in Macon, the Teva sandals. Her arms and legs, pale two weeks ago, were tanned now, and Bernadette looked healthier, too. It would be hard to tell from looking at them what it was like that first week.

She heard the doorbell ring.

"Come on, Berry!" she called. "Mom's here."

Bernadette flung open the bathroom door and they went downstairs together. Mrs. Davis was just opening the door, and Mr. Lee came in, looking years older than he had only a day or two ago. He was standing aside now, and their mother's eyes fell on them, and Cate could not remember such a feeling since she was a small child. They ran at each other, and the three of them hugged as though they could squeeze themselves into the same body. Their mother held their faces, kissed their eyes, and finally stepped back to ask what they had been doing.

Had they been to Mass on Sunday?

Yes, they had.

After a minute or two, Cate stood back, wiping her cheeks and smiling. Hermia Watson was behind her with Mr. Lee.

"I don't know what you think you're doing coming to my house," Tricia said in a venomous tone, "much less why I'd tell *you* anything about *my* son."

In the shock of it, they all stared at Mrs. Davis and Miss Watson. Mr. Davis took his pipe out of his mouth and said, "Varina, let's—"

"Why don't you lay off the booze, Tricia?" asked Mr. Lee, and when Mrs. Davis looked at Mr. Lee, there was such hurt and accusation in her eyes it was terrifying.

"You brought *her*."

"Yes I did, Tricia," he said.

"Do you know *who she is*?" she hissed. Cate was horrified to see her so unkind.

"Does Judah here know who your son is?" Chick asked.

"My son is none of his business and never will be!"

"Now Varina," Davis started to say, but she whirled on him furiously, and he took a step backward.

"Girls, come on," said their mother, pulling them toward the door.

"Mrs. Davis," Miss Watson started to say.

"Get out of my house!" shouted Mrs. Davis. "Get out! I can't believe you're standing in my—*get out!*" she screamed, her face distorted by loathing, and Mr. Lee caught her arm before she struck Miss Watson, who turned, stricken, and stumbled heavily against Cate as they went through the door.

27

Marisa was coming.

Chick Lee's call woke Forrest from another dream of the gray women. This time they were disguised as women from his childhood, sitting with their teacups in a parlor Bible study. His tall, blonde mother, so out of place among them, listened with dismay to the childlike superficiality of their comments about the travels of St. Paul. She was like a winged thing caught in some paralyzing web of unsuspected subtlety. How was it that amid such pious talk, in the clatter of cups, the bland comments about the pound cake, the small questions about Mrs. Hayes and sympathetic references to her late husband, she felt so unmistakably the stir of emotions so predatory and so cold?

Forrest was very small. This was another time, when his mother was not there. He stood in front of the white shelves in the sitting room. The figurines on the top shelf were above his head. He had to reach up to retrieve the one he liked best, a sleeping white cat curled on itself, the two little points of its ears breaking the smooth white surface. He liked to feel the ears under his thumb. He needed to go to the bathroom, but he didn't want to leave yet.

The wind was blowing in through the windows, and the white curtains filled up like sails and then let the wind go and it came and washed over his face, cool and pleasant. He could hear them talking in other rooms, but no one was looking at him, and he liked being by himself. When they were with him, the old ladies said things about him as though he were not there. They would look right at him and say things to each other. He did not like the old ladies.

Nobody except Mary Louise was nice to him.

He stood right in front of the windows, holding the porcelain cat in his right hand, and let the wind blow the curtains over him. The cloth was cool and silky, and when he stood still, it slid up his body and across his face and then let go, and a little gust of wind splashed him. Through the window, he could see the shadows going down the side of the hill, and a black man was out there mowing the grass. He looked like a shadow in clothes. The mower made a harsh, whirring, rasping sound when the man pushed it, and the blades curving between the two wheels would whir so fast he couldn't see them, and the cut grass would leap up behind. He loved to watch it. Sometimes the wind would catch the grass bits and blow them all away in a little cloud. Big grasshoppers went leaping away in front of the mower. Closer to the house, a sprinkler was on, spraying the water out in a wide arc, and then coming back *chuck chuck chuck chuck* in short fat bursts.

He needed to go to the bathroom. He started toward the door, but the voices of the women were coming down the hall. Many women, many old ladies. He was still holding the porcelain cat, and his grandmother Miss Sybil, the meanest one, would say something about it in front of the other old ladies. If he went over and put it back, they would be in the room before he could leave. He didn't want them to see him, so he crawled behind the sofa that sat up on its eagle legs—each one a big talon grasping a ball. The legs scared him a little, they were so fierce, but the back of the sofa curved out from the wall and left him a little space to hide, and he was just pulling his feet out of the way when the old ladies came trooping in.

He needed to go to the bathroom.

"Well, Sybil, I don't think he looks a bit like Robert. He looks just like his mama. Now where is she from?"

"I swear to goodness"—he recognized Miss Sybil's voice —"I never can remember. Somewhere up north."

"Wasn't she a Peterson?"

"No," said Miss Sybil. "Something ugly. Blatt? *Glatt*, that's the name, from somewhere in Minnesota."

"Minnesota," another old lady said, as if there was something wrong with it.

Minnesota was where Mama was from. They were talking about his mama, and so that must mean they were talking about him. He didn't look like Robert, who was his daddy who had died. Suddenly, his face burned. It felt red, his ears felt red.

He had to go to the bathroom.

"No, you can't tell he has a bit of Forrest in him, except for his disposition," Miss Sybil said.

"Temper, you mean? Does he have the Forrest temper?"

"My gracious. He and little Harry Bridges were playing out in the backyard yesterday, and little Harry did something that made him mad, and we heard this bloodcurdling scream and we rushed out and Harry's head had blood all over it."

"What happened?" all the old ladies asked in horror.

"Hit him in the head with a brick."

"You don't mean it!"

"I most certainly do mean it! On top of that, he's so big, and always wanting something." She sounded like she despised him. That was the word his grandmother used for things she didn't like to eat. *Oh, I despise boiled cabbage.* Or okra, or runny scrambled eggs with slimy white stuff in them. *Despise* had that spitty sound in the middle. "If it weren't for Mary Louise, I don't know what I'd do with him. She's the only one who can put up with him. I'd just as soon send him straight to reform school."

"Well, Sybil! He can't be more than five years old."

They all laughed.

More and more, he had to go the bathroom, but they were all starting to sit down. He could see the strange high-heeled shoes of the old ladies, fat ankles and stockings sagging over the leather. Just above him, the springs of the sofa creaked under broad bottoms and squeezed him tighter into his hiding place. He smelled dust and wanted to sneeze, but if he sneezed they would find him.

He could not tell where exactly Miss Sybil was. He did not remember ever hating anybody before. But she talked about him to people he didn't know, and he hated her. It was bad to hate, but he couldn't help it, and it felt almost pure, like ice, like hitting Harry Bridges with a brick for saying things about his father. Like something that happened inside him

318

that he just watched. He wanted to hurt her.

But he had to go to the bathroom.

Further away, across the room, he could see fat calves, the hems of dresses, a few purses leaning against the legs of chairs.

Suddenly, there was a burst of noise from the hallway. All the old ladies stopped talking, and he could hear Mary Louise somewhere in the house saying, "No, now, Miss Emily Barron, she got company. No, now, honey—not in there, if you got to do it, you can't take those dogs in there."

"I'll do what I please, Mary Louise. Get out of the way!"

Then he saw the feet of dogs skittering sideways on the wood of the floor on their hard nails as they came around the corner, straining to get loose of the leashes. Immediately, one of them saw him and growled, putting his head close to the floor.

"Well," said Cousin Emily Barron Hayes, "are you ladies enjoying my house?"

No one said anything. Two of the dogs now had seen him, and they were straining, whimpering to get at him. He had to go to the bathroom so bad it hurt like an ice pick stuck into him down there.

"It's not your house yet," said his grandmother weakly. Her voice shook. Cousin Emily Barron Hayes scared his grandmother, and he almost liked Cousin Emily Barron for that.

"Oh! Oh, yes it is," said Cousin Emily Barron Hayes. "As far as I'm concerned, you're just a poor relation who won't leave."

"I am the widow of—"

"Mary Louise!" cried Cousin Emily Barron. "Mary Louise!"

"Yes, ma'am." Mary Louise's feet appeared in the doorway. She had plain, scuffed shoes that could not be still. "I'm sorry to disturb you ladies. Miss Emily Barron, now —"

"Give them the steaks."

"Miss Sybil was saving these, Miss Emily Barron."

"Those are my steaks!" said Miss Sybil. "I bought those for the board members visiting tomor —"

"*You* don't meet with *my* board. You have nothing to do with Forrest Mills. Do you understand me?"

There was no answer. He could hear the dogs panting, whimpering, but all the old ladies were deathly still.

"Are you going to give them those steaks or not, Mary Louise?" said Cousin Emily Barron coldly. He could hear that she hated Miss Sybil, too, and it made him feel strange to hear what hate sounded like out loud.

"Miss Sybil," said Mary Louise, "I got to, it looks like. Mrs. Cox, all y'all ladies, y'all excuse me now. Please, Miss Emily Barron."

"Give them the steaks!"

And with a wet slap, a huge, thick, raw steak hit the hardwood floor just in front of the feet of the ladies on the sofa. They all gasped at once, all the feet disappeared as the ladies above him screamed, and all three of the dogs surged forward, free of their leashes, growling and snapping at each other. Fighting, they nudged the meat up under the sofa. A set of paws broke free to the side, scrambling around to get at it from the back, and he found himself staring up at a snarling dog a foot away trying to wedge himself behind the sofa.

Panicked, he screamed, trying to back out the other way and get to his feet and flee, but the fat sofa held him fast, and he felt a hot release all down his thighs. A moment later, the acrid smell flooded his nostrils. His mind went away in pure terror and humiliation. There were shouts, kicks, screams, and the dogs disappeared with a chorus of yelps. Someone pulled the sofa back, but when he tried to stand, he slipped and fell to his hands and knees in the pool he had made.

He heard gasps and clucks. *Oh my good Lord*, somebody said. Old ladies stood in a half-circle around him, gazing down. He could not look up at them.

He tried to be nowhere.

Then he heard sharp footsteps retreating down the hallway and Cousin Emily Barron Hayes telling Mary Louise to get a bucket and a mop, for the love of Jesus. He heard the word *pathetic*. He did not know that word, but it felt like *despise*.

"There. You see?" said Miss Sybil above him, her voice trembling. "You see?"

Their feet went away, but he still did not look up. Then he heard steps and Mary Louise's shoes appeared on the floor in front of him, with a thick mop head beside them, and he still did not look up.

"You ladies go on now."

They were still there, looking.

"Y'all go on."

When they moved away, murmuring, he let go a great sob.

"It's all right, sugarpie," she said. "Wash your hands in this. Then you run upstairs and get out of those clothes."

Just in front of him, she set down a gleaming tin bucket. Into the cool water, gratefully, he plunged his reeking hands.

"Oh good Lord," someone was saying. "Maureen took out his catheter too soon."

Marisa was coming. What would he say? But it was not Marisa who worried him. He felt someone else beside him now. Not Mary Louise, not Bill Fletcher.

It was Brother.

Brother! he said.

He hadn't seen Brother for a long time, and he was happy to see him again. Brother stood over the field notes, but he wasn't looking at them. His eyes seemed to be measuring Forrest. He held up a plumb line.

Forrest felt a wild desire to hide.

Are these your notes?

I guess so. It's been a long time.

It doesn't close.

Doesn't close? What do you mean?

It has to close or it's no good. It's all just wasted unless it closes, and it won't close.

I went over it. I went back there and went over everything. All the angles and distances.

Did you?

He drove back again. He saw Mo Woodson setting up the transit in the pine woods near the river. Forrest was wheezing, his eyes were swelling shut, and he needed to sit down. He saw a stump and he was already heading toward it when he saw a yellow jacket settle on it and disappear down a hole. The sight of it seemed magnified, a close-up in a movie; another yellow jacket, another. Now one flew out, and just then Tony Wright stepped in front of him, his mouth full of mockery.

Forrest's arms came up murderously. He hurled Wright onto the stump.

He saw it again. *There*: the recognition of yellow jackets even through his blurred vision. *There*: the furious intention in that split-second of reflex.

I killed him, he said to Brother.

The eyes were pitiless. *It has to close.*

Furious golden things crawled in a live mosaic on Forrest's heart, and each hot spasm of their loaded undercurling stingers softened the tissue for the next sting and quilted him with pain.

And he was back in the car with Marilyn that last night. They were sitting outside her house after she told him she was pregnant.

That man said terrible things to me.

Who? Tony Wright?

No. That man right there. Deacon Ray Watts.

I'll kill him.

Deacon Ray always said he knew the truth about me. I would ask him who my daddy was, and he would laugh at me and tell me he was dead. He would tell me I ought to be glad somebody fed me and put clothes on an outrage like me. He said there wasn't no point in something like me even trying to be good, because I was marked out for God's despising.

Who do you think your daddy was? Who do you think he was?

He said my mama was my daddy's sister and I was a walking abomination. Her voice rose, quavering. *Nobody's going to call my baby an abomination. Nobody.*

Who did he say he was?

He wouldn't tell me who it was.

Her face took on an extraordinary tenderness.

But Miss Mary Louise, she told me.

Mary Louise told you?

That's right. She found me and told me yesterday.

She found you?

Will you come get me after I get my shots?

Of course. So who was it? What did Mary Louise say?

She drew his face close with both hands and kissed him.

It's all right. I'll send you a message where I'll be and you come get me. I'll let you know, baby.

So she didn't tell me.

Brother held his hand over the white scroll of paper, and Forrest could see the wilderness there, the rivers and thickets, mosquitoes thickening in the shadows, yellow jackets, and the lines of the survey cast over this living thing like a white net.

It has to close.

But I didn't know. I swear to God I didn't know.

And it was the same night and he had just left Marilyn. He was driving down Sharp Street. He turned left onto Catalpa Lane and right on Gant Street and pulled up at the house where his mother used to pick up Mary Louise.

He sat there watching the grayish flicker of television light in the window. Mary Louise had worked at Stonewall Hill. She had grown up there, more or less. She used to tell him stories when she'd get him alone, away from his mother and Harlan Connor. She'd tell him she knew more about those folks than they knew about themselves. Once when he asked her why he didn't live at Stonewall Hill if he was a Forrest, she told him he might live there later, but he would have to wait until he was older.

Right now, she would say, *you need to put up with Mr. Harlan and stay with your mama.*

He thought: *How did Mary Louise know who Marilyn's father was, unless...*

He saw himself put the car in gear and drive away. Tomorrow, he was telling himself. Tomorrow I'll come by and ask her.

But the next day was Tony Wright's death, and early the next morning Mo called him about finding the dress.

So that's it, he said to Brother. I already knew. I knew she was my sister, but not really, not like you know something real.

It has to close.

And he saw himself that day like a man who had just staggered from a burning house, the only survivor. He had lost everything—and he was free of it. He remembered now the relief and shame he felt.

He saw himself going into Rockwell's Pharmacy when it was still on the courthouse square and Jed Rockwell's father still ran the store. He was standing at the counter buying aspirin, still dazed by seeing the dress nailed to the tree, and Jeremiah Rockwell saw him. Jeremiah Rockwell, Coach Fitzgerald's best friend, who had praised Forrest and given him free ice cream since he first went out for football in fifth grade. He came from behind the pharmacy counter and took him by the elbow to lead him over to an empty corner of the store. He would not look Forrest in the eye.

You heard that girl turned in your name?

Yes sir.

You let us take care of this, you hear me? You just sit tight.

He could have said something then. He could have spoken for her, but here was this man who had been a kind of father to him.

It's already been taken care of, Mr. Rockwell.

The older man stepped back, scrutinizing him, searching his eyes now, and Forrest withstood the scrutiny, his heart burning, crucified, and then Jeremiah Rockwell shook his hand.

Well, I'll be damned. Everybody said you—well, good, good for you, Cump. You've got your whole life ahead of you. You go on to Georgia now, you hear me, and you show Vince Dooley how we play football in Gallatin.

His whole life ahead of him.

He saw himself through the scope of the transit, the crosshairs steadying with the last fine adjustments, the spaceless vertical and horizontal tuned onto the central spaceless point of his inmost lie. He had tried to hide it from himself, cover it up, but it had eaten into everything he did and turned the most serious things of his life into irony, until he could not inhabit his own heart or take any heart seriously. It was as though Adam were allowed back into Eden after Eve took the punishment alone.

What good was it to know himself unless he could somehow make it right, make the past right, but how could he make it right? How could he undo what he was? Marilyn had been given back to him. Was that his second chance? But now she was truly and forever dead. Forever and forever dead.

How can I change it? What do I—

It has to close.

And it was late in the game. The opposing quarterback took the snap and gave a play fake as the line charged off to the right away from Forrest, but then the quarterback set up to pass, and Forrest saw him pump toward the wide receiver and at once knew he was going to throw it short over the middle to the tight end. He sensed a block coming and leapt back. The boy had left his feet for the contact and Forrest pushed him down hard into the grass, and then broke to his right just as the quarterback released the ball. He caught it in front of the tight end, already running at full speed. Behind him the play kept its momentum in the other direction, the offense still unaware of what had happened, and he streaked down the field untouched to score the winning touchdown and the state championship and everyone was screaming. It was a clean thing, a good thing. A glorious thing.

But the lights in the stadium were fading into darkness behind him and he seemed to be running on and on in the dark.

She's coming. Mr. Forrest? She's almost here. Can you wake up?

And now he was flat on his back and traveling at a stupendous speed into the thick darkness and he could see nothing above him but the brilliant wilderness of stars in the thickness of the Milky Way. He needed to get out of the big horseshoe yoke that came over his shoulders and held him fast. He struggled loose and tried to stand. Out the window he saw the black arc of the moon's horizon cutting off the stars. A light was growing behind it. He unwound his plumb bob to let it run to the end of the string, but it drifted mildly sideways, turning slowly over and over. Earth came into view, heartbreakingly beautiful, and he tried to will the string into straightness. Brother needed this shot, or the survey would never close.

"Mr. Forrest, please get back in the bed. Oh, look. Here she is. Here are your girls."

He held the tail of the white string as the plumb bob snaked in a lazy cursive toward that lovely apparition. If he pretended hard enough, with enough show of concentration, it might close, it might still close. And then, to his delight and gratitude, the line turned and straightened, not toward anything he could see, but heavy and sure toward the spaceless point at the center of everything. Taut and clean, shining like the sun, he felt the line coming still, centering all the way through him, an absolute vertical in a wilderness of stars.

"*Good*," he called to whoever was looking at him, knowing it was true. "*Good*," he said again, carefully not looking up. "*Good*."

EPILOGUE

1

December 24, 2009

When Cate came out of her room and down the stairs, tiptoeing, she found her mother already standing in the cold foyer in her robe and slippers, flipping through Christmas cards and junk mail.

"They already brought the mail?"

Her mother jumped and put her hand on her heart. "Cate! You scared me to death! What are you doing up so early?"

"I woke up and couldn't go back to sleep. So the mail came already?"

"No, it came so late yesterday I didn't see it until I went out to get the paper. Why couldn't you sleep?"

"I got a friend request last night from Hermia Watson."

"You're not serious." Her mother put the mail down and stared at her. "What did she say?"

"Nothing. Requests just show up, you know. You either click to accept them or you don't."

"Well for heaven's sake don't accept it."

"I already did."

"Cate!" she said, whispering now. "What are you thinking? Don't you realize what that woman has done to our family? To your father?" she gestured toward his room.

"Mom, I know. I just feel so bad for her. Everybody hates her. She doesn't have anybody, and she didn't mean to hurt Dad."

"Oh, sweetheart." Her mother embraced her, stroking her head, hugging her hard, and Cate burrowed her head into the soft nap of her bathrobe collar, suddenly sobbing. "Oh, baby," said her mother. "Don't cry, sugar. You didn't do anything wrong."

Cate cried harder.

"Well, did you hear back from her after you friended her?" her mother said, smoothing her hand down the nape of her neck and pressing between her shoulder blades. When she nodded into her mother's neck, her mother whispered, "Do you want to tell me what she said?"

She broke the embrace and stood back wiping her eyes.

Her mother had already turned back to the mail. She deftly opened an envelope with the letter opener, scanned the card, lifted out the photograph, and murmured, "Look at those precious children!"

"Did you know she has a son?"

Down went the photograph.

"Hermia Watson has a son?"

Cate nodded. "She sent me his name on Facebook, and I looked him up. I mean, he's this gorgeous football player in Dallas a year younger than I am. She gave him up for adoption, and he doesn't even know she's his mother."

Her mother was shaking her head. "That woman, I swear, Cate. She's so lovely, so educated, and just such a disaster." She turned back to the mail. "Are you headed to the kitchen?"

"Can I have some coffee? Is there any left?"

"Are you drinking coffee? Okay, well I'll make some more. Do you mind giving these to your dad?"

"He's up?"

Marisa nodded and handed her two envelopes, one large manila one from the Benson and Pitts law office in Gallatin, the other one square, hand-addressed to the Forrest family from Lee Ford.

The big dining room table was covered with long rolls of shiny red wrapping paper, spills of gift tags, spools of red ribbon and gold ribbon, press-on bows, a stack of white, collapsible boxes. The door to the old TV room, now her father's room, was half closed. She knocked lightly and pushed inward. He did not hear her. He was sitting in his chair in jeans and old slippers and a big hooded robe, staring out the window. They had moved down the big recliner and some of his books, and they had replaced the bigger couch, now upstairs in his old office, with a single bed. He had the smaller television from their bedroom and a loveseat so she and Berry could visit and watch movies with him. His hair had mostly grown back, but it was still far from being the mane he used to have, and his face had lost the quality of arrogance she had grown up seeing. He did not seem defeated, exactly, just older.

When they first returned to Portsmouth in early September, he had gone up the stairs to their bedroom, but when he started back down, he stood there panicked, gripping the railing and yelling for help, unable to get his bearings. Her mom had called her. They made him sit down like a two-year-old and lower himself step by step on the steep stairs. He had refused to go upstairs ever since.

Sometimes he would watch Turner Classic Movies for sixteen hours straight, but some days he never turned it on. He would sit in his chair and stare at the traffic on Marcy Street as he was doing now and never say a word. Lately, he had been trying to read, but it took an effort for him to concentrate, and when he wrote, his handwriting was like a first grader's. Last week he had asked her for his laptop so he could work on his book manuscript—a good sign—but his fingers no longer knew the keyboard. One of his mother's friends had brought over an icon that he liked, and sometimes she would find him holding it, just staring at the Virgin holding a child who seemed to be made of fire and air.

He still did not know she was there, and the expression on his face was so forlorn, she felt her heart give dangerously.

"Dad?" she said. He turned and looked at her.

"Cate. Sweetheart. Have you been standing there? Come in. You can watch the drawbridge going up." He pointed and she stooped down to look. Through the bare trees of Prescott Park, she could see the central part of the old bridge over the Piscataqua River lifting to let a boat through. "You can't see it in the summer," he said. "It reminds me of—wait," he said, holding up a hand. "Your smiling, or the hope, the thought of it/ Makes in my mind such pause and abrupt ease...... It goes on about a drawbridge."

"That's pretty."

"It's Richard Wilbur. About the traffic backing up. How when she smiles everything else has to stop. Why do I remember that and I can't remember how to type?"

"Mom asked me to give you these," she said, putting a hand on his shoulder and handing him the envelopes.

He took them distractedly and opened the larger one. He pulled out a large piece of paper that had been folded to fit inside the envelope. It looked like a map of something. He spread it across his knees and stared down at it.

"Good Lord."

"What's that, Dad?"

"The plat of Stonewall Hill. I got them to survey the property and make a plat of it. I didn't realize how big—so look, this is the front of the property along Johnson's Mill Road. It goes all the way from the fork in the road"—he traced a line with his finger—"down to here. You see this?" He showed her a figure printed along the line. *S 19 41 05 E 1863.52*. "That means that from this corner of the property the line goes south 19 degrees, 41 minutes, and five seconds, and the distance to the next corner is 1863.52 feet. That's the compass bearing and the distance."

"Okay," she said, not understanding his excitement.

"That's just on the road," he said. "Look at it, sugar. Almost a thousand acres right on the edge of town, still in one piece. Here's the house, and all this—the woods, the creek, you see? This is ours. This is what your great-grandfather bought more than a hundred years ago."

"Are we going to move there?" she asked, suddenly full of dread.

"Move there?" He looked up at her. The expression on his face made him look even older. "No. God, no. We can't move there, not now. Maybe you can later, if you want to."

"Why would I want to move there?"

"I don't know. I'll think of something to do with it."

He opened the other envelope, glanced at the card, and took out a folded sheet of white paper. "I don't remember anybody named Lee Ford. It looks like one of those things people write to brag about their children."

He handed it back to her. She didn't know whether he was joking.

"I guess Mr. Lee sent it from the Ford dealership," she said. She skimmed the first paragraph about a successful sale that had made 2009 an unexpectedly good year.

"Why don't you sit down and read it to me?" Forrest said.

"It's just about how many cars they sold. You want me to read that?"

"Why not? It's Christmas."

"Let me get some coffee," she said.

"What are you doing drinking coffee?"

"I need something to wake me up."

He held up his cup and she took it with her to the kitchen, where she found her mother shaking fresh coffee beans into the grinder. Bernadette wandered in wearing pink flannel pajamas and huge fluffy slippers that looked like rabbits in sunglasses. Her hair was such a mess and she looked so comical that Cate smiled. Bernadette went over and affectionately bumped her mother with her hip as she got down a cereal bowl from the cabinet.

"Hey," her mother said and bumped her back halfway across the kitchen. Undaunted, Bernadette got a spoon from the drawer and a box of Cheerios from another cabinet and headed for the kitchen table beside the windows.

"Mmmph," she said to Cate, setting everything down and turning to get the milk from the refrigerator. Just then her mother pushed down the top on the coffee grinder and ran it until the clatter rose to a whine.

"Good morning, dear Bernadette," said Cate when the noise stopped.

"Gosh, why are you even up?" Berry asked, making an exasperated face. "And why did you make so much noise?"

"I couldn't sleep."

"Does your dad want more coffee?" asked her mother.

Cate nodded.

"Mom, she calls him Dad," she said. "Miss Watson. It's just kind of weird, Miss Watson calling him Dad. I mean, I get it, I know we're half-sisters."

Her mother did not turn as she measured coffee into the French press. Bernadette gave Cate an exaggerated shrug and a look of accusing incredulity.

"You mean because she's so much older?" asked her mother.

"I mean, she has a son almost my age, older than Berry."

"She does?" cried Berry.

"John Bell Hudson," Cate told Berry. "They call him JB. He's gorgeous. And she wants me to call her Sis."

"*Sis?*" said her mother. "Unbelievable."

"Mom..."

But her mother was shaking her head. "Sis," she repeated flatly, in a way that silenced them. "She wants you to call her Sis." As the sound rose in the electric kettle, she stood over it, still not turning. Cate could see the tension in her shoulders. When the automatic switch flipped, she poured the boiling water over the grounds, pushed the filter down to the top of the water, and set the timer before turning to face Cate, her arms crossed over her chest.

"Sis," she said again.

"Sis," Cate said, suddenly smiling. She yawned hugely and stretched until her whole body trembled.

"Why are you smiling about it?"

"I don't know. I guess because this boy—I mean, he's like 6'3" and colleges are already trying to recruit him. So he's my nephew? Seriously? Do you want to see him?"

"No!" Her mother shook her head adamantly. "Don't get me into this."

"Come on, Mom. I'll be right back."

She ran upstairs, snatched her laptop from her bed, and brought it back to the table, where she opened it and found John Bell Hudson's Facebook page. When she clicked on it, Berry crowded close to her to see him.

"You already friended him?" Berry whispered, and she nodded. Her mother came over, glanced at the image of the tall football player in uniform, and went very still.

"Oh my lord," she said.

"Isn't he, Mom? Isn't he gorgeous?"

"He looks just like your father."

"Is that what Dad looked like in high school?"

"I've just seen pictures."

The buzzer went off and her mother went over to push the filter down. "Don't forget what day it is," she said over her shoulder. "Tonight we're doing the Feast of Seven Fishes. If you want to ask any of your friends over, it's fine with me. Then we'll do the posada."

"Not again," said Cate.

Her mother turned and said sharply, "It used to be one of your favorite things."

"Mom, I'm seventeen."

"I don't care if you're thirty-five, which is what you seem to think. Bernadette, it's your turn to put the baby Jesus in the crèche tonight. And then we'll go to Midnight Mass."

"I got up so early," Cate complained.

"Take a nap. Besides, it's not really midnight. I think it starts this year at nine." She poured coffee in her father's mug, put Cate's in a smaller one, and waved her over to add milk and sugar.

"When you take this to him, don't mention Hermia."

"You mean Sis?"

Grinning, she carried the two mugs across the dining room to her father's door and pushed it open with her hip. He was holding the piece of paper from the envelope.

"Do you know what Chick Lee did last summer?" he said. "He had a sale to celebrate the fortieth anniversary of Woodstock and the moon landing. 'The Moon Madness and Stardust Sale.' Can you believe he came up with that?"

She handed him his coffee and he took a sip. "I don't know what it means," she said.

"The moon landing and Woodstock in 1969? They sold so many cars they had to bring in more from Macon and Atlanta. When they had the drawing to see who won the car at the 1969 price, who do you think got it? Take a guess."

"I don't know, Dad. The Baptist preacher?"

"No, your boyfriend."

"What boyfriend?" she asked, suddenly nervous about what he'd heard.

"Your photographer. Humpty-Dumpty. Judah Davis."

"Oh, gross, Dad. Seriously, that's not funny."

"Chick broke the Georgia record for the most cars sold in one weekend. The company gave him a special commendation and tried to make him a regional sales manager, but Chick told them he was happy where he was. He said it was a one-time inspiration." Her father held out his hand to her and she took it. "Are you doing okay?"

"I'm doing okay. Just don't remind me of Mr. Davis."

He folded the sheet, and as he opened the envelope to put it back, he said, "What's this?"

He pulled out a newspaper clipping and opened it. She stood beside him to look. It was an obituary with the picture of a stern-looking man in a state patrolman's uniform. She put her hand on his shoulder and leaned over to read it. Robert Honeycutt Foster, 1970-2009. Killed in the line of duty. Highest honors in the history of the Georgia State Patrol. Rescued a mother and four children trapped in a burning car before being caught in the explosion. Miraculously saved the fifth child, an infant boy, who was found alive and virtually unharmed under his body. Survived by his wife Lucy and their sons Joshua and David, his father Larry Foster, and his mother Varina H. Davis.

She heard her father's agonized, unsteady breathing. His whole body was trembling.

"Who is it?" she asked. "Is it somebody you knew?"

"No!" he cried, startling her. "No!"

She did not understand why he was so upset, but she came around to the front of the chair, and leaning awkwardly, put her hands against the chair back and kissed him on the cheek. He encircled her waist, pulling her down against him, and squeezed her against his chest until she felt hot and small. His neck smelled sour. His unshaven whiskers scratched her. He did not say anything, but she felt long, convulsive shudders go through him, then, with alarm, wetness on her cheek.

"Dad," she said, trying to push away, but he clutched her tighter. "Dad, please," she said, and she felt his body begin to tremble again. He began to jerk. As his arms fell from her, she saw his eyes rolling back in his head.

"Mom!" she shouted.

When her mother burst in and saw him, she moved the coffee from the table beside him, pushed the chair back into the fully reclined position, and turned him on his side, holding his jaw open as he shuddered and spasmed helplessly.

"You just have to keep the breathing passages open."

"Why does it happen so much?"

"It's only when he gets emotional. What did you say to him? I told you not to talk about her, Cate."

"I didn't!" she protested. "He was just reading the card from Mr. Lee."

Bernadette watched from the door, her spoon poised above her cereal. Cate started to cry again.

"He'll be okay," their mother said firmly. "I promise. I promise you."

2

She sat in the borrowed BMW two blocks from the Hudson house on Armstrong Avenue. The second time the Highland Park police came by—Bella Davenport had told her how suspicious they were—the SUV paused, and when his window went down, she flashed the officer a big smile. He asked why she was there, and she told him she was supposed to meet a friend of hers for some last minute shopping, but her friend was running late.

That seemed to satisfy him. He said that the police had to be careful, because thieves scoped out neighborhoods to see which houses were empty over the Christmas holidays, just like in *Home Alone*. She asked him if she looked like a thief. He told her she'd be surprised what thieves looked like, but he tipped his hat and drove on. The third time he came by, she made an exasperated face and tapped her watch, and he tilted his head sympathetically.

One more time and he'd either arrest her or ask her to dinner.

Her friend Bella Davenport, a classmate at Northwestern, had made partner in a Dallas law firm. Two years before, in a conversation about a client's troublesome daughter who knew she was adopted, one of Bella's colleagues had mentioned a star athlete in Highland Park who had no idea he was adopted. The Hudsons, unable to conceive, had found the boy in Chicago during a one-year assignment for the husband's company. When they went back to Dallas with the new baby, no one suspected that he wasn't theirs. But then his extraordinary athletic ability began to be evident in junior high, and the Hudsons foresaw the media interest he would generate and the kind of prying that would follow. Jenna Hudson told her secret to a few close friends to get their advice; the real mother, she intimated, had been a Ph.D. candidate at Northwestern. Bella's colleague told her that now everybody in Highland

Park knew he was adopted except JB himself.

Bella had been the only friend present when Hermia signed the papers giving up any claim to information about her child, and she knew how bitterly Hermia regretted it later. She wrote an email—Hermia had been in Cambridge at the time—with links to the sports stories about him. Hermia had clicked on the links. And there he was: the young Braxton Forrest her mother must have seen forty years before. Since then, she had followed everything about him obsessively, even inventing a Facebook identity to friend him and shadow his every move.

She'd written those letters with John Bell Hudson in the back of her mind—wasn't that it? But not once when he came to Gallatin had she even hinted to Forrest that JB existed.

Forrest had come out of the summer better than she had. He had missed the funeral, of course—that disaster. Hermia never wanted a double funeral. She might have succeeded in staving off the worst if Rev. Marvin K. Love III had not believed he was part of God's plan. He seemed to think of the deaths as the reason he was called into the ministry. Why else had he been on Dutrelle Jones' high school football team? *I've known Trainwreck since we were little boys.* He had been the one Dutrelle came to when he wanted to divorce his wife and marry Adara Dernier. Since God in His mysterious purposes had called him to join them as man and wife, he was going to see that they were buried together, side by side.

He was the one who had held Gloria Jones at bay, mildly misleading her about his actual plans, while working with two funeral homes and arranging to buy a new plot in a new cemetery in Macon. Anticipating crowds, he was the one who had asked the minister of the white First Baptist Church, which had the largest sanctuary in town, to accommodate the funeral, "because Dutrelle Jones rose above the divisions of race."

Well, and so did Marilyn Harkins, after her fashion.

On that Friday morning in late July, people from all over the country had gathered in the big church that occupied the block in front of the house where Braxton Forrest grew up. Three plushly cushioned pews in the front of the church creaked with the weight of the huge former teammates and rivals of Dutrelle Jones. Judging by the reactions of the townspeople behind them—ducked heads, whispers, discreet pointing—some of them must have been famous. She herself remembered Herschel Walker, and she thought she recognized some of the sports personalities from network television. Chick Lee, carefully avoiding eye contact, occupied a distant pew with his wife and daughter.

All the prominent citizens of Gallatin were there to mark the tragedy of Dutrelle Jones, but it was Marilyn who drew the real attention. Rumors of her identity had spread through the town, and curiosity-seekers overflowed the pews, flooded the aisles, and rose against the walls, eager to hear what Rev. Love would have to say.

As it turned out, Hermia never knew what he said. Gloria Jones came in, veiled and dramatically bereft, supported by three men from the funeral home as though she could hardly walk. When she saw two coffins at the front of the church instead of just one for Dutrelle, she shucked them off and charged down the aisle like Tina Turner. *You got that whore in the same church as my son?* She would *not* have that whore next to her son, not in *God's house.*

The more others tried to hush her, the more she shouted and pointed. It took a cadre of linemen from Dutrelle's team to escort her from the sanctuary, but not before she had spotted Hermia and pointed her out to the whole congregation, her arm trembling with righteousness. Hermia had instinctively genuflected as she left.

She survived a few weeks of the town's prurient curiosity, because no one even suspected the whole truth. At least Chick Lee was there to help her. His solemn gratitude and tearful renunciation of her hurt her most of all. She had felt again the abyss: a ragged emptiness, a sheer deletion, the Missing All. A glassy, teetering imbalance had made her curl up naked on the floor of the shower until Eumaios' frantic barking prompted Mrs. Russell to call the police and LaCourvette came to find her.

A week in the hospital in Macon. Behavioral Services, they called it now, as though the meaning of all things were a matter of behavior. And after that came Mrs. Hayes' death, the unattended service presided over by the same priest who had heard her confession, the burial in the Forrest plot, and the last visit to Stonewall Hill to get the envelope.

Back inside the huge, empty house for the last time in September, she had found the envelope with instructions for Mrs. Hayes' funeral, as she expected. There were also old bank statements and documents of accounts in various places, most of them handled by a lawyer in Atlanta whose name she recalled Mrs. Hayes mentioning once. There was a key to a safety deposit box at the Gallatin County Bank, where she had found documentation for equities, bonds, and mutual funds worth several million dollars. Mrs. Hayes also had properties on Pawley's Island in South Carolina and in the mountains of North Carolina. Untouched for years, apparently forgotten, was an Atlanta checking account with over thirty thousand dollars in it. Nowhere did Hermia find a will from Mrs. Hayes. But the manila envelope in the desk contained T.J. Forrest's will, which stipulated that upon the death of Emily Barron Hayes, the Forrest home and her share in Monroe Mills would revert to Braxton Tecumseh Forrest, the son of Robert Forrest.

But those discoveries were merely the prelude. Folded in a smaller envelope were a thousand shares of Texas Instruments stock issued to Robert Forrest and apparently hidden since his death. The Macon lawyer whom Chick had retained for the Forrest family took them to a broker, and the man could hardly contain his astonishment. The distributions had been plowed back into more shares for nearly sixty years, and the eight stock splits since the early 1960s meant that Braxton Forrest, Robert's legal heir, now owned a stake in the company with a worth in the tens of millions. After a month or two of work, the lawyer, Chick's accountant, and the broker—all anticipating steady employment—managed to get regular distribution checks sent to the Forrest family in Portsmouth. It would take years for everything in the old Forrest estate to clear the probate courts, but in the meantime, Forrest's leave of absence from Walcott College would not pose a financial problem.

Nothing for her, of course. Nothing for Hermia Watson. Who was she, after all?

A ghost, a curse, a nobody. The undertaker's daughter.

She could live on what Daddy Loum had left her. Her mother's money, which was considerable, was still tied up in probate, too, but it would eventually come to her as well. Anything her mother had owned jointly with Dutrelle would go toward his outstanding debts, and if there was a little left over, it would go to Dutrelle's children from his first marriage.

All that was behind her now. Three weeks ago, Bella had called to invite her to spend Christmas in Dallas. Just this morning, Cate Forrest had friended her. Sis, she would be, and now Sis was in Dallas to see her son.

All up and down the street were the professionally designed Christmas decorations that people from all over the city came to see, according to Bella. Earlier today, Christmas Eve, she had seen the mailman deliver the big envelope that she had carefully lettered.

Now, at last, around the corner came a vintage white Triumph Spitfire. She sat up. John Bell was pulling into the driveway. He got out, running his hand through his hair, glancing down the street. He got a bag out of the backseat and held it casually over his shoulder—tall, elegantly loose, with an athleticism that was evident even at a glance. She had read all the newspaper stories about him; she knew every statistic, every detail. He was already all-state for the second time and considered as good a prospect at quarterback as Matthew Stafford. Oklahoma, Texas, and Alabama had scouted his games for his whole junior year.

She turned on the car and eased forward down the block, watching as he went through the side door. After a moment, the front door opened, and he came out to get the mail. She saw him flip casually through the cards and letters and find her envelope. He looked at it, curious, turned it over, shook it lightly. As he went inside, his hand on the door, he glanced up and saw her in the BMW, leaning across the seat to stare at him, and as their eyes met, her heart rose with fear and longing. Then he closed the door, and she drove down to the stop sign, picturing what he would find.

A copy of a photograph, first of all. It was in the kitchen at Stonewall

Hill. Robert Forrest, in uniform, a cigarette dangling from his lips, was holding the hand of Emily Barron Hayes and smiling down at her feet as they danced, both of them facing the camera. She looked happy, almost beautiful. The radio sat on the table behind them, and some other soldier, his back to them—Hermia thought it was Capt. Rufus Hayes—knelt as he adjusted the dial. It would have been very early in the war. They must have visited Stonewall Hill so Emily Barron could see her aunt and uncle and cousin. Off to the right side of the picture, turning to smile from the sink, was a pretty, slightly plump, middle-aged black woman in a maid's uniform with a broad white collar. That would be Aunt Ella.

And standing beside her in a plain shift was Ella's daughter of fourteen or fifteen. She stood with her weight on her bare left foot, her right ankle behind it. Her whole figure had an extraordinary grace that reminded Hermia of the Verrocchio David. Her left hand was cocked on her hip and her right rested lightly on her mother's shoulder, as though Aunt Ella had just beckoned her to look at the one thing that would testify for them. Her light eyes ignored everything else in the room and focused directly on the camera—not on the photographer but on the camera's lens, on the person looking at the picture.

Pearl met your eyes, whoever you would be. She seemed to know that Hermia would someday be there looking. And not just Hermia. Now John Bell Hudson, Hermia's child, her blond great-grandson.

Who had taken the picture? An army friend, maybe.

Or Mary Louise Gibson.

Hermia had lightly circled the faces of Robert and Pearl, and an arrow led to the side of the page. He would turn the picture over, and he would find the message written in her own hand, undisguised.

These are your great-grandparents. Aren't they beautiful? I think it's early in the war. There's so much to say, John Bell. Perhaps the best way to start is with a paradox: You are the one I kept, the one I gave away.

And he would stare at the signature.

Your loving mother

His handsome head would come up then, puzzled. He would stand there, holding the photograph, wondering what it meant. After a moment or two, he would wander down the hallway, perhaps, or into the kitchen. *Mom?* he would call. *Hey, Mom?*

Glenn Arbery, the descendant of generations of Southerners and the father of eight children, grew up in the small-town South during a time of great change and strife. He attended the University of Georgia before taking his Ph.D. at the University of Dallas, and he has taught literature for over three decades. He is the author of *Why Literature Matters* (ISI, 2001), and the editor of *The Tragic Abyss* (Dallas Institute Press, 2004) and *The Southern Critics: An Anthology* (ISI, 2011). He now lives and teaches in Wyoming with his wife Virginia. Much as he loves the courtesy and humor of his native place, much as he admires the heroes of the Confederacy—Lee, Jackson, and Forrest, in particular—he has spent much of his life elsewhere. Yet he feels no sympathy with those, ever increasing in number and forgetfulness, who seem easy in their ideological dismissal of the graces and pieties of this land that gave rise to William Faulkner, Allen Tate, Caroline Gordon, Flannery O'Connor, and Walker Percy—this region whose tragic experience and comic hope reflect and deepen the biblical and classical strains that form the Western tradition.

Made in the USA
Lexington, KY
07 October 2015